the

more they

disappear

the

more they

disappear

jesse

donaldson

thomas dunne books   st. martin's press ≈ new york

This is a work of fiction. All of the characters, organizations, and events portrayed in this novel are either products of the author's imagination or are used fictitiously.

THOMAS DUNNE BOOKS.
An imprint of St. Martin's Press.

www.thomasdunnebooks.com
www.stmartins.com

Library of Congress Cataloging-in-Publication Data

Names: Donaldson, Jesse, author.
Title: The more they disappear / Jesse Donaldson.
Description: New York : Thomas Dunne Books, 2016.
Identifiers: LCCN 2016002482| ISBN 9781250050229 (hardcover) |
    ISBN 9781466851337 (e-book)
Subjects: LCSH: Murder—Investigation—Fiction. | Drug traffic—Fiction. |
    Drug addiction—Fiction. | Kentucky—Fiction. | BISAC: FICTION /
    Literary. | FICTION / Crime. | GSAFD: Mystery fiction.
Classification: LCC PS3604.O5344 M67 2016 | DDC 813/.6—dc23
LC record available at http://lccn.loc.gov/2016002482

Our books may be purchased in bulk for promotional, educational, or business use. Please contact your local bookseller or the Macmillan Corporate and Premium Sales Department at 1-800-221-7945, extension 5442, or by e-mail at MacmillanSpecialMarkets@macmillan.com.

First Edition: August 2016

10 9 8 7 6 5 4 3 2 1

For my family

This soul, or life within us, by no means agrees with life outside us.

—VIRGINIA WOOLF, *THE COMMON READER*

You can forget everything.
The least little thing bothers you, you run to them.

—DANNY SHELLEY, INMATE

the

more they

disappear

prologue

OCTOBER 1998

The sheriff's cruiser swung onto Highway 68, a winding track of asphalt laid over a centuries-old buffalo trace that had been carved from salt lick to water's edge. Its driver headed north toward eight turn-of-the-century city blocks wedged between limestone cliff and muddy river. People had taken to calling these blocks "downtown" Marathon ever since the county seat began its expansion out from the shores of the Ohio. Behind the cruiser, strip malls and neon signs advertising gas prices and fast-food specials lined the highway until you reached the Walmart on the edge of town. Suburbs had formed along the newly paved roads that crisscrossed the highway, and attached to those roads were lanes that snaked into the hills and led to neighborhoods with names like Redwood Estates and Thousand Lakes, names that had nothing to do with their surroundings. It was this part of Marathon where most people lived and they simply called it Marathon.

Sheriff Lew Mattock crested one final rise before the river, dropped into third gear, and revved his engine. He believed this was how a competent man kept his valves clean. Ahead of him lay a quarter mile of open space and sky—the distance between two Marathons. The sheriff had been one of the first to buy property atop the hill, so he considered himself a trailblazer of sorts. Over three consecutive terms his acre of land had doubled in value and the best place to drum up votes had become the Walmart on a weekend. Downtown was dead. A few stodgy holdovers who romanticized the town's pioneer past kept calling for its restoration but they were outnumbered and unpopular.

The steering wheel ran loose and easy in Lew's right hand as he watched a window-tinted Camaro cross the double line to pass a lumbering dually. He could have issued a citation but he didn't particularly care to put on his flashers and go through the headache. Instead, he rolled the window down and sucked the crisp fall air like it belonged to him alone. At some point, he placed his hand atop a manila envelope sitting passenger-side to keep it from fluttering away in the breeze. Inside was a grant check from the DEA to help wage the federal government's never-ending war on drugs.

Lew had time to kill before a campaign fundraiser, and at the T-junction by the river, he parked along a scenic overlook the highway department had cleared a month or so before. He snapped off the dispatch and turned on the radio—the talking guitar of Peter Frampton following him as he stepped out and spit a stream of tobacco juice. Lew put one foot atop the guardrail and stretched his thick thighs. A cobalt sky extended above him, banded by the golden light of a waning sun. In the valley below a thicket of trees lined a creek that splintered out from the Ohio. The birches and maples and sycamores had turned golden and ochre and crimson. A bronze historical marker pointing out the remains of a log cabin told the story of the McGoverns, a husband and wife with four kids who'd moved to Kentucky from Boston for the *abundant lande* and *clean aire*. Apparently, they'd headed west again ten years later, *fearing Kantacke awash with new blood*. Lew read the placard and imagined McGovern as a hippie with shaggy hair and necklaces, his wife in long, fluttering dresses. He knew the type. Living off the grid, they called it, but it was more like death than living. A man made his mark on the world through other people. Lew kicked a chunk of gravel over the edge, pulled his sagging pants to a point just below his ample stomach, and offered McGovern his middle finger. Then he laughed at himself for gesturing to a dead man.

As he pulled a handful of index cards from his pocket, Lew started addressing the air, ad-libbing off his stump speech every now and again, letting his voice echo over the stereo. He was guaranteed four more years. He'd won the Democratic primary unopposed and Marathon was Democrat country. The only person stupid enough to run against him was a nut-job anarchist who looked homeless and spoke nonsense. Not a single Republican had stepped up to challenge him despite a lefty president who couldn't keep it in his pants. Lew considered adding a couple Clinton jokes just to let people know how goddamn independent he was—things he'd heard about four cigars and what you could do with them. Lew was Marathon's president. Four more years. And who knew how many after that? He was fifty-two years old, and he had at least three more terms in him if the voters did their job.

As he gestured toward the sky, Lew imagined he was being watched and he wanted to make sure his audience knew that before them stood a man who commanded respect. By the time he finished, ending in a flourish of "God bless this" and "God bless that," spittle was raining from his gummy maw onto the valley below.

Satisfied with his performance, Lew continued along the river road. At a four-way, he flipped his flashers to run the stop. It was a habit the mayor had fielded complaints about but Lew did little to change. *A quirk of mine,* he said.

Downtown had been built atop the footprint of the original settlement and was still laid out like a western outpost. Main Street included a clapboard-church-cum-perpetually-closed-visitor's-center, a diner wedged between vacant storefronts, and various county offices. The side streets were filled with row houses, but unlike a western outpost, Marathon had been built with brick—its houses modeled on those the town's founders had left behind in Philadelphia and Boston and New York. Across the street from the stone courthouse, the sheriff's department sat in shame. It was the ugliest building in town—a concrete box built in the 1950s with little regard for windows. An ancient, dying beech towered over the building and killed the grass. Lew had petitioned the mayor to chop the tree down, but the city council landmarked it instead. An arborist from Lexington had even come out to cable its heaviest branches.

Lew parked in his usual spot. Every day he imagined men in suits walking down the courthouse steps, belittling his ugly little piece of the pie, and as if on cue, the county's newest public defender walked by and waved. Lew barely returned the gesture. He didn't like lawyers. He believed justice could best be served by a single, exceptional man. Lawyers were on-the-one-hand-on-the-other-hand men, could convince themselves of damn near anything if they thought long and hard enough about it.

Lew cut a straight line across the sheriff's department's dirt in short, determined steps. "Did Harlan get me a grill?" he asked his secretary as he plowed into the office.

Holly finished stuffing an envelope before answering. "I believe so," she said.

Lew smiled. What his chief deputy lacked in brains, he made up for in stick-to-it-iveness. "Is it a good one?"

"I wouldn't know," Holly said. "I don't ask questions about the important stuff."

"I intend to grill fifty pounds of prime Kentucky beef, so I consider this pretty damn important."

"If you're worried, drive on over to see Harlan and get out of my hair."

Lew strode up to Holly's desk and rested his substantial heft against the small section free of paperwork. Holly was proof a person could age with grace. The wrinkles on her skin didn't make her look old so much as skeptical. Near seventy, she dressed in the fashion of a bygone era—square, gold-rimmed glasses, monochrome ladies' jackets, skirts that fell below the knee. On her left hand she still wore the ring of a husband who'd died young. Lew knew she didn't like his demanding nature or crude jokes, but together they helped an undermanned department keep the relative peace. Occasionally Holly annoyed him with her insistence on dotted i's and crossed t's, but given their lackluster deputies, hers was the only opinion besides his own that Lew respected.

"Will I see you at the barbeque later?" he asked.

"Social functions and I don't mix."

"But I can still count on your vote?"

Holly gave him a thin smile. "I have to think on it."

Lew slid the envelope with the DEA check onto her desk. "Does this change your mind?"

Holly removed and studied the check. "Depends on whether this goes to giving me a raise."

Lew grabbed the check back. "That sounds like extortion, Ms. Dilts. But maybe if you nice up a little, I'll consider it."

Holly rolled her eyes as Lew continued on to his office, where he pressed Play on his voicemail and listened to people spout various forms of recorded bullshit. He fixed his thirst with a pull from his desk flask as he hit Delete over and over.

Soon enough he was back in his cruiser and heading down the river road to Josephine Entwhistle's waterfront spread. As he pulled onto her pea gravel drive, Lew spotted Harlan crouched with a tent stake in one hand and a hammer in the other. Josie was squawking at Harlan about something or other. The rotted lean-to that Josie's ancestors had built stood behind them in a nest of hackberry and scrub oak. Josie liked to remind people that she descended from Marathon's founders, that her land had been passed down for over two hundred years. Lew couldn't stand when she started regaling people with her history, couldn't stand any of the families who thought their last names still mattered in Marathon. Lew didn't live in the past. He'd escaped his own, which began in the mountains of eastern Kentucky, and started anew along the banks of the Ohio, succeeding on his own intelligence and fortitude, not some passed-down privilege.

Josie claimed not to care much for politics, but she'd been more than happy to loan Lew her patch of riverside. In Marathon you couldn't refuse Lew Mattock a favor regardless of your last name. Josie had a dope-smoking grandson with a girlfriend he'd knocked up, and the last thing she needed was for Lew to make a point of arresting said grandson when he inevitably fucked up.

"What're y'all screaming about?" Lew asked as he stepped from the cruiser.

Josie pointed at Harlan. "He's ruining my lawn."

"Well, why would he do a thing like that?" Lew turned to Harlan. He couldn't help smiling as Harlan stood up from his crouch, his gangly limbs slow to straighten. Harlan's every movement seemed strained by his height. Physically he was everything Lew wasn't and this made Lew think less of him. Harlan was a head-in-the-clouds kind of man, figuratively and literally; Lew was a feet-on-the-earth man.

Harlan didn't answer Lew's question; he just fidgeted with the hammer, letting it smack an awkward rhythm against his thigh. "Harlan," Lew cooed. "Earth to Harlan."

"There're gonna be kids around," Harlan said, "running barefoot and all, so I figured I'd set up in this grass."

"What do you think of that, Josie?"

"I'd say that's a damn shame reason to tear up my lawn."

Lew cocked his head, as if considering the issue. "I have to agree with Josie on this one, Harlan. Now I know you're a bachelor, so I'm touched you were thinking of the kiddies and all, but kiddies are resilient. Don't matter if they're playing on grass or dirt or rocks. Hell, a kid can run over broken glass if they're having enough fun. Besides, Josie here has a vote in the election and kiddies don't, so move everything where she tells you, okay?"

Harlan nodded and followed Josie to a weed-strewn patch of dirt.

"Crisis averted," Lew mumbled to himself before going to inspect the stainless steel grill in the bed of Harlan's pickup. Harlan's truck was so old it had been his daddy's when his daddy was a young man. Lew had driven by a broken-down-on-the-side-of-the-road Harlan countless times, but he always sped by to avoid commiserating about what had broke and why. Harlan was oblivious anyway, the curved bill of his sweaty ball cap pulled low while he tunnel-vision-tinkered.

Lew ran his hand over a slipshod patch of welding along the truck's gate and shook his head. Flecks of rusted metal broke off where his fingers pressed. The grill put the truck to shame. Its cooking surface boasted a second level for toasting buns and there was an extra burner on each side. Harlan had done good. Lew even considered lowering the grill from the truck to help, but when it came time to hammer a stake or set up chairs in the grass, Lew became bored. He believed fervently in the separation of tasks. Harlan's time was best spent preparing for the fundraiser while his was best spent looking at a freshly inked government check and ruminating on the future.

A couple of early birds parked on the shoulder of the river road, and when Lew noticed a familiar white SUV, he grabbed a bottle of Basil Hayden's from the trunk of his cruiser. The bourbon was left over from the bust of a truck loaded with stolen booze and cigarettes. Lew had kept a couple of crates as a finder's fee, and since it was election season, he'd hand delivered most to wealthy farmers and difference makers. There'd been a time in Finley County when the man who distilled the best moonshine won the election, and Lew figured that time wasn't so far removed as people liked to believe.

He made straight for Stuart Simon, the editor of the *Marathon Registrar*. "Gonna make a fortune on parking tickets today," he said, his right hand extended. Stuart had moved from Chicago and liked the folksy quality of Marathoners, the one-line jokes and thick accents, so Lew hammered it up.

"Is that what this shindig is all about?"

"Ever lil' bit helps."

"It can't be 'cause you're worried about losing the election."

"Not a thing in this world is set in stone but the Lord's commandments." Lew handed the bottle over. "Kentucky's finest," he said. "I figure you mightn't've had the pleasure."

"I've been here three years." Stuart studied the bottle.

"Has it been that long?" Lew excused himself. Brevity was key in his dealings with other men. He couldn't abide a lagging conversation, considered pointless chatter a weakness.

While he looked for someone else worth talking to, Lew's son pulled up with his armpiece of a wife and their twin daughters. Lew's own wife was conspicuously absent. He hadn't expected Mabel to show up and it was just as well. He felt uncomfortable whenever he saw her moping along the edges of a party. Lew crouched down and beckoned his granddaughters, who ran and jumped into his arms. He lifted them up and spun a circle, smiling wide for anyone who might be looking. As he set the girls down, a claw of a hand gripped him by the shoulder; Lew turned to find Trip Gaines's smug face. Trip was family by way of his son's marriage—the armpiece's father—but Lew didn't feel like listening

to his long-winded bullshit, so used their granddaughters as buf-
fers and said, "Hug your Pappy Gaines now," winking at Trip as
the girls reached up their arms.

The guests kept trickling in and Lew kept busy pumping hands
and telling jokes until it was time for him to man the grill. Someone started playing music, a rocking bit of country that had him
shuffling his feet as he slapped steaks onto the fire. It was going to
be a bash of a party—the best yet.

one

Mary Jane Finley was late. She'd changed her outfit three times but nothing seemed to fit. It was the mirror's fault, the way it reflected her body lumpen and plain. She had new curves, new skin— had for a while now—and no amount of makeup could bring back the face that had twice been Finley County's Junior Miss Harvest. Those years, from twelve to fourteen, had been her best. After that her body ran its own course, and no diet, fast, or finger down the throat could help her regain the promise she'd shown. There always remained twenty pounds she couldn't shed. After futilely changing her clothes one last time, Mary Jane scowled at the mirror and said, "Fuck you."

She drove her red coupe past the house where her boyfriend, Mark, had lived before he left for college. She knew Mark was back in town, waiting by the window for that moment she drove by, and she resisted the urge to honk hello. The finished homes started to thin out as she rolled down the street at a steady twenty-five. In countless plots there lay only the expectation of a house— floor plans staked with wooden boards, electric boxes rising from the emptiness, scraggly seedlings of trees. Mary Jane parked in a deserted cul-de-sac next to the bones of a two-story and slipped on a backpack before hiking into the woods.

It was bow season but the trails were quiet. Most hunters waited for gun season to bag their bucks. The occasional bird flitted from branch to branch and called out, but Mary Jane paid them no mind. She adjusted the backpack, which held a broken-down rifle that weighted itself awkwardly against her shoulders. Her impulse was to step into the thickest woods and move under the cover of brush, but she knew her feet would kick up leaves that way and a stray limb might scratch her face. No. It was better to stay on the worn paths.

She moved with a certain grace through the woods, though that grace wasn't the result of years spent hiking so much as years spent walking down the hallway in heels. "Down and back," her mother would say until blisters formed on Mary Jane's feet, Mary Jane refusing to show pain. Down and back. Mary Jane a plaything to order around. Down and back. A mindless animal.

She was not a born killer, nor an experienced one, but she'd prepared. If she was in over her head, she didn't realize it, and if she had doubts, they didn't show. She was buoyed by thoughts of her and Mark together. She thought of this act as not altogether different from a marriage—something that would bind them.

In many ways she was the perfect criminal. She came from a respectable family—her father was an investor, her mother a socialite. She descended from the Revolutionary War general who at one time owned all the land in the county that still bore his name. No one in Finley County would ever believe Mary Jane Finley had committed a crime. No one knew about her sadness, her addictions, or her faith that Mark Gaines would carry her away to a better place.

She reached a clearing along the ridge overlooking the river and the wind died down. Months before, the hike would have left her breathless, but no longer. To the west a few abandoned trailers hunkered along the river road and to the east Mary Jane could make out downtown. In the distance lay Josephine Entwhistle's house and behind stood only the skeletons of unfinished homes.

By the time Mary Jane arrived, the party was in full swing. She briefly considered turning back, but there were expectations, a plan to follow through with, and if it worked, Mary Jane would no longer she be trapped in Marathon, would no longer feel so damn alone.

She pulled a Ziploc of pill dust from her backpack—a mix of Xanax and Adderall that she snorted in bumps off her car key. She'd learned there was a pill for every need and Mark fed each one of hers. Afterward she took out the stock and barreled action of a .308 Winchester. The smell of gun oil calmed her. Her grandfather had taught Mary Jane to shoot when she was just a girl, the lessons his way of stemming her mother's influence, of showing Mary Jane there was more to life than beauty pageants. They'd gone hunting every deer season until he passed away, and when it wasn't deer season, there'd been wild turkey and dove. Somewhere in the basement the mounted head of Mary Jane's first buck—a four pointer—gathered dust. In a strange way she'd discovered that shooting a rifle wasn't altogether different from walking down the runway. Both required great balance, great composure.

She attached the stock and barreled action, tightened the action screws, and checked that the chamber was empty, then wrapped her index and middle fingers around the trigger, and pulled. A smooth click. The action was sound. She'd started to develop a kinship with the Winchester and regretted she'd have to get rid of it. The .308 was right on the edge of kicking too hard and she liked that about it, too.

She attached the scope, cradled the barrel in a tripod, and looked down the sight. Partygoers mingled. The mayor, the judge, and other politicians stood around laughing at one another's stale jokes— men with names that went as far back as Finley, names like Craycraft and January and Estill. Mary Jane could wipe the whole town

THE MORE THEY DISAPPEAR

clean if only she had the bullets. A .308 with a good scope: that's all it took. She moved the gun from face to face—a god above them. She wished Mark was there with her—to feel this, to see her as no one else could. She wanted Mark's hand over hers as she cupped the trigger—Mark caressing her, her caressing the gun—the power all theirs. She chambered a round and set the butt of the rifle against her shoulder. Theirs was a fated love. A sacrificial love.

The last of the pill dust went up her nose and her thoughts about the future dissolved and turned to smoke. Her fears drifted away and fell into an abyss. She was patiently numb to consequences—her mind focused by one pill, her doubts erased by the other. The shot was a touch under two hundred yards and it was quiet along the Ohio.

She peered through the scope and found Lew. Oblivious. Flipping meat at the grill. She drew a deep breath and aimed the rifle at his chest, let the world come into focus and thought of nothing but the pressure against two tips of fingers. When she exhaled, she drew those fingers toward her heart and the rifle kicked.

The smell of gunpowder floated in the air. Mary Jane felt the warmth of the barrel and looked back through the scope. Lew fell forward onto the grill. For a moment nothing else changed. Then came the distant sound of screams. Mary Jane watched the crowd scurry like ants as smoke rose from the grill. Her body convulsed and knocked the rifle from its cradle. Then she vomited a thin, weak stream onto the ground. She cursed and struggled to regain composure, started humming "Twinkle Twinkle Little Star"—an old runway trick to calm the nerves. In less than a minute her body steadied and her stomach settled. She kicked dirt over the vomit, loosened the action screws to break down the rifle, and placed it in the backpack along with the casing before she headed back in the direction from which she'd come.

———

It may have been the music blaring from the speakers of a souped-up Mustang or the noise of the crowd or the fact that people had become accustomed to cars backfiring; whatever the reason, no one connected the boom from the hills to Lew Mattock's collapse. The spatula slipped from Lew's hand and spun to the ground, where dirt clung to its greasy edges. Harlan Dupee watched him double onto the grill and assumed heart attack, though he couldn't seem to move his legs and help.

It was Lewis Mattock who ran to his father's side, pulled him to the ground, and yelled, "Shooter!" The crowd scattered. Some ran for water, others the woods. Most ran in circles to nowhere particular. Harlan dropped to the ground and watched Lew's legs jangle until his massive belly—a mound rising from the cracked clay of a dry October—stilled. Lewis Mattock slumped back on his knees, a look of horror across his face. Time must have passed. When Trip Gaines, a local doctor, checked for a pulse and shook his head, Lewis wrapped one burly arm around his wife and the other around his twin daughters before shouldering them into the safety of Josephine Entwhistle's house. Dr. Gaines laid his suit jacket over Lew's wounded face. The smell of burnt flesh hung in the air.

The crowd waited for someone to give the all clear, and even though no more bullets rained down, Harlan lay on the ground a long while before getting to his feet and asking people to please seek shelter inside the house and stay there until told otherwise. Most rubbernecked glances at Lew's body as they passed. A couple retched. More than a few sobbed in fits and starts. Two other deputies, Del Parker and Frank Pryor, joined Harlan around the body. Blood had begun to pool through the weave of the doctor's jacket, which Harlan lifted. Lew's right eye was gone and his face had become a pulp of meat and bone and yellow flesh. The earth swallowed what blood coursed from the hollow in his skull. Harlan dropped the jacket back in place and started giving orders. He did his best to sound confident, but it had been years since he'd asked the deputies to do anything other than what Lew told him to pass along. He had Del radio Paige Lucas, the rookie out patrolling roads, and tell her to stop any suspicious vehicles. After that Del was to get the neighboring county's dogs and search for evidence. This left Harlan with Frank, an overweight deputy with a ruddy face and a chip on his shoulder. "Head inside and get the contact information of everyone here. See if anyone noticed something unusual." Frank shrugged before spitting on the ground and joining the crowd as they herded themselves into Josephine's.

Harlan marked off the area around Lew with caution tape and radioed Holly from the sheriff's cruiser, explained to her what had happened, and asked her to send someone out from the state police, the crime lab in Frankfort, and the coroner's office. Then he pulled out a textbook on criminal investigations from the toolbox of his truck. He hadn't worked but a couple of murders, and Lew had always been there to guide him. The textbook was left over from a correspondence course he'd taken years before, and the mere fact that he kept it made him the best deputy in an otherwise apathetic department. He flipped to the chapter on murder investigations, found the gunshot section, and started making checkmarks as he completed each step. He started by removing the blazer from Lew's face and snapping photographs with a point-and-click. Then he drew badly scaled sketches of the scene with a shaky hand and redrew them to keep from examining Lew up close. He wrote his account of the murder, trying to recall the details. He waited for help.

The witnesses came out of Josephine's one by one, hurried to their cars, and sped away, as if putting distance between themselves and Lew's corpse would help them forget. But it wouldn't. They would talk about it at dinner and dream about it at night and even people who hadn't been there would claim to be haunted by the sight of Lew Mattock's dead body.

Harlan stared at Lew as if he might provide some guidance, and when a burly hand touched down on his shoulder, he jumped. "Jesus," Frank said. "Relax."

"What are you doing?"

Frank pinched a load of snuff and showed his bean teeth. "I'm finished."

"Already?"

Frank tapped his notebook. "I talked to every last person." A thin man wearing a fleece jacket stood behind Frank with a pen and paper. Harlan looked to Frank for an explanation. "This guy's with the newspaper," Frank explained. "I told him you're in charge."

"Stuart Simon," the man said. "I edit the *Registrar*."

Harlan shook his head. "Not now."

"Just a couple questions, Deputy. . . . It's Dupee, isn't it?"

"Frank, can you escort Mr. Simon to his vehicle?"

"I just want to know—"

"Now," Harlan yelled.

Frank took Simon's arm. "Come on, Stu," he said.

Simon started to wage a halfhearted protest but stopped as the dispatch from Lew's cruiser crackled with Holly's voice. Harlan couldn't make out what she said and asked her to repeat herself. "Fire," she said. "Over at the Spanish Manor. The volunteers are on their way. Want me to do anything else?"

Harlan looked at Frank. "Head over there, but on your way pull over every car with a busted taillight or expired registration. Look for guns."

"I don't think hoping the shooter has a busted taillight is much of a plan," Frank said.

The editor slipped Frank's grasp and started writing in his notebook.

"Just do it," Harlan snapped. He radioed back to Holly that Frank was on his way. He was thankful the textbook had been safely hidden in the cab of his truck. He didn't need Frank or the other deputies doubting him. And he definitely didn't need some reporter doing the same. Harlan had grown soft since he joined the department. They all had. You kept your job by avoiding any police work that might cause extra paperwork. Harlan had been promoted because of those through-the-mail criminology courses, but whatever policing knowledge he'd learned was rarely put to use. Now was his chance to prove himself. He'd always wanted the sheriff's badge on his chest—not like this, of course—but you didn't get to choose what life threw your way. Or when.

Along the river road an ambulance-style hearse pulled up with the coroner who serviced Finley and the neighboring counties. Behind him came a state police cruiser with lights flashing. The state policeman came down first, took a look around, and said, "Damn shame." He put out a thick hand and introduced himself. His eyes were almost all pupils and he wore a gray-flecked mustache. "You want me to take samples from the body?" he asked. "I didn't know the man, so it won't affect me the same."

"I'd appreciate that," Harlan replied.

The coroner joined them a minute later. He was new—a kid with a two-year degree, fresh pimples, and a talkative manner. The sun started to set as they worked and the sound of crickets chirping rose from the woods. Harlan held a flashlight while the coroner labeled plastic bags the Statie handed him. At some point, he looked up to watch a sports car speeding along the river road before it disappeared into the coming dark. He realized, perhaps for the first time, that his life of writing traffic tickets was over.

"I can't believe someone shot Lew," the kid coroner said, trying to sound like some wizened old-timer. "He seemed invincible."

"No one's invincible," the Statie replied.

The crime lab investigator from Frankfort showed up just in

time to say "nice work" and collect the samples. He told Harlan to
develop and send him the pictures. The sooner the better. They
bagged Lew and the Statie helped lift him onto a gurney while the
kid coroner struggled with his end; meanwhile, the investigator
and Harlan loaded the grill into a van. Harlan closed the lid so as
to not see the burnt flesh along the grates.

He examined the crime scene one last time, and just as he was
ready to call it, he noticed a small depression that had been beneath the body. It led to a fragment of bullet buried four inches
into hardpack.

"That's good police work," the Statie said as Harlan sealed and
marked the evidence.

"More like good luck."

The kid coroner had lit a cigarette by the side of the road, and
Harlan walked up to join him, rolled a smoke of his own, and
listened to the Ohio murmur its song—a gurgling chorus of choking mud.

Mary Jane chewed her last bite of Big Mac and searched along the
bag's bottom for stray fries. Tara Koehler had been working the
drive-thru, and as she handed the order over, Mary Jane mentioned
she was going to see a movie to set up an alibi. Tara had added a
fried apple pie on the house, so Mary Jane finished off her meal
with dessert, licking the last bits of sugary glaze from her fingers.

It had been a long time since she'd seen another car, which should
have been comforting, but the emptiness made her nervous. She
kept checking the rearview mirror expecting to see flashing lights
where there was only blackness. After her dinner, she lit a Marlboro Light and one cigarette turned into two turned into a quarter
pack and soon enough she felt nauseous again. The burger and fries
sat heavy in her stomach and Mary Jane stifled the urge to pull
over and jam a finger down her throat.

Mark had told her to drive out to the West Virginia border and toss the rifle into a wide branch of the Big Sandy, but Mary Jane couldn't make it that far. In the darkness, she had trouble figuring out how far she'd traveled. The names of the small towns she passed weren't written on any map, and even though the rifle was stowed safely in the trunk of the car, she felt like it was sitting beside her—chatting away. When the stereo began losing its station, she snapped it off and heard nothing save the wind rushing through a seam in the window. She downed another dose of nerve pills but it didn't work. *Lose the gun,* she told herself over and over. *Lose the gun.*

A sign marking a one-lane bridge flashed in her headlights, and Mary Jane banked onto the road paralleling the water. Her wheels caught a pothole in the dark and the wind snatched the cigarette from her hand and flung it to the backseat. Flustered, she hit the gas, cursed, hit the brake, and pulled sharply to the side of the road before rescuing the still-burning Marlboro and bringing it to her lips. Crickets whirred and animals scurried in the woods. A small hole had burned where the cigarette came to rest and she fingered its scorched edges. Through a cut of trees, the river muttered. It wasn't wide like the Big Sandy but in the scant moonlight it looked deep enough, and if she couldn't return to find this place, how could anyone else?

She stuffed every last trace of the crime in the backpack and hiked to the river before swinging it two-handed into the dark. After the bag plopped in the water, she lit one last Marlboro. A ceremony of sorts. It had been that way ever since she took up smoking. A cigarette for making it to school, for making it to lunch, for making it through the final bell. A cigarette while driving, while walking, while staring out the window and thinking important thoughts. A cigarette to celebrate the arrival and a cigarette to celebrate the leaving behind.

On the road home, Mary Jane could almost trick herself into believing she was returning from some innocent adventure—that she'd been lost but found her way. After an hour, she passed the sign that marked twenty-six miles to Marathon. There were three such signs on the roads that led east, west, and south from town. The road north lacked one despite the mayor's best attempts to weasel himself a square of Ohio dirt. Mary Jane offered the sign her middle finger, a rite of passage Marathoners learned as soon as they were old enough to drive and had the good sense to head someplace else.

Her father was sitting alone on the porch when she returned. The lit end of his cigar pulsed and Jackson tilted his head to blow smoke toward the stars. In his other hand he swirled a highball glass that Mary Jane guessed was more gin than tonic. "I'm afraid you're on your own for dinner," he said as she climbed the stairs. "I haven't heard from your mother. Do you think you can manage?" Jackson tried to pass this last bit off as a joke, but Mary Jane knew it was a barb meant to draw blood. Ever since she'd been rejected from colleges six months before, her father couldn't help reminding Mary Jane that she was a disappointment.

"I already ate," she said.

"What did you have?"

"McDonald's."

Jackson laughed. "Your mother would love that."

"You know she wouldn't."

"On that matter, at least, I agree with her. Do you know what that trash does to your body?"

Mary Jane opened the front door. "Yeah," she said. "It makes you fat." She let the door slam and ran upstairs to her room where she opened the window and screamed into the night. Her room looked onto the street and she could hear the groans of the porch swing echoing as Jackson rocked back and forth, could smell the smoke of his cigar rising. If he had more commentary, he kept it to himself. Mary Jane fingered a hole she'd cut in the window screen for her hash pipe. For years she'd worried her parents would ask about it, but they either didn't realize what the hole meant or didn't care.

She stepped back from the window and grabbed a teddy bear off the bed. It had been a present from her father when she was nine. The bear had come with a name—Teddy Ruxpin—and a tape deck so he could tell stories. In a way the bear was a substitute for Jackson himself, who rarely told Mary Jane stories or tucked her in at night. She opened the tape deck and removed a bag of pills. Pills were her ticket out of Marathon. Mark called Oxy a "miracle" drug, and the first time he gave Mary Jane one and taught her to grind it to dust, she came to understand the meaning of the word. Oxy wasn't like pot, which made her paranoid, or booze, which made her sloppy. It didn't skew the world or make things funny; it offered separation. Separation from her father's passive-aggressive insults and her mother's chain-smoking sadness. Separation from the fat girl in the mirror. Separation from a life that stalled out in high school. Oxy offered oblivion.

She crushed a blue pill between two spoons and snorted the dust. "I love you," she said to the bear, pretending it was Mark. She understood why Mark wasn't there, why it was smarter for them to stay apart, but that didn't make her feel any less alone, and for a brief moment her doubts about Mark, about his love or his capacity to love, reared their ugly heads before skittering away on a sea of painkiller. Mary Jane stretched herself like taffy over the bed; her head lolled over and her mouth hung slack as she stared out the window at a starless sky. The house and the street outside fell asleep.

When she came to, it was to the sound of her parents yelling, their voices snaking through the empty halls and up to her room. Mary Jane heard her name bandied about but drowned out the specifics. The specifics didn't matter. Her parents fought because they knew no other way, had lost whatever drew them together in the first place. The older she became, the more Mary Jane understood her parents' marriage was based on something other than love, that they stayed together because neither was strong or merciful enough to walk out the door. And Mary Jane was just another part of the problem, fuel to toss on a fire. It seemed her parents were forever blaming each other for whatever deficiencies they saw in their only child.

Mary Jane put on her headphones to drown out the noise, lit a candle, and pulled the atlas from her bedside table. Pencil lines connected Marathon to Montreal. As she read the names on the map, she savored the way the vowels formed on her tongue. She'd taken French in high school at her mother's insistence and it turned out to be the one class she enjoyed. She imagined herself speaking French at the grocery store, ordering wine at a restaurant. She imagined her and Mark starting a family there, a better family than the one she'd grown up in—because their kids would never be Finleys in Finley County. She knew a couple of girls who already had rings on their fingers and husbands who bought them pretty things and sometimes she doubted she'd ever have that life for herself. Now, for the first time, it seemed within reach.

Mark had been indifferent to Montreal when she came up with the idea, but the more Mary Jane told him about the city, the more she repeated things she'd learned from high school textbooks, the more excited he became. Montreal was across the border and far away from his father and that was a good start. There was even a university where he could study once they got settled. McGill. The Harvard of Canada. Mark said they needed to stay in Kentucky a little while before leaving, just to play it cool, though Mary Jane would have left that moment if he were willing. She didn't care who might chase them. She knew how to press the gas.

Lewis Mattock answered the knock at the door, which turned out to be the pizza delivery guy. He'd ordered a large cheese because, despite everything, the girls still needed to eat. Lewis tried to talk to the guy about sports, the weather—anything other than his father—then handed over a too-generous tip. The phone continued to ring nonstop, streaming a steady diet of calls from people asking for news. Each time Lewis told the caller his father had passed on, they offered the same canned condolences and he offered the same canned responses. An assembly line of conversation.

Sophie followed him into the kitchen as Lewis got plates ready for Ginny and Stella. She opened a bottle of Merlot and popped a Xanax from her stash, but still she talked and talked. "Give your mother one of these," she said, cupping a pill. "She's in shock."

Lewis looked out to the living room, where his mother was sitting statue-like on the couch watching a movie with the girls. "We're all in shock," he said. "I think she just wants to be left alone."

Lewis let the girls eat in front of the television to distract them, not that they weren't used to eating in front of the TV. His mother liked to tell him that his daughters would rot their brains away but tonight she kept her opinions to herself. Mabel Mattock was always wrinkling her nose at Lewis and Sophie's parenting. She disliked the mess of toys that dotted the living room like land mines, the gaudy oil paintings of Ginny and Stella that hung over the fireplace, the general lack of discipline.

Once the girls were fed, Lewis turned off the phone's ringer and poured himself a bourbon and Coke. He offered his mother a slice of pizza and a glass of wine, but she politely declined. None of the adults ate. Sophie wanted to leave the ringer on in case her father called with news, but Lewis was done with the phone. He was tipsy by the time Sophie's father came back from the morgue. Trip talked as men do in times of crisis, told Lewis that his father didn't suffer, that he was in a better place, that there would be justice. Sophie prodded her dad with questions and the doctor continued to fill the air with words as the girls sang along to some Disney song on the TV. Lewis drowned out the noise with booze.

His mother came and hugged him good-night and told the girls to sleep tight before retreating to the guest bedroom. A digital clock on the wall flashed half past nine but it was an hour off from the time change in the spring. Not much longer and it would be right again. "I should put the girls to bed," Lewis said, more to himself than anyone else. Sophie took a break from the conversation with her father to tell Lewis that was a good idea.

He turned off the television over the girls' weary and halfhearted protests, guided them to their room. Ginny asked about Grandpa. Again. Neither girl understood what was going on, but Lewis didn't know how to explain. They were just five, mature enough to think for themselves but naïve about the world and the people in it. He told Ginny they'd talk in the morning. Earlier he'd said they'd talk after dinner. He found that parenting was often just stalling on the questions you didn't want to answer and hoping your kids forgot to ask again, but Ginny and Stella never seemed to forget. Stella asked why his breath stank and he said he didn't know. One day he'd answer their questions. *I'm drunk,* he'd say. *Grandpa's dead.* But for now he said, "I love you" and waited for the girls to repeat it back to him, their voices rote and robotic but comforting nonetheless.

It was near midnight by the time Harlan left the office with the paperwork for Lew's murder in hand. He stopped by the ruins of the trailer park fire, which was just down the road from his place before going home. The town's volunteer crew had managed to keep the fire from turning the whole place to ash. The trailer's bent and scorched frame prevailed against the night sky even though the windows and doors had blown out and broken glass littered the grass. Harlan's flashlight revealed a couch reduced to coils and a stovepipe that leaned at an unholy angle, its sheet metal no longer moored to the remains of the roof. Other than the couch, the home looked empty. A few discernible odds and ends were buried among the debris—mugs, the blade of a kitchen knife whose handle had burned away. Frank's report claimed the place had been abandoned and that the fire was likely started by faulty wiring. Given what else the day had wrought, Harlan was inclined to go along with Frank's assumption and leave good enough alone. He doubted anyone would come asking the sheriff's department to do a thorough investigation, and it didn't make sense to bring an arson investigator out for a fire that no one cared about.

He called it a night and headed home, but as he pulled into the dirt drive of his property, his headlights hit upon two specters in the grass—a rail of a girl working herself atop a fat boy whose body writhed beneath her. The girl moved in slow circles, hips falling from the side, taking whatever the boy had to give. The boy's pants were clasped around ankles, and when the girl let gravity carry her, his legs kicked and made to rip them in two. She wore a long white T-shirt that he kept lifting to reach for her breasts, but she pushed him down easily, her palms burying into his fleshy, hairless chest. A quarter moon dangled low in the sky behind them like a lure at the end of its line. The boy pointed toward Harlan's truck and the girl turned to stare into the headlights, never stopping her up and down.

Harlan had caught prowlers before—dope-smoking refugees from the Spanish Manor—but nothing like this. He honked and the horn tinned into the lonesome, quiet night. Spurred to action, the boy rolled the girl over, slipped out, and ran buckshot for the woods, hitching up his pants as he went, his pale ass flashing like some prehistoric firefly through the cypress trees. Harlan cut the lights and let the girl get decent, a process she took her time doing.

"I was almost finished," she yelled when he stepped out. "That tubby was gonna come. I could see it in his eyes."

"Guess he should've stuck around," Harlan said.

She buttoned the waistband of her cutoffs and stuck out her hand, straight ahead and rigid like a man. Harlan ignored it. He knew her from the backs of cars he'd pulled over, had seen her running from house parties and caught her getting drunk in places she shouldn't. She was a tough case—a mother absent, a mean streak of a father. "You're trespassing, Matilda," he said.

"If you want to arrest me, go ahead. And call me Mattie." The girl's lips quivered and her belly heaved. Her eyes darted all over and beyond. She was high on something.

"All right, Mattie. I'm too tired to arrest you, so why don't you head on home."

The girl put a hand to her hip, shifted her weight, and jutted out the bone on the other side. "That's it?"

"What more do you want?"

"I don't know. Yell at me. Give me a lecture. Call me names or something."

Harlan started for his porch. "Next time," he said.

When he heard her feet moving, Harlan turned to watch the girl lope into the woods, her fingers hooking a bare belt loop to keep her shorts from falling. The quiet returned and he slumped onto a rain-soaked couch that barely fit his porch. The house was a shotgun, a glorified shack, but it faced the river—the view the sole reason Harlan had bought it. Graying clouds pulled themselves across the sky and stretched over the moon and stars. Headlights glinted through the cables of the suspension bridge connecting Kentucky to Ohio and the orange globes atop it gave off a soft glow. Harlan could hear the whir of a riverboat casino chugging along the water. He pictured desperate gamblers throwing their last dimes and found himself wishing he possessed even an ounce of their faith.

He scanned the write-up on Lew's murder. The dogs had found the shooter's spot along a ridge overlooking Josephine's, even turned up a small bit of bilious spit, but by the time Harlan reached the clearing, it had been dark and pretty much combed over. He and Del walked the woods with the dogs but came up empty. Frank and Paige spent the evening visiting a few of the county's most frequent offenders, taking their pulse, and Holly was coming up with a list of hard cases and inmates Lew had locked away that were recently released. Harlan and Lew had never seen eye to eye when it came to running the department, but no one deserved to go out like that—face disfigured and scorched. It made Harlan's stomach twist like a quirt.

The barbeque was meant to be a celebration of Lew, one in a series of campaign events leading up to his coronation as Finley County's first-ever four-term sheriff. Now the election was a month away and the lone candidate was an end-of-days crazy who headed up a militia of one. People would expect Harlan to run. Before Lew came along, Finley sheriffs and their chief deputies had carried on a tradition of trading terms back and forth like dueling banjos. At one point Harlan suggested he and Lew might do the same, but Lew didn't care much for tradition. He preferred being the boss. He kept the politicians happy and avoided bad press, and most people in Finley County had forgotten that anyone else had ever enforced the law.

A decade spent observing Lew taught Harlan that being sheriff was more about politics than policing anyway, and Harlan wasn't much of a bullshitter. But now the job was his, and there was a good chance it would be after the election, and if that happened, Harlan would change things. Lew had catered to Finley County's rich and powerful, but Harlan cared more about the people eking out a living along the fringes, the unfortunates whose drunken fights ended in assault charges and whose kids died of drug overdoses. He'd grown up watching his dad beat his mom and his mom threaten his dad, stood by while both of them drank away any semblance of their lingering humanity. In his early twenties, during his first years as a deputy, he'd pushed Lew to do outreach in the worst parts of the county, had lauded the benefits of preventive policing—a term he'd learned through his schooling. But Lew didn't care for newfangled ideas. Eventually Harlan stopped trying so hard. His ambitions were back-burnered and then one day they were forgotten. Lost, really. The only woman he'd ever loved died, and that took something out of him. Ever since he'd laid Angeline to rest, each successive sunup to sundown seemed a sort of accomplishment.

Marathon was the only place he'd ever called home, but Harlan had never fit in. He'd been too raggedy, too scatterbrained, too much a loner. He'd grown up poor, wore oversize, hand-me-down clothes patched with iron-ons, spent his weekends by the side of the highway selling junk his father salvaged and quilts his mother sewed. Every now and then, when he booked a former schoolyard bully, they would retell jokes from that long-ago past. *Harlan the dupe. Harlan smells like poop.*

Something had kept Harlan in Marathon and maybe this was it: he was *meant* to be sheriff. It wasn't happiness that kept him. Nor obligation. His father had drowned in the river. His mother followed not long after, her last days spent in a mental hospital. But if Harlan found Lew's killer, things would change. The other deputies would start to respect him and the town would do the same and his name might become as synonymous with "sheriff" as Lew's had been.

Harlan put the paperwork for the murder back in its folder and rolled a joint from a plastic bag hidden in the couch cushions. Cave crickets hopped across his lap, but he paid them no mind. He'd come to terms with the crickets, the snakes in the grass, the den of opossums burrowed beneath the house. There'd been a raccoon one summer that squatted on its hind legs and stared at Harlan while he smoked and to whom Harlan spoke when he was lonely.

Then one day it stopped showing up. That loss felt like any number of losses Harlan had experienced—random and raw. He mouthed her name—Angeline—and toked the joint as he sunk deeper into the couch. She would have been proud of him.

"Sheriff Harlan Dupee," he said to the crickets. He said it again, changing the cadence of his delivery, pausing to accentuate the word *sheriff*, speaking through clenched teeth, offering up a quick grin or handshake. He said it over and over, like a mantra, repeated it aloud until sleep overwhelmed him.

t w o

Harlan woke to the ringing of the phone and stretched his long limbs. He couldn't remember the last time someone other than a telemarketer had called him, so he let it cry out until it was obvious the person on the other end of the line wouldn't take no for an answer. "Good morning," Holly said as he picked up. "Making sure you were up."

"I am."

"So I'll see you soon."

"Are you at the office?" Harlan asked. "What time is it?"

"Time to get moving."

Holly hung up and Harlan staggered to the porch for the day's first cigarette. A heavy damp hung in the air and bursts of wind shook the trees and knocked river birds from their paths. In the east a rolling mass of reddish clouds danced with the rising sun. Harlan wanted to walk the ridge where they'd found the shooter's spit-up in the light of day but the rain was coming to wash it clean.

Holly, who tended to ignore him when he walked in, pushed a stack of folders into Harlan's arms before he could say hello. The phone was ringing but she didn't answer. "Judge Craycraft is going to be in soon, so go over there and get sworn in. Also, the coroner needs you to fill out the forms in this top folder. The second is the write-up on what we sent to the crime lab. And the third is empty. That's for your investigation."

Harlan shuffled through the paperwork as the phone continued to ring. "Are you gonna answer that?" he asked.

"Jesus Christ," Holly said. "I just told you what all that crap is. And leave the phone to me. You need a coffee?"

"You got an Ale-8?"

"Real men drink coffee in the morning," Holly said before making a big show of grabbing a soft drink from the fridge. "Listen, we're gonna be working like dogs until you find out who shot Lew. The phone is ringing off the hook. Parents are scared to send their kids to school. We've got bum tips from every jackass in the county who hates his neighbor. All anyone knows is that Lew was the law and Lew's dead, so get yourself looking presentable and go see the judge. You can't be sheriff until he goes through the anointing ceremony or whatever the hell it is. In the meantime, I'll put these folders in your new office."

"New office?"

"That's right. The one that says 'sheriff' on the front. A town needs a sheriff, a sheriff needs a sheriff's office, and by God, you're about to be sheriff." She tossed a set of keys to him. "You're driving Lew's cruiser now. I had it brought back this morning."

The phone rang again.

"On second thought," Holly said, "take the coroner's forms and fill them out while Craycraft makes you wait."

She picked up the call and covered the mouthpiece while Harlan stood there like a rock. "How do you know he's gonna make me wait?"

"'Cause he wants to prove he's got bigger balls than you," she said. "That's the way men do things. Now get."

The judge did make Harlan wait. Craycraft passed him on the way into his chambers, said he needed a minute to get settled, then took a good ten before calling for Harlan. Craycraft talked about Lew and what a good man he was and how shocking his murder was and who would do such a thing and so on, and by the time he bestowed upon Harlan temporary authority as sheriff, the first drops of rain had started to hit the Ohio. Harlan sprinted from the courthouse hoping to reach the ridge before the storm was more than a drizzle, but as soon as he started the cruiser, the dispatch buzzed with Holly's voice asking if he wanted his old files in his new office.

Harlan sped away from downtown. "Can this wait?"

"Sure. But I think it would be good to show the other deputies you're the new boss."

"I'm sure they'll figure it out."

"You'd be surprised. Speaking of the deputies, they're complaining about the extra shifts."

"What extra shifts?" Harlan nearly missed his turn, banked hard left.

"I have Paige flanking school busses so parents feel safe. Del is checking in on everyone recently out of lockup, and Frank is following up on the best tips that have been phoned in."

"That sounds good."

"I know, but that's everyone, Harlan. Short term it works but we can't all work twenty-four-hour shifts."

"Can this wait, too?"

"Sure. Whatever you want. I'm just keeping you in the loop."

Harlan pulled the cruiser to the side of the road. "Is anybody else in the office with you right now, Holly?"

"Nope."

"Good. Then here's the deal. I don't care which office is mine and I don't want to explain a schedule I didn't make. I'd like to do a little real police work first. So call the state police and ask them to up their presence in the county. Otherwise, as much as I'm sure it will pain you, deal with it." There was silence on the other end. Harlan laid his head softly against the steering wheel. He couldn't afford to piss off Holly; she was the glue that kept the department together. "You still there?" he asked.

The dispatch crackled again. "That's the first sensible thing you've said all day."

Harlan sighed and pulled back onto the road, though as soon as he turned in to a subdivision that bordered the ridge, the clouds opened up and rain started collapsing in sheets across the windshield. The subdivision was a lagging project started by Square Homes, developers who'd invested heavily in northern Kentucky but had yet to see a profit. Each year a handful of newcomers moved into one of the prefab houses and slowly a neighborhood formed but just a half mile in from the entrance you came upon a wasteland the builders deemed "potential." Plumbing snaked through the ground, and electric was strung on poles, but the fruits of labor—the houses—were nowhere to be seen. Barren lots bordered by paved roads and sidewalks.

Harlan didn't know what he expected to find that the dogs hadn't, but he couldn't think of any other place to start. He parked next to a home the builders would be lucky to complete come winter. Rain raced through the frame and splashed against the foundation, which was fast turning to mud. Above him heavy gumdrops beat against the cruiser's roof with no apparent rhythm and no sign of letting up. Harlan stepped out.

Leaves slicked the wooded paths and he slid down a couple embankments in his boots. The trees provided cover but by the time he reached the clearing, the storm was full bore. He stepped to the edge and looked east toward the soggy downtown. The river had crested a couple times in the past but more often it was the runoff from the hills that caused flooding and sent mud slides oozing through the streets of downtown. A halfhearted waterfall formed by his feet and pitched small rocks and leaves below. Harlan rolled a cigarette from under the cover of trees and looked across the murky river.

The Ohio side hunkered down against a low fog. The widest banks protruded from the mist like tiny islands veiled in silk. Harlan cupped the cigarette to his mouth. Through the haze he could make out the Entwhistle place. The tent and chairs were still set up for the party—the tent sagging with rain, the chairs sinking into the ground. It looked like a mistake, a party planned on the wrong day. Harlan wondered how long it would be before Josephine called the department and asked them to clean up their mess.

He tried to imagine the shooter but his mind drew a blank. Harlan could understand the petty criminals of Marathon—the drunks and small-time thieves who started fights and stole because they were bored, desperate, and depressed. Their sort of impulsive wrongdoing made sense but shooting another person, that he couldn't understand. He crouched down and pretended to be the culprit. The river road cut a clean path to Josephine's and the rock beneath him was flat. It wasn't an easy shot but not impossible, not for a person with a steady hand. Whoever wanted Lew dead had planned it, that much was certain. Harlan made a note to have Del check in with C. Alistair Noll, the end-of-days crazy who was running against Lew in the election, but he doubted Alistair was involved. He was more local eccentric than criminal, liked to run for sheriff every four years by promising not to enforce drug laws or issue parking tickets.

Until the crime lab finished their work, Harlan wouldn't have much to go on. Murders in Finley County were usually straightforward: wives fed up with abusive husbands, cuckolded husbands exacting revenge on unfaithful wives, friends and families turned against one another for reasons of money or pride or sin. Harlan walked the clearing once more, looked for something, anything, that might give him some direction—found nothing.

———

Mary Jane scanned the street from her bedroom window. Except for a heavy rain, it was unremarkable in every way. No police. No angry mobs. No reason for pause. She walked by the guest bedroom and noticed her mother—still asleep—though there was nothing unusual in that either. Lyda Finley spent more time sleeping in the guest bedroom than she did beside her husband. Mary Jane hesitated at the door. For the first time in as long as she could remember her mother *looked* vulnerable. Lyda's mouth hung slack and her horsey teeth, once so striking, protruded. They'd yellowed from cigarettes and strands of her golden hair had faded to silver and the skin between her breasts was spotting. For all her harping on Mary Jane about letting herself go, about needing to put down the ice cream and pick up the jump rope, Lyda was aging in a way that would devastate her.

Mary Jane drove through the downpour to a gas station pay phone, hunkered under the store's awning, and dialed Mark. She needed to know that he was out there, thinking about her just like she was thinking about him. She needed connection. As the phone rang, she practiced saying hello casually and was caught off guard when he picked up.

"Hey," she blurted.

"MJ," Mark said. "Is everything okay?"

"Yeah. I mean . . . yeah. I wanted to hear your voice."

"Oh," he said. "Okay."

"Everything is fine. I did it. I mean, we did it."

Mark hushed her before she said more.

"It's okay," she said. "I'm at a pay phone. Like in the movies." The rain beat down behind her in a steady rhythm—the soundtrack to their story.

Mark sighed. "We need to act normal and not call attention to ourselves. And calling me from a pay phone is *not* normal. Do you understand?"

"Sure. It's just . . . I'm sorry." Mary Jane hesitated. She didn't owe Mark an apology. It was easy for him to decide what was normal. He hadn't been there. He hadn't watched Lew die. She searched for the right thing to say, came up empty, listened to Mark breathe. He was the one person in the world who might understand what she was feeling, though what that was she didn't exactly know. "Just tell me everything is going to be okay," she said.

"Everything is going to be okay."

Mary Jane took a deep breath. "Okay," she said. "Let me hear some of your French."

"Je voudrais un œuf, s'il vous plait."

"That's good," Mary Jane said. "I hope you like eggs."

Mark gave a small laugh. "Hang tight, babe," he said. "There's no reason to worry." But Mary Jane did worry. She worried. She couldn't stay in Marathon and listen to people talk about Lew, couldn't hold up under that stress. "Just act normal," Mark said again, as if it were that easy. "We're almost there. I'm going to get the money and then we'll leave. Just like we planned."

Mary Jane cracked a smile. She liked when he referred to them as a pair—we, us, our. "I love you," she said, but Mark was talking over her.

"I've got to run to class," he was saying. "Stay strong."

The line went dead.

Mary Jane couldn't be sure if he'd heard her. He'd told her he loved her before, but his love always followed hers. An *I love you, too,* as if his was conditional. One time she'd become angry with him over it, but Mark claimed the more you used the word love, the more you became accustomed to it, and the less that love meant, which sounded like BS to Mary Jane.

She hurried back to her coupe through the storm, hands shaking as she fit the key in the ignition. She'd said it. Why didn't he? Why couldn't he even hear her? Mascara ran from the corners of her eyes, whether from the rain or the tears, it didn't matter. Her lips trembled as she turned the rearview mirror on herself. Was this the face of the girl Mark would build a life with? That he would love? "Fucking ugly." Mary Jane wept. "Fucking monster!" She slapped herself hard across the cheek, then banged her fist against the steering wheel. The horn sounded and a couple of people pumping gas glanced in her direction, but they didn't see her, they didn't care. She fumbled in her purse and pulled out a pill, hesitated, then swallowed it dry. Swallowed another. The world was such an easy place to fade away.

Mary Jane pined for those days when other girls clamored to be her friend, when boys—men even—had stopped to look at her. People had seen her then. Mark was the one person who'd stayed by her through the worst years, the guy who took her home from the party, the friend who listened when she complained about her parents, the boy who took her virginity. Theirs was a clandestine but long-standing love, an understanding. She belonged with him. *I love you* was just a phrase. Just words. Actions spoke louder than words. And Mary Jane had acted. They were in the darkest part of the story but the dawn lay ahead. She imagined driving north with Mark through Ohio, Pennsylvania, New York, crossing the border into Quebec, into a whole different country. She closed her eyes and started the coupe, kept the car in park as she pressed the gas and listened to the rattle of the engine as if it were taking her there. She imagined snowflakes melting on the windshield, tires crunching along icy ground, Mark pointing the way beside her.

Mark Gaines's left hand moved robotically across his notebook, copying whatever the professor wrote on the board even though he was busy thinking about Mary Jane. He wished he could be in Marathon with her—put a pill in her hand if need be—but it was better to keep his distance in case the situation took a bad turn. Mary Jane wanted to run away that moment, as if the cops were chasing her, which they weren't, so far as he knew. He could tell she was scared and he was scared, too, and that united them, but Mark was scared because she'd done her part and now it was up to him to follow through on his.

He looked at his notes—chemical compounds he didn't recognize and phrases he couldn't parse. The professor droned on, switching dry erase markers from blue to green to red, as if the rainbow of color might make what he said more interesting. Mark gathered his books. He'd seen other students leave midlecture but he'd never been so bold himself. He half-expected the professor to stop him or his fellow classmates to *tsk tsk*, but no one so much as raised an eyebrow as he climbed the auditorium steps and escaped into the bright hallway.

He hadn't skipped a class in college yet, a fact he was proud of and occasionally wrote in his planner to remind him of how hard he'd worked since beginning at the university. But that achievement was over. He needed to put school behind him. Another student came barreling out of the classroom not long after and said, "BORE-ing." Mark forced a smile, listened to the guy complain, and nodded along without offering much in return.

It was a blustery, wet day, and Mark kept his head down as he trudged across campus toward the library. His pager went off and he checked it even though he knew it was Chance. In his backpack Mark carried thousands of dollars in prescription pills, and in less than an hour he'd be making his final deal—the end of an era he was all too happy to see pass.

He settled himself at the usual nook in the library basement and waited. Chance marched in like clockwork thirty minutes later wearing a ripped shirt, warped cap, and steel-toed boots. The backpack slung over his right shoulder seemed out of place. With his pinched face, tattoos, and graying stringy hair, Chance didn't pass for a college student. He looked more likely to be fresh out of jail, though he'd once bragged to Mark that he'd never been arrested, never even been pulled over for driving too fast. This fact he chalked up to his intelligence and the authorities' lack thereof. Every time they met, Mark wondered what onlookers would make of them— the student and the menacing hillbilly.

"Hey Boo Boo," Chance said as he set down a stack of library books and slung himself into a leather armchair. Mark pulled the books from his backpack and left the pills inside, placed the backpack under the table. Afterward Chance put his own bag down and in this manner they made the exchange. They'd learned to trust each other more or less. Mark wondered what Chance would do the following week when he didn't show up, wondered if Chance would come looking for him or leave the past alone. He hoped it was the latter, hoped that whatever rapport they'd built counted for something.

He'd met Chance during his freshman year. Before college Mark had dealt pills in Marathon, and not long after he joined the pharmacy program and started work at the campus clinic, he'd found ways to game the system. There was outright theft, pocketing from bulk stock, but there were also Medicare patients with multiple prescriptions. Mark learned to target the clinic's most beleaguered clientele, then visited their houses and told them about a pill buyback program for terminally ill patients who couldn't afford medication. He never pressured people but he offered cash, and those in need accepted. Soon Mark had more Oxy than he could sell. The clinic scheme was how Chance found him—Chance by way of his mother, Linda Goodenow, who was one of those beleaguered patients. Linda told her son about the nice young man from the university and how she had money for groceries now and

Chance didn't need to keep driving all this way and handing over his hard-earned paychecks to take care of her, and no, she didn't really need the OxyContin because she also had a prescription for Vicodin and she didn't like the way the Oxy made her feel anyway.

Chance had waited for Mark's next visit, then followed him to the library and told him that if he kept making handshake deals in the quad he would get caught or piss off someone he didn't want to piss off. Then Chance explained that he too had business in the pill trade and no matter how careful Mark thought he was, someone like Chance would find out about him eventually. "'Between two worlds life hovers like a star, twixt night and morn, upon the horizon's verge,'" Chance said. Mark didn't know whether he meant it as a threat or something else. Chance explained that it was a quote from Byron and that Mark was that hovering star, which meant Chance was both night and morn.

Mark was scared, convinced he'd end the night in a ditch—dead or dying—but Chance suggested a partnership instead. "I need another supplier," he said, laying an envelope on the table. "That's five G's. Come back next week with ten thousand milligrams and we'll have ourselves a partnership. But if you don't come back, I'll find you. And it'll hurt."

Mark stared at the envelope. "Why me?"

"A kid like you doesn't want to get caught and fuck up his life," Chance said. "And I don't either. I got a good life. What's good for the goose is good for the gander, you know?"

"The gander?"

"That's the male goose. The big-dick kingpin. And that's me. You're the female goose 'cause you're scared. You don't even realize I'm the best thing that's ever happened to you."

Mark had nodded along as if this made sense, picked up the envelope, and sealed his fate. What else could he have done?

A year had passed since that first meeting but not much had changed. Now, Chance opened the backpack, took a cursory glance at the pills, and zipped it back up. "So how're classes?" he asked, his voice filled with fake cheer.

"Fine."

"Just fine?"

"Yeah. Fine."

"My mama says 'fine' stands for fearful, insecure, negative, and emotional."

"Is that right?"

"Yeah, but my mama is full of shit. You know that. Sometimes fine is just fine."

Mark shrugged.

"Just keep studying hard, Marcus Aurelius. You're gonna make a hell of a pharmacist one day." Chance turned his head, pressed his chin to pop his neck, and set his boots up on the table before cracking open a book.

Mark felt the eyes of other students on them. "Are you going to stick around?" he asked.

"I believe this library's open to the public, Mark, so I thought maybe I'd set here and expand my mind. Don't let me bother you."

"I have someplace I need to be." Mark put his books in the backpack Chance had brought. As he zipped it up, Chance grabbed his arm.

"Just remember I'm the one in charge," Chance said. "And when I want to read some fucking history book, I will read that fucking history book. Do you understand?"

Mark pulled his arm away. "You want me to stay and keep you company?"

Chance smiled. He liked seeing Mark show a little spine. "No," he said. "Go on home and yank your little nubbin or whatever it is you college boys do."

Mark gave a half smile and turned to leave. When he glanced back, he saw that Chance was reading intently—pen poised in hand as if ready to take notes.

Harlan drove the beat-down county roads inland past trailers and tobacco fields, past crumbling stone fences and Amish homesteads. The Amish had started moving down from Ohio a few years back to buy up eyesore farms. Lew had called them "backwoods motherfuckers," but Harlan liked to watch the Amish work, liked that they used the old-time methods and cared enough to paint their weather-beaten homes. The wipers made loud, futile whipping noises against the rain, and Harlan could barely see the road ahead but he didn't need to. He knew the county like a map etched into the backs of his hands.

In the hills south of Marathon, the cruiser planed across the slickwater ponds that formed in the dales. Harlan wished he could drive his pickup on the job. The tight steering and touchy brakes of the county's Impalas put a man on edge. His truck wasn't sleek but steadfast. Growing up, Harlan's daddy had preached the values of the Ford Motor Company, claimed he'd rather push a Ford than drive a Chevy, and though Harlan didn't care much for his daddy's opinions, that one he'd adopted as his own.

He crossed the county line and parked on the muddy-rut road of a tobacco farm cut clean of its burley. He probably should have been out with the other deputies breaking down ex-cons or looking over Lew's case files, doing something more hands-on, but he needed time to think. Lew always hated that about Harlan; what Harlan called prudence, Lew called dawdling. Lew, whose cruiser was a mess. Beneath the driver-side window tobacco stains from misdirected spits splotched the vinyl. Harlan cleaned them with rainwater and the bandanna from his pocket. Under the driver's seat he found a plastic bag from Walmart and a half-empty bottle of bourbon, which he poured onto the soggy ground. He used the bag for trash, picking up crumb-filled packages of chips, Styrofoam cups stained with coffee, tins of Skoal. Among the maps in the doorside compartment, he picked out loose change from the sticky remains of soda. The cruiser's filth spoke to Lew's various faults. He drank too much, dipped too much, ate too much. Even though he was good at his job, good at telling his deputies where they needed to be and when, the rest of Lew's life was a mess. He rarely took days off and he spent those drinking in the office, looking for someone willing to shoot the shit.

In the glove box Harlan found a cell phone among a mess of candy wrappers and used napkins. He didn't recall ever seeing Lew with a cell phone, had never used one himself. The first time Harlan ever saw someone on a cell, he mistook the man for a lunatic, though more and more he'd seen people walking down the street and talking into their hands. Harlan couldn't understand the desire. There wasn't one person he'd like to talk to so bad it couldn't wait.

He dialed the number for the sheriff's department but nothing happened. Then he examined the keypad and pressed the green button—green for go—and the phone started to ring. When Holly answered, her voice surprised him, the way it rose out of a thin, staticky air, and Harlan, as if caught in a prank, pressed all manner of buttons to hang up. In between the pings, he could hear Holly cursing, and at some point, he stopped trying to end the call and said hello.

"Harlan," Holly said. "Is that you? What the hell?"

Harlan could barely hear her. "I found this cellular phone in Lew's cruiser," he shouted. "Do you know if it's his?"

"I don't know," she said. "But you don't need to yell about it. Maybe he confiscated it off someone."

Harlan lowered his voice. "You think you could get me the phone records?"

"I don't see why not."

"Okay." Harlan looked at the phone. "I don't know how you hang this thing up, so why don't you do that on your end."

"Gladly," Holly said and the line went dead.

Lewis took his mother's feather-boned fingers into his own and returned them to her lap. "Let's not listen to the radio," he said. Like most people who knew Mabel Mattock, Lewis thought her a touch odd. He'd been close with his mother as a child but over time adopted his father's attitude toward her—mild embarrassment coupled with condescension. His father's loud talk, his sheer size, had lured Lewis away. It was a split he recognized in his own family, the way he favored Ginny and Sophie favored Stella. As soon as the girls had started to form personalities, it seemed like sides were taken for a lifelong tug-of-war. When his mother reached for the stereo a second time, Lewis wondered if it was an early sign of dementia. She was a decade older than his father and frailer; Lewis never once thought his dad would be the first to go.

Mabel settled on a song with screeching guitars and a loud singer, something like Van Halen or AC/DC, and turned the volume up until the floorboards rumbled. Then she opened the window and took big breaths of damp air.

"Mom," Lewis said, as he turned the volume down. "It's cold outside."

She turned to him and said, "How are you *really* doing, Lewis?" Her questions always sounded like accusations.

"I'm fine," he said.

"I don't know how I'm doing," she replied, not that he'd asked.

"I'm sad and shocked. That's what I'm supposed to be. But I'm also . . . at peace."

Lewis pulled in front of the Baker Family Funeral Home and parked. "You're probably just confused," he said. He walked around the Explorer to help her down, but his mother didn't move.

"I don't feel like doing this," she said.

Ezra Baker watched them from the front step, smoking a cigarette. Lewis raised a hand hello. "You don't have to do anything. I can handle it."

"Just make sure he gets a fancy casket," she said. "Your father liked fancy things."

"You're okay here?"

"Leave the keys. I'll listen to the stereo."

Lewis didn't particularly feel like planning a funeral either, but these sorts of tasks were his responsibility now. He took the sheriff's uniform from the backseat. Olive piping ran down beige pants and there was a matching olive tie. The starched shirt stood stiff on a hanger to which Lewis had tied a plastic bag of insignias and a badge. It was a uniform he respected but had never worn. His father wasn't keen on the idea of Lewis becoming a deputy. "It's not a line of work that suits you," he'd told Lewis after he graduated with a two-year degree. That was always the way with his father. Lew Mattock never thought anyone as capable as himself, especially not his son. No matter what Lewis achieved—a college degree, his own business, a wife and kids—it never seemed to make his father proud.

When he reached the top step of the funeral home, Ezra Baker tendered a limp, sweaty hand and muted condolences. Inside the vases of fresh flowers failed to mask the smell of bleach and the plush carpet swallowed Lewis's steps. Through an open arch, he could see a coffin. "We have a service later," Ezra explained before closing the room off with heavy drapes. "I see you chose the uniform."

"I doubt Dad even owned Sunday clothes," Lewis replied, handing over the hanger. "There's a specific location for each honor, so if you need help—"

"If we have questions, we'll ask." Ezra fingered the metal pins through the plastic. "But we should be fine."

Lewis shoved his hands in his pockets.

"Why don't we go into my office and discuss the details." Ezra put one of his clammy hands to Lewis's shoulder but Lewis drew back. He didn't care about the details. And he didn't want to spend another minute in the presence of Ezra Baker's practiced solemnity.

"There're a lot things I need to get done," Lewis said. "I'm sure you can imagine."

"Of course. This won't take long."

"Just make sure he has a nice casket."

"I can show you a catalogue—"

Lewis shook his head. "No need. Just pick a nice one. He already has a plot at the cemetery."

"We should discuss a few matters at least," Ezra said. "A pastor? A budget?"

Lewis took out his checkbook. "What's suitable?"

"I really—"

"A couple thousand to start?"

Ezra straightened his thin tie. Its black had turned purplish from too many washings. "Three would suffice."

Lewis scribbled the check and handed it over.

"If you change your mind and want to help—"

"I won't."

"And you don't have a family pastor?"

"No," Lewis said. "Anyone is fine. Really, Ezra, I have to go."

Ezra followed him out and lit another cigarette on the porch, drew the smoke deep into his lungs and out his nose. Death. It was a good business. The sort that thrives when things go wrong.

Harlan put the car in drive and crossed back into Finley County. When he reached the sheriff's department, he found his office empty save a rectangular desk and bare shelves. Holly had moved everything into the sheriff's office proper, though photos of Lew still hung on the wall and Lew's belongings were scattered about. On the desk a mug filled with Harlan's favorite pencils sat beside neat stacks of files. There were Post-it notes on everything. One pile of papers was marked, "Things for you to sign." Another, "Things for you to ignore." Four banker's boxes in front of the desk said, "Lew's case history" and a note on the desk itself said, "Harlan's desk." The filing cabinet was locked and Holly had written, "Couldn't find the key" on a pink Post-it. When Harlan asked about it, she said, "I don't know, but that cabinet's not exactly Fort Knox."

He picked up the folder of witness statements Frank took following the murder. Frank's apathy for the task was apparent in his chicken-scrawl writing, and Harlan could make out little more than the names, but the more he read, the more he was reminded of how close Lew kept the kingmakers of Marathon. And it wasn't just local politicians. There were heavy hitters from the state Democratic Party—men and women who decided which candidates to back in the primary—and, since Finley was longtime Democrat country, pretty much decided who would run things. There were a few lines from Lewis Mattock about pulling his father off the grill, a few from Josephine about nothing being out of the ordinary that day. Little else. Harlan put down Frank's notes and started in on Lew's case history, earmarking repeat offenders and files that caught his eye.

In the desk's top drawer, he found Lew's flask and had a taste. Lew had hidden his drinking when Harlan started as a deputy—it was the sort of thing you smelled on his breath and pretended didn't exist—but over time Lew tired of the charade. For years

Harlan had envied Lew's position, his swagger and easy talk, but aside from a grate-covered window that looked onto a patch of dirt, Lew's office wasn't much different from Harlan's old one. It wasn't even Lew's anymore. Soon someone would come along and scratch his name off the wire-hatched glass, ship his belongings home to his family.

Harlan opened his new window and lit a smoke, started taking down Lew's photos and plaques one by one. There was Lew and his son holding a gigantic catfish. Lew shaking hands with the governor. Lew brandishing his service weapon. A collection of MATTOCK FOR SHERIFF signs leaned against the wall and Harlan lifted one up to study it. Lew's last name was in white over a blue background. A large red star anchored the top left corner. Lew had a flair for the patriotic; he liked to pepper his speeches with phrases by Lincoln and Jefferson—bits of wisdom borrowed from inspirational quote books. Harlan carried the sign to his desk, cigarette dangling from his lips, and started drawing his own campaign logo. At first he just copied Lew's, but Harlan's last name didn't have the same weight as Mattock. "Dupee for Sheriff" wouldn't work. Even as an adult Harlan was embarrassed by the name—its strange French pronunciation, its damning link to the men who'd come before him. His first name was better, taken from a great-uncle who'd been named after the county where he was born, but even that didn't have the same ring as Mattock. Harlan decided on his full name, started sketching pictures around it. A flag. A line of stars. A badge. None of them seemed right and he settled for simplicity—HARLAN DUPEE FOR SHERIFF—no ornament. He liked the way the black ink looked against the background of his yellow pad.

As he admired his work, Holly barged in and said, "No smoking in the office."

"I thought I was in charge," Harlan replied.

"Sheriffs have rules, too," she said. "Snuff it."

Harlan pushed the butt through the window grate and put up his hands like an innocent. "I thought I'd go grab a bite to eat. You want anything?"

"Clean air would be nice."

His mother asked Lewis to drop her off at her house. The thought of leaving her alone made him feel guilty—it was Lewis's responsibility to comfort her—but then again his mother didn't seem to need much comforting, and Lewis didn't know what to make of that. His father hadn't exactly treated his mother well; there were reasons Mabel Mattock might not be heartbroken over her husband's death, but it would have been easier if she just came out and said so, if she didn't just sit there like some enlightened nun while the world teetered around her.

He parked in the driveway of his childhood home and killed the engine. The house sat matter-of-factly at the end of a cul-de-sac, the street's other houses a straight-line procession leading up to it. The lot was double-sized but the house itself, unremarkable—vinyl siding, small windows, a taped-over doorbell. Two dogwoods that had never learned to flower leaned at an angle in the yard and the shrubs that bordered the front were scraggly and thin.

"Let me help you," Lewis said, opening his door.

"I can manage," his mother replied. As she made her way to the house, Mabel's stooped back straightened ever so slightly, and she waved before closing the front door. The street went silent. The house pressed flat as if Lewis was looking at a poster and not the real thing.

He club-footed the gas and headed downtown. He needed a cup of coffee and could stand a gravy biscuit, but when he reached the diner, he saw that a table of his father's buddies had gathered inside. If he walked in, a hush would fall over the place, and Lewis couldn't bear the thought of more condolences. He watched Susie, the Korean woman who'd married a vet and saved the diner from being boarded up, set a bucket of beer at the table. The men would sit there all day, drinking coffee and beer and eating fatty food when it suited them. Some of them were so old they'd worked in the mills when cargo boats still tread up and down the river.

When he was a kid, a different table of old-timers had regaled Lewis with tall tales about dinosaur fish in the river and Simon Kenton, who'd owned half the state and lost it all because he couldn't read. It was as if the men had lived since the dawn of time. They talked about Daniel Boone like he was an old friend. But when Lewis repeated their stories, his father would chide him. "Don't put stock in those fools," Lew would say. "A man shouldn't live in the past."

In that, at least, his father stayed true to his word. Lew Mattock always looked ahead. In high school Lewis had been a decent foot-ball player; he played both ways—linebacker and tight end—and during his junior season, he single-handedly won a game with a forced fumble and a last-second touchdown grab. He'd been given the game ball, a rousing cheer from the stands, and a headline in the newspaper, but what Lewis remembered most about that night wasn't the adoration of strangers, it was the ride home with his father. Lew reminded him he'd missed a tackle at the end of the first half and dropped a pass on third down, that he could do better next time. "Never be content," he'd said. They'd driven the rest of the way in silence, and when his mother cut out the newspaper article a few days later and suggested they get it framed, Lewis told her not to go to the trouble, to wait until he did something truly special.

Knuckles rapped against the passenger-side window of the Explorer, and Lewis looked up to find the crooked face of Harlan Dupee staring back at him. Harlan removed his ball cap and brushed his stringy hair behind his ears as Lewis lowered the window.

"I saw you setting here," Harlan said. "And I didn't want to bother you but I felt I should tell you we're all real broken up about what happened. Shocked. And we're going to work around the clock until we figure out who did this."

Lewis nodded. He'd never minded Harlan but he'd never thought much of him either. Harlan had been a few years ahead in school, but he never stood out in any particular way, a loner then just as he was now. He looked older than his thirty-some years but then again he'd always somehow looked old. Harlan had only been promoted to chief deputy because his father wanted a patsy in the position. Lew had worried a capable second-in-command might campaign against him one day. Now that plan had backfired. It was Harlan who was left to find his dad's killer. Harlan, who'd been cowering on the ground while Lewis pulled his dad from the grill.

"You have any leads?" Lewis asked.

Harlan looked down. "We're coming at it from a couple angles. There's evidence down at the crime lab and we're checking in with people he arrested recently. That sort of thing."

Lewis changed the subject. "I came to get a cup of coffee," he said. "But I don't feel like dealing with those old liars."

"Wait here." Harlan headed inside and came back a minute later with a Styrofoam cup and boatloads of cream and sugar. "I didn't know how you take it," he said.

"I appreciate it," Lewis replied.

Harlan opened his mouth as if he had something more to say, then closed it.

"I should be heading home," Lewis said.

Harlan put out his hand to shake before Lewis raised the window. "I'll be by at some point to talk. Just standard investigation stuff."

"I don't know how much help I can be. You were there, same as me."

"Like I said. Just standard procedure." Harlan donned his cap. "Take care of yourself, Lewis."

Lewis watched Harlan head back into the diner, then headed home for a drink.

Jackson opened Mary Jane's door just enough to poke his head in and say he was going to the country club for dinner. "Your mother seems to have left," he said. "I don't know where to, but I doubt it was the grocery store."

"That's fine," Mary Jane said. "I'll manage." She hoped this might end the conversation. She understood that her father wasn't inviting her to join him; he just needed a sounding board to complain about Lyda. Sometimes she felt less like a daughter than a warehouse to store her parents' grievances.

"Maybe tomorrow we'll all eat Sunday dinner together," Jackson said. "Like a proper family."

"Maybe," Mary Jane replied, unable to mask her sarcasm. Formal Sunday dinners were a relic of her father's childhood that he futilely tried to maintain, though they usually ended in raised voices and at their best were filled with awkward silence.

"I don't know why I try with you," Jackson said.

Mary Jane couldn't let this pass. "Yeah," she said. "You try real hard."

Jackson huffed dramatically. "I don't know what's going on with you, Mary Jane, but you need to look in the mirror and start making some changes."

She flicked him off as he closed the door and tried not to cry, tried not to care. She'd never felt close to her father. As a child her grandfather had filled the void. It wasn't until she started spending the night at friends' houses and met fathers who played games and hugged their kids good-night that she realized her own dad was notable mostly for his absence. Most days Jackson could be found hacking the golf ball at Idle Haven; most nights he could be found at the bar trading bullshit stories with other old rich men. As a kid, Mary Jane had loved swimming at Idle Haven's pool, but she grew to hate the rules about what you could wear and who you could bring and when. The Haven, as its members called it, was a throwback to old-guard southern conservatism, a place with separate lounges for men and women and black porters in white gloves. Her parents found comfort in Idle Haven's defense of status quo, but as Mary Jane grew older and learned to think for herself, she came to hate everything about the club. She didn't want to become her mother playing doubles tennis, didn't want to become her father talking about what kind of "stock" this person or that came from.

It was only after she failed to get into college that Jackson's fatherly indifference turned into outright disappointment and that disappointment morphed into resentment. Both his and hers. Jackson tried to persuade the University of Kentucky to rethink their decision—it was his alma mater after all—but Mary Jane's grades and test scores were an embarrassment. They couldn't talk anymore without fighting. It was the same with her mother, though Lyda's shortcoming had never been indifference. Her mother had tried to shape Mary Jane into a version of herself, as if she were a nesting doll, but Mary Jane stopped fitting the mold. Every once in a while she told Mary Jane she could still be beautiful, but it was always couched with the words *if you only* or *if you would just* . . .

Mary Jane climbed the stairs to her father's third-floor office. Jackson's desk was that of a man who spent too much time with his work. Papers paralleled edges in perfect stacks. Ornaments sat catercorner. A gilt pen was clipped to a notepad with a list of letters and numbers that had something to do with investment. Mary Jane licked the coating off an OxyContin, crushed it, and snorted a line of blue dust. Her life had become a routine of drug-induced ups and downs, but the office was a special treat—the best room in the house to get high. The windows were two squares that touched both the floor and slanted ceiling. She'd liked to stand between them as a girl: big as a wall!

Mary Jane couldn't spend another night in the house sad and alone; she wanted to go out into the world, to revel. She decided to call Tara Koehler. Even though Tara was a year younger and they'd never been that close, Tara liked to party. Besides, Tara was as close a thing to a friend as Mary Jane had left in Marathon. Almost everyone she'd known growing up had moved on—to college, the military, jobs in other towns. Mary Jane was supposed to have done the same but she'd stalled out.

She snorted the rest of the Oxy, pulled out the phone book, and dialed Tara's number. When a voice said hello, her thoughts cobwebbed. "Hello? Hello?"

Mary Jane's eyelids fluttered as the Oxy pulsed through her. "Tara?"

"Yeah. Who's this?"

"It's Mary Jane. Finley."

"Mary Jane? You don't sound so good."

"I'm okay. I took some pills."

"Hold on." She heard the cupping of the receiver, followed by a whisper. "What did you take?"

"An Oxy. Will you pick me up and take me somewhere?"

"You got any more?" The room shifted. The ceiling bore down. Mary Jane became lost in the pattern of a rug. "Mary Jane?"

"Sorry. I . . . I have more."

"If you can get me high, I'll take you to the dirt track."

"Sure. Anything. Just come over."

Mary Jane hung up and looked down at her legs. They jangled but she didn't control them. Parts of her raced, flew, and hummed.

Parts of her stayed numb. She grabbed the desk and swiveled the chair. Come on feet! Come on legs! She stood. She stumbled. She walked. What freedom!

The office *was* the best place to get high. Streetlight slanted through the cat-eye windows and the musty smell of books filled the air and the faces in the photos that hung along the wall stared back at her. She studied a pair of Civil War soldiers in a split frame— both of them kin. The Confederate rested an arm across a saddle, his hand loosely gripping a pistol. An unlit cigarette dangled from his lips. He was handsome and cool, nothing like the Union man standing rigidly before a bullet-marked wall with his arms crossed like he didn't know what to do with them. Next to the soldiers hung tintypes of toddlers in church clothes, their eyes dead and stern. Mary Jane moved down the wall, photo after photo. Generations of Finleys smiling into the flash. There was her grandmother in a black one-piece that made Mary Jane think of a penguin. Alongside her a photo of her grandfather. Pappy, Mary Jane called him. Anything-for-Mary-Jane Pappy. Her grandfather had been the one to tuck her in at night and tell her bedtime stories. He brought home leaves and taught her to identify the trees, and on Sundays they made pancakes in a century-old cast-iron skillet that Lyda once washed with Palmolive. Pappy hadn't spoken for a week. Mary Jane was thirteen when he died, a girl a year away from starting to grow awkward. It had all been downhill after that. "Why'd you have to go and leave me?" she asked.

The most recent photos added color. There was her mother in a beach chair, hair nested, smoke drifting from her lips. Jackson beside her. Jackson staring at her. Mary Jane's heart slowed. Not even the faintest tendrils of affection held her parents together anymore. In the wall's last photo, Jackson held Mary Jane, just a baby, just a whiff of hair on her head, which Lyda stroked with slender fingers. Mary Jane's colorless eyes stared straight ahead. It was as if her parents had thought that by holding her they were holding each other. And then the story stopped. Her father hadn't hung any photos of Mary Jane as a girl or as a teen or as a young woman, but that seemed to make sense in its way. Because when she looked back at the thin, drawn faces of her ancestors, their fair skin and hair, Mary Jane didn't feel like part of them. She didn't feel like part of anything.

three

A bulleted sun beat onto Mary Jane and sweat-dampened strands of brownish hair clung to her pale skin. She woke as if from a bad dream and wiped the grit from her eyes. She was in the backseat of Tara's car. Alone. All the proper buttons were buttoned and zippers zipped but her mouth tasted like stale cigarettes and she had scratches and a bruise along her left forearm, bits of crushed leaves ground in her hair.

She decided she must've fallen down and started making up an excuse to tell her mother in case Lyda asked why she hadn't come home. She'd stayed at Tara's. Tara had been upset over a fight with her boyfriend. That's how Tara was—high drama. Mary Jane had stayed to comfort her with rom-coms and ice cream. Lyda knew how it was with girls. Mary Jane smiled at the story, how easy it came, how believable it seemed.

She coughed as she opened the door and something loosed in her throat that she spat on the ground. The world was washed out in bright light and amplified sound. Birds chirping like jackhammers. The horrid hangover of a morning after. Tara's car was one of a handful scattered among the beer cans and cigarette butts of the dirt track parking lot. Mary Jane looked for her—checked on a pair of bodies huddled in the field grass, checked under a tarp

roped between two trees, finally found Tara naked as the day she
was born and stretched across the bench seat of a truck with a boy
wearing only his socks. Tara's little tits stood at attention, her
nipples bumpy from the cold. The boy had a long, thin penis. Un-
circumcised. Mary Jane had never seen one like that.

Tara got the boys now. Once upon time it had been Mary Jane,
but when it mattered, when it meant getting felt up and fucked
instead of passing notes in class or playing spin the bottle, Mary
Jane had faded into the background.

"Tara," Mary Jane said. "Wake up."

The boy whimpered in his sleep.

The keys dangled in the ignition so the stereo could play but the
speakers were silent. Mary Jane hoped Tara didn't make her stick
around to give the boy a jump. She leaned in through the open
window and pressed Tara's pink knee. "Tara," she said. "Tara, wake
the fuck up." Tara wouldn't move, so Mary Jane yanked her hair—
just a little tug at first—then a harder one. Tara flinched and opened
her eyes. They radiated fear for a moment before she recognized
Mary Jane. Then she glanced over at the boy and smiled. Mary Jane
wanted to tell her to fuck off but she needed the ride. "Let's go,"
she said. As she walked back to the car, Mary Jane noticed a
small clump of hair in her hand. She studied the delicate blond
ringlets and opened her fist and watched them float away in the
breeze.

Harlan walked into the sheriff's department and was greeted by the
sight of Frank sprawled over the couch with his boots kicked off and
his holey socks perched on an armrest. He held a cold pack to one eye.

"What happened to you?" Harlan asked.

Frank dropped his hand and revealed a bruise more yellow than
black but ugly enough.

Harlan shrugged. "Well?"

"I pulled this guy over outside the dirt track and had him step out to fail his sobriety test when bang!" He smacked his hand against the cold pack. "I never saw it coming. Next thing I know there're four, five guys pounding on me." Frank didn't look like he'd been worked over by more than one good punch but Harlan didn't press the finer points. Paige came out from the break room and Frank pointed at her. "Ask Paige. I radioed for backup and she come out there."

Harlan tipped his head toward Frank. "What do you know about this?"

"Whoever did it ran off," she said. "It was *ugly* out there. No one wanted to help the cops much, you know?"

"What kind of car?"

"White sedan," Frank said. "A Toyota, I think."

"You write down the plates?"

Frank didn't reply and Harlan crossed his arms.

"Give me a break, okay?" Frank said and put the cold pack back to his eye.

Harlan pointed at Paige. "You and me are going out there. Frank, put your feet up on your own couch. And next time write down the plates." Frank groaned and shifted his heft as Harlan tossed his keys to Paige. "You're driving," he said.

He felt crackerjack as they walked outside, buoyed by the confidence that comes from giving orders and having them followed. For the first time, he felt like the sheriff of Finley County and not some interloper. Paige kept turning toward him with her mouth half-open as she drove, but whenever Harlan looked back, she returned her eyes to the road. She was new to the department, less than a year in. Lew had been against hiring a woman but the mayor insisted, not that Lew's objections kept him from spouting some high-minded rhetoric about gender equality to the newspaper when it ran an article about the hire. Paige was cautious around the other deputies, seemed to know her place was tenuous. "If you have something to tell me, speak up," Harlan said.

She took a moment before replying. "It's just . . . last night was a shit show. Frank's beat up and cursing those kids and they're cursing me and who knows if one of them has a gun. Half of them are high. I was afraid. And what am I supposed to do? Call you? Call in every deputy? We'd still be outnumbered. You get what I'm saying?"

"You're saying there're more criminals than cops."

"I'm saying I don't see why we don't shut the dirt track down."

Harlan cracked the window and lit a smoke. The dirt track was the brainchild of a petty criminal named Leland Abbot. After inheriting his father's spread, Leland turned the property into an ATV park by building an oval track and cutting trails through the woods for off-roaders. It was the closest thing to a legit enterprise he'd ever dreamt up and the most happening nightspot in Finley County. He charged parking fees and looked the other way when underage kids brought in beer. There'd been talk of trying to shut the track down—through tougher enforcement or by passing new laws—but nothing came of it. "It's a legal-type situation," Harlan said. "Lew looked into it. The track's on private land and we don't get noise complaints 'cause it's in the middle of nowhere. Leland doesn't break any building codes 'cause there aren't any building codes to break. It's like a giant house party. One time we tried going in with the Staties—half the people ran into the woods where we couldn't find them, the other half ran to their cars and sped off bombed out of their ever-loving minds. The next night nothing had changed. Same party at Leland's. Same problems."

Paige pressed the gas. "I think we should enforce the law even when it's inconvenient."

Harlan liked that she cared. The department could use more of that. "We're heading there now, aren't we?" he said. "And if we find the guy who punched Frank, I'll shake his hand and then cuff him for assault."

Paige cracked a smile. "Poor Frank," she said.

The listing fences of Leland's property were newly topped with barbed wire and a snagged grocery bag fluttered in the breeze. A purple Grand Am was stuck nose down in the ditch that bordered the front gate—its trunk open. Whoever wrecked had salvaged their cooler. The gravel road onto the farm was lined with trees and switchbacked up a steep incline. As Paige eased the Impala up the grade, another car crested the hill and started down. She put out a hand to stop it, and the compact's brakes squealed as the driver cranked her window down.

"Tara?" Paige said, peering at the driver. "Tara Koehler?"

The girl didn't respond—a bit confused, a bit afraid.

"I'm Paige. Paige Lucas. I was friends with your sister."

"Oh," the girl said. "I remember you. How's it going?"

"Good. How about you?"

"Long night," she said and laughed. Harlan craned his neck to get a better look.

"Well, I'm glad you didn't drink and drive," Paige said. "But I don't think you should be hanging out here. Your mom wouldn't like that."

The girl shrugged. "I doubt she'd care."

Harlan leaned over. "You hear anything about a deputy getting punched out here last night?"

The girl shook her head.

"What about your friend there? What's her name?"

The passenger leaned forward. "Mary Jane," she said.

"You hear anything about a deputy getting punched, Mary Jane?"

She shook her head. "No, sir."

Harlan tapped Paige's shoulder. "Let's keep moving."

"You girls get home safe," Paige said and rolled her window up. In the side mirror, Harlan watched the compact continue downhill. "Her older sister and I were friends," Paige said. "Alexis went into the navy. Looks like Tara's taking a different path."

At the top of the hill, the road opened onto a grassland-turned-parking lot. Fifty yards out the racetrack, banked by concrete barriers and chain link, sat in the middle of a field. Scattered along the outside were piles of rubble from wrecks and pieces of stone stacked like shrines. The gravel road continued up to an abandoned farmhouse. Somebody had busted the windows, and where kudzu hadn't taken hold, the paint was stripped. Next door stood a brand-new trailer. The house had belonged to Henry Abbot before he died one morning feeding his chickens. Harlan remembered when Lew had been called out to meet the coroner. He came back talking about how the chickens pecked poor Henry blind. Leland lived in the trailer.

The parking lot was littered with empties and Harlan played kick the can while Paige rapped her knuckles against car windows and questioned a bunch of couldn't-give-a-fuck degenerates. Most of them had to be told where they were. All of them claimed ignorance when it came to Frank's busted eye.

A skinny tattooed punk with a shaved head stumbled out of a van and slurred, "Fucking 5-0 pigs." Harlan heard a girl giggle from inside the van. The punk, who was barefoot and naked save his jimmy shorts, stepped gingerly on the ground as he told Paige to suck various manners of cock. Paige turned to Harlan for guidance. "Have at him," Harlan said.

Paige stepped forward and punched the punk in the stomach, then lifted her knee to his crotch and put him on the ground, where he whined like a sick cur. Harlan expected the girl in the van to step out and take up the cause, but she didn't have a horse in the race. "She must've found your little willy-nilly," the girl called out and kept on giggling. Paige smiled despite herself. Harlan had never been one to work over the assholes he met on the job, but he understood the impulse, and he wasn't so holy as to think they didn't deserve it.

He had Paige drive him up to the trailer and told her to stay in the cruiser. You never knew what you were gonna get with Leland, and he wasn't exactly kind to women or authority. The front door was ajar, and when Harlan knocked, it swung open to reveal a naked man drinking a beer. The moans of a porno pulsed from the TV, but Leland had a newspaper folded across his lap and seemed to be doing the crossword. He squinted at the light that came through the door. "You have a warrant, Harlan?"

"Nope."

"Well, come in anyway."

"You wanna get decent first?"

"Not really."

"How about turning off the sex show?"

"That I can do. Have a seat." Harlan settled onto a recliner as Leland searched for the remote and snapped off the TV. "Hey, I'm sorry about your boss," Leland said when the room was quiet. "I'd come to think he was pretty decent."

"Is that right?"

"Yeah. He didn't give me too hard a time. I appreciated that."

"You know anything about who shot him?"

"Nope," Leland said. "Not a thing. It's too bad, though—what happened."

Harlan nodded. "I had a deputy get clocked out here last night."

"Is that right?"

"Yeah. Frank Pryor."

"That fat-ass probably deserved it."

Leland was sharp; he knew Harlan wouldn't lose sleep over Frank's black eye.

"Look, I know why you're really here," Leland said.

Harlan leaned forward on his elbows. "Enlighten me."

Leland grabbed his wallet off the coffee table and pulled out a couple hundreds. "This should cover me for a week or so. Lew was by not too long ago, but I figure you gotta pay the new piper and all."

Harlan didn't reach for the money. "You've got the wrong idea."

Leland folded the bills back into his wallet. "Whoops," he said.

"Let's start again. Do you know anyone who had it out for Lew? Hear any gossip around the track?"

"I don't know anyone personally, but I'm sure I wouldn't have to search hard. Lew threw a lot of people in jail. And then again, there's a lot of people Lew didn't throw in jail."

"What do you mean by that?"

Leland shrugged. "I mean what I mean."

"What about guns?" Harlan said. "You own any rifles?"

"Man, you know I don't truck with guns. It's in my parole agreement."

"You buy your way out of trouble?"

"I practice nonviolence."

"What was your deal with Lew?"

Leland shrugged.

"I could book you right now for bribing an officer, and given your past, that's not a good thing, so why don't you talk. Besides, I don't feel like handcuffing a man in all his God-given glory."

Leland glanced down at his member and lifted the newspaper to give Harlan a better look. "Depends on how hard up Lew was for money," he said. "A couple hundred would usually buy me a week of peace and quiet. It wasn't exactly a steady trade, more as-needed."

"Why pay him off? You dealing drugs?"

"Man, I don't mess with that trash." Harlan rolled his eyes, and Leland shrugged. "I don't go kicking people off my property either. See no evil, hear no evil. But me, I live off the gate receipts and enjoy the festivities. It's a simple life. There's easy pussy and plenty of booze. I paid Lew to make sure I got to keep living that life."

Harlan stood up. "I'm gonna shut you down, Leland."

"Come on, Harlan. You and I both know this place helps you keep the peace. You can't patrol the whole county with four deputies."

"Is that what Lew told you?"

"That's just the truth. Lew came here trying to bully me same as you, but he understood what was in his best interest."

"I'm not Lew."

"That's too bad." Leland turned the TV back on. "But I'd think about it first. You close me down, you might not like the results."

Harlan slammed the door on his way out, the sounds of fake pleasure following him. Paige was sitting on the hood of the cruiser, waiting for a report like she was the boss. "So?" she asked.

"Maybe it's time to start making life harder on Leland."

Lewis fought off his hangover with increasing doses of aspirin but still the girls' tinny laughter and applause from Sophie's talk shows bored into his temples like a blunted drillbit. He swallowed the harsh words he wanted to say about Sophie's choice in television, bit his tongue when Ginny pulled Stella's hair. In his hands he held a copy of the *Herald-Leader*, the Lexington daily, which had a photo of his father as a young man printed below the fold and a short article about his death. There'd been phone calls from reporters but nothing Lewis said made the story. He'd tried to come up with the sort of feel-good anecdote you share with strangers but none of the stories that popped into his head had been of the feel-good

variety. Most were tinged with disappointment and broken promises. The television cut to commercial just as Stella stole Ginny's
favorite stuffed squid, Mr. Inkhead. Rather than arbitrate, Lewis
escaped to the backyard and let himself be blanketed by the cool
wind.

He untarped a cord of wood he'd bought off a down-on-his-
luck farmer and grabbed his ax from the toolshed. He felt so lost.
How were you supposed to mourn a father? A man you'd both loved
and hated? He raised the ax and the muscles stretched down his
back. He pictured Sophie in front of the television, and chopped
down. Pictured Stella throwing a fit, and chopped down. Pictured
Ginny staging a hunger strike, and chopped down. He pictured his
mother, all alone in her house, and chopped down. Then he pictured the faceless killer of his father, and chopped down. The face
of his father, and chopped down. He chopped until his arms shook
and his wrists rang, until he'd made a heap of kindling.

When he went back inside, nothing had changed except the
show on TV. Lewis needed to leave before he said something he'd
regret, so he told Sophie he had to check in at the office. She mumbled goodbye and offered him a cheek to kiss, though her eyes
never left the flickering screen.

He sped down the curved roads of his neighborhood, ignoring
the ridiculous 24 MPH speed limit signs the developer claimed
made streets safer, flew past the unmanned guard post, and after a
mile of open road, pulled up to Riverside Security, where his partner, John Tyler, was locking up. "What are you doing here on a
weekend?" Lewis asked.

John Tyler was an old high school buddy, a fellow football player
who'd let himself go soft after knocking up his then-and-still girlfriend. "I gotta do a fucking install," he said.

"You?" Lewis let his jaw drop comically low. When they started
the business, he and John Tyler installed the security systems them-

selves, but a good reputation, the Mattock name, and financial help from Sophie's father changed the game. They ended up hiring two employees away from Diebold in Cincinnati and became office men. Ever since they'd spent their days behind desks watching ESPN and making the occasional phone call.

"We're swamped," John Tyler said.

"In just the past couple days?"

"Think about it, Lewis."

"What?"

"Your dad."

"What about him?"

"I don't want to be unfeeling or whatever, but it turns out the sheriff getting shot is good for business. It sets people on edge."

Lewis didn't know how to respond, so he asked John Tyler if he needed an extra set of hands.

"I don't even know why you're here," John Tyler replied. "You should be with your family."

"I was."

"I get it. When my mom died . . . it's like . . . you don't know what you're supposed to do." He clapped Lewis on the back and pulled him into a half hug. "But I don't think it's installing security systems. There's beer in the fridge if you want to hang."

"You going to the funeral?" Lewis asked.

"You know I am." John Tyler picked up his toolbox. Lewis wished he'd stick around so they could talk about the Cats or watch football, but he didn't want to seem needy. "Your old man gave 'em hell," John Tyler said and put out his fist for the bump they'd used as hello and goodbye ever since they were dopey-eared kids. Lewis met him knuckles on knuckles.

Inside the office, he cracked open a Bud Light, and when he couldn't find the remote, he walked up to the television to turn on the Bengals game. He paused at his reflection in the black glass.

Everyone told Lewis he was the spitting image of his father, and growing up it had seemed like his dad was training him to become the second coming, that one day he'd drop the *is* from his name and take over. What did it matter that he hadn't lived up to expectations? That he'd never stopped being a boy cast in his father's shadow? He'd tried to make his dad proud and that counted for something. That was a type of love.

Lewis took a long, hard swallow of beer. Even after the funeral, there'd be no closure. He imagined himself tracking down his father's killer, bringing him to justice, but that was just a daydream—the sort of make-believe his father abhorred. Because living in an imagined future was just as bad as living in the past. If his father taught Lewis anything, it was that a man defined himself by his actions in the here and now. The present was his burden.

Built in the seventies, Marathon's medical plaza was an L-shaped single-story with space for five practices, though only two—the dental offices of Spiller, Wise, and Toth and Trip Gaines's medical clinic—had managed to stay in business. As Mark pulled into the parking lot, his tires rumbled over potholes and broken concrete. He parked next to a tree that had died before growing tall enough to offer shade.

As a kid Mark had failed to notice the sad state of the medical plaza; he didn't yet have an understanding of the word *shabby*. They'd moved to Marathon from Cincinnati when he was just three, and he didn't remember that previous life, though his sister, Sophie, often told him how much better things had been in Ohio. There'd been the zoo and the children's museum and a big brick house with a swing set in the back. There'd been a mom, too, though she left not long after Mark was born. When Sophie felt like being especially cruel, she would tell Mark he was the reason Mom left, that before he came along their parents had been happy. Growing up the dead look in his father's eyes told Mark all he needed to know about his guilt.

In Cincinnati his dad had been a surgeon, but around the same time Trip Gaines's ex-wife remarried—to a former family friend— he was served with two malpractice suits amid rumors of surgeries performed under the influence. He nearly bankrupted himself settling out of court and joined A.A. The hospital fired him anyway and the state's medical board took his license. Given his past, Trip had limited options. When the lone GP in Marathon died from a heart attack, he packed the remains of his family and zeroed his bank accounts to lease space in the medical plaza. The state of Kentucky issued him a medical license—they needed doctors in rural places, after all—but revoked his right to perform surgery. The clinic in Marathon was less a second chance than an exile, a precipitous drop for a man who'd once dreamt of hospital wings named in his honor. Mark was a dutiful son, willing to do whatever was asked of him in the hopes that it might bring him and his father closer together, but his dedication never seemed to make much difference. He grew up feeling like a stray, as fatherless as he was motherless.

The landscaping in front of the medical plaza was littered with cigarette butts, and inside the lobby's fluorescent lights hummed and flickered as if browning out. Computer-printed signs pointed left, toward the dentist, and right, toward the clinic. When Mark walked in, his father's longtime receptionist, Bea, started peppering him with questions. He assured her he was studying hard and that, no, he hadn't met a pretty girl to bring home. To his left two patients waited, a man in a wheelchair breathing oxygen from a tank and an overweight woman sitting on a pillow. In the corner, an undersized plastic table and chairs bowed beneath a mess of broken toys and battered *Highlights* magazines.

Mark spent most of his childhood at that table, being watched over by staff while his father worked. Sophie hated the clinic because of the germs and "gross" patients, so she got to spend her time in after-school programs for dance and piano. Mark had wanted to take his own after-school classes, but his father invoked the cost and reminded him that it was free to have Bea watch him. Trip Gaines didn't seem to care about the discrepancy between son and daughter. And so Mark was the kid who sat silently at the sad table and waited for his dad to finish so they could drive home in further silence.

He took a seat in the waiting room and buried his head in a magazine as the fat woman farted into her pillow. His dad came out a minute later, patient in tow, and did a double-take. "What are you doing here?" he asked.

"I was hoping you had a minute to chat."

Trip checked his watch as if it would confirm he was too busy, but Bea stepped in and said, "We're ahead of schedule, Doctor," despite the two patients in the waiting room.

When they were alone in his father's office, Mark pulled the envelope of cash from his backpack. "Five thousand from Chance," he said.

Trip reached his hand out for the envelope. "That's good but this could have waited. All things considered."

Mark did know. All things considered. His dad never seemed in a rush to do anything that might benefit him. Trip took the money that Mark "earned" dealing and put it in an account that only he could access. Mark's nest egg, he called it, though Mark doubted he'd ever see a dime. For so long Mark had been too afraid to question his father, had been conditioned into submission, but now he was prepared to demand what he was owed.

He pulled the envelope back from his dad's open hand. "The way I figure it you still owe me twenty thousand, even if I keep this." It sounded ridiculous when he said it. Like he was some street tough. His father grinned and Mark tried not to wilt under the sheer amusement in his face. Even the amount sounded childish. He and Mary Jane had calculated that twenty-five thousand was enough for them to live on for a year. At the time it had seemed a fortune.

All of a sudden Mark felt small, demanding so little for something so great, and he got the distinct impression his father could tell as much. Trip paged the front desk. "I'll be a few minutes here, Bea. Please put my next patient in the examination room." He lifted his finger off the intercom and turned back to Mark. "Hand it over," he said, as if Mark were nothing more than a dog, as if when he said "lie down" Mark would abide.

Mark clenched the envelope in his left fist and placed it back in his bag. "I'm keeping it."

"Keep that money and I won't pay for your college or your apartment or the lease on that ridiculous car you drive. You do the math."

"And maybe I'll stop selling to Chance. How would you like that?"

Trip laughed. "You don't think I'd figure something else out?" He stood up, came around the desk, and grabbed the backpack from Mark's soft hands. Mark shrunk into the chair. "Don't fuck up a good thing," Trip said, taking the cash and sliding it into the front pocket of his slacks before tossing the empty bag back in Mark's lap. He gripped Mark's shoulder and dug his fingers deep as if he was giving a massage but there would be bruises. "This isn't the time to buck, Mark. You're being shortsighted. Now that Lew's gone, the profit is all ours. Don't you get it? We're going to be rich."

"You're going to be rich."

"And that makes you rich by proxy. You're my son."

Mark wanted to tell his father that he wasn't going to be pushed around anymore, but instead he mumbled assent—ever the dutiful son. Satisfied, Trip released his shoulder and patted it. "I've got patients," he said, and slipped away but not before reminding Mark to close the door on his way out. Mark tried not to cry.

There were photos of Sophie scattered around his father's office, but just one of Mark and even that was in a hinged frame he shared with his sister. Sophie favored their mother; it was uncanny how alike they looked. Mark had never stood a chance, would never be loved like Sophie, who had only to walk into a room to be admired. This was supposed to be his chance to break free, but he'd failed. Himself and Mary Jane both.

He wiped the snot from his nose and dried his eyes. It was time for him to fight back, not by standing up to his father—that wasn't in the cards—but by doing something that fit his nature. He stooped behind his father's desk, pulled open the bottom left drawer, and stole a prescription pad. If Mark couldn't collect what he and Mary Jane were owed, he could at least use the pad to load up on pills and make a big deal, enough to help them start over in Montreal. With the prescription pad in his bag, Mark felt like he had the upper hand; for once he was the gander and his dad was the goose.

The pinging of the fax brought Harlan out of his office and he crowded around the machine with Holly as she read line after barely inked line from the crime lab in Frankfort. The bullet had entered below Lew's right orbital and exited at the base of the skull, which suggested an elevated shooter and jived with what they already knew. The fragment was 150 grain and came from one of three rifles— a 30-06, .308, or 300 Win Mag. There were partial markings that could be matched to the murder weapon, and they'd preserved the spit sample to do a DNA test, but only for trial. Holly stopped reading. Harlan waited for more. "That's it," she said. "I guess we have to find the gun."

"That shouldn't be hard," Harlan replied, knowing it was damn near impossible. Just about every man, woman, and child in the county owned a rifle, and the 30-06 was popular with hunters. He'd have a deputy stop by the Walmart and check their sales, but it was a long shot at best.

Harlan had planned to keep the information about Leland and Lew to himself but decided it was better to tell Holly. Holly knew Lew better than just about anyone in Marathon, maybe even his wife. She shook her head at the news. "You think Leland was telling the truth?"

"I don't think he intended to let it slip."

Holly twisted the wedding band on her ring finger. "I wouldn't put it past Lew, but I also think he left Leland alone for those reasons he talked about. Concentration of crime and so on. It's likely Lew saw a way to profit from what he was already doing."

"I'm more interested in how it might relate to the murder," Harlan said. "Don't you think that's the sort of deal that could come back to bite someone?"

"You think Leland killed Lew?"

"No. It wasn't that much money. But there might be other bribes." Harlan stopped. "Forget I mentioned it."

Holly started packing up her purse. "I don't care about defending Lew's legacy, but I also don't see him doing anything so corrupt as to get shot. Lew wore his faults like badges of honor."

"Maybe you didn't know him as well as you think."

"Maybe not. I'm just giving you my opinion." Holly snapped her purse shut and put on her jacket. "Find the gun. That's the fastest way to wrap this up."

As far as Harlan was concerned, Leland was his best lead. Let the other deputies search for the gun, that was a needle-haystack job. Let them follow up on bunk information from the tip line. Just because Lew was dead, Harlan wasn't going to pretend like his former boss was some idealistic lawman. Lew had plenty of enemies besides the people he arrested, and Harlan was willing to bet he carried his fair share of secrets. If he found out *why* Lew was murdered, he was certain it would lead him to *who*.

Harlan took advantage of Holly's absence and lit a cigarette as he examined Lew's old office. Inside various cabinets and closets he found paperwork Lew had neglected to file, old campaign paraphernalia, and stacks of *Field & Stream*, but nothing of consequence. Lew's funeral was slated for the next morning. After that Harlan would have to meet up with Mabel Mattock and search Lew's house. He'd need to talk with Lewis as well.

He took a seat at the desk and sifted through its drawers, searching for clues among the pens and paper clips. The filing cabinet was still locked, and with a cigarette dangling from his lips, Harlan used his clasp knife to break in. An upward shove popped the pins and the drawer came sliding out. It was crammed with files tagged in Lew's mix of cursive and print. Budget files and employee files. Various official forms. Harlan read through his own file first. It was clean. No discipline cases, no commendations—just a decade of service and a promotion.

Near the back of the drawer, he uncovered a folder of correspondence between Wesley Craycraft and Lew. It seemed Lew liked to offer the judge suggestions for parole and sentencing—his way of being judge, jury, and executioner. Harlan sorted though the file and stopped at a familiar name.

Wes,
We talked about the parole hearing for inmate 165198. Given the lack of prior offenses and prison overcrowding I don't see

any benefit in keeping Doyle Chapman behind bars. He has
family in Arkansas and intends to move there. The sooner Doyle
is gone and forgotten the better. I never believed he intended to
kill Angeline Chapman. As far as I'm concerned Mr. Chapman
must reckon himself with God more than the state of Kentucky.
I suggest an early parole and an end to this unfortunate incident.
—Mattock

Harlan ran his fingers over the type as if reading braille, pressed them against her name. Stapled to Lew's letter was a copy of Doyle's court-ordered release, signed by Craycraft.

For two years Angeline had curled into Harlan like a scared potato bug and rested her backside against him—a pretty girl with a round face. In the morning they'd flirt over fried eggs and figure out to the minute when they'd see each other again. She worked at a dental office and liked to tell Harlan he drank too much soda. He picked up groceries after his shift and cooked her dinner. They talked about plaque and criminals, kissed each other softly, and made sweet love. Harlan promised her a ring on her finger when he could afford it and then, all at once, it ended.

Harlan found Angeline dead in the kitchen of her father's place the day after she decided it was time to move in with him. Her body was covered in flies. Doyle Chapman had pushed his only daughter harder than intended into an object not made for contact with the head. A plastic bag filled with Angeline's meager belongings sat next to her body like trash. Later, Doyle would claim that he'd only meant to have a heart-to-heart, to teach Angeline a lesson about family. He'd only wanted her to stay. Maybe he'd been drinking. He was sorry. Things had gotten out of hand.

By the time Harlan found her body, Doyle was already on the run, though he didn't have many places to go. Harlan treated it like a crime scene and called Lew for help, a decision he'd regretted ever since. They'd looked at Angeline's misshapen face together. Lew had seen the crater in her skull, the skin a loose bowl, her bangs falling into it—the frightening lack of blood. How could the man capable of that reckon himself with God? If Harlan were a better man, he'd have tracked Doyle down and beat him to a pulp, he'd have brought him back to the house and made him bear witness to what his hands had wrought, but Harlan had trusted in the law.

Lew gave him an extended leave, which Harlan spent in various stages of drunkenness. People brought casseroles and buckets of fried chicken, left them on the porch when he didn't come to the door. Doyle pled guilty and people talked about the tragedy of Angeline Chapman for a while but soon they forgot. At some point, Harlan took her belongings from evidence and offered them to the river. Everything sunk save one white dress, which floated downstream, rippling beneath the surface like some sort of water flower. Afterward, Harlan asked Lew if he could please return to work. Doyle served a few years on a twenty-year manslaughter charge and moved on. Early release. And all because of Lew. Harlan had vowed to find Doyle in Arkansas, but the weeks passed and he stayed in Marathon—working all day and getting high deep into the night—his dreams of revenge drifting away on a cloud of smoke.

Nearly four years had passed and Harlan had never woken up the same. He still loved Angeline, could conjure memories of her that made him ache—her soft body, the way she sneezed twice whenever she sneezed, the nonsense she spoke in her sleep—but the girl in those memories had grown faint. He no longer remembered the hint of red in her summer hair, the smallest scars of her skin. She'd slipped into the fog of his past. A ghost. There was only one thing left of her in the house, a bottle of apple-scented shampoo that he brought to his nose whenever the loneliness became too much to bear.

Harlan balled Lew's letter in his fist and punched the cabinet.

The metal buckled and he punched again, an uppercut that sliced his knuckles. Blood pooled in his hand and dripped onto the carpet but Harlan didn't care. He punched again. And again. Over and over. He punched because he'd failed to protect her, because he'd done nothing to avenge her, because she was gone and he'd started to forget her.

When Paige came in to take over dispatch, she asked, "What happened to your hand?" Asked, "Are you all right?" Asked, "What's going on?" Harlan wrapped his bloody hand in a bandanna and shoved the crumpled letter into his pocket. There were always more questions than answers. Why even reply? He left the rest of Lew's correspondence on Holly's desk along with a note telling her to find out what Craycraft decided in each case.

Outside, crows perched on power lines, black forms above the glow of a streetlight. They squawked warnings to anyone who'd listen. Harlan had once known a crow with a forked tongue. His owner cut him that way, taught the bird to say, "Damnation is coming to us all." The crow squawked it to whoever would listen. Harlan launched a rock at the crows with his bandaged hand but missed. They flapped their wings and sang an ugly song. Damnation coming.

In that hazy hour between night and day, just after the sun fell but before the sky went dark, Mary Jane's mother knocked on her door. "Your father insists you join us at the table." Lyda started to fold Mary Jane's discarded clothes and pair her scattered shoes. "It's a mess in here," she said.

"Mom," Mary Jane groaned, letting the vowel extend. "Stop."

Lyda opened the closet and pulled out a dress that still had its tags attached. Lyda's tastes tended toward floral print and cable-knit, and she rarely brought home anything in a size twelve. She bought Mary Jane fours to "inspire" her and help her envision the pretty girl she might become again. "This looks nice," she said. The dress complemented the shimmering skirt and blouse Lyda had on for dinner. Wearing it would turn Mary Jane into an accessory no different from her mother's dangly earrings or diamond tennis bracelet.

"I'm not wearing that," she said.

"Well, you can't wear sweatpants. You father has it in mind to enjoy a proper meal and we should play our part."

"Like puppets."

"Like ladies." Her mother gave a dramatic curtsy to make a joke of it. Mary Jane burrowed deeper into the covers. "Why are you always so tired?" Lyda asked.

"Maybe I take after you."

Lyda ignored the insult. "Did you sleep at all last night? Were you even here? What's going on? Are you smoking marijuana?"

Mary Jane moaned. Caring wasn't something her mother got to turn on and off whenever it seemed convenient. "Yeah," Mary Jane said. "I'm smoking pot and snorting cocaine and dancing at a strip club where my boyfriend works as a bouncer. It's a great life."

"I guess I don't find that funny," Lyda said. "Besides, the girls who dance at those clubs are fit. Maybe that would be a step in the right direction." Satisfied that she'd gotten the last word, Lyda turned to leave. "Ten minutes," she said. "And put on some makeup."

Mary Jane dropped her head back to the pillow. She and her mother had been close once. After Mary Jane's pageants they'd get tea—"lady time" Lyda called it—and her mom would talk about how she'd wanted to go to New York to model or L.A. to act, dreams that were silly looking back, but growing up they made Mary Jane think her mother a star. For a long time she'd wanted those same things. Pageant titles. Attention. Compliments. But when Mary Jane stopped rehearsing for the stage and trying on sequined dresses at the store, they lost whatever connection they'd had. For a while Lyda kept trying to fit Mary Jane in a box and slap a bow on her but eventually they drifted apart for good.

The difference between Mary Jane's stagnant life and her mother's was that Mary Jane had been born into it and Lyda had chosen it. Her mother was born a Fieldhouse, the daughter of a tobacco worker and a homemaker; she married into the Finley money. Her mother barely spoke about that past, but the way Mary Jane's father told the story, it wasn't hard to win her affection. He told her his last name, bought a big diamond, and soon enough they were walking down the aisle. After one too many gins, Jackson liked to pay Lyda back for years of icy stares and noncommittal I-love-you's by recounting their wedding in glorious detail—hillbillies on one side, respectable folks on the other. Mary Jane had heard her mother crying after a few particularly unpleasant dinners and came to realize those tears might not be from shame over the life she left behind but the life she chose. Because the Finley name wasn't a badge of honor; it was a burden to live up to.

Mary Jane took a nerve pill from an Altoids box and popped it to get through dinner intact. Then she tossed her mother's dress on the floor and trudged downstairs in her sweats. The chandelier was dimmed and a pair of candles sat perfectly spaced on the table. Jackson was at one end, Lyda the other. A plate for Mary Jane sat between them. "I thought you told her to wear something decent," Jackson said.

"I pulled out an option," Lyda said. "I can't very well hold her down and dress her."

"It didn't fit," Mary Jane said and sat down. A thin slice of breaded meat, dollop of mashed potatoes, and three stalks of grilled asparagus sat on the plate. A meal for a bird.

"It's my famous Beef Wellington," Jackson said, taking a large bite and swallowing it down with a drink from his highball glass.

"I'm not hungry," Mary Jane said, which was a lie. She wanted her mother to see how she starved herself. Lyda forked an asparagus and took a bite from its end. Then she rested the fork back on the plate, dabbed the corner of her mouth with her napkin, and folded it in a perfect triangle as if she were done. The tip of her napkin was marked with lipstick that looked like a bloodstain. "Delicious," she said. Mary Jane wanted to scream.

Theirs was a playhouse—phony at its core, every detail designed to show off the family's wealth and taste. They ate off china and spread their butter with silver knives. Their furniture was antique, their carpets Persian, their towels monogrammed. Oil paintings hung on the walls in ornately carved frames. All to keep up appearances.

Appearances. That's what had kept Mary Jane from reaching her potential. She didn't *look* like a Finley, didn't grow into the lady the girl foreshadowed. Her story was the opposite of the ugly duckling's; it was the tale of a swan turned homely.

"How is it?" Jackson asked.

Mary Jane looked down. In her hand, she held her fork and knife. Half her food was gone even though she hadn't remembered taking a bite. She looked over at her mother's plate. It had barely been touched. "Delicious," Mary Jane said.

"Now," Jackson said. "We have to discuss our plans for the funeral."

"What funeral?"

"Lew Mattock's." Jackson looked across the table at Lyda, then turned to Mary Jane. "Make sure you wear something appropriate. And black jeans and a black T-shirt are not appropriate."

"Why do I have to go?"

"Your father insists," Lyda said.

Mary Jane's hands started to go clammy and she dropped her fork—the first pangs of a panic attack. "No," she muttered and shook her head. "I don't want to."

"It's not up for discussion," Jackson said. "We're Finleys and the town expects it."

Mary Jane heard her mother stand up. "Excuse me. You two can sort out the details while I smoke a cigarette."

Jackson put his hand out and grabbed Lyda's arm as she walked by. "You don't want to be part of the discussion?" He squeezed. "I thought you'd have an opinion."

Mary Jane stared at her shoes. Black Chuck Taylors. Black Chuck Taylors.

"You tell me where I need to be and when," Lyda said. "We get along better that way."

Jackson grinned as she tapped out a Virginia Slim. "That sounds easy enough," he said. "How about you, Mary Jane? Are you as agreeable as your mother?" Black Chuck Taylors. Black Chuck Taylors. "Mary Jane?"

"Can I be excused?"

"You didn't answer the question."

"Fine. Whatever. Now can I be excused?"

Jackson downed the rest of his drink. "Go ahead. The both of you." Mary Jane heard her mother step onto the porch, then stood up from the table and ran upstairs. She couldn't find a pill fast enough.

four

The morning of Lew's funeral, Holly called to tell Harlan the cell phone he'd found was registered to Lyda Finley. Whatever Harlan expected to learn about the phone, this wasn't it. "Why would Lew have Lyda Finley's cell phone?"

"I don't know, but maybe she'll be at the funeral and you can ask her yourself."

"What about the note I left you at the office?"

"That's a lot of court records to sort through."

"It's worth it, right? I mean first we find out Lew was taking bribes and then we find out he lobbied on behalf of felons."

"It sure sounds suspicious, but you know how Lew was. He wanted his hand in all the honeypots. It's not exactly surprising. He and Wesley were old friends."

"And that makes it okay?"

"No. It doesn't. But I worked with Lew for twelve years, so excuse me if I'm not exactly thrilled to find out he might have been crooked. And maybe I hold out hope he was just an asshole and not a criminal." She took a deep breath. "I'm also worried this is personal for you, Harlan. Lew never treated you right but he didn't shoot himself. Don't forget that."

"Let me know what you find out," Harlan said and hung up.

Harlan hoped to forget about police work at the funeral, to put aside his feelings about Lew and simply pay his respects, but as soon as he arrived, Stuart Simon of the *Marathon Registrar* came up and asked about the investigation. That morning the paper had run a special edition complete with photos of Lew throughout the years along with sentiments from various friends and luminaries. Harlan looked Simon up and down; he was a hack for certain. "I'm not sure this is the best place."

"I called but I keep getting the machine," Simon said. "It still has Lew's voice on the message."

"And?"

"Do you have any leads?" Harlan walked away but Simon followed at his heels like a needy mutt. "People have a right to know," he said.

Harlan stopped and let Simon bump into him, then leaned in close to the man's ear. "Fuck off," he growled. Simon took the hint and left him alone, though Harlan didn't look forward to reading what he wrote in the next edition. Tragedies seemed to bring out the worst in people or maybe they brought out the worst people.

Harlan stood along the outskirts of the service in his wedding-and-funeral clothes, a hand-me-down suit with roughed-up cowboy boots and a thin black tie. The other deputies wore uniforms and lined up alongside Lew's casket as if it were a military affair. They looked ridiculous, like the saddest of regiments at the end of a lost war. Harlan wished he could slip away and skip the charade, but if he didn't put in an appearance, people would notice and then speculate on what that meant—guilt over a lingering investigation, jealousy, gutlessness.

At least Lew would have been happy with the size of the crowd. His funeral was the social event of the season. Mabel Mattock was front and center, flanked by her son and Holly, who kept her head bowed. Lewis's daughters sat between him and his wife, who leaned the slightest amount of weight against her father, the doctor, who didn't so much watch the ceremony as the clouds above. All around them sat prominent Marathoners—politicians, lawyers, doctors, gentleman farmers. Wesley Craycraft sat back row center beside the mayor and his mother, herself a former mayor. Lyda Finley sat near the back, flanked by her husband and daughter, who looked uncomfortable in a black dress and cardigan. Harlan recognized the girl as the passenger from the car Paige had stopped at the dirt track.

The pastor's canned sermon droned on. Harlan wondered how so many lives could be summed up by the same rote words, wondered how much any single person there truly knew Lew. Harlan felt like it would take the words of all those gathered to tell Lew's story, to tell any man's, for that matter. He tried to think of who would speak at his own funeral, couldn't come up with a single soul.

The service ended around the time the pastor realized no one was listening. When he said, "Amen," the deputies drew their guns and shot blanks in the air. Frank invited Harlan to take part, but he'd declined, which led to Frank muttering about Harlan being stuck up. The crowd covered their ears as the shots rang out. Frank looked proud as punch, bruise and all, as he aimed for the sky. The sound reminded Harlan of the day Lew died, only this time nobody cowered. They just stared at one another in dull, dumb shock.

As the echoes from the gunshots died down, Lewis and Mabel stepped forward and tossed dirt onto the casket from something that looked like a giant saltshaker and a cemetery employee lowered the casket with a crank. Lewis returned from his burial duties and wiped away his daughters' tears. Mabel Mattock's face held more true sorrow than any of the others but she did not weep. She did not need to.

Harlan slipped away and headed for the far edge of the cemetery. Unlike Lew's final resting place, Angeline's wasn't blessed with shade from an ancient sycamore and didn't have a view of the pond. Angeline had had a body made for water. In the summer, she and Harlan would hike to hidden eddies along the river and swim in the shallows. Angeline could spend hours floating on her back and looking at clouds, could swim across the river and back if challenged. Harlan had wanted her to spend the afterlife near something she loved but the only plot he could afford was weed-strewn and within earshot of the highway.

Standing above Angeline's sparse grave, Harlan became tongue-tied. She was just a name and dates. Angeline Chapman. Dead at twenty-two. Dead four years. When they'd met, their hearts had been unworn. Untested. Now Harlan's was broken. That was his cross to bear but Angeline's fate was so much worse—she would never know how it felt to be broken-hearted. Harlan couldn't remember the last words she'd said to him. *I'll see you soon. I'll see you tomorrow. I love you.* It could have been any of those or none. Maybe she hugged him. Or maybe they kissed goodbye. Or maybe she ran excited to her tiny two-door car and drove off waving. He hadn't made a point of remembering. There'd been so much future then. Now it all felt like make-believe.

How could he explain to Angeline that he'd just been to the funeral of a man who'd helped free her father? That he'd gone to keep up appearances? It was a shit reason. Keeping up appearances was just another way of saying scared. Scared to do the right thing. And it was fear that had kept Harlan from hunting down Doyle. All those times he told himself he'd go when the time was right and yet it never was. Years. Years had passed. And still the fear. All the flowers and honeyed phrases spoken to the dandelions that grew above her grave meant nothing.

Harlan imagined Doyle free and easy. Doyle strolling down an Arkansas street. Doyle flying a lure over a green river. He pulled a half-sunk rock from the ground and pounded at that name she'd inherited. Chapman. A simple Angeline would have been enough. A simple "A." He bashed at the headstone but nothing changed. Centuries would pass before the name wore away. And by then it would be the work of God. Of wind and rain and hail.

Even though the casket was closed, Mary Jane could feel Lew staring at her. She was reeling from pills. She'd been popping them all morning. Even Jackson seemed to notice she was acting strange and kept asking her if she was all right. She kept saying fine. She was fine. I'm fine. Don't worry about me. Fine. She distracted herself by counting the people sitting in front of her as if counting sheep. Whenever she reached the end, she started over.

She watched Mark's father and tried to picture Mark as a grown man. Trip Gaines didn't know she and Mark were dating, didn't know that Mary Jane knew his secrets. The drug lord of Marathon. What a crock. Mark thought his father was evil incarnate; Mary Jane just thought he was a jerk. Their unhappy home lives had brought her and Mark closer together, though sometimes she liked to pretend they were orphans who'd met on the streets. It made a better story. Didn't matter that it wasn't true.

When Mark came back to Marathon on college breaks, he'd call the private line that had been her twelfth birthday present and they'd meet at the dollar movie theater one town over or along the dock for late-night make-out sessions. Those secret rendezvous and clandestine hand grabs, those midnight fucks in the back of his car, made her feel alive, made life mysterious and exciting. Together they shared secrets. Bonnie and Clyde.

Imagining a future with Mark sustained Mary Jane through the funeral, sustained her as the preacher recited scripture, sustained her when Lew's wife and son approached the casket, when the ceremonial gunshots rang out in the air, when her mother wiped a tear from her eye. Because Mary Jane knew why her mother cried. That was her cross to bear—a memory that refused to stay buried.

It had been her freshman year, during the last months of her waning popularity as a pretty girl, before her future as just another face in the crowd. A group of juniors invited her to skip the homecoming pep rally. One of their brothers was a clerk at the Motel 6 and would let them party in an empty room for a joint and twenty dollars.

They played a drinking game called Kings. At some point Mary Jane volunteered to get more ice so she could boot and rally. It was then—the moment she was contemplating vomiting outside a neglected motel the color of an ashtray's bottom—that she saw her mother and Lew Mattock climbing the concrete stairs in a desperate clutch. She tried to convince herself that it was a mistake, that it was some other woman who only looked like her mother, but she couldn't ignore the throaty laugh that rang out as Lew ran his hands over the woman's body. She'd heard that laugh her entire life.

She knew she should turn around and return to the rented room with the double beds and drink until memory became a blur, but instead she carried the empty ice bucket up the stairs, as if drawn by an invisible string. Through a sliver of space between the blinds, she saw Lew fucking her mother, pounding her as if he didn't care how much damage he did. Lyda's arms were tied to the bed and Lew's fingers were clasped around her throat but they couldn't stifle her voice. Her mother sputtered, moaned, begged for more, and Lew gave it to her, gave it to her until something broke inside Mary Jane.

She ran down the stairs and into the parking lot but she didn't have anyplace to go. She was stuck at the motel and soon her new friends would come looking for her and she couldn't let them see her upset so she sat next to the ice machine and had a good cry. After the tears stopped falling, she filled the ice bucket and returned to the party, where she turned the nearest bottle up until she passed out. The others reveled around her slumbering body.

She'd never confronted her mother about the affair, but that was the moment her life began its downward spiral. She'd never been able to talk to her father and then she lost her mother when she needed her most, when she needed guidance through the vagaries of adolescence. Her skin became oily and pimples followed and then one of her boobs grew bigger than the other and both of them sprouted dark hairs around the nipples. The optometrist prescribed glasses she never wore and she lost all the friends she'd ever had— the girls who'd come to her slumber parties in middle school— and all because she no longer looked like part of the tribe. Mary Jane blamed everything on that moment she caught her mother with Lew.

It was Mark who'd kept her from spiraling completely. Mark, who she'd dated for a couple weeks in middle school the way kids that age date—bashful kisses in the hall, hands held in the movie dark. She'd broken up with him because that was how the world worked at twelve. Two weeks seemed like an eternity. Besides, Mark was odd. Shy. A bit of a loner. In a way, the same traits that caused her to break up with him in middle school drew her back to him in high school. They explored their bodies and Mark called her princess line so they could talk deep into the night about the teachers they hated and the classmates they hated and the parents they hated and it was all so comforting. They never made anything official—boyfriend-girlfriend—they were above all that; they had an understanding. When he left for college, Mary Jane's profound sadness caught her by surprise. Mark had been her best friend, her fuck buddy, the one person who didn't abandon her, but it wasn't until he left that she realized she'd fallen in love.

The funeral plodded along and Mary Jane slunk into her cave. She wouldn't allow herself to be sad that Lew Mattock was dead. Fate had brought her and Mark together for a reason. He was the boy who wanted the sheriff dead. She was the girl with a buried grudge. Lew's funeral wasn't a misfortune. It was a triumph. Proof they were capable of anything—terrible deeds, sure, but greatness, too. It was revenge. And when the popping sound of the crank that lowered the coffin started to ring out in a steady drone, Mary Jane lifted her head to watch the crowd scatter and realized she'd made it through the trial.

She skipped out on her parents' postfuneral brunch plans by feigning sickness. It wasn't hard. Her father had been asking her if she was okay all morning and her mother was practically catatonic. They dropped her off at home, and Mary Jane's heels clicked along the brick walkway and up the steps to the house. The paint along the banister of the porch had flaked to reveal the wood beneath. It needed to be sanded and given a new coat—the sort of task her father would begin but never finish. She smoked a cigarette but her hand wouldn't stop shaking. She could barely hold the filter to her lips. Her nerves were on fire, her skin clammy. Mark had told her to stay in Marathon but she saw no reason to stay.

She walked into the house and wrote a note. "Gone to Lexington. Back in a couple days." It was vague but truthful enough to keep her parents from worrying. Then she climbed the stairs to her room and packed a bag. Her teddy bear's battery bay reeked of pot, so she stuffed him beneath the bed. She imagined a private eye scanning the room for clues, but she wouldn't leave any. Her face would be on milk cartons. She wondered how long it would take until her mother turned the room into something else. A guest bedroom? A yoga studio? Before she left, she considered taking a photo from the dresser—a photo of her on the stage or blowing out birthday candles—but the girl in those photos was dead now.

———

Lewis invited the pastor to lunch out of some misplaced sense of obligation. He thought the man would decline and was surprised when he said he supposed he should be there to comfort the family in their time of need. His father hadn't been much of a churcher, but the man Ezra Baker hired left plenty to be desired. The cuffs of his suit had frayed and strands of hair swept his balding head like pieces of pulled cotton. He chain-smoked and bounced nervously on the balls of his feet whenever he wasn't holding a menthol. When Lewis told Sophie to expect one more, she gave him an exasperated look, eyed the pastor, and mouthed, "Why?" Her father, standing nearby, chuckled softly.

"It seemed like the right thing to do," Lewis replied. Sophie nodded like this was the sort of answer she expected. She liked to tell Lewis he put too much stock in *doing the right thing,* liked to tell him he didn't understand the way the world worked, but Lewis didn't know what qualified her to judge. Sophie never seemed to *do* much of anything.

Trip told Lewis he would buy lunch and bring it to the house, acted as if he was doing him a big favor when it was exactly that sort of mundane, achievable task that had brought Lewis comfort in the days since his father died. "Isn't that nice of Daddy?" Sophie said, skilled at asking questions in a way that told Lewis how he was supposed to answer. He nodded.

There'd been talk of having a wake and sending his father off in style, but the plans never materialized. Lewis didn't have it in him to organize it and his mother wasn't much help, so they settled on a small family brunch. Mabel set the table while the pastor smoked one after another on the back porch. Lewis checked on him now and again and the man would offer some halfhearted words of consolation. It's a blessing to be with the Lord. He'll live on through his family. Those sorts of things.

At some point, his mother whispered, "I don't know how you'll get rid of that man," and Lewis laughed. Sophie, who was pouring her father a Perrier with a slice of lemon, eyed them suspiciously. She was stoned on one pill or another. Red wine and pills were Sophie's social bread and butter, a crutch her father fed.

"It's nothing," Lewis said. Sophie didn't look pleased. She hated being left out of the conversation, and whenever someone laughed, she assumed it was at her expense. She hadn't always been so touchy or maybe she had and he'd never realized it. They'd been so young when they married, just a couple years out of high school. Sophie, for better or worse. Sophie since middle school. Everyone thought they were the perfect couple—the doctor's beautiful daughter, the sheriff's strapping son.

Trip walked into the kitchen and sniffed the air. "Something sure smells good," he said, lording over the spread he'd brought, though if he expected compliments, Lewis didn't oblige. He was busy dealing with the yardbird the doctor had picked for the girls. The hen had been halved and its body cavity would produce in Ginny and Stella a volatile mix of fascination and revulsion. Lewis asked his mother to make Wonder Bread and game hen sandwiches slathered with salad dressing.

Trip joked that they were butchering the poor bird a second time, and Mabel said, "The girls are still refining their palates." Lewis laughed. His mother seemed more alive than she'd been in years. It felt wrong, laughing with her so soon after burying his father, but maybe it was just some bizarre form of grief. Everything about the day seemed so close to normal. His family could have been getting together for any other occasion and they would have acted the same way. The only piece missing was his father but his absence wasn't felt. Not really. Except for the shabby pastor who hardly knew him, no one said a word about Lew Mattock. There were too many particulars to deal with—tables to set, glasses to fill. There was small talk about the weather, the never-ending task of entertaining Ginny and Stella.

Trip took a sip of sparkling water and put his arm around Sophie. "You like my lunch, don't you, baby girl?"

"You know I do," Sophie replied, always her father's china doll. Lewis wondered if Sophie would ever love him as much as she did her "daddy."

Mabel finished plating the food and Lewis went to tell the pastor lunch was ready. Trip slipped out behind him and said it was time they had a heart-to-heart. Lewis hoped he wasn't about to get a lecture.

"What do you know about Harlan Dupee?" Trip asked, catching Lewis off guard.

Lewis watched the pastor light a cigarette and examine the backyard trees as if he were a botanist. "Harlan's all right."

Trip opened his suit jacket and put his hands on the rail of the back porch. On another man the suit would have been gray but on Trip it shined silver. Everything about him sparkled. His white hair, his platinum watch, his gleaming, toothy smile. If ever there was a man who could polish a turd into gold, it was Sophie's dad. "I ran into the mayor and he told me they're going ahead with the sheriff's election. Anyone who files papers can run. It'll be a bunch of nobodies, but Billy figures Harlan will throw his name in the hat. Needless to say, no one's too excited about that. Your father's a hard man to replace." Trip paused, as if to give Lewis's dad a moment of silence. "So I was trying to figure out who wouldn't let the sheriff's department go to heck and came up with the one man who might be able to fill your father's shoes."

"Who's that?"

"You."

"Me? I don't know the first thing about being sheriff."

Trip put a hand to Lewis's shoulder. "How much do you think your father knew before he started?"

Lewis shrugged.

"People like having a Mattock as sheriff. Besides, you've been running the security business for years. People trust you. And if you don't run, Harlan will win, and I don't want to badmouth the poor boy, but don't you think you could do better?"

"I guess."

"Damn right you could." Trip clapped him on the shoulder.

Lewis tried to picture himself as the sheriff, but the image kept morphing into a portrait of his father. "What would Sophie say?"

"She'd support you, of course. Running for sheriff is a great testament to your father. To your family."

"What would I need to do to run?"

"File paperwork with the county commissioner. I'd let it slip to a few people that you're a candidate and the rest will take care of itself."

Trip made it sound easy, and even though Lewis didn't like going along with his father-in-law's plans, he often found himself doing just that. It was Trip who'd found their house and put the money down, Trip who'd told Sophie it was time to have children, Trip who'd extolled the virtues of the Volvo that Sophie used to shuttle those children to and from that house. The doctor had a way of phrasing things so that any other course besides his own seemed foolish.

"So it's settled?"

Lewis liked the idea, not because it was a testament to his father but because it was a chance to do something for himself. He was tired of the same old, same old. He could spend the rest of his days goofing off at Riverside Security or do a job that made a difference. He needed a change and maybe this was it. He put out his hand for Trip to shake. "I'll give it a shot," he said.

Trip pulled him into a clipped hug. "Your father would be proud," he said, but Lewis didn't believe it. Lew Mattock would have called his son foolish, but his opinion didn't matter anymore. Lewis would run for sheriff and prove his father wrong.

Harlan parked his truck across the street from Jackson and Lyda Finley's red brick Victorian. He hoped showing up in the Ford made Lyda less anxious to talk. Nobody wanted their neighbors seeing a cop car out front and speculating on the reason. A wrought-iron gate ornamented with fleur-de-lis creaked as Harlan pushed; it looked like something that had long ago come up the Mississippi from New Orleans. Downtown was filled with such flourishes—things that had been lost along their journey north. Harlan's kin had been in Marathon then, working the docks, but any wrought iron they owned they had stolen. Knaves, criminals, and gamblers—these were Harlan's stock.

The roots of a dying ash surfaced along the yard like eels cresting a river. They'd loosened the brick walk, which was covered with fresh clippings from a boxwood hedge. The front door was propped open, and through the screen Harlan could see a wide staircase with a large, rounded banister. Lyda Finley appeared in the frame and stepped out as though she'd been expecting him. Harlan still wore his suit from the funeral and Lyda wore her black dress, now accented with white gardening gloves.

He introduced himself and Lyda put out a gloved hand, laid it softly in his grip. "What can I do for you, Sheriff?"

"Do you have a moment to chat, Mrs. Finley?"

"Have a seat." She extended an airy arm toward the porch-swing and perched herself on the edge of a metal folding chair before removing her gloves and lighting a thin white cigarette. She had a strong, square chin that seemed out of place on the rest of her face. "Dupee," she said, pronouncing his last name with an accent. "That's French."

"That's right."

"*Parlez-vous français?*"

"I'm sorry?"

"I suppose not."

"You asked if I spoke French. I don't. Not much anyway." She seemed disappointed, took a long draw, and ashed in a china bowl set atop the porch's railing. "My father spoke it," Harlan said. "I guess I didn't take after him."

"It's a beautiful language," she said.

Harlan forced a smile. He felt ridiculous on the porch swing. It shook at the slightest movement. To keep from rocking back and forth, he set a wide stance and planted his feet like bricks. "I wanted to talk to you about Lew."

She furrowed her brow. "Lew Mattock?"

"Yes. Lew Mattock."

"I don't know what I could tell you." Inside there was a loud whistle and Lyda stood up. "I was making tea," she said. "Wait here."

Harlan relaxed his legs and the chains holding the porch swing cried out. The neighboring houses were masterpieces of construction—worn brick exteriors, bay windows, wraparound porches. They were nothing like the shoddy craftsmanship of Harlan's home. A place like the Finleys' could be passed down through generations. The only drawback was the view. Neighbors everywhere. Neighbors watching you come and go. Neighbors judging you. The trailer park next to Harlan's place could be a headache, but better trashy neighbors on the other side of some woods than nosy housewives steps away. Harlan had the crickets and the opossums and the deer and that was enough. In the winter, when everything but the cedar and pine died back, there was a clear view to the river, and up until a coal barge or gambling boat went by, he could almost believe the world was his alone.

Lyda walked out with two steaming mugs. She'd changed into jeans and a sweater. "I felt so dreary in that dress," she said. She was the sort of woman who looked fashionable no matter what she wore. Harlan had seen the catalogues that clothes like hers came from, their pages covered with models who looked like younger versions of Lyda herself. "Where were we?"

"Lew," Harlan said.

Lyda cupped her mug in both hands as though to warm them. "Right," she said. "What do you want to know?"

"Did you know Lew?"

She shook her head. "I voted for him but that's about it. I guess we saw him at the occasional social event."

"You were at the funeral today."

"Jackson felt we should go." She relaxed and her shoulders dropped slightly. "He has this sense that people expect the Finleys to show up at such things, as if our mere presence gives the town succor. It's ridiculous, of course, but I find it best to let Jackson have his delusions."

"So Jackson and Lew were close?"

"No, I don't believe so. Not unless Lew spent time at Idle Haven. My husband practically lives at the country club."

Harlan knew Lew wasn't a member at Idle Haven, though it wasn't from lack of effort. The Haven was famous for its exclusivity. Newcomers needed to be sponsored by current members and even then the board rarely voted in their favor. Lew had wrangled a sponsorship but been denied by the board. Harlan remembered because Lew retaliated by setting up a speed trap down the road from the club. Harlan sipped his tea in silence and waited for Lyda to say more.

"I don't know what to tell you, Mr. Dupee. I didn't know Lew that well."

"The day after he died, I found a cell phone in Lew's cruiser." Harlan pulled the phone from his pocket. "Looks like this." If he'd surprised her, Lyda hid it well. She blew over the rim of her mug, took a sip, and waited for him to continue. "Does it look familiar?"

"I have one that looks like that."

"I know. We subpoenaed the records. This phone's registered to you."

Lyda rubbed her nose. "That's strange," she said. "I don't know why Lew would have it. Maybe I dropped it and he picked it up." She put out her hand.

"You want to know the strangest thing," Harlan said. Lyda stared at him, not blinking. She couldn't be bothered to ash her cigarette and its dead end grew silently. "This phone—*your* phone—dialed one number over and over, so I called it and got a recorded message of your voice. Strange, right? That you'd be calling yourself?" A neighbor walked by with a little boutique dog—a fluffy mess of a thing. Lyda turned and waved hello as the dog paused to pee on a shrub. Harlan let the neighbor continue down the block before getting to his real question. "Were you and Lew having an affair, Mrs. Finley?"

She smiled tightly. "Please, Mr. Dupee. Call me Lyda."

"Lyda."

She tapped out another long, white cigarette from her pack and offered it to him. Harlan put it to his lips and let her light it, took a drag. "Lew gave me something my husband couldn't. He was a respite from reality."

"How long did it last?"

"Not long."

"But you had phones to reach each other. This wasn't a one-night fling."

"A year. Maybe less. Maybe more. I bought the cell phones so I wouldn't have to call his office or home. Lew didn't know how it worked, but once he figured it out, the bill became sky-high. He loved gadgets. Sometimes he'd get on the phone right after we slept together. The reception barely works out here, but he didn't care. I had to lie to Jackson about taking French classes to help pay for it."

"Who did he talk to? What did he talk about?"

"I don't know. Nothing important. He called people to say hello, to tell them he was on a cell phone. He had nicknames for everyone. It was Big Boy this, Billy Goat that. I told Lew if he didn't stop calling other people, I'd take the phone away." She smiled. "Like he was a child." Her voice started to waver and she sniffled once before rescuing the cigarette for a final drag.

"And he stopped calling other people?"

"He did. He turned it into a game, like what would I do for him in return. Though I'm sure you don't need those details."

"Do you know anyone Lew might have had a disagreement with? Someone who would have wanted to harm him?"

She shook her head.

"What about Jackson? Did he know about the affair?"

She kept shaking her head, looked down as if she'd been chastised. "No," she said. "Of course not."

"Where is Jackson now?"

She raised her head to look at Harlan again. "We had brunch at the club. He wanted to stay. I'll pick him up when he's good and liquored."

"Does he own any guns?"

"Jackson? Obviously, you haven't met my husband. He prefers cooking to hunting."

"There aren't any guns in the house?"

"His father's are in the basement gathering dust. Jackson wouldn't even know how to load a bullet."

"Can I borrow them?"

"Do I have a choice?"

"Not unless you want me to get a warrant, in which case I tell the judge about the affair to justify probable cause. Either way, I get the guns."

"Whatever you want," she said. "But I didn't have anything to do with Lew's death, Mr. Dupee. And neither did my husband. Part of me wanted out of the affair, and I'm sure part of Lew felt the same. The problem was we fit well together, so it was hard to end. I hope that makes sense."

She opened the front door and led him through a dining room with glass-fronted shelves to show off silver and china. A chandelier loomed above a long mahogany table. In the kitchen she paused and picked up an envelope. "Do you have children, Mr. Dupee?"

"No."

"My daughter left a note today that said, 'Gone to Lexington.' That's it. No 'Dear Mom and Dad.' No 'Love, Mary Jane.'"

"I'm sorry to hear that."

"You try not to mess them up but sometimes you can't help it." She sighed and dropped the envelope back on the table before leading him into a dimly lit basement.

He stood at the base of the stairs while Lyda searched through boxes. The mounted head of a four-point buck stared at him from a perch on the wall. Spiderwebs stretched across the rafters where the house's plumbing and electric snaked. A brown spider was hard at work and Harlan thought he could make out his initials in its nascent web. "Your daughter who ran off," he said. "Any chance she knew about the affair?"

Lyda pushed a plastic bin out of the way. "Mary Jane barely knows I exist."

"And you're not worried about her having up and left?"

"I'm not asking you to find her, if that's what you're asking. She'll come home when she needs money or a warm meal. This is nothing new." Lyda stopped and opened a wooden chest. "Here we are," she said. "It's heavy."

Harlan came over to help, and as he grabbed the chest by its leather straps, Lyda put her hand atop his. "Will you be talking to Jackson about this?" she asked.

Harlan pulled his hand away and handed her a card. "Call me if you think of anything else that might help, Mrs. Finley." Then he lifted the gun chest and hiked up the stairs.

When he passed through the dining room a second time, it didn't leave the same grand impression. The heavy wood and delicate glass made Harlan feel like he was in a museum, like nothing was meant to be touched, and he thought he could understand why a woman like Lyda might be so terribly bored, why she might have found something in Lew.

By the time he'd hefted the chest into the bed of his truck, Lyda had stepped back outside. He watched her pick up the hedge clippers and start back on the boxwoods, one of those thin cigarettes dangling from her lips as she opened and closed the blades.

As Mary Jane headed south for Lexington, weather-beaten fences gave way to the bright white planks and low stone walls of horse farms with elegant names. Denali and Claiborne, Gainesway and Calumet. The black eye of an occasional thoroughbred flashed in her headlights, and she wondered each time if it was a million-dollar runner or a broken-down nag. She never understood how someone could tell the difference. The highway's shoulder reappeared as the first hint of the city—the Big Blue Building—flashed on the horizon. Mary Jane passed a Travelodge and Shell station that bordered the crossroads at I-64 and I-75, passed a strip mall empty save a Chinese buffet, a fenced-in mental hospital that divided historic Victorians from public housing. Downtown boasted a smattering of office buildings surrounded by empty sidewalks and fountains no one was around to appreciate. On the other side, the suburbs began—two-story homes with clipped lawns and circular drives.

She turned down Euclid, a mix of boutique stores and college-town standards—a pub, a record store, a skate shop. Closer to campus the houses turned modest. In the front yards students had slung couches, bleached and blotchy from sun and rain. Beer cans littered the grass like shell casings. At a stoplight Mary Jane watched a couple of girls in skirts too short for the cold stumble arm in arm down the sidewalk while the rolling bass of a stereo shook her coupe—a tricked-out truck with two pasty white boys in backward hats. They lowered their music and hollered at the girls, who ignored them, then turned their attention to Mary Jane and said something crass. Mary Jane stared straight ahead until the light turned green. When she glanced over, the passenger mouthed "Bitch" as the driver spun his tires.

A few blocks down, she turned onto Mark's street and parked in front of his fourplex. The windows of his apartment were dark. On the porch of the unit below, two girls sat drinking a bottle of wine. Mary Jane considered driving to the library and looking for Mark there but the scratching pens and clicking keyboards always made her feel like a failure.

One of the neighbors came over and knocked on the passenger-side window. "What's up?" she said.

"Nothing."

"Are you spying on us?"

Mary Jane wished that were the case, wished she were doing something more interesting than waiting for a boy. She flipped off her headlights. "I'm a friend of Mark's."

"Who?"

"He lives upstairs."

"Oh."

"We grew up together."

"Oh."

Mary Jane didn't add any more.

"He comes home late," the girl said, checking a silver watch clasped loosely around her bony wrist. "Later than this." She put her thin arm through the window, extended her hand. "I'm Audra."

"Mary Jane."

"I think he keeps a spare key beneath that empty planter outside his door."

"Really?"

"Yeah, but I didn't tell you that. Especially if you *are* casing the joint."

"I was waiting for Mark, but now . . ." Mary Jane let her voice trail off as if she was up to mischief. Audra gave a throaty laugh and asked if she wanted a glass of wine.

The porch was lit by flashing Christmas lights, and every few seconds Mary Jane could make out the color in Audra and her roommate Megan's faces before they faded back to gray. The wine stained their teeth purple, and Megan dribbled some onto her sweater. Mary Jane watched the stain spread along the fabric like blood in the flash, flash, flash. She wanted a cigarette, but neither Audra nor Megan seemed to smoke, so she made do without. Audra asked what she studied and where she lived. Mary Jane lied and said she was taking acting classes and looking for a place of her own. "You should join our sorority," Audra said. She alternated between twirling her wristwatch and twirling her hair.

Megan started singing. "High, low, everywhere we go, on Kappa Gamma we'll depend! We are Kappa Kappa Gammas; we're sisters 'till the end!" She swung her arm with a final flourish and knocked her glass onto the porch, where it shattered. Everyone laughed.

Mary Jane watched her feet appear and disappear in the flashing lights, the reflection of broken glass. She was still wearing her heels and black dress from the funeral. "Maybe I'll check it out," she said, and for a moment she believed the lie, believed she actually was a student.

Audra unscrewed the top off another bottle and they passed it around as if in ceremony. The conversation turned to sex, each girl sharing her disappointments and lies, each girl slurring her words ever so lightly.

By the time Mark showed up, Mary Jane was giddy drunk. "Hey baaaby," she called out. Mark hesitated and walked toward her. She stumbled along the ledge of the porch, fell into his stiff arms. "My hero," she said in a breathy voice.

"MJ, what are you doing here?"

"I came to see you."

Mary Jane tried to make introductions, but Mark barely said hello before starting up the stairs to his apartment. "I better go," she said. "He doesn't like surprises."

"Go ahead." Audra nodded toward Megan, whose eyes were half-lidded in stupor. "I'll clean up this mess."

Mark started lecturing her as soon as Mary Jane walked in. He told her this wasn't the plan and that they needed to stick to the plan, which was for her to stay in Marathon until he arranged for them to leave. Didn't she understand? His hands made ridiculous chopping motions in the air while he talked. Mary Jane wished he would shut up and jam his tongue down her throat instead of speaking to her like a child. "And to top it all off you get drunk with my brainless neighbors," he said. "Telling them Lord knows what."

Mary Jane rolled her eyes. "I didn't tell them anything and I'm not going anywhere." She took a seat on the couch and turned on the television but left it mute. An awkward silence filled the air.

Mark crossed and uncrossed his arms. "I'm sorry," he said. "It's just . . . I'm a little stunned. That's all."

"I thought you'd be excited to see me."

"I am." He sat beside her on the couch, put a hand on her leg. "Excited and surprised."

Mary Jane wriggled herself behind Mark, let her legs straddle his hips, massaged his stiff shoulders. "I did it," she said, softly. "We did it." She nibbled on his ear and the tension in Mark's body loosened. *Touch me,* she wanted to tell him. *Touch me right here.* She walked her fingers down his back and held his sides, moved her hands to his hips. "Come here," she said, and brushed her hand over his crotch. Mark fell back into her arms and Mary Jane savored the moment. His bony back against her chest—that's all it took.

"You shouldn't be here," he said again, softer.

"But I'm here now." She kissed his cheek. "Okay?" She kissed his lips.

"Okay." Mark kissed her back and stood up from the couch. All the tension seemed to return to his body. He took a bottle from his backpack and stepped into the kitchenette where he crushed a couple pills on a cutting board with the blade of a chef's knife. "What a weird night," he said. "Let's get high." He snorted a line before Mary Jane even responded.

She joined him in the kitchen and together they got high and soon enough Mark was close to comatose on the couch and said he should go to bed. Mary Jane wasn't tired and what she really wanted was for Mark to fuck her but that wasn't in the cards. Before he said good-night, Mark made a big show of taking a handful of pills from his bottle and leaving them on the cutting board. "These are for you," he said, as if he were offering her diamonds.

Mary Jane nodded and thanked him but she didn't care about the pills. Not really. She wanted Mark inside her, wanted him to treat this night as if it were a wedding night. They were together now. She needed that to mean something.

The lightness in her head—the wine's feelgood—scampered away on a biting wind that snaked through a stuck open window. Mary Jane's veins pulsed like hammer strings and her muscles

clenched. She breathed deeply to calm herself but her breath remained ragged until she walked into the kitchenette and snorted
another line.

She peered into the bedroom and closed one eye to see better.
Streetlight snuck through the busted blinds. After a minute, she
could make out Mark's body—wrapped in the sheets and lying
diagonal across the bed. No room for her. His chest rose and fell in
a steady rhythm and she mirrored it with her own to find some
deeper connection. She told herself tomorrow would be better. And
all the tomorrows after that.

She scavenged in the kitchen for food but the fridge was mostly
condiments and Coke. She settled for a plate of leftover fries,
which she ate cold. Then she opened the front door and looked for
Audra and Megan but they'd gone inside. She sat in the dark and
listened to the wind bend the trees. The cars race the streets.
Thoughts slipped from the back of her head on a river of wine and
pill dust. The oil from the fries coated her fingers, and she licked
them. Then she lay back on the couch and slipped her fingers under
her dress. She worked in small circles and imagined Mark on top
as her fingers warmed, but the drugs coursed through her and her
limbs went heavy and no matter how close she seemed to coming,
it escaped her.

five

Mark woke in a panic—his legs pumping as if biking uphill and his hands pulled tight to his chest in prayer. The remains of a nightmare lingered. Mary Jane pointing a finger that turned into a pistol. And then a gaping hole in his abdomen but instead of blood, a black sticky tar. He'd touched it, put it to his lips. It tasted like licorice. Booming from the heavens above was his father's voice—amplified and reading the weather report. *Monday: partly cloudy, highs in the sixties, lows in the forties overnight with a thirty percent chance of rain. Tuesday: partly cloudy, highs in the sixties, lows in the . . .*

He dressed in the shadowy half-light of a street lamp and poked his head into the common room. Mary Jane was asleep on the couch. He started to slink by her but reconsidered. It wasn't that he didn't want Mary Jane there; it was just that her arrival complicated things. He hadn't followed through on collecting the money and she wouldn't understand why. She'd expect him to go back to his father and demand what they were owed, as if it were that easy. He rubbed her shoulders and her eyelids fluttered. "MJ, I've got work to do. You should sleep in the bed." She muttered nonsense as he helped her to the bedroom, pulled the covers over her, and sealed the blinds to turn the room an inky dark. Mary Jane trusted him to get her to Montreal and he'd pretended he could deliver.

He was the steady half of their relationship—the planner, the pragmatist—but he wished he could harness Mary Jane's faith. Sometimes he felt like he carried all the doubts and she carried all the dreams. To Mark, Montreal wasn't a place, it was a state of mind, and he wasn't sure how to get there. He kissed Mary Jane softly on the forehead and left a note and his spare key on the coffee table, along with twenty bucks in case she'd come empty-handed. You never knew with Mary Jane.

The sun winched itself up over the suburbs. The sidewalks were empty save a couple of professors carrying leather satchels, and the first students Mark came across were still up from the night before, howling as they took turns posing atop a statue of the university's first president. One girl put a cigarette in the statue's mouth. Another sat in his lap as if telling her desires to Santa Claus. A boy did his best to make it look like the statue was sucking him off, and when the girls called for him to pull it out, he craned his head around to look for witnesses. Mark tried not to draw attention.

Outside the library a maintenance crew blew leaves into piles and crisscrossed the grass with mowers, the din of motors buffeted by a strong wind. Mark ducked into the coffee shop next door, where a pair of basketball players sat drinking smoothies and signing autographs for a blond coed. The town treated its Wildcats like celebrities; it seemed ridiculous that in addition to dunking and posing for photos, they had to attend class and go through the motions of being actual students. Mark supposed the attention could become overwhelming at times.

The black-haired barista treated him with her usual indifference, put his coffee on the counter without a hello and held out her hand to swipe his meal card. On the receipt he noticed his balance was under a hundred. Normally he would phone his dad and ask for money and deal with the lecture that accompanied the funds. Everything came down to money in the end. The money his father kept from him. The money Lew had extorted from his father. The money Mark and Mary Jane needed to start over in Montreal. Everyone carried a balance, was owed or past due. Everyone was greedy for more.

It had started with money, too. And lies. Right around the time he'd learned to drive, Mark started making gas money by pinching drug samples from his father's office and selling them at school. It didn't matter what drugs he stole from his father's supply, because Mark could sell a week's trial of anything for twenty bucks. For nearly three months, the business kept his tank full of premium. Then one night at the diner he was careless and handed codeine cough syrup and hypertension pills under the table to a guy in his biology class named Luker. As he started to pocket Luker's twenty, Lew Mattock's beefy hand came down and pinched the back of Mark's neck. "If it isn't my good buddy, Mr. Gaines?" Lew said. And then, to Luker, "Whatever he gave you, leave it and get gone."

Luker had glanced at Mark and did as he was told. "What about my bill?" he muttered.

"Get."

Lew slid into the booth and studied the drugs. "Now the cough syrup I understand. Drink enough and maybe you have visions. But the heart pills. That's a surprise to me. A kid so young shouldn't have coronary problems." Mark didn't respond. He took the twenty from his pocket and put it on the table, as if that might erase the crime. "Oh you keep that," Lew said. "You earned it."

Mark expected to be charged with a crime, but instead Lew sat him on the passenger side and drove him home, talking all the way about how the good doctor wouldn't be happy when he found out his drug samples were making their way around town. Lew never asked Mark to explain himself, didn't seem to much care about the circumstances. When Mark's dad came to the door, Lew suggested he send his son up to his room and let the grown-ups chat.

A half-hour later, Mark learned Lew had agreed to keep him out of trouble (and keep his dad out of trouble, by proxy) in exchange for "fair" compensation—a deal he was willing to make because they were family of a sort. His father explained this to Mark in an even tone, but Mark could tell he was roiling inside and that it was only a matter of time before he blew. It happened when he finally got around to asking Mark what he was thinking? What *the fuck* was he thinking? Trip raised his hand as if to strike and Mark cowered into a corner, blubbering an apology. His father, disgusted or fed up or unsure what should happen next, lowered his hand and slammed the door.

For a couple of silent but tense days Mark barely left his room. Then Lew showed back up with a different proposal for his father. Mark eavesdropped on the conversation. Lew explained it like this: Trip would supply Mark with pills and drive up demand by prescribing pain meds without refilling them, Mark would sell the pills to dealers at the dirt track whenever Lew told him to, and Lew would provide protection from the law, along with a measure of comfort that it would all work out. To Mark's surprise, his father said he'd heard worse ideas. And when Lew revealed how much they could make on just one bottle of painkillers, a measure of excitement entered his dad's voice. When he explained the deal to Mark, his father claimed it was in everyone's best interest. Back then Mark hadn't questioned this. He'd already been dealing drugs and now he was promised protection from the law.

In another way he felt like his father had opened up to him because of what happened with Lew, had trusted in him. Maybe Trip didn't have any other choice but the end result was that dealing drugs brought them closer together than anything they'd ever done. Within a month, it became apparent the arrangement was successful beyond what they could have imagined. And a lot more complicated. Lew introduced Mark to a world he didn't know existed. Instead of handshake deals for gas money, he was selling entire prescriptions for nearly a thousand dollars. His father had to start finding ways to make the profits look legitimate.

A few times Mark expressed concern over what they were doing, but his dad had a way of making the drug trade seem normal. After all, weren't prescription drugs safer than illegal drugs? And did Mark know that more people died taking Advil than OxyContin? And didn't Mark want to help him rebuild the life they'd lost in Ohio? And Mark did, so he continued doing what was asked of him and his father kept treating him more and more like an equal. They started eating dinner together and Trip leased a Mercedes for himself and a yellow Mustang for Mark. He even talked about buying a piece of riverside property where he could build a dream house, the sort of place that could be passed on when the time came. A legacy.

Mark thought the drug dealing would stop when he left for college, but neither Lew nor his father would let it end. Paying Mark's tuition became contingent on his enrolling in the pharmacy program. Trip had big visions of opening a drugstore alongside the clinic and making a fortune. Mark came to realize he wasn't a partner but a pawn.

His father and Lew both possessed voracious appetites, and in the end, that drove them apart. Lew kept demanding a bigger share of the profit and his father started calling Lew a liability. Mark couldn't pinpoint the exact moment a switch flipped and his father turned from a desperate man into an evil one but it was around the time he started talking about Lew as if he weren't a flesh-and-blood person. Lew increased their "exposure"; he was an "encumbrance," and there was little "residual benefit" to keeping him around. The relationship became, in his father's words, "untenable." That was the cloying word that led to murder. Untenable.

Mark had gone along with it all. Out of fear, mainly. But also because it sounded logical in its way. He too stopped seeing Lew as a person, started viewing him as an obstacle. When he finally came clean and told Mary Jane the full extent of what was going on—because he couldn't keep it inside any longer—she helped him see the situation as an opportunity. He could demand the sort of money from his father that would allow them to start new lives. Otherwise his option was to stick around Kentucky until his father or Lew screwed him and he ended up in jail.

Mark's sneakers squeaked along the library's marble floor and echoed through the atrium. He passed a handful of students coming down off all-nighters, each of them curled up in a leather armchair, and took the elevator to the fifth floor, where a large skylight let through the watery morning sun. He spread his books on a long table. It was a Monday. Normally he would have popped an Adderall and made precise outlines of the week's reading. Getting B's in college had given Mark a greater sense of accomplishment than anything else in life; he'd never felt particularly smart or talented but he'd earned those grades.

He wanted desperately to travel back in time, erase everything that had happened since he'd first stolen a drug sample and sold it. He wanted his textbooks to offer the same comfortable escape they had for the past year, but the time for magical thinking was over. The sun continued to rise and the atrium filled with a dusty light. Mark stacked his books on the table and left them. A symbolic gesture. His life as a student was over and he needed to come to terms with that.

———

Harlan ducked out of the office and picked up two boxes of campaign signs he'd printed on the cheap. He figured it was okay to
start campaigning now that Lew was buried, okay to at least put
the word out. When he dropped the signs off at his house, he found
the neighbor girl, Mattie, crouched on his porch steps and picking
at a scab.

"You need some help?" she asked, jumping to her feet as Harlan
grabbed a box from the truck bed. She scrambled up onto the Ford,
her tattered sneakers knocking rust from the tailgate. "Man, this
thing is older than my daddy's car," she said, turning her attention
to the rust and scratching at it much as she had the scab. Blood ran
a thin course down her leg and pooled in a loose, white sock.

"It's old," Harlan admitted and pointed to the second box. Mattie
lifted it over the side and onto his shoulder. "What's your daddy
drive?" he asked.

"Drunk," she said and Harlan tried not to smile. "Naw, he
drives . . . I don't know what you'd call it. The body is an El Camino
but the engine is from a Ford. Other parts he grabbed out of whatever junked-out beater he could find. It's a mutt car." She rushed
ahead to the porch and put out her hands to stack the boxes. "I'm
taking the driver's test next month, and I told my dad that if he lets
me use his car, I'll rip off one of those Mercedes hood things and
solder it on the front all classy-like."

"You think it's smart to talk about breaking the law in front of
the sheriff?"

"Don't be rude now," she said. "I didn't have to help you carry
these."

"I didn't ask."

Mattie put a finger to her mouth and bit it, scrunched up her
nose. She had large, open pores, some of which had turned into
pimples, and her legs were rubbed red, like she'd shaved with a
dull razor. Her clothes were secondhand things, pillowed over her

lanky body, but she was sturdy—every inch of her muscle or bone.
"You wanna come pick through the ashes of that fire with me?" she
asked.

"I've already been there. You won't find much of value."

"It's just something to do."

"Maybe another time."

She tapped her fingers on one of the boxes. "What's in these
anyway?"

"Stuff."

"Sounds interesting." She lifted a necklace with a pocketknife
charm from under her shirt, cut open the box, and pulled out one
of the signs, reading it aloud. "Harlan Dupee for sheriff," she said,
butchering his last name.

"It's 'Du-pay.'"

"Oh, Du-pay. Classy. I thought you was already sheriff after
that last guy died."

"Not for long unless I win the election. You gonna vote for me?"

"Not old enough. Sorry."

"Maybe you can put up signs at the Spanish Manor."

"Sure. But dogs'd just piss on them. Or people." She returned to
the scab, picked at the dried blood. She licked two fingers and
swirled it in a mess. "You already knew that, though. My daddy
told me you was once poor like us, that you wasn't bigger than your
britches 'til recently."

"Guess your dad knows everything, huh?"

"Naw. He's a puffy bastard. Like how he taught me to work on
cars as if it was father-daughter bonding and now he just orders me
around. Mattie, fix this, Mattie, fix that." She pulled a pack of Pall
Malls from her pocket. "He don't pay, so I steal my wages in smokes."
She lit a cigarette, inhaled, and coughed like an amateur.

"He sounds pretty rough," Harlan said. "Maybe the sheriff
should pay him a visit."

Mattie beamed. "Yeah right." She threw a couple of phantom punches. "Henry would make mincemeat out of you." A bee buzzed nearby and came to rest along the lip of an Ale-8 bottle to suck syrup. Mattie pointed and said, "He looks just like one of your advertisements."

Harlan studied the sign she'd pulled out. Some of the ink came off on his fingers. He'd used his full name in all caps across the top—black over a yellow background. HARLAN DUPEE. Most people just knew him as Harlan. Harlan that drives the old truck. Harlan whose daddy drowned in the river. Harlan who lives in that run-down shack. Below his name the words FOR SHERIFF were printed. He was proud of the sign—its simple honesty, the future it portended. "Maybe I should've gone with red, white, and blue."

"Naw," Mattie said, "everyone does that. You're different." She crouched close to the bee and blew smoke on it.

"You're gonna make him angry," Harlan said.

"Nuh-uh. This stuns 'em." She blew another cloud and the bee stumbled along the edge of the bottle, its legs twitching.

"So that boy from the other night, is he your steady?"

Mattie straightened up. Her reddish-brown hair was uncombed and she shook it before her face, peering through the tangles while she rubbed the hairs on her wrist. "Why do you want to know?"

"Just making conversation."

"I wouldn't date a chubster like Lard. That's his name you know. His real name is Lawrence, but people been calling him Lard ever since he was a fat baby. It's good you showed up. He would have blabbed about it otherwise."

"Why'd you have relations with him if you don't like him?"

"First off, we were fucking. Second off, it was a transaction. Lard gave me something for my trouble."

"What's that?"

"Something you don't tell the sheriff about."

Harlan sat on the porch steps and patted the space next to him. "How about I promise immunity."

"You promise?"

"Promise."

Mattie accepted the invitation reluctantly, held out her pinkie and made him swear. "Lard gave me a couple pills," she said. "Nothing much."

"What kind of pills? Tylenol? Birth control?"

She rolled her eyes and offered him a fake smile. "Just some stuff for aches and pains."

"Where'd Lard get the pills?"

Mattie made a big show of avoiding the question, stood up, and stomped away. "I thought we was gonna be friends," she said, "but you're just trying to get me to snitch."

"I'm not taking out the handcuffs," Harlan said. "I just want to chat, maybe convince you to stop having sex and doing drugs. That sort of thing."

She put her hands on her hips, thumbs forward, elbows cocked back. "Do you like me, Harlan Du-pay?"

"I'd like you more if you started taking care of yourself."

She cat-walked up to him. "Let's roll a joint," she said. "I know you smoke."

"No."

"You're a good guy." She sat next to him again, rested her head against his shoulder.

Harlan looked into the dusty dandruff along her scalp and shrugged her away. "Time for you to go home, Mattie," he said. "I've got grown-up business."

"What'd you think I was suggesting?" she asked, pursing her pale lips. "'Cause I don't think it would work. You want to be sheriff, and I'm just trailer park trash. People wouldn't understand our mismatched love."

"Funny," Harlan said.

Something about the girl put him at ease—the way she jumped from subject to subject as the boredom set in, the way she couldn't keep still. "What do those pills do?" he asked. "They must do something if you sleep with boys named Lard to get them."

"Oh. They just make your body go numb," she said. "Send this sort of cool water through your veins and turn all your worries away. Some people take uppers so they can keep doing stuff. I did that once, but it made me feel like my arms weren't mine. I didn't like that. I like the lay-in-the-grass-and-look-at-the-sky pills."

"Kids have died taking them."

"I ain't dead," she crowed. "Besides, I can't even afford the good pills. Those are for rich kids now. I wouldn't let Lard stick his stubby in me for nothing."

"So Lard deals?"

"Oh, Jesus Christ, Harlan. You being a cop again? Lard sneaks them off his daddy who's got this back thing. He takes a couple and convinces some girl to fuck him. Lard likes skinny girls."

Harlan didn't want to know more. Mattie acted as if her life were normal, which in its way it was, but that didn't make it right. She was still just a kid. "You want a Coca-Cola?" he asked and opened the cooler he kept on his porch. The tepid water floated a couple of sodas and some dead insects. A waterbug had managed to make a home there and skated across the surface with frog-leg kicks.

"You know how I like my Coke?" she said. "With big chunky ice in a Styrofoam cup."

"Settle for lukewarm in a can?" He handed her the soda and popped his own. "You know, I hate to sound like an old fart, but things have changed since I was your age. Not so much kids breaking the law. They've always stolen what isn't theirs and started fights and gotten high. It's just that now they rob houses and the fighting involves guns and the drugs can kill you. I've caught twelve-year-olds sucking nitrous from Reddi-wip canisters and drinking cough syrup. I even found one kid setting a plastic garbage pail on fire and huffing the fumes."

"That's pretty desperate."

"I don't know what to do about it."

"Why do you have to do anything? It's their choice to get high. And they don't hurt nobody besides themselves."

Harlan thought about his own father—all boozy breath and heavy belt, purple fists and white rage. He could still touch the scars from a nail-filled two-by-four swung into his shoulder. "Your daddy told the truth," he said. "I grew up poor." He motioned toward the house. "Shit, this ain't a castle. But I saw how all that getting fucked up hurts someone eventually." He pulled down his collar and showed her the scars, scattered like buckshot.

Mattie clutched the Coke in both hands and brought it to her mouth, looked away. "Let's say you caught me with pills," she said. "What would you do?"

"I'd ask you where you got them."

"And I'd say they're for my grandma. She forgets to take them, so I remember for her."

"I'd check on the prescription."

"And you'd find out I don't even have a grandma."

"So I'd arrest you."

"Okay, but what if I had a doctor's note of my own. 'Cause maybe I have some pain, too. Most people do. And maybe I'd go across the river to a doctor in Ohio and get a second note for all that pain."

"You're not telling me anything I don't already know."

"You don't want to be sheriff, Harlan. Deep down you're like us over at the Spanish Manor. We don't care who the sheriff is." She drained her Coke, stood up, and kicked at the boxes. "It's a shit job anyway."

Mary Jane pressed her palms against the wall and stretched the length of Mark's bed. It felt good waking up away from her parents' house. Mark was gone but she had a dim recollection of him helping her to bed and kissing her good-night, almost like a dream. The sheets were steeped with the salty smell of him. She doubted they'd been washed in months. She sat on the edge of the mattress and pictured the bedroom with a more feminine touch—art on the walls, clean carpet, lavender-scented potpourri. Imagined a pair of heels kicked beneath the bed, a small box of jewelry atop the dresser, their clothes side by side in the closet. Two lives braided like rope. Visions of their future threatened to overwhelm her. With happiness. With doubt. She'd risked everything for Mark. Lew Mattock was dead. And the memory of it cored her. His slumped head on the grill. She stood up and searched for an Oxy to fill the void, hesitated once she'd found one because it was still so early, then popped it in her mouth. She reminded herself she'd done it to save Mark—that they'd done it together.

When Mark first told her Lew was going to arrest him, Mary Jane brushed it off as false bravado. She'd always considered Mark more pharmacist than drug dealer and couldn't imagine him in an orange jumpsuit. Prison wasn't a place for boys like Mark Gaines. He'd just finished his first year at UK with good grades, and he was home for the summer but acting strange. Mark had never been a heavy user but that summer he invented a game where they both snorted so much Oxy they passed out, and the "loser" was the first one to wake up. That person had to write a note with a joke or a funny drawing welcoming the other back to the world of the living. Mary Jane tired of the game but Mark insisted, thought it was hilarious when he found a note telling him how much better off he'd be dead.

Then one terrible night Mark's concerns about Lew became real to her. They were sitting on the docks tossing stones in the river. The town had thrown a party for the Fourth of July, trying to one-up the pyrotechnics set off by their neighbors to the north. Remnants of the celebration littered the riverbank—trash cans vomiting beer bottles and half-eaten burgers, tufts of exploded paper and plasticware lapping against the shore. Mark was quiet, and when Mary Jane asked him what was wrong, he said "nothing," which had become his standard response to any question. She leaned over and kissed him—the only way to break through—then took a walk. She worried she was losing him. Her plan had been to join Mark at UK, but when the university rejected her, that idea went up in smoke, though Mark never wanted to talk about it.

It was only a couple of minutes after she left him on the dock that Mary Jane heard Mark arguing with someone. She hurried back to find Lew harassing him. "I will make your life a living hell, you stuck-up prick," Lew barked as he balled Mark's shirt in his fist.

"You're drunk," Mark replied in an eerie monotone.

Lew pushed Mark to the edge of the dock. "Five thousand," he said. "You or your daddy. Do you understand?"

Mark didn't respond, so Lew unholstered his gun and let it shimmer in the moonlight. Mary Jane couldn't stand by and do nothing. She stepped out of the shadows and screamed, "No!" In the pale glow of night, she could see Mark's eyes—dull and unimpressed. He shook his head.

Lew took a step back and swiveled his eyes between Mark and Mary Jane, the gun swaying loose in his hand. "That's cute," he said, lifting the gun languidly toward Mary Jane as if it was a crooked finger. "You got a girlfriend. I didn't think you were the type." He bent his wrist effeminately and laughed. Smiling, he turned away from Mary Jane and pointed the gun back at Mark. "Take off your clothes." Mark hesitated and Lew cocked the hammer. Mary Jane

stood in shock as Mark pulled his shirt over his head and unbuttoned his jeans. His belt buckle thudded against the wood with a
dull knock. "All of it," Lew said and tapped the gun against Mark's
crotch. Mark slipped off his shoes, methodically peeled off each
sock, then dropped his boxers to the dock. He looked as vulnerable
as a plucked chicken and his lip quivered slightly as he cupped his
genitals.

"Stop," Mary Jane said, her voice a whisper. And then louder,
"Stop it!"

Lew holstered the gun and in a flash his arms uncoiled and sent
Mark toppling into the river. Mary Jane ran to the edge of the
dock as Lew kicked Mark's clothes over. "Say hello to your mama
for me," Lew said before walking away.

Mark paddled in the water after his clothes, tossing them up
before hoisting himself with two scrawny arms. It took a minute
for him to catch his breath and despite the warm, humid night,
goose bumps rose along his skin. "I hate him," he said, shaking. "I
fucking hate him."

Mary Jane wrapped Mark in her arms. "It's okay," she said. "I
won't let him hurt you. We'll do whatever it takes. We'll kill him
if we have to." She'd been high—just talking shit—but the words
ended up prophetic.

Now Mary Jane was in Lexington and she needed to forget about
that past. She raised the blinds and looked out as students scuffled
toward campus. It was midmorning but most wore pajamas or sweatpants, had hair freshly slept on. They looked less like scholars than
junkies and those who made an effort stood out. A boy in a crisp
blazer and jeans, his thumbs cocked under the straps of his backpack. A girl wearing motorcycle boots, peacoat, and a long red scarf.

It was the first day of her new life and Mary Jane decided to
make the most it. At least Lexington wasn't Marathon. She ran a
hot shower and pretended she was spaghetti boiling in a pot, soft-

ening and loosening and letting go. Afterward, she put on her favorite oxford shirt and a black skirt, did her makeup and straightened her hair.

Out on Euclid Avenue, she fell in lockstep with the other students, even stopped at the bookstore to pick up a backpack and reading material. The shelves were arranged according to course. Most held heavy textbooks stamped with boring titles, but a class titled Acid Trips and Flower Power: Literature of the Sixties caught her eye. She bought copies of *On the Road* and *Divine Right's Trip*, the back of which said it was about a Kentuckian driving across the country in a VW bus. Mary Jane had never been much of a reader but she thought she could use the books as guidance for her own journey.

With the backpack slung over her shoulder, she moved with the confidence that comes from belonging. She followed a girl with pink streaks in her hair to a grease spot named Tolly-Ho, where muscled line cooks worked the flattop while punk-rock waiters poured coffee. She took a booth next to a grimy window where dead flies lay on their backs and a fluorescent sign hummed. The tattooed forearm of a waiter shoved a menu onto the table. The tattoo was of a mermaid clutching a rock. Behind the mermaid, a sinister castle rose to a quarter moon and a horde of bats flew to the elbow. "Drink?" the waiter asked.

"Coffee," Mary Jane said as she looked up.

He had a scruffy beard, white boy dreads pulled into a tall, colorful cap, and a barbell in his left eyebrow. "The corned beef hash is on special," he muttered.

The sound of pans clanging and the smell of bacon frying filled the diner. The chatter of students melted into the din as Mary Jane cracked open one of her books. "Here comes D.R. Davenport, Divine Right he calls himself after that incredible stoned-out afternoon. . . ."

Mary Jane paused and thought about how she'd tell her own story. "Here comes Mary Jane, MJ she calls herself, after that fateful day in Marathon. . . ."

A coffee mug came down with a clang and sloshed onto the book.

"Damn," the waiter said.

"It's okay." Mary Jane dabbed the pages with a paper napkin.

"It's been a shit morning."

"It's okay," she said again.

His face relaxed into a grin. "My bad." He had a crooked, toothy smile.

"I like your tattoo," she said.

The waiter looked down, as if noticing it for the first time. "My brother did it. He works at True Blue down the block."

"It's awesome."

"He's good. And cheap. Just ask for Madcap."

"Maybe I will."

"How about something to eat while you think on it?"

Mary Jane bit her lip softly. "The hash sounds good."

"Hash always sounds good to me," the waiter said.

Mary Jane laughed. "Me too."

"I'm Vince," he said.

"Mary Jane."

Now it was his turn to laugh. "The hash for Mary Jane," he said. "You gotta be kidding me."

The food was oversalted and undercooked but Mary Jane didn't complain. She picked at the plate long after other customers had come and gone, and Vince refilled her coffee time and again. They talked whenever the flow of customers slowed down. He was older, almost thirty he said, without getting specific. He wasn't a student. He was busy living and that was hard enough. She told him she wasn't a student either and when he asked about the books, she said she didn't need some professor telling her how to think. He liked that, told Mary Jane she was wise for her age.

It had been so long since she'd flirted with someone who wasn't Mark that she'd forgotten the thrill of a stranger's attention. She didn't want to leave, but she worried that if she stayed, it would become awkward, so when Vince went to pick up an order for a four-top, she left a tip with an Oxy beneath the bills.

A couple of buildings down, she stopped in front of True Blue. Its walls were graffitied with tattoo stereotypes—an anchor, an arrow-struck heart, a rose, and a cross. A pair of gutterpunks with a dour pitbull sat against the building smoking cigarettes and pan-handling for change. As Mary Jane hesitated in front of the door, a hand touched her shoulder softly. "Hey," Vince said. She turned to look at him. "You know that tip you gave me?"

Mary Jane gave him a sly smile.

"Can you get more?"

She nodded.

Vince took a pen from his ear and the waiter's pad from his pocket. "I'm having a party in a couple days. You should come." He handed her the address, stooped to kiss her cheek, and she returned the gesture. He was the tallest boy she'd ever kissed.

"You getting a tattoo?" he asked.

Mary Jane nodded again. She would have nodded to anything.

"Say hi to my brother for me."

Mary Jane turned back to the tattoo parlor with a new confi-dence. Mark wasn't the tattoo type, but maybe she was. She'd never much thought about tattoos; her parents wouldn't approve—tattoos were low-class—but her parents weren't in the way any-more. She undid the top button of her oxford shirt and flared the V so that the top of her bra became visible, adjusted her skirt so that it rode high on the hips, and stepped inside.

The girl behind the counter had a face full of piercings and a star tattooed above each breast. She lisped a syrupy hello and introduced herself as Eva. When Mary Jane asked after Vince's brother, Eva pointed to a stocky man with close-cropped hair dancing to drum and bass. He wore tight black jeans and a ripped T-shirt, held together by safety pins, that said DISMEMBERED across the chest. It looked as if he'd been attacked by a slasher and Frankensteined back together. Nearly every inch of his skin, even parts of his face, were tattooed. When he came over and put out his right hand, she noticed the word *mad* inked from his ring to index finger. The left had *cap* from index to ring. "Madcap," he said in a soft voice. There were bits of gray above his temples.

"You here for a tattoo or a piercing?" Eva asked.

Looking at the tattooed man and pierced girl, Mary Jane was torn. "Both," she said.

"A double-dipper," Madcap hollered. "Awesome. Eva here does the piercing."

"Where can I put a hole in you, hon?" Eva asked. A stud flashed from the back of her mouth.

"The tongue," Mary Jane said.

"And I do the tattoos," Madcap said. "Did you have something specific in mind?"

Mary Jane shook her head. "No. But Vince said I should come see you."

"Well, a friend of my brother's is a friend of mine. As long as you have cash."

"How much?"

"Well, that depends on the tattoo."

"I have about five hundred."

Madcap nodded. "That should work," he said. "Let's look through the binders while Eva sets up."

A flood of images filled the pages. There were ten roses, thirty decorative bands, dragons, bosomy ladies, and birds. So many birds.

Chinese symbols. Love. Peace. Strength. A page of black cats, a few nymph fairies. "There're so many," Mary Jane said.

"Most people want something personal," Madcap said. "Not just a pretty picture. Each one of my tattoos has a story behind it." He asked her what she was passionate about.

Mary Jane didn't know. "I'm moving out of my parents' house," she said. "You know, being on my own."

"That's a great reason for a tattoo," Madcap replied, all positivity. "It makes me think of this painting I saw. It was this girl—this woman, really—walking along a dirt road. She was alone but she was strong."

"That sounds cool."

"Let me draw it for you." Madcap pulled a pen from behind his ear and inked the woman's dress and then her legs. It seemed like she was walking away—into the page—but she was walking on air. Then he added two curved lines around her feet. A path. When he finished her body, he drew hair blown by the wind.

"Could you add some trees?" Mary Jane asked.

With a couple strokes of the pen, there were trunks and branches arcing over the path, protecting the woman. Madcap took out a gray pen to add shadows and blurred the edges as if she were in a fog. Mary Jane couldn't believe how quickly he'd drawn it, how much she felt like that woman. "It'd be cool on the back of your shoulder," he said. "The fog thinning out over the top."

"Right," Mary Jane said. "It has a certain *je ne sais quoi*."

"What's that?"

"It's French. A phrase for something that's hard to describe."

"Spell it," he said, and soon he'd inked the words beneath the woman in cursive. "Now it's yours."

Mary Jane signed the consent form and snuck away to the bathroom to chew another Oxy. As she opened her mouth for the stud, Eva cooed sweet nothings to distract her and Madcap held her hand. She squeezed when Eva's muscles tensed and the needle pulsed through. It hurt despite the Oxy but it felt right. Salty blood pooled in her mouth, and Eva said, "Here, let me get that," and daubed gauze around the stud. "Sometimes the tongue bleeds." She held up a mirror and a little piece of silver glinted from the hollows of Mary Jane's mouth. A bright red outlined her gums. She looked like a cannibal.

Madcap moved her to his tattoo chair and asked her to take off her shirt. Normally she would have felt too self-conscious but Madcap put her at ease, and when the tattoo gun buzzed to life, he placed a reassuring hand to her skin and said not to worry. The needle touched down and he kept saying "good" as he dabbed the excess ink. To her left, painted on the wall, was a big pool of goldfish. Mary Jane counted them, named them, closed her eyes, counted again, renamed them. Madcap talked the whole time and asked her questions. She kept saying yes or no without really listening. She kept telling him it didn't hurt and he kept saying, "Good. Good." It did hurt though, and she liked that, and she liked the way the Oxy dulled it and made it a hurt she could bear.

When Madcap finished, Eva turned up the stereo, and Mary Jane examined her new body in the mirror. The glass rattled to the pounding bass of a rap song. The trees around the woman shook. An earthquake. Mary Jane imagined Mark's reaction when she showed him. Mark was square. He wouldn't understand. And for a moment she imagined showing Vince, imagined leaving with Vince, imagined kissing Vince.

Mary Jane smiled as a deep voice came over the speakers, cool and unaffected. *Yeah, Mista Busta, where the fuck ya at? Can't scrap a lick, so I know ya got your gat.*

Madcap came and stood beside her. "You like it?" he asked.

Mary Jane nodded.

Jim Gardner didn't stand up so much as lean his substantial self over his oak desk and wave Lewis and his mother into the office. Jim was a friend of the family and the only lawyer whose presence his father had been able to stomach, and for that reason alone, he was the executor of Lew's will. As they sat across the desk from Gardner, the secretary brought Lewis and Mabel each a miniature bottle of water. It seemed very official. Gardner started by talking about the estate and held up a blue folder. Two identical folders sat on the desk before them. It was a funny word, *estate*. It made Lewis think of plantation homes and pasturelands—not a house in the suburbs.

Gardner talked broadly, told them that Lew had been concerned with providing for his family after death and that he dreamt of buying a vacation home. As Gardner talked, Lewis studied the framed certificates and commendations that hung on the walls behind him. There were diplomas from UK, a thank-you for serving on the Democratic Council, a miniature Confederate flag in a frame. On the desk sat a gold paperweight shaped like a golf ball and on the shelves were rows of hardback books that looked brand-new. "In many ways, Lew lived up to the goals he set," Gardner said and opened the will. Lewis followed suit and turned to page one while his mother left her copy untouched. "Lew paid off a mortgage, earned a steady income, and carried term life insurance, but just as his occupation was about taking risks, he took risks as an investor. Some were questionable and his liquid assets— cash, stocks, and the like—were hit hard. He tried to correct these losses by borrowing against his pension and his life insurance."

"What's that mean?" Lewis asked.

"It means there's no money," his mother said.

"Not exactly." Gardner put up his hands, as if asking for calm. "It's true that your father's investments didn't pan out. He owed money at the time of his death and the estate assumes those debts, but he also held assets. He didn't borrow the full amount against his life insurance, so there will be a check coming from Commonwealth Annuity. Not what you would have expected but something. And there's the house, of course."

"Wait," Lewis said. "You're telling me there's no savings? No retirement account?" He turned to his mother. "Where'd it all go?"

Mabel looked at Gardner. "That's a good question, Jim. Where'd it all go?"

Gardner knitted his fingers together, rested them over the high hillock of his belly, and sighed. "Lew tried to correct his losses by gambling. He lost more, then borrowed more. It was a vicious cycle. I advised him to seek help, and I think he was on his way, but then this tragedy and well—"

Mabel interrupted. "Didn't you and my husband get together and play poker, Jim? Is that how you helped?"

"Now that's unfair." Gardner craned his head to look at Lewis. "Your father and I played penny poker. Nothing like what got him into trouble." He wheeled back to Mabel. He was working them both. "I provided a breakdown of known debts on page six. You might be able to make arrangements with Lew's creditors. I'd be happy to help."

"With a fee for your services?" Mabel said.

Gardner frowned. "For free. As a friend."

Lewis sat slack-jawed. He felt like the kid in a room of adults. He seemed to react a half second late to each new bit of news.

His mother finally picked up her copy of the will. "That bastard," she said and pointed to a number on page six. "We owe the Silver Spoon fifty thousand?"

None of this made sense. His father had praised the twin values of hard work and common sense above all others, had railed against people who felt the world owed them something or believed in luck. Lottery players, welfare parents, heiresses, ambulance chasers—Lew Mattock disdained them all. But apparently he didn't hold himself to the same high standards, was all too willing to double down and chase the straight.

"I know this looks bad," Gardner said. "But not all of the money Lew borrowed was gambled away. Some of it helped pay your bills. Kept the lights on, so to speak. Heck, if I remember correctly, Lew loaned Lewis money to expand his business."

Lewis glanced at his mother, a tinge of shame over having accepted that money. She worked the water bottle anxiously in her hands while Gardner continued to fill the air with babble—noise sitting atop the hum of the heating unit. At some point he waved his hand in the air to get Lewis's attention. Fat fingers glinting golden.

"Jim," Mabel said, putting up her own hand up to keep him from talking over her. "Let me see if I understand you correctly. Even if I get enough insurance money to pay my husband's debts, there will be nothing left. I need to know because I haven't worked for many years—my husband was against such silly notions—and I'd like to keep the electricity on without taking loans against what future I have left."

"I understand your concerns," Gardner said. "But remember, you've inherited the house and that is a significant asset. You can sell if necessary—"

"I don't intend to sell the house," Mabel said, "nor do I intend to be bullied by my husband from the grave."

"I'm sure we can figure something out. Maybe you both need time to look over this in private. We can meet again later. Given the nature of Lew's death, I'm sure his creditors will be understanding."

"How fortunate," Mabel said.

Gardner didn't take the bait, continued to assure them everything would be okay as the secretary came to show them out. For some reason Lewis went through the motions of shaking Gardner's hand.

He wanted to forget everything he'd learned, but how could he? The printed proof sat heavy in his hand.

Outside, his mother tossed her copy of the will in the trash.

"Did you know about the gambling?" Lewis asked.

"I thought he was losing twenty bucks here and there. Nothing like this."

"But you didn't seem shocked."

"Just about nothing your father did would shock me at this point," his mother said, her voice starting to tremble. She handed him her water from the meeting. "Open this for me. My hands are too weak and I'm thirsty."

Sitting in the dark cab of his truck and staring out at a lifeless street, Harlan felt more like a movie detective than a small-town sheriff. He'd downed two bottles of Ale-8 for the caffeine and now he needed to take a leak something fierce. He looked at one of the soda bottles and started devising a plan when the Finleys' porch light came on. Jackson trotted down the front steps a minute later and climbed into his big beige Cadillac.

Harlan didn't keep much distance between the vehicles, though staying back and creeping in the shadows wouldn't have been any more effective than riding Jackson's tail. Jackson never once glanced in his rearview mirror, and Harlan wondered how a man could go through life so certain. When the Cadillac turned onto Lucas Ferry Road, Harlan eased back and pulled over to see a man about a mule. There wasn't but one place Jackson could be headed down that road and it was just as well to let him have a couple of cocktails at Idle Haven before making him discuss his wife, the dead sheriff, and issues of fidelity.

Harlan parked the Ford along the far edge of the country club's parking lot, away from the polished cars and trucks of its members. There was a uniformed lackey working the valet who came over and knocked on his window. "Can I help you?" the valet asked.

"I can park myself, thank you."

"I'm sorry, but this club is for members only. You can't be here."

"I can't be in the parking lot?"

"Not unless you're a member."

Harlan handed over his sheriff's badge. "I think I'll park here anyway."

"Sorry," the valet said. "I didn't know. So you want to stay in the parking lot or actually go inside?"

"You know Jackson Finley?"

"Yeah."

"I figure he's at the bar, and I wonder if you might poke your head in and let me know when he's ordered his second drink."

The kid shook his head. "I don't think I should do that."

Harlan pulled a couple of twenties from his wallet. The boy eyed the money. He was gawky, dressed in a polyester shirt, cheap vest, and secondhand, old-man glasses. He couldn't have been over twenty—burdened with bad teeth and hair that wouldn't sit down—a country boy trying to pass.

"Okay," the boy said and slipped the twenties into his front pocket. "But don't tell him."

Harlan raised two fingers. "Scout's honor."

Not but fifteen minutes later, the kid returned. "Already?" Harlan said.

"He's doesn't exactly sip."

"Okay then." Harlan stepped out, checked the tuck on his shirt, and made his way inside. The brick building spanned three stories, the topmost a ribbon of gable windows, the second ornamented with large arches of clear glass, and the first a series of French doors that opened onto covered porches, pea gravel walking paths,

and trim grass that bordered the golf course. Through the front
doors, the foyer opened up the full three stories and the soft glow
of wall lamps led to a wide staircase. A plush crimson rug swallowed the heavy heel of Harlan's boots.

The valet pointed him in the direction of the bar, where he
found Jackson with tumbler of gin and tonic in his hand. A television rebroadcast the UK football team's first game of the season,
a blowout loss in which the starting quarterback had been knocked
unconscious on the first play from scrimmage. "Looks like another
long season," Harlan said. A couple of men sitting in wingback
chairs around the fireplace looked up.

"Do I know you?" Jackson asked

"Harlan Dupee," he said. "Sheriff."

"And?"

"I wanted to talk to you for a minute." The bartender, a black
man with a thin mustache, headed in their direction.

The bartender stopped in front of Harlan, mentioned something about not recognizing him, and asked Jackson if everything
was okay. "We're fine, Charles. Mr. Dupee asked me for a favor
and made the mistake of coming here to discuss it. He'll be leaving
shortly."

"Of course." The bartender turned away without offering Harlan
a drink.

"You shouldn't barge in here and make a scene," Jackson said.

"Barge?" Harlan said. "A scene?"

"Call me and we can set up a time to talk."

"I'm not sure that works for me, Mr. Finley. What I want to
talk about is of a sensitive and, I suppose, timely nature."

Jackson looked at him, waited for more.

Harlan let his voice go soft. "It's about Lew Mattock." He hesitated. "And your wife."

Jackson spun the ice in his glass with his pinkie and took a drink. "I see," he said. "How about you let me finish this and when I'm done I'll meet you somewhere more appropriate. Do you know the revival house?"

"It's a couple miles back down the road."

Jackson nodded. "We can talk in private there. Like gentlemen." Jackson lifted his glass and tipped it toward Harlan as if offering a silent cheers. Harlan stood up. "Next time you're seeking donations, please call me at home, Sheriff," Jackson said, loud enough for the bartender and the men by the fireplace to hear.

Harlan smiled wanly, nodded at the men in wingback chairs. "Of course, Mr. Finley. I'll remember that."

Jackson took his sweet time, likely ordered another drink or two, but he showed up like he said, parked around back next to Harlan's truck. Harlan was studying the structure. Pioneers had built the meetinghouse before Kentucky was a state and Protestants of varying ilk—Baptists, Disciples of Christ, Pentecostals—had worshipped there for almost two hundred years. A few years back, after being abandoned by its latest God-fearing tenants, someone— Satan worshippers or bored kids—tagged the place with pentagrams and signs of the beast. The county repossessed the property and sold it to the Quakers for a dollar. Now a small group of men and women met there every Wednesday and Sunday and sat in silence until one of them felt moved to speak. Harlan figured that was about the time the service started going to shit.

"I bet it gets cold in there come winter," Harlan said, pushing his hand into one of the gaps between logs.

"Surely mankind has made architectural advances since this was built, Sheriff." Jackson took a handkerchief from his pocket, wiped it over the hood of his Cadillac, and rested his backside.

"Do you know why I want to talk with you, Mr. Finley?"

"You hinted at it clearly enough. My wife. Your former boss."

"Do you know why?"

"I suppose it's because they once had a relationship. How you found out, I don't know. But that was a long time ago, Sheriff."

"How long is a long time ago?"

"When Lew first came to town. Twenty years or so. Before we even married. Lyda admitted the whole thing to me. It was a difficult time for us but we worked through it."

Harlan took out his notebook.

"Do you mind?"

"I'd prefer you keep this confidential and off the record."

Harlan shoved the notebook back in his pocket, made a mental note of the discrepancy between Jackson and Lyda's time line. One or, more likely, both of them were lying.

"And way back then. That's when the affair ended?"

Jackson shrugged. "As far as I know."

"I'm sorry to tell you this, Mr. Finley, but they were still seeing each other when Lew died. They had cell phones to set up . . ." He let his voice trail off. Jackson didn't need the details. "I'm not trying to be cruel. You have a right to know."

"And now that I know, now that you've been so gracious as to air my wife's infidelities, how does that change things?"

"I'm trying to clear your name, Mr. Finley. You're a suspect. I've already confiscated the guns from your basement. They're at the crime lab right now."

"Like I said, Sheriff. I'm not worried." Jackson pushed himself up from the hood of the Cadillac and peered through the gaps in the logs and into the dark.

Harlan lit a cigarette and offered one to Jackson. "You really didn't know they were still having an affair?" he asked. "I mean, if the first time was two decades ago, how many times do you think they've been together since?"

"I'll try not to think about that if you don't mind," Jackson said. His voice was slowed from drink. "The truth is Lyda and I have come to terms with our marriage and its limitations. And I'm no choir boy." He drew hard on the cigarette and coughed.

"So do I need to worry about you taking out your anger on your wife? I don't want to get a domestic call because we talked about this."

Jackson shook his head. "I'm not a violent man." A strange look spread across his face and he shook his head as if remembering a private joke. "Let me tell you a story. When my father died, he left us the ugliest mongrel you ever saw. Muldoon was some sort of terrier with cataract eyes and alopecia. Anyway, our daughter said she'd walk and feed him but that lasted all of a week. Lyda, she liked the dog or maybe the dog liked her, but she didn't like Muldoon enough to walk him two times a day or drive him to the vet every now and then. So I took to putting Muldoon in the backyard to do his business. Sometimes I'd put him out before bed and forget to let him back in. Then the next morning, I'd open the door and find Muldoon sitting there scratching behind his ear or chewing on his tail. This went on for years. Muldoon wouldn't die. And all through those years Lyda would ask me, 'Do you know where Muldoon is?' And I would say, 'Outside.' I stopped even wondering whether or not I'd actually put him out there. She'd ask and I'd say, 'Outside.' Like a reflex. Didn't matter if it was true or not. Then sometime last year, Lyda comes up to my office and asks, 'Where's Muldoon?' And I say, 'Outside.' Well fifteen minutes later, she comes back and says she can't find him. So we search, start with the house and move into the neighborhood, calling his name, as if Muldoon ever came when called. I gave up first, returned home, and damned if we couldn't find Muldoon anywhere. At some point Lyda comes back and asks, 'Are you sure you put him outside?' I lie and say yes. Then my daughter, Mary Jane, comes back and yells at me for being negligent, which is a laugh coming from her. Next morning I wake up and reach into my closet to get some shoes and what do I find but Muldoon. Cold and dead. And you know what I did?" Harlan shook his head. "I carried him outside and hid him behind some bushes by the fence. Then I made coffee and read the paper and waited for Lyda to wake up so I could tell her I'd found Muldoon. *Outside*."

"That's a good story," Harlan said. "But I'm not sure I get the point."

"In a marriage you'll do just about anything to prove you're right. You'll carry a dog's corpse past your wife while she sleeps. You'll do this as if it's normal. You get so accustomed to the lies you don't even realize they're lies anymore. I knew Lyda and Lew had a history, and maybe I learned to look the other way so long as she was kind enough to be discreet. I didn't know she was back together with him before he died, but I'm not surprised. And maybe she and I will have a talk about it, but I doubt it will change whatever understanding we have of our marriage. These are complicated matters and best dealt with in private. Of course, I'm hoping this helps put your mind at ease regarding my involvement in Lew's death. I will do what I can to help you, Sheriff, so long as you keep my private business private. Tact is the hallmark I value above all others."

Harlan risked putting a hand to Jackson's shoulder, a soft pat to let him know he was sorry for having to ask in the first place. "One last question," he said.

"Shoot."

"I remember a few years ago Lew tried to join Idle Haven. The mayor sponsored him, I think. Did you have anything to do with his being denied?"

Jackson smiled for the first time since Harlan had sat next to him at the bar. "I believe the decision to deny Lew membership was unanimous, though I'm not ashamed to say I was among the nays. He didn't fit the Idle Haven mold."

six

Mary Jane woke to the sound of Mark munching dry cereal in front of an early-morning action flick on TNT. She was sprawled on the couch, still wearing her clothes from the day before. Mark must've thrown a blanket over her, though she couldn't remember when. She'd returned from True Blue with a bottle of peach schnapps she convinced some creep outside the liquor store to buy, rifled through the apartment for loose pills, and proceeded to drink and snort away the pain. She remembered worrying when Mark didn't return but her concern lessened the more she drank. At some point, she must've fallen asleep. Mark must've returned.

As she sat up, her feet kicked over the empty bottle of schnapps.

"You sure tied one on," Mark said. "You were passed the fuck out when I came back. I tried to wake you up and you just went limp."

"What time was that?"

"I don't know. Not late."

Mary Jane's head felt like it had been rattled by a paint mixer. Each shudder of her eyelids pierced like a needle. "You had cereal here?" she said.

"In the cabinet. But no milk."

"I don't think I ate dinner." Mark held the bowl in her direction but she closed her eyes and cradled her head in her hands. "Can you not chew so loud?"

"I'm having breakfast." He turned the volume down a notch on the TV, continued to talk with his mouth full. "Why'd you get so drunk?"

"I got a tattoo," she said, as if it was no news at all.

On the television a man with wavy hair praised his shampoo. "What's that?"

She unbuttoned her shirt and showed him. "A tattoo," she lisped. She winced as she spoke; her tongue felt like an overgrown slug. "And a piercing."

Mark shook his head. "Of all the things. Why would you get a tattoo?"

"Because I wanted to," she said, and something in the way the words formed snagged the stud and broke loose the scab. She rushed to the kitchen sink to spit out a pink mass. When she closed her mouth, it felt like she was choking.

"Good God," Mark said. "You're a mess." He stepped into the bathroom and came out with a hand towel and hydrogen peroxide. The peroxide fizzed as it touched raw skin but Mark blew to cool the pain. "It's a woman in the woods," he said. "And what's that French?"

She shrugged.

"Tattoos aren't really my thing but . . ." Mark's voice trailed off. Mary Jane's mind sharpened with each burning flash of peroxide. She didn't feel guilty about the tattoo. What had Mark been doing the day before that was so important? Where was the money he was supposed to collect? He owed her answers; she didn't owe him anything.

She reached up and grabbed his hand. "We need to talk," she said.

"Okay."

She turned to face him. "When are we leaving?"

"It's complicated."

"Complicated how?"

Mark put his hands on the counter, locked his elbows, and leaned into them. "There are a lot of loose ends to tie up, and . . ." He started drumming his fingers. "I didn't get the money."

"Why not?"

Mark mumbled something she couldn't hear and she told him to speak up.

"He refused," Mark said, his voice whiny with despair. "He said I still owed him."

"Fuck," Mary Jane said. "Fucker. You don't owe him anything."

Mark nodded. "I know." He seemed less like a man than a little boy.

Mary Jane punched him in the shoulder. Hard. "Well, what are you going to do about it?"

"I'm figuring that out."

The sounds of gunfire rang out from the television and she looked over to watch the Terminator lay waste to a police force. She found the remote and snapped off the television as the Terminator cocked his shotgun. She remembered the pressure of the trigger, the butt of the rifle kicking her shoulder. "Let me deal with your dad if you can't."

Mark shook his head. "You don't know what he's like."

"We killed someone," Mary Jane said. The words were blunt and to the point and saying them out loud felt good. "I pulled the trigger but you aren't innocent."

Mark couldn't look at her. "I know," he said. "I set the fire to help you escape, remember? I helped."

"But you weren't there," she said. "You didn't see. There was blood everywhere. On people we know." And even though what she said wasn't exactly true, it felt true. "His wife was there, screaming. I swear I wanted to die, Mark. Right then and there. But I did it. For you. For us." Mary Jane's mouth burned and she swallowed a syrupy gob of blood. She ached in a way she'd never ached before and she could no longer hold it inside—the blood, the fear, the tears—and there wasn't a pill strong enough to heal her. She grabbed Mark and turned him to face her. She needed him to stand up and take responsibility. "*We* did that," she said, her breath ragged and loud, like a train stuttering up a mountain.

Mark tried to pull her into his arms. "I didn't realize what we were getting into."

"It was your idea," she cried. And it was true. Mostly it was true.

It had been a couple of weeks after the incident with Lew at the docks. Mark took Mary Jane on a long drive, gunning his Mustang through hairpin turns as they smoked dope and soaked in the summer sun. They tried to forget that if he wasn't arrested first, Mark would be returning to school and Mary Jane would be left behind. Again.

In the middle of Nowhere, Kentucky, Mark pulled into an abandoned farm and bounced over unpaved roads until they were all alone in the world. At first she thought he wanted to get high and play the game where they pretended to die, but then Mark said he had something he wanted to show her and a small part of Mary Jane thought he'd drop down on one knee and pull out a ring. Instead he popped the trunk and showed her the rifle, asked Mary Jane if she would teach him to shoot.

She tried to convince Mark he was overreacting. If reasoning with Lew didn't work, he could run away. They could run away together. Mark said she didn't understand. There was evidence that could put him away for a long time and Lew wouldn't just let him go. "You have to cut off the head of the snake," Mark said, as if he were some wizened master.

Mary Jane didn't want to imagine her life without Mark. Mark seemed destined for bigger things and she seemed destined to be with him. And so Mary Jane picked up the rifle and tried to remember what her grandfather taught her all those years ago. "Never assume a gun is unloaded," she said. "This is a bolt action, so you rotate this handle up and pull it back to make sure the chamber is empty. . . ."

Of course she had regrets. She'd taken a man's life, but as Mark held her and promised he'd be there for her, she trusted that it had been for a reason. She reminded herself that Lew Mattock was no innocent. Mark had failed to deliver the future he'd promised and Mary Jane was afraid, but together they could muddle through. Mark was there to catch her tears, and for the moment, that was enough.

"I'm sorry," he said as he rubbed his hands up and down her back. "I'll fix it."

"How?"

"Just trust me, MJ. I'll fix it."

She wanted to believe him so badly she said, "Okay." Because okay was better than nothing at all.

"I mean it. We'll be fine."

"Okay." She dried her eyes on his shirt and pressed her lips into his. "No regrets."

"No regrets."

She felt the beginning of his erection press against her thigh and moved her hand beneath Mark's shirt and kissed him despite the flashing pain in her mouth. His hand scraped against her tattoo and she gasped. "Be careful," she whispered and taught him to touch her new skin.

She took off his clothes and pushed him down on the couch

and rode him to keep the tattoo in the open air. She felt triumphant. And when she closed her eyes, she focused on her own pleasure. And when the boy beneath her didn't do the trick, she imagined he was someone else. And after she came and came, she took Mark's cock in her hand and helped him along. One day he might grow into the sort of man who took charge, but he wasn't that man yet. She'd need to teach him. Because when they stopped talking, when all that mattered were their bodies, she spoke the language fluently and he just stuttered. And as they lay on the couch naked, the dull pain of her body throbbed like a heartbeat. And there was no pill for that.

Harlan received word from the crime lab that none of the Finley rifles were a ballistic match with the crime scene bullet and put a question mark next to Jackson's name on his yellow pad. Later, Del knocked on his door and handed over a list of names compiled from the gun sales at Walmart, few of which were promising. Frank followed Del in and said, "You ask him about Cynthiana?"

"Not yet," Del mumbled in his soft drawl.

"What about Cynthiana?" Harlan said.

"Frank's buddy is a cop down there. Says they booked an illegal last night who shot a local outside a bar. The vic's on life support at Chandler, but the bigger news is they impounded an unregistered Camry from the parking lot with a brick of marijuana, a bag of MDMA, and a couple guns in the trunk."

"MDMA?"

"Ecstasy," Frank said. "People take it and fuck like bunnies." He grinned wide, happy to have come up with a lead he could rub in Harlan's face, but Harlan didn't mind giving credit when it was due. "That's good work," he said. "Why don't you two go down and check it out."

Harlan copied Del's list of names onto his yellow pad, added a note about the unidentified perp in Cynthiana, then flipped it closed. On the front of the pad was a to-do list he'd made the day after Lew died, including a reminder to visit Mabel Mattock. Harlan told himself he'd been giving Mabel time to grieve. The truth was he didn't want to look her in the eye after finding out about Lew's affair, but the time for dawdling was over.

Mabel stood outside her house, wearing a wide-brimmed hat and staring at some needy-looking shrubs. "I saw that car coming up the road and it gave me déjà vu," she said.

"I'm sorry," Harlan said. "I wasn't thinking about how strange that might be."

"Oh, be quiet. I'm just making small talk. Come on inside."

Where other people found Mabel awkward and aloof, Harlan found her honest and humble. A welcome contrast to her husband. "I should have stopped by sooner," he said. "At least said hello at the funeral."

"I figure you've been busy." Mabel led him into the kitchen and poured them two glasses of milk. "I need to make a run to the store. This is all I've got."

"I could use the vitamins," Harlan said. "I haven't exactly been taking care of myself."

"It's been a rough week," Mabel admitted. She pointed him to a Formica table and vinyl-cushioned chairs above which a calendar from the year before dangled by a nail.

"I have to admit this isn't entirely a social call."

Mabel sat down across from him. "You're here to ask about Lew?"

He nodded. "We've checked in on plenty of people he locked up and we're still tracking leads, but there comes a time when you have to start finding out more about the victim—"

"You don't have to beat around the bush, Harlan. I was married to a lawman for nearly thirty years."

Harlan grinned tightly; maybe it was a wince. "Was Lew acting strange in the weeks before he died? Did he meet with anyone out of the ordinary? It doesn't have to be a big thing, any small change you may have noticed."

Mabel laughed a little. "Gosh, Harlan. I'm about the worst person you could ask. Turns out I wasn't very good at knowing what Lew was up to."

Harlan wondered if Mabel knew about the affair. "What do you mean?"

"We went over Lew's will yesterday, and I learned that he was in debt and left me with a list of creditors."

Mabel started to sniffle, and Harlan reached over and took her hand. With his other he pulled the bandanna from his back pocket and handed it over. He hated that he'd need to keep asking questions, that his job was to make people talk about their sorrows.

"How did he— Where'd the money go?"

"Cards," she said. "He lost it playing cards." She dabbed the creases below her eyes and handed the bandanna back. "I knew Lew liked to gamble but nothing like this. Poor Lewis. He was shocked. He idolized his father. No matter how poorly Lew treated that boy, Lewis came back to him like a lost puppy dog." She looked around the kitchen. "You know I might have to sell the house."

Harlan shook his head. "I'm sure that there are steps you can take—legal and whatnot."

"I should have known. I would overhear Lew on the phone. He was always promising the person on the other end of the line that 'they'd be fine' and 'not to worry.' That's how most of his conversations ended. 'Don't worry about it.' And you know if you're always telling people not to worry, they are, and things aren't going to be fine."

"You can't blame yourself, Mabel. None of this is your doing."

"People keep calling to offer condolences, and I keep accepting them, but what I really want to say is that my husband was a two-hundred-and-sixty-pound burden that pushed me onto a sliver of bed each night and kept me awake with his snoring. He bullied me and I let him." She started to cry again, and Harlan offered the handkerchief once more, but she shook her head. "When we moved here, he was so full of . . . enthusiasm. He was just a deputy but he wanted to make a difference. And he was a good husband, too. When the doctor put me on bed rest with Lewis, Lew would come back on his lunch break to pour me a lemonade and dab my head with a cool towel. And at night he'd sing to Lewis in the womb. I don't know when it all changed. Pretty early on, I suppose. But it wasn't always bad."

Harlan nodded. He knew better than to respond, to make light of her words by telling her marriages are tough or that men contain multitudes or some other false truism.

He sipped his milk in silence while Mabel stared off into space and waited a good long while before asking if she had a copy of the will. She shook her head. "I threw it in the trash." A smile crossed her face. "Where it belongs."

"Where it belongs," Harlan repeated.

"I can get another from Jim Gardner for you, but the gist is that Lew owes a lot of money to the Silver Spoon."

"The gambling boat?"

She nodded.

"How much?"

"Fifty thousand."

"You know, Mabel. If there's anything I can do—"

She cut him off. "You're a good man, Harlan. Don't worry about me." She stood up and refilled his glass from the fridge. "Now sit here and let's talk about better things. I was thinking it might be nice to plant a garden. What do you know about roses?"

On the door to Riverside Security, Lewis taped up a computer-printed piece of paper that announced: CAMPAIGN HEADQUARTERS. A minute later John Tyler came outside clapping a slow, sarcastic applause. "What the fuck am I supposed to do when someone calls here asking political shit?"

"First," Lewis said, "keep the cussing to a minimum. Then take a message."

"And when someone calls wanting a security system?"

"That's still our job, right?"

"We need a second phone line."

"It's only going to be a few weeks."

"Do you really want to be sheriff?"

It wasn't a question Lewis had asked himself when Trip mentioned the idea, but now he was certain. Some hesitation had disappeared when he learned about his father's gambling. The public perception of his dad would remain the same, but Lewis knew the truth about Lew Mattock. There was no more mantle to maintain.

"It's the right thing to do," Lewis said. "Maybe I'll even deputize you."

"No way. Writing speeding tickets isn't in my DNA."

John Tyler pointed over Lewis's shoulder as Trip Gaines's Mercedes pulled into the parking lot and sounded two honks hello. Sitting beside Trip was Arthur Blakeslee, a big-shot lawyer from Cincinnati and the doctor's best friend. In the back Sophie sat with the girls. "Looks like the whole clan is here," John Tyler said. "I'll make myself scarce." He avoided Trip whenever possible and tried his best to ignore the doctor's passive-aggressive comments about how lucky he was to have befriended Lewis and become part owner of a successful business.

"Stick around," Lewis said. "He won't be here long."

"Long enough." John Tyler shook the keys to the van. "Besides, I have work to do."

Stella scampered from the backseat, pulling Sophie along after her while Ginny followed a few steps behind. Sophie wore a plaid skirt that Lewis had never seen along with a white blouse and beige cardigan. She'd looped a scarf around her neck and styled her hair so that stray strands fell in arcs across one cheek. She looked stunning. Lewis stepped up to kiss her. Then he hunched over and pretended to be a monster tromping after the girls, all loose limbs and grunts. Sophie said, "Don't you have a campaign to run?" but Lewis kept playing his part and growled in response. He caught Ginny in one arm and Stella in the other, snarled and snorted and zerberted them until they begged him to stop. Their lives seemed infected by new possibility.

Sophie pulled a box of his father's MATTOCK FOR SHERIFF signs from the trunk of her father's sedan and started attaching "Lewis" adhesives to them. "Isn't this smart," she said. Lewis wasn't sure. He thought maybe it was disrespectful or maybe he wanted signs of his own, but when she handed him a sticker, he took pleasure in smacking his name atop the placard. She kept on with the stickers and recruited the girls to help her line the grass that fronted the building with campaign signs. Lewis had to admit it looked pretty neat, seeing them lined up there like a low fence.

"Have you met our future sheriff?" Trip asked as Arthur Blakeslee came up to greet Lewis.

"Great news!" Blakeslee exclaimed. "Great news!" He extended a thick hand bearing a white envelope. "For the campaign."

"Go ahead," Trip said. "Open it." Inside Lewis found a check for twenty-six hundred dollars.

"When Trip told me, I was thrilled. Couldn't get out the check-book fast enough."

"Thank you, Mr. Blakeslee," Lewis said. "But I don't know if I'm allowed to accept this."

Blakeslee laughed and Trip put an arm around Lewis. "It's not only okay to accept," Trip said, "it's necessary. You have a campaign to run and to run a campaign you need money. Arthur here is your first benefactor, and I'd like to be your second." Trip pulled an envelope from his suit jacket. "I took the liberty of soliciting donations from other friends as well. Those are on the way."

Lewis hadn't considered raising money. "This is very generous," he said. "But I planned on walking door to door."

Sophie came up and wrapped her arms around Lewis. "Gifts make Lewis uncomfortable," she said.

"I just don't know what these gifts are buying."

Blakeslee stepped back into the conversation. "They don't *buy* anything, son. This is standard procedure. As a lawyer, I wouldn't do anything that wasn't legally on the up-and-up."

Lewis tried not to laugh.

"And it's not just about this election," Trip added. "It's about building a career."

"I guess I don't know what to say," Lewis said.

"Say thank you." Trip clapped his hands together to end the discussion and handed a piece of paper to Sophie. "Call this number, honey, and buy us a little time on the radio. We need to get the word out that your husband is going to be this county's next sheriff."

"Do I need radio ads?" Lewis asked.

"I don't think it's wise to go knocking on doors," Trip said. "Your father's passing is pretty fresh. It might not look right. We'll record one spot where you talk about how you are inspired to pick up where your father left off, extend his legacy, and so on. Then

Sophie can record another with the girls. Those, along with a speech to announce you're running, should be enough. If it becomes necessary, we'll send you to knock on doors."

Sophie beamed at Lewis. "Don't worry," she said. "You're in good hands. Daddy knows a lot about this sort of thing."

Blakeslee grinned.

Lewis couldn't help feeling he was getting sold something but what that was he didn't know, so he said his thanks and didn't ask too many questions.

Sophie hugged him and said, "I'm so proud of you." Her eyes were shining.

Lewis had felt this way before—during that first year of marriage, when they'd found out Sophie was pregnant, the day he'd opened his business—but he'd begun to doubt he'd ever feel so good again. The times in between hadn't been filled with discontent so much as tedium.

Trip's pocket buzzed, and he stepped away to take a call on his cell before coming back to Lewis. "We should go to the bank and make a deposit," he said. "Do you have the checks?" Lewis shook the envelopes. He'd never seen eye to eye with his father-in-law, but he was glad to have Trip leading the way. He felt confident he'd win the election, and then he could start building his own legacy. Lewis had thousands between his fingertips but little idea what they meant.

When Harlan mentioned Lew's financial woes to Holly, she handed him an official-looking envelope. "What's this?"

A smile slipped across her face. "A subpoena to look into Lew's bank records."

"When did you—?"

"I started on the paperwork after you had me look at those court records. If Lew was accepting bribes, you might find evidence at the bank."

"How'd you get Craycraft to sign the subpoena?"

"Look close."

Harlan examined the legalese, stopped at the signature line. "Lee Smoot? The judge over in Mason?"

Holly nodded. "I didn't tell him my reasons, but he and Craycraft had a falling-out over a golf game, so he was more than happy to help out."

Harlan smiled and called Paige in to cover dispatch so Holly could go with him to the bank. With Del and Frank in Cynthiana, there wasn't a single sheriff's deputy on patrol, but that wasn't the end of the world. The Staties had kept a couple extra officers in the county since Lew's death and the phone had stopped ringing off the hook and life had generally returned to normal just about everywhere except inside the sheriff's department.

"Does this mean you're on board with my investigation?" Harlan asked as they walked to First Federal.

"I've spent a couple sleepless nights thinking about Lew and the possibility he was crooked. If this helps us find who shot him, then we should do it, but I still hope you're wrong."

"And if I'm not?"

"Then you'll track the leads that come from it. Regardless, it sounds to me like you need to get in touch with Little Joe O'Malley."

O'Malley was a former flyweight who'd made a name for himself by taking punches and staying upright. Now he managed the Silver Spoon for an out-of-town conglomerate. Harlan asked Holly what she knew about him.

"Slow-footed," she said. "But when he landed a left hook, it was over."

The bank manager looked skeptically at the subpoena, adjusted his pale pink tie, and asked why Wesley Craycraft didn't issue it.

"I guess he was busy," Harlan replied.

The manager looked unconvinced and Holly spoke up. "I believe it has to do with where the account was opened," she said. "But it doesn't really matter, does it? Lew isn't the subject of the investigation. He was the victim. We think these bank records might help us find his killer."

The manager didn't seem reassured—the law didn't come asking for bank records without expecting to find dirt in the account. "We prefer not to disclose our clients' private information," he said.

"It is a subpoena," Harlan said. "It doesn't matter what you prefer."

The guy faked a smile and called over a teller with horsey teeth that she tried to keep hidden. He explained the nature of Harlan and Holly's inquiry in such a way as to tip the girl off that he wasn't thrilled by their presence. The girl said for them to follow her and tottered toward a back office in a stiff skirt and heels she hadn't perfected.

She logged on to a computer and brought up Lew's account, asked if there was anything in particular they wanted her to find. Harlan had her scroll through the transactions. "This sure was a busy account," she said as the numbers flashed on the screen. "Thank God for computers, right?"

Harlan found the data dizzying. "I don't even own a calculator," he said.

Holly giggled. "They have their merits," she said and pulled a chair next to the teller, asked the girl if she could handle the mouse.

Harlan and the teller watched Holly methodically click through screens, occasionally making marks on a pad of paper. "You find what you're looking for?" the girl asked.

"It's not quite that simple, honey," Holly said.

The girl started to make her own notes, wrote each time Holly stopped on a screen and made a mark. She was the bank manager's eyes, but Harlan didn't blame her. She was just a kid following directions and most people following directions have no idea what they're doing. Harlan had been like that for years—just following Lew's directions.

He didn't feel comfortable talking in front of the teller, so he asked her if she'd get the manager for him. The girl was conflicted. Her boss wanted her to keep an eye on Harlan, but then again Harlan was the sheriff and you did what the sheriff asked. She looked once more at Holly, who kept scrolling through transactions. "Sure," she said and picked up her notes. "I'll be a minute."

As soon as she was out the door, Holly said, "Lew's financial situation was a mess. He kept zeroing his balance, bouncing checks, then adding large deposits. The cycle repeated."

"That sounds like someone who's taking bribes."

"It does. Especially since almost every deposit that isn't a paycheck is cash, which makes the money hard to track."

"So what's the verdict?"

"I thought we'd be out of luck, but three months ago a check from Lingg Pedersen bounced. I remember him from those letters. His son Adam had a drug charge reduced."

Harlan knew the kid, knew his dad, a surly Scandinavian tobacco farmer. "By God," Harlan said, reaching down and rubbing Holly's shoulders. "I should give you this badge."

"No thanks," she said. "I don't want the responsibility."

Harlan could hear the teller returning with her boss, heels and wingtips clicking in an even rhythm, and asked Holly if she'd seen any checks from a Chapman.

"As in Doyle Chapman?"

"Yeah," Harlan said. "As in Doyle."

Holly reached up and took his hand in hers. "I looked, Harlan. There wasn't anything unusual around the time of his release. I'm sorry."

"I don't know if it would have been better or worse."

"I don't think what happened to you and that girl could be any worse." She squeezed Harlan's hand once and let go as the bank manager pivoted on his polished Oxfords and asked Harlan what he needed.

"I was wondering if y'all have a john I might use?" Harlan said.

"Excuse me?"

"A restroom."

Holly snickered.

"Down the hall on your right." The manager glanced at the teller. "Amanda could have told you that."

"I know." Harlan soaked in the manager's confusion, then said, "Holly here has some stuff she wants y'all to print out. She'll tell you all about it." He clapped the bank manager on the shoulder as he walked by and thanked him for his help.

On the way out, Harlan and Holly bumped into Lewis Mattock, who was with his father-in-law and a third man Harlan didn't recognize. Holly gave Lewis a hug and told him not to be such a stranger. Harlan muttered something about making headway in the investigation. Lewis didn't offer much response. It was awkward running into Lewis right after digging up dirt on his dad and soon everyone was standing around without much to say. The third man didn't introduce himself, so Trip Gaines ended everyone's discomfort and said to Lewis, "We should really get a move on."

Mary Jane's new tattoo worried Mark. Even though she'd taken it well when he'd come clean about his father, he didn't know how

long the calm would last. Mary Jane could become unpredictable if
she wasn't stoned or fucking or otherwise distracted and the clock
was ticking. For the moment she was content, napping on the
couch. The air smelled heavy with sex and Mark pressed his nose
into the crook of her neck and breathed deep. If Mark couldn't
whisk her away that moment, the least he could do was keep Mary
Jane happy in Lexington.

He slipped away to buy her flowers at the Kroger, and as he
walked back to the apartment, he stopped in a boutique and scanned
the racks of dresses. They needed every dollar he'd saved, but he
considered the navy dress with a white collar more investment
than gift.

"I love that one," the salesgirl said from behind him.

Mark lifted the dress; he had no idea how to shop for women's
clothes. "It looks like it would be too small."

"What size is she?"

"I don't know. She's my height. A bit rounder." He hoped he
hadn't made Mary Jane sound fat. She was self-conscious about her
weight, but how could Mark explain to the waif of a girl in front of
him what fitting into clothes was like for Mary Jane? "She'd be
about a medium in men's."

"So maybe a ten or twelve."

"I really don't know." Mark was on the slight side for a boy—
five-eight, pushing 140. Sometimes he felt that if he and Mary
Jane fit better, their lives would be easier, not that he'd ever told
her that. She'd take it too personally. It wasn't an indictment of her
size and shape any more than it was of his own.

"Give me one minute," the girl said as she scanned the racks
and pulled out the same style dress in black, along with a white
leather belt. "This should be the right size and this belt would give
the dress some shape, especially for a woman with curves."

Mark hadn't thought about a belt but it was a nice touch. A minute later, he was back on the sidewalk, heading home with flowers and the dress. He opened the apartment door and announced in his most gallant voice, "I'm taking you on a date."

Mary Jane was sitting on the couch watching TV. "What's that?"

Mark brought out the flowers and she jumped off the couch to hug him. "And . . ." He handed over a bag stamped with the boutique's bird logo. "Something to wear."

Mary Jane unwrapped the dress and blushed. She wanted to give Mark a fashion show and took her time changing. When she came out, she'd straightened her hair and done her makeup and the dress clung to her in all the right places, even flared out as she spun. "What do you think?"

Mark could see the Mary Jane of his past in that dress, the vision he'd fallen for years before. She was almost stunning. "Beautiful," he said.

Mary Jane cat-walked up to the couch and straddled herself over him. The dress lifted, and as Mark started to get hard, she ran her fingers through his hair and over his chest and grinded against his cock. "We'll deal with this later," she whispered and licked his ear. Mark wanted to deal with it right then, but Mary Jane stood up and told him to get dressed for dinner.

He changed into slacks and a button-down shirt, ran a comb through his hair. Tonight, he would be an admiring Romeo. So much of their relationship had been lived in the dark. Their first kiss had been in middle school at a basement truth-or-dare party, and for a couple of weeks afterward they'd "dated," which meant making out in hallways and after school. Eventually Mary Jane broke it off. She could have had any boy she wanted.

Then, in high school, as other girls matured into their bodies, Mary Jane grew heavy. Mark would find her after parties and they'd go someplace hidden. Mary Jane wasn't considered a catch anymore. By then, it was Mark who kept Mary Jane at arm's length, who didn't want people to know what he did with the heavyset girl who liked to say yes. Eventually they lost their virginity together, and even though he wanted to keep their coupling secret, Mary Jane never complained or tried to make it "official." Mark felt closer to her because of that. He tried to date other girls but it didn't work out. Other girls found him too quiet, too brooding, and in time he started to think of Mary Jane as something more than a fuck buddy, as someone he could trust—a girl who was smarter than she let on. During his lonely and sexless freshman year of college, he'd kept returning to Marathon to be with her, came to realize that she was the only person he'd ever confided in, came to realize that even though he wasn't sure what it meant to love, this was as close as he'd ever come.

As he came out of the bedroom, Mark kissed Mary Jane deeply. On the way to the restaurant, he opened the car door, played slow jams, and piled compliments upon compliments. When the hostess at Chili's asked how many, he said, "Table for two" and put his arm around Mary Jane.

It was a proper date—something to take their mind off all the what-ifs—the perfect illusion. Then midway through dinner Mary Jane forked a bite of chicken fettuccini into her mouth and asked, "What are you going to do about the money?"

Mark stared at the television above the bar.

"When are we leaving, Mark? What's the plan?"

Before the situation with Lew reached a point of no return, Mary Jane had told him he should make a run for it, that kids ran away all the time, but he'd missed that chance.

"Tomorrow is the day I usually pick up prescriptions," he said. "So we'll do that. Then we'll hit up pharmacies and by the end of the day we'll have a stash of Oxy."

"And?"

"I'll sell it."

"I don't understand why we can't leave now."

Mark sighed. Part of him wanted to believe they would make it no matter what, but he was a realist at heart. He knew it took means to make it on your own. "How would we survive?" he asked. "I mean honest-to-God survival. Maybe we'd have enough money to pay for gas and food to get to Canada. But what then? This way we'll have enough to rent an apartment, get settled."

"And we're just going to forget about the money your dad owes us?"

"We're moving ahead."

"Because you're scared of him?"

"Because it's not going to happen."

"Even after what we did?"

"I'm sorry," Mark said. It was the best he could offer and it wasn't much. "But what we did kept us together. Made tonight possible and all the tonights to come." He stared at her, unblinking, tried to convince her he was telling the truth. There was something beautiful in the hazel eyes that looked back, the hazel eyes that had driven boys wild with desire all growing up, but there was skepticism, too. Mark wanted to give Mary Jane everything she wanted but he knew he wasn't capable. She asked too much; he offered too little. He could only do his best. It was the try that mattered. If he could erase it all now, he would. He'd return to school, complete his degree, get a regular job, move to a town with suburbs, buy them a house, lead a normal life. He'd never wanted fame or fortune. The most he'd ever tried to weasel was a little gas money.

"What?" she said, as he continued to look into her eyes.

It was one of those questions that you don't really answer, that you're not supposed to. Mary Jane didn't want to hear the what, didn't want to know that Mark was afraid they would get caught, that even if they made it to Canada he worried they wouldn't find happiness. "Nothing," he said.

"Seriously. What?"

Mark didn't know how to feel. "I love you," he said.

Mary Jane's face relaxed into a smile. "I love you, too."

seven

A sad herd of bedraggled cows lolled across the road leading into Lingg Pedersen's homestead. Harlan had to shoo them by waving his ball cap as if it were a Stetson. He'd read up on the Pedersen case since visiting the bank. Lingg's son, Adam, was a common punk facing jail time after having swung through his third strike—the last one for carrying a couple of grams over the misdemeanor limit of dope. Lew's letter to Craycraft had mentioned how the weighing of drugs was an imperfect science and that he might consider this when adjudicating Adam's future. Craycraft ended up dropping the charge to a misdemeanor, and Adam walked out with a fine and community service. Not long after, Lingg sent his son on a bus to his mother's place in Pennsylvania. A week after that, a check from Pedersen to Lew bounced. There wasn't a second check.

When no one came to the door of Pedersen's house, Harlan continued on to the barn. He found Lingg checking his tobacco, which hung on inch-thick poles to cure. "Good yield this year, Lingg?"

"Doesn't matter if the market's down," Pedersen replied before turning to see who'd asked.

"I wondered if I might talk to you," Harlan said. "About Adam."

"That boy. So much potential, so little drive. He's at his mother's place."

"I remember when you sent him up there. Pretty soon after his court date."

"Yep."

"Pretty good fortune for Adam."

"I suppose."

Pedersen grabbed a broom and started brewing up a dust storm of barn-floor dirt.

"Do you know why the judge reduced the charges?"

"Nope."

Harlan pulled out a bandanna and covered his mouth, took hold of the broom to make Pedersen stop. "You wrote Lew Mattock a check around that time."

"Now there's a tragedy," Pedersen said.

"We're all broken up about it," Harlan said. "But the check. Do you remember it?"

Pedersen scratched through his beard and thought. "Probably a campaign donation."

"That's strange," Harlan said. "It didn't go into a campaign account. It went into Lew's personal savings. And then it bounced."

"Did it now?" Pedersen shrugged. "I never put much stock in banks."

"None of this sounds familiar?"

"It sounds familiar," Pedersen said. "But that doesn't mean I recollect it." He was playing dumb but he'd perfected the art.

"That check wouldn't have anything to do with Adam's arrest, would it?"

Pedersen started fiddling with the engine of his International. He couldn't keep still.

"Did you know Lew wrote the judge a note on Adam's behalf?"

"Is that right? Maybe he was a better man than I thought."

"What do you mean by that?"

Pedersen pulled a rag from the pocket of his overalls and rubbed his face. "All these questions."

"I'll stop asking when you start answering."

Pedersen methodically folded the sweat rag into a pocket-sized square with his gnarled but nimble fingers, then slipped it back into his overalls and focused his attention on Harlan. "Lew asked for a campaign donation around the time of Adam's court date. He didn't say anything about the donation getting Adam off the hook but I knew it couldn't hurt. When the check bounced, Lew was some kind of angry, so I offered to butcher him a couple cows instead. Damned if he didn't pick my two best heifers. I butchered one that day but he asked me to fatten the other one up, came over a couple weeks ago, told me it was time to bolt the poor girl. Adam wasn't locked up, so I figured I owed him what was due and paid." Pedersen pulled a flathead from the back pocket of his overalls and continued to tinker with his tractor. "Look, I'm sorry Lew's dead, but what kind of asshole takes advantage of a down-on-his-luck farmer?"

"Sounds like you had an ax to grind."

"Naw. It worked out in the end. Adam, he's doing better. Wants to write poems or something. I might be out two cows but I don't need much to get by."

"You own any guns, Lingg?"

"Yep."

"How about a 30-06 or a .308?"

"Probably."

"You mind if I take a look at them?"

Pedersen put the flathead down. "You got a warrant?"

"Nope."

"Then I suppose I mind. On principle. But you don't need to worry about me, Sheriff. I didn't want to hurt Lew. Hell, the fact you told me he wrote that letter for Adam makes me feel like this was all worth it."

"It's a crime. What you did."

"You wouldn't have done the same?"

Harlan shrugged. "If I called you into court, would you tell the truth about the bribe?"

"Campaign donation," Pedersen corrected and reached above him to finger some still green tobacco. "Besides, what are you gonna do? Dig Lew up and put him on trial?"

"No. I don't know. But maybe not all the people Lew wrangled campaign donations from were so forgiving." Harlan put out his hand and gripped Pedersen's calloused paw. "I'll be back with that warrant," he said.

Mary Jane rubbed the goose bumps along her pale arms warm. Mark had cocooned himself in the sheets and slept as if he were a rock, so she settled for big spoon and dealt with the cold, and when she couldn't fall back asleep, she tickled the bottom of Mark's feet with hers. He squirmed and fidgeted and eventually sat up, his dime-sized nipples erect from the cold. "You need to turn on the heat," she said and ran her fingers through his tousled hair. "It's not like we'll be here when the bill comes."

Mark glanced at the alarm clock. "Shit," he said. "We need to get moving." He jumped out of bed, tucked a button-down into khakis, and told Mary Jane to wear her new dress.

She'd never seen how Mark's business worked up close, but he gave her a crash course as they got ready. It was all about acting, he said. They'd have new names—Stephen and Ashley—and new personalities. They were two college kids out doing a good deed.

The first house they visited was a two-story brick with plantation windows. Elm trees lined the street and neglected flower beds led to the front door. Mark carried a couple of flowers he'd stolen from the bouquet he'd bought Mary Jane. Black tape covered the doorbell, so he used the knocker, which was shaped like the head of a Labrador. When the door opened, a woman with a bathrobe draped loosely over her wrinkled body stared out. Gray hair twisted atop her head. Behind her the house was shrouded in dark.

"Good morning, Ms. Morrow," Mark said, exaggerating the southern lilt to his voice.

"Oh my, Stephen. I forgot you were coming," the woman said. "And you have a friend?"

"This is my girlfriend, Ashley." Mary Jane gave a polite half wave and a wide smile. "We brought you some flowers." He checked the time on his watch as he handed them over.

The stately brick of the house gave way to a run-down interior. The woman led them through a shade-drawn living room flooded by the rank odor of cats to a kitchen of peeling wallpaper and chipped tile. A tabby rubbed against Mary Jane but hissed as she bent to pet it. Three plastic tubs filled with kitty litter and shit sat before the stove. The cats had kicked large piles of litter to the floor, though the barefooted Ms. Morrow didn't seem to notice or care. "I'll be a minute getting dressed," she said.

Mark stopped her. "You know, Ms. Morrow, I have class today. Do you mind if we chat another time?" He winked at Mary Jane as a sadness stretched across the woman's face. How terrible to be so old and alone.

"I understand," she said. "Young people keep very busy." She tightened the bathrobe around her sandbag breasts. "The prescription is on the counter."

Mark picked up the bottle and took three twenties from his wallet. A dollar a pill he'd explained to Mary Jane. "I hope this helps," he said. Ms. Morrow nodded and assured him that it would, it would. Then Mark pocketed the pills, took Mary Jane's arm, and guided them out as quickly as they'd come in. Mary Jane glanced back at the woman—stranded in the kitchen—the cats swarming her like sharks.

Outside, Mark explained that Ms. Morrow had been selling her belongings to pay for a degenerate son's legal fees. When Mary Jane told him she found the woman and her cats depressing, he said, "We need the Oxy, don't we?" Mary Jane couldn't help feeling he'd missed the point.

Their second stop was in a black neighborhood on the other side of town. Every third house looked empty and run-down but none were empty. Mark called the pickup a twofer since both husband and wife had prescriptions. The third stop was an old Victorian, not unlike her parents' house in Marathon. An older, half-deaf man lived there. He wore a big, bushy beard, carried a cane, and kept calling Mark "dahling" in a long southern drawl. At each pickup, Mark presented himself as an eager student doing a public service. If anyone asked, he had a lie prepared about giving the drugs to cancer patients without insurance, but no one ever asked. They just needed the money.

Mary Jane asked if he ever worried about getting caught, and Mark explained that dealing drugs wasn't like in the movies. He didn't stand on street corners and run from cops. "The reality isn't very exciting," he said. "I'm a middleman. I collect pills in bulk and sell to dealers. It's hard to bust someone like me. I barely pop up on the cops' radar. I make sure my suppliers have other pain meds and tell them about doctors that are sympathetic to pain. The dealers need me because the suppliers wouldn't trust them. It's symbiotic."

"What's that mean?" Mary Jane asked.

"Mutually beneficial. See, a lot of these old people don't have enough money to pay for basic shit like food and electricity. Apparently, Social Security doesn't cut it. Selling their Oxy is good income because Medicare covers the cost of the drug, but they need me to get their pills into the hands of the dealers. I'm a pharmacy student, so I seem legit."

Mary Jane nodded as if it all made sense. Drug dealing was nothing like she'd expected. Driving around dressed in their finest, she felt more like a yuppie than a criminal.

As Mark headed out of the city, Mary Jane opened one of the new prescriptions and held a blue forty between her thumb and forefinger. "You know," she said, "my tongue hurts pretty bad."

"Didn't I give you some already?"

"I used them for the pain from my tattoo. And I tipped one for good service."

"You shouldn't sell to strangers."

"I didn't sell it. I tipped it."

Mark rolled his eyes, but he wasn't mad. Not really. He put out his hand. "Give me one, too," he said. "But don't crush it. We need to be functionally high."

They each swallowed a pill, and while Mark focused on passing a hay truck, Mary Jane pocketed a couple extra for later. "That *stranger* invited us to a party," she said. "If we're still in town, we should go. It could be a last hurrah. Goodbye, Kentucky. See you never."

"Sure," Mark said. "Whatever you want." He drove them north along the road that led to Marathon, which made Mary Jane anxious, and she told him as much.

"We're just going to Paris," he said.

"My mom begs my dad to take her to Paris," she replied. "You'd think he wouldn't mind since it's only an hour away." It was an old joke but Mark laughed anyway.

The sun beat into the dash, beat into Mary Jane's skin. Oxy always seemed to suit her mood and today it offered a mellow, mature high. Her bones radiated a steady pulse, as if plucked like strings from a bass. Her insides turned watery and slushed through her undammed.

Driving the state highways reminded Mary Jane of those end-of-summer days when she and Mark would go to an abandoned farm and practice shooting watermelons nestled in the branches of trees. The plan to get rid of Lew had still seemed like a game then; it was as if they were living in a movie. Mary Jane would teach Mark to measure his breath and keep his hand loose, but he proved a terrible student. He possessed a restless energy ill-suited to aiming a weapon and each miss seemed to sap his confidence. A couple of weeks into their lessons, Mary Jane peppered the targets to demonstrate, and Mark admitted he was hopeless, which only made her love him more. When Mary Jane could prove to Mark there were things he didn't know, things he couldn't do, he turned soft like putty, and she liked when he was putty. "You're amazing," he said after she sent three straight bullets into the target. "I wish you were there to pull the trigger." And that was all it took. It wasn't much. Mary Jane said maybe she should. She saw the logic in it but that wasn't the real reason she said yes. She said yes because she yearned for a moment like this, a time and place where she could take center stage and do something grand. Most people wanted the same. They were just too afraid to admit it, to follow through.

In the weeks that followed, Mark crafted plans and burned the evidence as Mary Jane bull's-eyed targets. Afterward, they'd fuck in the backseat of his Mustang. Life had never been better. If ever Mary Jane had a moment of pause, if ever she thought about how in movies criminals get caught, she convinced herself that they would be the exception, that together they were unstoppable. And if that didn't soothe her, there was always an Oxy nearby.

Now they were on the road again. Working together. Partners. Mark stopped at a pharmacy in Paris and grabbed a cane from the backseat. "I should do this one alone," he said and pulled a prescription from the glove box. Mary Jane watched as he faked a limp into the pharmacy. Across the street, people went in and out of the Get-on-Down Deli, and Mary Jane stepped out to buy lunch.

By the time she returned, Mark had the engine running. The cane sat passenger-side and she moved it to sit down. *"Bonjour,"* she said. "I got us some sandwiches. I wanted wine since we're in Paris, but the clerk asked for an ID." Mark dug into the grocery bag and shoved a ham and cheese into his mouth. Mary Jane looked up at the soft blue sky, the bare sun. The piercing made it difficult to eat, so she picked at her sandwich like a bird. Her new diet. Mark finished his in a few minutes and started the car again. "Back to work," he said. Mary Jane had barely touched her lunch and ended up tossing it out the window for the animals to eat.

They drove to towns all around Lexington—Winchester, Richmond, Versailles. Mark perfected his limp as the day lingered. He pretended he was new to town, pretended he was a traveler passing through. He'd been in a wreck. Been hurt on the job. Each time, he came back with another prescription.

Mary Jane wanted to help, so Mark taught her how to hustle a pharmacist. If the pharmacist seemed skeptical, she was to insist on getting her medication—always use the word *medication*—and cause a scene. The pharmacist would fill the prescription just to get her out the door. In the end, Mary Jane didn't need antics. The pharmacists barely looked at her. A couple of times, she found a way to mention bone cancer or a tragic accident to make the game more interesting, but the pharmacists barely reacted. They were numb like cows.

And by the time the sun set and the small-town pharmacies closed, Mary Jane and Mark had more than two dozen prescriptions— orange plastic bottles rattling with opportunity.

————

Harlan didn't consider Lingg Pedersen a serious suspect. Pedersen's bounced check was a pittance compared to the amounts coming in and out of Lew's bank account. What Harlan really wanted to know was why the Silver Spoon extended Lew such a large line of credit, but his messages to Little Joe O'Malley had gone unanswered. The Pedersen check opened one other avenue, so Harlan walked across the street to chat with Wesley Craycraft.

He found his path to the courthouse blocked by a crowd of people, and at the top of the stone steps stood Lewis Mattock in a suit. Beside him were his wife and two daughters, each holding a sign that read, CHECK MATTOCK ON YOUR BALLOT. Lewis stepped up to a podium and unfolded a sheet of paper. "I know some of you will find it surprising that I'm standing here days after laying my father to rest," he said, scanning the crowd before looking back to the paper. "But these are dark times and they call for action. Behind me this great courthouse represents justice." Another pause and a gesture toward the building. "And the people of Finley County deserve to feel like justice will be carried out. They deserve to feel safe. For almost two decades you gave my father the honor of protecting this community. I'm standing here asking for that same honor. That is why, after consulting with my wife, our daughters, and our families, I'm announcing my intention to run for sheriff of Finley County." Lewis nodded once, stepped back from the microphone, and hugged his wife. Applause went up from the crowd.

Harlan stood there gawping like a fish. "Looks like you got competition," the man next to him said. Harlan couldn't manage a response. He shouldn't have been surprised. When was the last time a Mattock hadn't been sheriff? And people would vote for Lewis. Some would vote for him because his daddy had died and some because he'd installed their security systems and others because they'd spent so long voting Mattock it was second nature.

Harlan slipped away quick and made for the back door of the

courthouse, climbed the stairs to the judge's chambers, and stepped into Wesley Craycraft's office only to find himself in the company of Lewis Mattock's father-in-law. "Harlan," the judge crowed. "Come on in." A bottle of Basil Hayden's sat on the desk between the men. Craycraft motioned to it. "Have a drink." Craycraft pointed Harlan toward a second chair next to Trip Gaines, who was holding a glass of water.

"I'm on duty," Harlan said.

"Oh, come on," the judge whined. "That never would have stopped Lew. Besides, Trip here is a teetotaler and I don't want to drink alone. It makes me feel self-conscious."

"All right," Harlan said. "Pour me a taste."

"Did you happen to catch Lewis's speech?" Gaines asked.

Craycraft poured a double and handed it over. "I did." Harlan sat up straight so that he could look down on the doctor. "It was short and to the point."

"I hope you don't take it personally."

Harlan didn't like the smug look on Gaines's face, but he tried not to let it show. "It's just politics."

"That's right," Gaines said. "It's just politics."

"And of course I'm neutral," Craycraft chimed in. "Let the people decide. Democracy and all that." He raised a glass. "To the union," he said.

Gaines lifted his glass of water. "I'd hoped to toast to my son-in-law but the union will have to do."

"And justice," Harlan added.

"And justice," Craycraft cried, as if he'd been dipping into the bottle all day.

Gaines downed his water and set the glass on the desk. "Gentlemen, I have patients to see. Wesley, it was a pleasure." He shook hands with the judge, then put his hand out for Harlan. "Sheriff, I wish you luck. May the best man win."

Harlan waited for the door to shut and turned to Craycraft. "What was that about?"

"That's my business, Harlan." Wesley pulled back the metal ball of a desk ornament and let it go. The ball was at one end of five, and when it crashed against its neighbors, the ball on the other end swung up. "But if you must know, Trip asked me to support Lewis in the election." The clinking ornament sounded out like a metronome, the two spheres flying up and down, up and down. "Like I said, I'm neutral. I won't be supporting either of you publicly. Of course, I'd rather Lewis had come to ask me himself."

"Well, I'm not here to ask for your endorsement," Harlan said.

"Oh, thank God."

"I'm following up with witnesses from the barbeque."

"Official business, then." Craycraft reached out a hand and stilled the desk ornament. "You know," he said, "ever since it happened, I've been wracking my brain to come up with someone who'd want to hurt Lew."

"And?"

"I don't enforce the law for a reason. I couldn't think of a single person. Everyone liked Lew. He was always good for a laugh." Harlan nodded. The Lew Mattock he knew could make people laugh but only at someone else's expense. "My guess is that some criminal he locked up came back for revenge."

"So I've been told."

"It's the only plausible explanation."

"I guess I'm not sure Lew wasn't mixed up in things he shouldn't have been." Harlan leaned forward and set the silver balls back in motion. "Maybe Lew put his hand in the wrong man's pocket or asked the wrong person for a favor."

Craycraft wrinkled his brow and poured himself another drink, swirled the remaining cubes in his glass. "I heard you had that idiot judge over in Mason County sign a subpoena for Lew's bank records. I'd have been more than happy to do that for you, Harlan."

"I'll remember that."

"It's just a matter of trust."

Craycraft put his feet on the desk, though his legs barely reached. Harlan never realized he was so short. In fact, he'd never considered Craycraft much at all. He just was. The judge. The man who'd let Doyle Chapman out of jail. Harlan wanted desperately to confront Craycraft about it but he bit his tongue. "I need a warrant to search Lingg Pedersen's premises for guns," he said.

"The farmer?"

"That's the one."

"What do you have on him?"

"He bribed Lew but the check bounced, so Lew settled for a couple prime heifers."

"Bribed him why?"

"To get his son off in court."

Craycraft removed his feet from the desk and leaned closer. "That little pissant pothead?"

Harlan nodded.

"Why would Lingg bribe Lew? That doesn't make sense. It's my court."

"Good question. Here's what I know: Lew wrote a letter to you on behalf of Adam, Lingg paid him for the favor, and a couple weeks later Adam's charged was reduced."

"Hold on," Craycraft said. "Lew wrote me hundreds of letters about defendants, and I humored his desire to be part of the process, but I never decided a case based on what Lew Mattock or anyone else wanted. So if you want to come into my office and question my integrity, at least have the decency not to drink my fucking bourbon."

"Why'd you reduce the charge on the Pedersen kid?"

"If I remember correctly, he was caught with some pot. It was his third offense—maybe he had a couple DUIs—so he was going to do hard time if I didn't reduce the charge. Now how would that help a kid like him? Being locked up with rapists and murderers? I gave him another shot and haven't seen him since, so maybe it worked." Wesley shook his head. "Now do you still want a warrant to search the Pedersen place?"

Harlan nodded. "I do."

"Okay. But let me be clear. If Lew was earning on the side, I wasn't part of it."

"And if I wanted to look at your bank records?"

"I'd sign the subpoena myself." Craycraft came out from behind the desk and took Harlan's elbow in his stubby fingers. "Now, let me show you out." He led Harlan to the door. "And don't go asking that mulligan-lover Smoot for any more favors. At least let me do my job."

When Lewis showed up at his mother's to share the news of his candidacy, he was surprised to discover the Plymouth sitting in the driveway like a snapshot from the past. As far as he knew, the station wagon hadn't been driven in years, but now, moving between the wayback and the yard with an armload of plants, was a man in a flannel shirt and mesh cap. A fifties doo-wop song drifted from the windows, but his mother was nowhere to be seen.

Lewis had spent half his childhood riding passenger-side in the Plymouth. His short legs always struggled to touch the floor and he'd slipped the seat belt's upper strap behind him so it didn't rub against his neck, but he remembered those days fondly nonetheless. His own daughters rode in car seats in the back, and Lewis often wished they could sit in the front with him and watch the world pass by. It made him sad to think that Ginny and Stella were forever staring into headrests.

His mother had loved driving. She'd let her hair loose and sing along to a worn-out tape of the Everly Brothers, drumming the beat on the steering wheel while serenading the straightaways. *Love is strange, yeah–eeh–yeah.* Even after his father leased a new car for his mother, she wouldn't let go of the station wagon. Keeping the Plymouth in the garage was the one thing she put her foot down about.

Above the crooning of the speakers, Lewis heard his mother call from the porch. "What's going on?" he asked, stepping out.

"We're planting a garden."

"You're planting a garden *today?*"

"I always wanted to . . . I just never—I put it off too long."

"It's almost November," he said. "None of this is even going to bloom."

"Don't be shortsighted, Lewis. It'll bloom next year. The man at Home Depot said a garden is a lifelong project."

"Sounds like he was trying to make a sale."

Mabel shrugged. "You sure look nice." He was still wearing his suit from the campaign announcement. Sophie's father had called in favors and a sizable crowd showed up. The editor of the newspaper even took photos and interviewed him.

The man helping his mother finished unloading the wagon and came over to them. His face was pockmarked and he had a gold cap on one tooth. "Mrs. Mabel," he said softly.

"Oh, it's just Mabel, Bonito." She turned to Lewis. "Lewis, this is Bonito. That means 'handsome' in Spanish." She gestured to Bonito. "Bonito, this is Lewis. *Mi hijo.*"

Bonito gave Lewis an awkward wave hello.

"Give us a moment," Mabel said to Lewis and led Bonito to an assortment of plants. "I think we should put *las rosas* here." She made a circle with her arms in front of the leggy shrubs that bordered the front steps. *"Uno, dos, tres,"* she said, stomping her foot three times before walking to the other side of the steps and repeating herself. *"Uno, dos, tres."* Bonito nodded. *"Nada* grass," she said.

"*Sí.* No grass," Bonito replied and picked up a worn spade from a pile of tools.

Some of the tools still had their price tags attached, and when Lewis pointed out that Bonito wasn't using the new shovel, his mother said, "Oh, I didn't buy those. Your father claimed he was going to plant a vegetable garden one year." She glanced over. "Besides, I'm sure Bonito knows best."

Lewis was oddly unsettled by his mother's newfound love of gardening; it didn't seem rational. Maybe it had to do with the fact that she might have to sell the house; maybe by planting new flowers she thought she was deepening her hold on the place. Lewis searched for some logic she'd understand. "I think it's . . . I mean, isn't it strange to plant a new garden so soon after Dad's funeral?"

"Is it?"

"I think so. Yes."

"I guess I don't know all the rules about planting a garden. And I certainly don't know all the rules about dead husbands."

"I'm worried about you, Mom."

"Hold on," Mabel said. "I forgot the compost."

She walked back to Bonito and waved for him to stop. *"Muy bueno,"* she said, toeing the freshly turned earth. He smiled. "Remember the good dirt." She pointed to a couple of bags and gave a thumbs-up. Bonito mirrored the gesture.

"Bonito doesn't speak much English," she explained to Lewis. "And I don't really speak Spanish. Just little bits like 'hello' or 'good.'"

"Wouldn't you rather relax and read a book?" Lewis asked. "Isn't this a lot of work?"

"This is my house now and I don't want to relax," Mabel said. "I want to do some gardening." Her voice started to rise like one of his daughters before they threw a fit. "I've been bored a long time, Lewis. I drove that Plymouth today and—"

"That's another thing, are you sure—"

"And I put the windows down and I listened to the stereo and I felt young again. It drives like a dream."

"Is it safe?"

"Listen to that stereo." Mabel took Lewis's hands and did a couple of shuffle steps while Bonito poured compost onto the dirt. "Let's go look at the soil," she said. "The man at Home Depot said roses like clay soil." Each turn of Bonito's spade brought up a mix of red and brown. With the black compost, it looked to Lewis like a finger painting Ginny might make for him to hang on the fridge.

"Perfecto," Mabel said, taking a handful and letting it slip through her fingers. Then she whispered to Lewis, "Let's make Bonito lemonade."

"I didn't ask you how you met Bonito," Lewis said as they walked inside.

"At the Home Depot in Flemingsburg. This teenager was loading my plants like an ogre, so Bonito came over to help. I managed to tell him I needed an assistant. I think I mimed digging and he nodded, so here we are. He didn't ask about pay, but I'll be generous. I've never been an employer." She plunked a cylinder of concentrate into a pitcher and handed Lewis a slotted spoon. "So what brings you here all dressed up?" she asked. "Besides putting a wrinkle in my garden plans?"

"I'm running for sheriff," Lewis said. It came out matter-of-fact, like it was no news at all.

"Is that right?"

"I talked it over with Sophie. She thinks it's a good idea. John Tyler can run the security business without me." Lewis tried to think of other reasons. "I think it's time for a change, and it would be good to give back to the community." He paused. "What do you think?"

"If you think that's for the best."

"Do you think I'd be good at it?"

"I think you'd make a better sheriff than your father."

"What do you mean by that?"

"I mean what I said. You'd make a better sheriff." She hesitated. "But you'll have to run against Harlan Dupee."

"I'm not worried about that. You know Dad didn't think highly of him."

"I wouldn't judge a man before you walk in his shoes. Harlan was actually over here yesterday; he wanted to know if I'd noticed anything strange before your father died. I told him about our meeting with Jim. I got the sense he thought it was useful."

"Maybe for the election," Lewis said. "He can use Dad's gambling against me."

Mabel took Lewis's stirring hand in hers. "That lemonade looks ready," she said. Lewis looked down. Some of the juice had sloshed onto the counter. "I don't think Harlan's built that way. Besides, he's not your enemy. He's trying to find the person who shot your dad. Don't forget that part." She grabbed the pitcher and a glass and walked outside.

Lewis held the spoon as if it were a tool that still had use and looked out the small window above the sink. It was the only window in the kitchen and on the wrong side of the house for sun. Opposite it a plain table with three chairs was pushed up against the wall. The table had only ever needed room for three. On Sundays, they'd eat dinner as a family. The talk was that of fathers and sons. Responsibility. Backbone. Right and wrong. His father told stories about the men he arrested, and when his mother tried to defend them, when she said circumstances could drive a man to steal, his father would down his drink and laugh. Lew Mattock had many laughs. Laughs for his own jokes. Laughs to warn someone they were close to crossing a line. Laughs to mock. Lewis's mother usually received this last kind. Afterward his father would turn to Lewis and say, "Women." Lewis learned to laugh, too. He liked being in on the joke. At some point near the end of dinner his father might promise a ride in the squad car or a round of golf, but those promises were rarely kept; they yellowed like the paint on the kitchen wall. Lewis slammed the spoon in the sink and the clang echoed as if he were nowhere.

He walked outside where Bonito stood drinking lemonade while his mother, thin and stoop-shouldered, dug futilely into the ground. The roses had been planted and a number of tall grasses were set beside them. It looked nice. Lewis examined a small, leafless cherry tree with a half-off sticker pasted onto the container.

"Find a place for that," his mother said.

"I wouldn't even know—"

"Anywhere is fine, Lewis. Really."

He hefted the container onto his shoulder. The tree looked like some misshapen antler grown from his body and soil spilled down his suit jacket. When he put the tree down, his mother walked over. "This looks perfect," she said. "What do you think, Bonito?"

"*Perfecto.*" Bonito handed Lewis a shovel, the one his father had bought but never used, and Lewis pressed it into the earth with his black, shiny shoes—the same ones he'd worn to his dad's funeral not a week before.

After his conversation with Craycraft, Harlan decided to knock off early and clear his head. He hopped into his truck, but as he pumped the gas, the Ford sputtered and hiccupped, and when he shifted into reverse, it went dead. He banged the steering wheel and the horn sounded harmlessly.

Under the hood, Harlan found coolant running down the engine block and realized the head gasket was about to blow. He managed to get home by feathering the clutch and laying off the brake on the downhills. By the time he rolled into his driveway leaking coolant, he'd concocted a story in which his truck problems were the work of some saboteur. The smug grins of Wesley Craycraft and Trip Gaines flashed into his head. He imagined them under the hood banging away with wrenches. The thought of it was almost enough to make him laugh until he realized they wouldn't be the sort to do their own dirty work; they were the sort to pay off some country boy with a case of beer and an envelope of bills. Division of labor and all that crap.

Harlan couldn't just lie down and let Lewis win the election. He needed to fight the grinning assholes at their own game, so he trampled through the pines and cedars toward the Spanish Manor carrying a stack of yard signs. People like the ones who lived in the neighboring trailer park were his best chance to drum up votes; the town's well-to-do would all support Lewis. The problem was, to the residents of the Spanish Manor, Harlan was just an asshole with a badge, and even if he could convince them otherwise, apathy was the most common emotion come election day.

He came into view of the trailers and waded through a swath of uncut grass littered with junk. A rusted-through wheelbarrow. A bent spigot. A pile of broken windows. Somebody from New York would have taken a photo and called it art. Then they'd have taken photos of the sunken faces that eyed Harlan warily and claim those faces were some deep comment on the world.

A couple of kids raced ahead of him calling, "Po-po. Po-po." Harlan pulled the signs tight into his armpit. The gravel roads were filled with driven-over dandelions that refused to die. At the edges dog shit moldered. The dogs themselves scampered between the trailers in packs like wolves, sniffing at trash and one another. Harlan thought he saw a woman smile in his direction and started walking toward her. "Johnny," she called out. Harlan heard the voice of a man bark in response. "What?" The woman wore a Kentucky-blue sweat suit and her stringy blond hair went every which way.

THE MORE THEY DISAPPEAR

She cocked her head. Harlan turned back to the road and she called out again. "Nothing."

A coal-colored cat heavy with pregnancy stretched itself on the gravel and yowled. "I wouldn't walk up on Maude Boone like that," a voice said from behind him. Harlan turned. A powerfully built man in denim and dusty motorcycle boots came up and loosed a heavy, amber spit at Harlan's feet.

"What's that you said?"

"The cat. Somebody wanted to name her Daniel but she puts 'em out like the world's about to end, so some other fucker came up with the name Maude."

"Rebecca," Harlan said.

"What?"

"Daniel Boone. His wife's name was Rebecca."

"Who fucking cares?" The man pointed to the signs under Harlan's arm. "My daughter put one of them in my yard."

"Is that right?"

"Yep. She must've got a handful 'cause I put a knife through it and damned if she didn't put another one next to it."

"I guess that means you won't be voting for me." Harlan put out his hand to shake. "Harlan Dupee." The man let Harlan's hand hang there until he pulled it back. "I'm guessing you're Mattie's father."

"That's right. Henry Dawson."

"She's a good girl. Mattie."

Dawson kicked the ground and pulled out a back-pocket flask. "Don't lie. She's rude and ungrateful." He twisted the top and had a taste.

"I've seen worse."

"She adores you all of a sudden. Comes around talkin' Harlan this. Harlan that. Makes a father wonder, you know?" Dawson took a step closer and his boozy breath beat on Harlan like a drunken moth. "Why don't you go on home?" he said. "Don't nobody want what you're selling." He was tall, an inch taller than Harlan and broader by more. When he knocked the signs from Harlan's grip, Harlan balled his fist, and Dawson said softly, "Don't do it."

They stood like prizefighters sizing each other up before the bell. Dawson stomped one of his black boots on the signs and ground them like a cigarette butt. "I'll see that my neighbors get these, Sheriff."

"I appreciate that, Henry."

Dawson took another pull from his flask. "You should get going," he said. "That badge won't do you no good over here." From behind him, Harlan watched Mattie step out of a slanted trailer holding a brindled mutt. The front yard was littered with spent shotgun shells—bright greens and yellows and reds. Joe-Pye weed grew between them and a vine wrapped itself around the front end of an engineless Chevelle. The split campaign signs stood on lone wobbly legs like ostriches. Mattie kept shock still, but the dog let out a pitiful whine. Dawson didn't flinch.

Harlan rolled a cigarette. Took his time. Then he turned away. He walked between two trailers among the pokeweed and trash, passed a pile of eggshells and coffee grounds dropped from a kitchen window. He fought the urge to look back at the girl, kept on walking until he reached the river where he found a landing of smooth limestone and breathed deep. He felt weak and cursed himself as he clambered over the rocks upriver toward the docks of what was once the paper mill.

Under the bridge to Ohio, some ambitious tagger had spray-painted a water-lapped pylon with a gigantic phallus and some indecipherable scrawl. A signature for all the world to remember. A truck rumbled across the bridge and a cluster of small stones pitched themselves over the edge and rustled the water. A fish jumped and splashed down before Harlan could sight it. The sun had started to fall—its rays poking over the horizon like in a religious painting, like that moment right before God arrives in all his blinding glory.

Most people would say a river is something made over time, that porous, thirsty rocks slaked themselves on the rains that poured into the valley, and that the more they drank, the more they disappeared, and that before long rock gave way to water and what became Kentucky separated from what became Ohio. Others would say that some god created that river and set it there for purposes only he could divine. But Harlan, he had this image in his head of some giant, crippled god, the heel of his lame foot dragging along as he pulled himself across the earth and carved out waterways. Such a god would be easy to hunt, his path marked by that useless leg—limp like an almost dead thing. Harlan tossed a stone. Then he unzipped his pants and added to the river's level.

e i g h t

Harlan's pickup grunted like a pig, coughed once, and then went dead for good, so he trudged to the shed and dug out a bent tenspeed tarnished with rust, and when he couldn't find an air pump, he stuffed his uniform in a plastic bag wrapped over the handlebars and rode flat tires to the mom-and-pop gas station down the road. The machine only took quarters and a droopy-eyed attendant made him buy something in order to break his five, claimed it was the only way to open the till. Harlan snatched a bag of pills meant to make men last longer, paid, and left them on the counter for the attendant's use. As he chunked quarters into the machine, he couldn't help wishing he lived in a time when the world didn't charge a man for air.

He guided himself gingerly along the shoulderless roads, his long legs pistoning up and down as he gasped shallow breaths. Most drivers gave him room but a couple of punks in a Dodge 1500 buzzed by and called him some less-than-polite names for homosexual. Harlan braked and managed to keep the bike upright on a slope of dirt and rock, but he couldn't make out the plates as the truck sped away. He felt the fates turning against him. Slashed signs that bore his name, a busted truck, getting run off the road: any one of these by itself might have seemed innocent enough, something born of chance, but put together they made Harlan feel as if he had a target on his back and all the world was taking aim.

When he finally steered into the office, out of breath and huffing, Holly said, "I don't want to know."

"I don't want to say," Harlan replied before retreating to his office. Lew's case file was open on his desk. He'd learned more about his former boss than he'd ever wanted to, but it hadn't helped him solve a thing. He checked his backlog of messages. There were a number from Stuart Simon at the *Registrar* prattling on about God knows and asking for comment but nothing from Joe O'Malley at the Silver Spoon. Harlan was tired of waiting around. He grabbed the keys to the cruiser, stepped into the lobby, and said, "I'm going to find O'Malley and make him talk."

Holly looked up from her paperwork as a toilet flushed. A couple of seconds later, Frank came out of the bathroom holding a copy of the *Registrar*. "What do you need with that punch-drunk horse's ass?"

Harlan came up with a lie quick. "Noise complaints," he said.

Frank tapped the newspaper. "Sounds to me like Joe's got bigger fish to fry. Says here the state is pulling some environmental protection bullshit and making the Spoon find a new home."

"What are they protecting?" Holly asked.

"Mussels." Frank laughed. "Apparently the docks are upriver from a breeding ground for"—he looked at the paper—"endangered bivalves." He handed the finger-dampened paper to Harlan. "There's an article about you in here, too."

Harlan scanned for his name and found an op-ed by Stuart Simon endorsing Lewis Mattock. Simon didn't have many kind words for him, so Harlan folded the paper and calmly handed it back to Frank. "Did y'all get anything good in Cynthiana?"

"That Mexican was a bad motherfucker. Teardrop tattoo. All scarred along his forearms. He spat on Del when we questioned him and this is after the boys in Cynthiana had worked him over."

"And?"

"He had an alibi."

"That you could check?"

"Turns out he was in lockup the day Lew was shot. The guys in Cynthiana let him go because their pen was full and the paperwork for an undocumented is hell."

"I guess that was a bad decision."

Frank shrugged.

"It was a good lead, though, Frankie," Harlan said. "Keep working. If you find the man who killed Lew, you might just become sheriff yourself."

Holly laughed and Frank turned to her, offended. "What?"

"Cold day in hell," she said.

Frank waved a fat, dismissive paw at her and lumbered out to his cruiser. After he left, Holly told Harlan that Little Joe had called that morning and said he'd be happy to meet with Harlan on the boat.

"That would have been nice to know before I blabbed in front of Frank."

Holly slammed her palm down and stapled a stack of papers. "Did you ever stop to think that you and the deputies should be working together?"

"I don't need them doubting me."

"I wouldn't be too tough on them, Harlan. You might not have noticed but they're working their tails off—checking gun sales, rustling up the suspects you're too busy to bother with. Even Frank."

"And you think I should be doing the same?"

"I'm just telling you they're working hard."

Harlan promised he'd do a better job letting everyone know they were appreciated just as soon as he had the oppurtunity.

From the road, the Silver Spoon materialized like a relic left over from the century before, but once you reached the parking lot, the illusion faded. The steamship was a recent construction—fiberglass and galvanized iron manufactured in some factory overseas.

Harlan crossed the dock and climbed aboard. A lone girl was tying off black plastic bags she pulled from metal trash cans bolted to the deck. The ship's railings were eight feet tall to keep people from tossing their empties into the river, or to keep desperate gamblers from ending it all. High above Harlan the red-and-white wheelhouse preened.

He ducked into the stateroom where gaming tables sat around a horseshoe-shaped bar. A handful of employees were setting up for the night. A croupier spun her wheel distractedly and waited for the ball to drop. A dealer flipped hands to an imaginary table. Harlan asked the bartender where he might find Mr. O'Malley and was pointed to a door marked RESTRICTED.

He climbed a circular staircase to the wheelhouse and found Little Joe in the captain's seat wearing a pressed suit and bolo tie. "Sheriff," Joe drawled, pivoting in the swivel chair and putting out his hand. "I saw you come aboard." O'Malley had cauliflower ears and a cloudy eye from years taking jabs to the head. Back in his day he'd been a tough son of a bitch, and eventually he'd earned himself a couple of paychecks as a punching bag for young contenders. After he retired from the ring, Little Joe bought himself some pristine dental work—a full smile of big white chompers—and took the job with the Silver Spoon.

Harlan studied the boat's control panel. It seemed unnecessarily complicated given a leather-wrapped wheel steered the damn thing. "Nice setup you got here," he said.

"It's decent," Joe replied, flashing those pearly horse teeth. "So tell me what can I do for you."

"I'm out here to get information about one of your—what do you call them—guests?" Harlan pushed against the steering wheel until it turned. "Suckers?"

"We call them patrons."

"I'm here to ask about one of your patrons."

Little Joe leaned forward, returned the steering wheel to its previous position. "Go on."

"I heard Lew spent time out here and I'd like to know more."

"Why would I talk about that?"

"I figure it isn't bad business to help me since I'm in charge now."

"I don't necessarily agree," Little Joe said. "You're in charge short-term, but I hear long-term may be a different story."

Harlan took a deep breath. "Even if I lose the election, I'm sheriff until the end of the year. We've already asked the state police for extra manpower. Maybe I can have one hang out by the docks and give sobriety tests."

"We're a legal business."

"That doesn't mean your patrons wouldn't notice us, drink a little less, make fewer bad decisions."

"You might have me there." Little Joe slapped his knee. "I stopped drinking when I left the ring and never once regretted it." He stood up. "Why don't you come down to my office and we'll talk proper."

O'Malley walked Harlan back through the stateroom, making banter with the employees as he went, led him belowdecks to a keypad-locked room filled with screens for the security cameras and an expensive vault. "This is the operations center," Joe said. "Aka my second home. At night we have two armed guards protecting me. Or, well, protecting this." He slapped the vault.

"Impressive."

"So Lew. What do you want to know?"

"Let's start with the basics. How often was he here? How much did he lose? Who did he come with? Those sorts of things."

Little Joe titled his head back and forth like he was amping himself up for a fight and launched into the story. "Lew was a good patron, which means he lost. A lot. And often. It didn't start out

that way. I remember his first night he cleaned up at the craps
table. Sometimes that's the best thing that can happen. Lew won
five grand and he was hooked. He kept buying drinks and flirting
with the waitresses, giving them hundred-dollar tips and pats on
the ass. More than a thousand of his winnings went right back into
our pockets. That must've been two, three years ago. He started
coming out every week or two but he didn't like people seeing him
here, so we invited him to our high-stakes poker games, where most
of the patrons are from out of town. Anyway, when Lew ran out of
cash, he'd ask me to extend credit. Usually he was good for it, but
he started taking on more than he could handle. He was the worst
kind of poker player. He had a short attention span and he bet with
a chip on his shoulder, like the game was personal."

"How much did he lose?"

"By the end? Tens of thousands. And pretty consistent."

"And you kept extending him credit?"

"That wasn't my decision. The bosses in Huntington told me to
keep letting Lew borrow. Maybe they were keeping the peace.
Toward the end things soured. Lew started telling me if I didn't
forgive his debt he'd shut us down and make my life a 'living hell'—
his words, not mine. I told him he didn't have the balls to mess
with me and that I wasn't scared of some small-town sheriff. Same
as I told you. But maybe I wasn't so polite with Lew."

"He didn't respond well to politeness?"

"I've dealt with tougher men." Little Joe cast a cloudy eye toward
Harlan.

"How was Lew coming up with the cash?"

"I don't know and I don't care. I'll tell you this, though. I got
tired of dealing with him. One night he got drunk and threw a
punch at me. Can you imagine? My days of throwing punches are
over, so I threatened to tell the newspaper about his gambling and
complained to the bosses. I was tired of the bullshit. Next day out

comes the father of that pretty girl Lew's son married carrying an envelope of cash. Motherfucker tells me he'd like it if I could keep his friend from losing so much. Like he doesn't understand what business I'm in."

"This is Trip Gaines?"

"Yeah. The doctor. Real cool customer. I wouldn't trust him to take my pulse."

"How much are we talking?"

"Fifteen G's at least."

"In cash?"

"Banded fucking bills."

"Did Lew mention anything about it?"

"Nope. Next week it was more of the same. I comped Lew a few vodka tonics to loosen him up and watched as he frittered away the coin." Little Joe cracked his knuckles like he was back in his prime, all pumped-up bravado.

Harlan could understand helping a friend in need, but Trip Gaines's benevolence went above and beyond. "You ever feel guilty about taking people's money?" he asked.

"Not my problem."

"Mabel Mattock might lose her house."

"If that's true, I feel for her. Truly, I do. But I didn't put her house on the line. Lew should have come to me for advice. I put my money in a portfolio and let some business school fucker handle it, live off the dividends. Everyone out here on the river trying to get rich quick should wise up and do the same."

Harlan stood up and shook O'Malley's hand, said he could show himself off the boat.

As he walked down the ramp, Harlan caught sight of divers downriver and made his way over to watch them pull mussels from the bottom. "So what's the story?" he asked a woman in a wet suit.

She handed him a three-inch pumpkin-colored mussel with

wart-like spots and a swirl of white at its base. "That's an orange-footed pimpleback," she said. "They're being killed off by zebra mussels and that albatross." She nodded in the direction of the Silver Spoon.

"I read today the boat might have to find a new home."

The woman held out a bucket of brown water that smelled like rot. Harlan placed the mussel back with its kin. "Depends on how hard the casino fights in court," she said, shaking the bucket and admiring her treasures. "A lot of damage can happen in the time it takes for a judge to make up his mind."

Harlan looked west, past the woman. The river wended through a series of bluffs where persistent scrub trees anchored into the rock face and managed to survive against all hope or expectation. It was almost enough to believe the mussels would survive as well, that no matter how hard man tried to fuck it up, the river would endure.

The sheriff's department looked no different to Lewis than it had when his father took over in the eighties. Even Holly, sitting behind the front desk, seemed unchanged. As a kid, she'd taught him to play solitaire, and, later, Texas Hold'em.

"Surprise," he said.

"I'll say. You come down here to visit an old woman?"

"Actually, I was hoping to catch the sheriff." On the wall newspaper clippings of his father hung in frames. "You look exhausted," he said.

"You sure do know how to charm a woman."

"I meant—"

"I know what you meant," she said. "I've looked in a mirror. I don't know whether to blame Harlan or all the knuckleheads running around breaking the law."

"Dad's murder to boot."

"That's a big part of it." She paused. "We're going to miss him."

"How's the investigation going?"

"I don't know. You should talk to Harlan so long as you two stay civil." She pointed him toward the sheriff's office. It still had his dad's name stenciled on the glass.

He rapped his knuckles on the doorframe. "You got a moment, Sheriff?"

Harlan was drawing on a cigarette by the window, his ball cap tilted down low as if he were napping. "What's on your mind, Lewis?"

Lewis shut the door behind him. "I heard you spoke with my mom."

"Guilty as charged."

"Shouldn't you be looking for the man who killed my dad?"

"What do you think I was doing?"

"I don't see how making her dredge up bad memories helps you."

"Are you worried about how I'm handling your dad's murder or are you worried about your campaign?"

Lewis felt the blood rise to his face but Harlan just set there sucking on his cigarette like it was his only care in the world. "Go bother the criminals, Harlan. Leave my family alone." Lewis turned to go but stopped short at the door. "Dad always thought you were an idiot," he said. "He was afraid if he promoted someone worth a damn, they'd campaign against him. Guess the joke's on him, huh?"

Harlan stabbed his cigarette into a soda can. "Your dad wasn't a saint. I suspect you know that better than most."

"Go fuck yourself."

Harlan lifted his hat. "What do you know about your father-in-law?"

This caught Lewis off-guard. "Trip?"

"Were he and your dad close?"

"Why?"

"Your dad lost a lot of money gambling. We both know that. But your father-in-law paid a big chunk of his debt. Now why would he do that?"

Lewis didn't follow. His father and Sophie's were never more than cordial. If anything, they'd seemed annoyed by one another.

"Tell you what," Harlan said, rolling another cigarette. "If you find out the answer, come talk to me. In the meantime, don't worry about me using your dad's gambling as campaign fuel or whatever. I'm not the sort of man to speak ill of the dead or make empty speeches." Lewis started to defend himself, but Harlan wasn't interested. He pointed to the door and said, "Close that on your way out." Lewis, flummoxed, did as he was told and staggered out the door, trying to decide where he should go next.

Harlan followed Lewis away from the sheriff's department. He figured there were only a few destinations Lewis might be headed, and when Lewis passed the turn that went up to Trip Gaines's place, Harlan guessed he was on his way to the Silver Spoon. He eased the cruiser back and pulled into the boat's parking lot a few minutes after Lewis. The dumb lug was talking to an employee on the deck, getting more and more animated as he talked, his arms flapping up and down like a fat bird that couldn't fly. If Harlan were a betting man, he'd wager his future held a phone call from Little Joe O'Malley asking him to not spout off about their private conversations.

Harlan backed the cruiser away and pointed it toward Trip Gaines's. He was glad Lewis hadn't run straight to his father-in-law. It meant Lewis was just as in the dark about what was going on as Harlan was. Harlan didn't really know Trip Gaines, but he didn't like what little he'd found out. He didn't like finding him in the judge's chambers or outside the bank, and he didn't like the way Gaines talked about the election or trust that he'd paid Lew's debts out of kindness. The doctor was the sort of man on whom even honey wouldn't stick. He lived in one of the ridgetop subdivisions that seemed in perpetual construction. Harlan realized he'd driven by the place the day after Lew's murder. Gaines's house was the nicest in the community—a newly built colonial made to look like an older colonial—but it stunk of fakery. The brick was only decorative and the siding a painted Hardie board. The driveway was newly lined with thin-trunked pin oaks cabled to keep them upright and it would be years—decades even—until the trees gave off the stately effect intended.

Gaines came onto the front porch and crossed his arms like a security guard. Harlan reminded himself to be cordial, apologized for the unexpected visit, even wished Lewis luck in the election. None of it softened the doctor. "What are you doing here?" he asked

"Money," Harlan said. "I'm trying to track a bit of money you gave the Silver Spoon."

"I'm not sure I can help you."

Harlan took out his wallet and looked inside. "I'm trying to imagine fifteen thousand dollars. Is it banded in hundreds?"

"Is that what you want to ask me? What money looks like?"

"That's a lot of cash to carry around."

"I'm not poor."

"Even for a doctor."

Gaines uncrossed his arms. "I paid a portion of Lew Mattock's gambling debts if that's what you're hinting at. And I can show you a loan contract that proves he still owes me that money." He rapped his knuckles against one of the porch's decorative columns, let the hollow sound ring out.

"So you're planning to collect?"

"No. I don't plan on causing Mabel any more trouble. As far as I'm concerned, it's a family matter." Gaines looked down on Harlan from the top step. "In fact, the only reason I can come up with for why you'd be asking is because you want to use it as blackmail in the election. Does that sound about right?"

"For me being sheriff isn't about winning elections."

Gaines laughed. "That's good. Because you haven't won any."

"What I really want to know is what your money was buying."

"Buying?"

"What did you get out of the deal?"

A glint came into Gaines's eyes. "You don't have a family, do you? A wife? Kids?"

Harlan shook his head.

"So you don't know what it means to provide. You don't have responsibilities. You see, I'm a provider, Harlan. I give money to charities. Medical care to the poor. And no one ever thanks me because they don't realize how valuable my time is. You don't seem to realize that either." Gaines cracked his knuckles like some Ivy League brawler. "I take care of my own, Harlan. When someone in my family gets in trouble, I help. Lew was a good man with one vice. Maybe you would punish him for that but not me. I tried to help him put his life back in order, but he never got that chance, and it's your job to find out who took it from him—not terrorize the people who helped. I'm a provider, Harlan. What exactly are you?"

Harlan didn't answer the question, wouldn't even know how, but he liked seeing the doctor get worked up. He decided not to push his luck and raised two fingers to the brim of his cap. "I appreciate your time," he said. "I'll make sure if I have any more questions, they're worth your while." He pivoted to leave, then hesitated. "In the meantime get me a copy of that loan agreement. As long as it's not too much hassle."

"I'll put you in touch with my lawyer."

"Good enough."

Harlan turned to go. Maybe Gaines was telling the truth. Maybe he was helping Lew out of a jam, but Harlan knew a snake when he saw one, and as soon as he backed out of the drive, he knew the doctor would be on the phone with one crony or another talking about the sheriff's surprise visit and what it might mean for his son-in-law's electoral outlook.

Mark put faith in his headlights as he wound through the curves of the Appalachian Mountains. It was a part of the state he tried to avoid, but ever since Chance tracked him down in the library, he'd become a cog in the eastern Kentucky drug trade. He'd trekked out to Chance's spread by the Virginia border only a couple of times and he dreaded the trip. He would get lost and stay lost for long stretches, unable to make sense of the unmarked roads or get his bearings amid the shadows of ragged mountains. And eastern Kentucky wasn't exactly the sort of place strangers went asking for directions, especially not strangers with drugs in the trunk.

Chance acted more roughneck on his own turf. He never gave Mark a tour of his property, which seemed to consist of various outbuildings, two small airplane hangars, and a house made up of four double-wides fused together. Mark once caught a glimpse into one of the hangars; there'd been a virtual army of classic cars and two gutted prop planes surrounded by wires and engine parts. The house itself was a mystery. Chance would come out front, hand over the money—no envelope, no rubberbands—and grab the pills before saying, "Get on outta here" or lobbing an insult Mark's way. It wasn't that much different from his usual trash-talking but there was less humor to it. Mark missed the Chance that came to the UK library, the steady businessman who spoke clean English and didn't delight in the role of hillbilly drug dealer; yet despite the hiccups, Chance never stopped being reliable. He paid in full, bought often, and never quibbled over price.

Now, for the first time, Mark needed a favor from Chance. He

carried fifteen thousand in Oxy—most of it in the trunk, a few
prescriptions hidden in his backpack—and if Chance bought the
lot, he and Mary Jane would have the cash they needed.

He passed through Evarts, the last real town before Highsplint,
crossed Bailey Creek, and inched slowly around the sharp turns
that led into the valley. Chance's hometown wasn't much of anything anymore—an abandoned post office and a few houses with
shuttered windows and slanted porches. No businesses to speak of,
no municipalities, no law.

As he turned onto Chance's property, Mark gripped the wheel
tight and kept his Mustang steady over the bumps in the road.
When he reached a couple bare bulbs strung on a pole thirty yards
out from the house, he slowed long enough for Chance to recognize him, then continued past various tin-roofed lean-tos.

Mark saw that Chance was sitting on a wooden chair in the yard
with a double-barrel sawed-off lying across his lap and his bare feet
stretched out beside a pair of work boots. Chance was grinning
wide, perfectly tickled by the surprise visit. "Boo Boo Bear," he said.
"You came to make a social call. That touches me right inside where
I'm all goopy and soft. I mean, I was ready to shoot your fucking
head off, but I'll buy you a beer instead." He grabbed a Silver Bullet from the cooler at his feet and tossed it to Mark, who cracked
the tab and drank off its sudsy top. "Don't be shy," Chance said,
making a sweeping motion with the gun. "Come over here beside
me." Mark did as he was told, and Chance tossed his empty to the
ground where Mark had been standing, raised the gun, and fired.
The can jumped and Chance let loose the second barrel, catching it
airborne and knocking it into the shadows. Then he put an arm
around Mark and said, "What the fuck are you doing here?"

"I came to sell."

"I didn't call you."

"I *need* to sell."

"That's not how this works. You can want to your heart's content, but you don't get to *need* anything from me." Chance moved his grip to Mark's neck, gave a squeeze.

A heavyset blonde poked her head out and said, "Who you shootin' at?" When she spied Mark, she crowed out, "You didn't tell me we had company." Chance told her to shut up and flung one of his mud boots in her direction, but the door slammed and the boot bounced harmlessly to the ground.

"Get that, would you?" Chance said. Mark heard him stand as he reached down for the boot, but he wasn't expecting the kick to the ribs that sent him rolling over the rocky earth. He shielded his face with the boot and readied himself for more, but Chance was busy hopping around on one foot and cursing. "Damn your bony ass," he said as Mark sat up. "I had to do that. On principle. You've gone too long without realizing what kind of business you're in." Chance reached down and rubbed his foot. "You're lucky I'm in a good mood or else I'd shoot you and take whatever pills you were dumb enough to bring out here. Now tell me what's going on."

"My girlfriend got herself in trouble and I want to help but I need cash."

"That doesn't sound like you. Helping out a damsel in distress."

"It's in my best interest."

"Now that sounds more like you," Chance said. "What, did *you* knock her up?"

Mark shrugged. The lie sounded good enough. "Yeah. And I'm not ready to be a dad."

Chance hesitated. "I don't get involved in matters of the heart. Or the pussy."

"Look," Mark said. "You may not care, but I trust you. And I have a stash that I'll sell on the cheap."

Chance cracked open another beer. "What's cheap?"

Mark wasn't in a position to bargain—he needed Chance—

so he dropped the price. "Let's say three hundred for a scrip of forties." It was two hundred less than usual.

Chance whistled. "You must be hard up. How much do you have?"

"Ten thousand would clean me out."

Chance clutched his heart as if having a cardiac event. "Wooboy. That's a lot of pain to cure. Let's see the goods."

"I stashed them down the road."

"Bullshit you did."

Mark shrugged.

"We're past the point I'd rob your dumb ass." Chance cracked the shotgun and emptied the shells onto the ground. "Come on inside. Let's talk more about your troubles."

The trailer they walked into looked like it had been ransacked. There were empty beer cans littering the floor and piles of books stacked like shrines. Books filled with Post-its, books on the stove in the kitchen, books as tables holding beer bottles and books. A blond girl about eight with pale blue eyes and freckles sat cross-legged on the floor playing Nintendo. Toys were scattered around her, as well as a power drill and socket set. "Say hello to our company, June," Chance said. The girl waved without looking away from the screen.

The woman who'd come out earlier was passed out on the couch. Her nightgown had lifted, and Mark could see her underwear and the fat and pubic hair inching out from it. A hash pipe sat on the couch next to her.

"What?" Chance said. "You were expecting Ethan Allen and shit?" He laughed. "This mess is Darlene's and she needs to clean it the fuck up." Chance yelled her name and another woman, the spitting image of the one on the couch, came out with a child clasped to her veiny breast. There were two of them. Twins. "Hello, Harvard," she said and bounced the child, who lifted her breast in his mouth. The other tit sagged like a cow's.

"That's Kenny," Chance said, motioning to the baby. "Kenny G. Like that bullshit saxophonist. Darlene named him. I wanted to name him Second Chance."

"How old is he?" Mark asked.

"Too old to be sucking on his mama's tit." The woman ignored the insult and coolly lit a cigarette with her free hand. "June is Deanna's," Chance said, motioning to the woman on the couch. "She takes after me, thank God." The girl didn't take note of the compliment, but Chance went over and kissed the top of her head anyway. Then he threw a blanket over the woman on the couch, but not before slapping her on the ass. She stirred and muttered for him to stop. "'For God's sake hold your tongue and let me love,'" Chance cried out and turned to Mark. "You know who said that?"

He shook his head. "June?"

The girl didn't reply.

"It was John Donne," Chance said. "But I think he was talking about a dude." He motioned for Mark to follow him and walked through the junk-filled kitchen, turning a corner where it seemed the trailer would end. He'd cut doors and joined the four double-wides together to make a square. The second was a stark contrast to the first, had been outfitted as a kitchen and dining room. The interior windows opened onto a courtyard garden where a few winter cabbages popped their heads out of the ground. Chance kept walking to the third trailer, which faced the back of the property and had to be opened with a series of keys. "I'm the only one allowed in here," he explained. "You can't trust those two bitches as far as you can throw them."

As soon as Mark stepped inside, he forgot he was in a trailer at all. The entire thing had been gutted and just about every square inch was lined with books and maps. Chance pointed to one of the maps above a captain's desk. "That's an original," he said. "My favorite part is where it says 'terra incognita.' That means 'unknown land.' Which doesn't really exist anymore, except maybe on other planets. Anyway, the cartographer drew these rad fucking sea monsters." Everywhere Mark turned, some new oddity showed itself. On a shelf sat three military helmets—one camouflage, another with a swastika, the third some sort of Spartan replica. In one corner hung two birdcages, one with a white bird that cooed softly and the other with a black bird that called out, "Hot dog. Hot dog." Chance ignored the bird and unlocked the captain's desk. "I'm a collector of sorts," he said, "And in my line of work you have a lot of free time, so this is my refuge." He pulled out a stack of hundreds, didn't even bother to count. "Eight is the best I can do and the only reason is 'cause the price is right." He held on to the money as Mark reached for it. "Don't ever come out here uninvited again, okay?"

Mark nodded and Chance released his grip on the money. Mark had hoped for more but he couldn't complain. The weight in his hands was a lifeline. "The Oxy's out in my car," he said.

"I thought so." Chance shook his keys. "Go ahead and get it while I lock up."

Mark noted the place settings as he passed back through the dining room and tried to imagine Chance sitting around the table with his kids and the two women like a proper family. In the front trailer, the taciturn girl was still fixed to her video game, her mother snoring on the couch.

As he stepped outside, Mark breathed deep and let his lungs expand. His plan had worked. A weight lifted and he felt proud as he counted out pills from the trunk of the Mustang. Then he heard the sound of a shotgun shell being chambered and froze. "Boo Boo Bear," Chance said from behind him. "I thought you were smarter than this." Mark wondered where he'd come from. Nobody had opened the front door. Out of his periphery he could see one of the twins holding the sawed-off.

"Can you ask her to lower the gun?" Mark said. His voice trembled as badly as his hands. His stomach unspooled and there was a rattle in his throat, but his mind stayed sharp. He worked through the situation and realized he deserved whatever happened next. If the woman shot him, it was because he'd helped take Lew Mattock's life. And if he was beaten by Chance, he would die in the company he kept. And if it was a joke—a cruel, frightening joke—if the woman put the gun down and Chance let him go, well, he deserved that too—because he was not the creator of this madness; he was just a bit player among other players and to start placing blame or meting out justice wouldn't make it better and wouldn't make it just.

Chance walked gingerly to the car and put Mark between himself and his gun-wielding girlfriend. "Boo," he whispered before grabbing a pill bottle and tossing a graceful hook shot in the woman's direction. Mark heard it rattle along the ground and watched her lower the gun and grab at it like an animal baited by bread crumbs. As she bent over, her finger pulled the trigger and the gun fired into the ground and Mark started pissing down his leg while Chance laughed and laughed. The woman kept screaming at him to stop making fun and help her ass up.

"Go on inside," Chance said after he'd finished hollering. "And leave the gun." Mark closed his eyes and prepared himself for the blow that would knock him out. "You wet your pants," Chance said. "I have a bathroom, you know." Mark couldn't have replied even had he wanted to. He had no breath to speak. Chance grabbed his chin and turned it toward him. "Open your eyes," he said. Mark did. "You shouldn't have come here like this. It's not fair to me. Bring all this shit out here and beg for money. A rich boy like you? How would it look if I played along and helped you?" It wasn't anger but disappointment that colored Chance's eyes. "I guess I should say something like don't hustle a hustler. But you weren't trying to hustle me. Or maybe don't trust a drug dealer but that shit's a given." Chance reached his hand inside Mark's pocket and took back the cash, then peeled off a handful of bills and dropped them in the trunk before taking the pills as well. "Gas money," he said and snorted. He craned his neck to look around. "It could be worse. I know you wouldn't have come out here unless you were scared, but you're still alive. That's a start." Chance sucked the cool night air and exhaled. "There's something else John Donne said that I like. I don't get to say it enough 'cause nobody around here appreciates poetry, but you might." Chance looked to the sky or to God or to the heavens, then closed his eyes and chanted. "'But I do nothing upon myself, and yet I am my own executioner.'" Mark cried in silence.

Lewis swung a loopy left after Joe O'Malley finished chronicling the details of his father's carousing. O'Malley ducked and gave Lewis a sharp punch to the kidney followed by a left hook that knocked him breathless. As he dropped to one knee, Lewis realized the smaller man could have done much worse. O'Malley set to apologizing—for punching him, for his shit father, for his mother's predicament. Then he said, "But it's just business, kid." Lewis tried to respond but he could only gasp.

Once his feet found purchase, Lewis staggered to the Explorer and made his way home. Sophie and the girls were gone. He started rereading his father's will while nursing a fifth of bourbon, and with each sip, the booze ate away at whatever lay inside him. By the time his family came home, most of the bottle was gone— hard at work corroding Lewis's better qualities. Though his drinking had long been on the verge of problematic, Lewis rarely lost his temper. He was a silent, apologetic drunk, but now his eyes were reddened from a stress that seemed primed to break him. He wielded the rolled-up copy of his father's will like a club.

"Go to your room," he snapped at the girls. Ginny and Stella froze—rooted by fear, but instead of backtracking, Lewis embraced the path he'd started down. "Now," he barked. Sophie glanced at the bottle, gave each girl a push in the right direction, and marched valiantly past Lewis to the kitchen.

"There's chicken and fish," she said as she put away the leftovers.

"So you saw your dad tonight?"

"He treated us to dinner. We talked strategy for your campaign, but I don't recall it involving getting drunk."

"Maybe if you'd consulted with me, I could have let you in on the plan."

"Consulting? Is that what we're calling it?" Sophie closed the refrigerator and faced him.

"I don't want your father around," Lewis said. "He's not welcome here."

"What are you talking about?"

Lewis tossed the will onto the counter. "You know that money my dad lost, how yesterday you felt so sorry for my mom, well, your father knew all about it."

"I don't know what you're talking about."

"He's a liar, Sophie. And he controls us with his money. He did it with this house. He did it to my dad. He's doing it with the election. He's playing God or the devil. Who knows?"

"You're drunk, Lewis. You're not making sense."

"He knew my dad was gambling but he didn't tell me or you or anyone else. Then he paid off my father's debts knowing he would just lose more. Why would he do that?"

"It sounds like he was trying to help."

"Right. He's always helping, isn't he? Has all the answers. He pushes the buttons and pulls the strings and we dance like we're fucking puppets."

Sophie shook her head. "Does he push buttons or pull strings, Lewis? I'm a bit confused."

Lewis felt tongue-tied and punched down on the will. The jars atop the kitchen counter shook and Sophie yelped before slipping past him. "Fuck you," he managed to say as she fled. He stalked her to the living room with the will in hand. She took up residence on the other side of the couch, which they circled like wrestlers.

"Don't do this, Lewis," she said. "You're scaring me. You're scaring the girls."

"Maybe I should hand you a couple pills like your daddy, drug you up so you don't feel anything, so that you're not scared. And maybe I should do the same, so we don't realize what a sham our life is." Sophie said nothing. Her eyes darted around the room. Lewis wanted to hurt her, not physically, but he had so much hurt to give. "Maybe if we take enough of them, we'll forget what a terrible mother you are. Maybe we won't think about how selfish you are, how you're just your father's plaything. Maybe I won't pay attention to the way he puts his arm around you like you're your fucking mother reincarnated."

Sophie started to cry. "Stop it, Lewis," she whimpered. "Stop it."

The door to the girls' room opened. Stella was standing there holding Ginny's hand. Sophie said, "It's okay, girls, just go back in your room. Your daddy and I are talking." The door shut softly— the girls afraid of breaking things more than they were already broken.

Lewis winced at what he was doing. "It's bullshit," he said and threw the will at Sophie. She ducked and it thudded against the wall. Pages scattered to the floor.

"Who's the creep, Lewis?" Sophie said, taking her turn. "Who's the bad parent? The lousy husband? Without my father, you'd be nothing. You're right. Our life is a sham. Because you've done nothing to make it better. You relied on my dad. And you relied on your own dad, too. Even fat Lew Mattock was more of a man than you." Sophie's words stung more than she could realize, and still she kept on. "You've never made me happy. I take pills so I don't have to look at the man I married and think about how I only stay because of the daughters *I* brought into this world." Lewis lunged to grab her, not to hurt her, but to stop her, to smother her words, but Sophie slipped his grasp, grabbed a candlestick from the shelves—one of her countless knickknacks—and hurled it at his head. When she missed, she picked up another and tried again. Then she ran to the girls' room and turned the lock.

Lewis slumped to the ground and cried into his hands, which he'd balled into fists. A quiet blanketed the house. In time his fingers relaxed and he picked up one of the candlesticks. It was spotted from lack of use and on the bottom there was a MADE IN TAIWAN sticker. Lewis had never seen the candlesticks before, never noticed them at least, but now, as he looked at the dents in the wall above his head, he knew he'd never be able to forget them.

n i n e

Harlan woke to the sound of scurrying outside his bedroom and mistook it for a creature that had risen with the sun. Then he saw Mattie's face peering through the window screen. "You driving that police car exclusive now?" she asked. "'Cause if you don't want your truck, I'll take it off your hands."

Harlan sat up. His chest was pale and flat as a pine board and his feet poked out from the bedrags like prairie dogs checking for danger. "That truck's the only decent thing I own."

"Then why ain't you drivin' it?" The sunlight pounded through the window around Mattie's head. There must not have been a cloud in the sky. Harlan closed his eyes. "You hungover?" she asked.

"No."

"You look hungover."

"I'm tired." He'd been unable to sleep the night before and tried smoking dope to relax, but it had just set his mind to wandering.

"I'll make coffee," Mattie said and disappeared.

Harlan heard her barge in the front door. "Shouldn't you be in school?" he called out.

"It's the weekend."

"Is it?"

"Yep." A minute later she walked down the hall into his bedroom. "Don't you even have coffee?"

Harlan pulled a pillow over his eyes and fell back into a restless sleep with dreams he couldn't remember other than that they weren't sweet. The noise of Mattie flitting about roused him every now and again but not enough to spur him from bed, and when he finally dragged himself back into the world, it was to a new home. Papers that littered the hallway were piled in neat stacks and the busted gasket, which had made a stain on the kitchen's splintering hardwoods, rested on a dish towel. Half-empty soda cans had been thrown away and the ashtrays were emptied and the dishes sat clean in the drying rack. Mattie had opened all the windows and a brisk wind swept the stale air from the house.

Harlan ran the shower. He was run-down and spread thin—the weight of things since Lew's death taking its toll. He felt good about the investigation, but there was nothing concrete pointing to the murder, and in the back of his mind a voice fretted that he was following the wrong track.

He found Mattie outside, wiping down the porch with a ragged, dun-colored mop. She picked up the fraying pieces of cord that fell from it and stuffed them into a trash bag tied to her belt. Another bag of trash was burning in the drum and sour smoke rose to the sky.

"We need to get you a comb," she said.

Strands of Harlan's wet hair had clumped together like muddy icicles before his face. He pulled them back and snapped on his hat. "That's what these are for." He looked at the house and whistled. "I don't think the place has looked this good since—" He paused, thought of Angeline. "Since a really long time. What do I owe you?"

"Not a dime. I was thinking we could spend the day together and hunt for sang or fish for channel cats or just pick up trash like good citizens."

"I'm pretty busy," he said.

Mattie planted herself before him like an emaciated sentry—skeleton fingers on bony hips. "Is that why you got fucked up last night?"

"I didn't get fucked up. I've been working overtime." He looked in the direction of the Spanish Manor. "Your dad know you're over here?"

"Nope."

"He didn't seem to like you spending time with the sheriff."

"Henry's full of it," she said but there was a hiccup in her voice.

"If he ever tried to hurt you, you'd let me know, right?"

She ground the ball of one foot on the ground like she was squishing a bug, muttered, "Yeah." He wished she'd look him in the eye but understood her hesitation. He hadn't exactly stood up to Henry Dawson when they'd met.

Harlan put out his hand for a formal shake. "I owe you, Matilda. How about a rain check?"

"I don't accept credit," she said. "How about you spend ten minutes looking at that burnt trailer with me instead. That's part of your job, right? Investigating fires?"

"I've been there already," he said. "Why are you so caught up on that fire, anyway?"

"Well, this morning I caught a big, black snake over there and while I was stringing it on a fence, this old man comes out and starts talking to me about how that fire weren't no accident."

"What old man?"

"Henderson Jones. Two last names. He's lived there like forever. People say he's crazy but he ain't. Anyway, he took care of that burnt property, so he should know. I seen him out there mowing. Hell, that trailer looked better than Henry's and mine."

"What did he say caused the fire?"

"He didn't. Maybe you can get it out of him with your policeman ways."

Harlan looked up at the sun. "Ten minutes," he said.

Mattie led him through the woods on a path that came out along one of the trailer park's gravel roads. From a distance Harlan could see her father's place but she took the long way around. When they came upon the remains of the fire, he tried to entertain Mattie's suspicions, but Harlan couldn't tell arson from an accident. The trailer looked the same to him as it had the night it burned. Mattie was right about the lawn, though—the grass was shorn neat. And the site backed up to a rocky, less used road into the trailer park—something Harlan had missed earlier. If you wanted to set a fire and get away, there wasn't a better property in the Spanish Manor.

"Who'd you say took care of this place?"

"Henderson Jones. He lives right there." She pointed to a trailer with mums in containers and a collection of garden gnomes.

Harlan climbed the steps and knocked. An ancient-looking black man came to the door and asked him what the hell he wanted. Harlan apologized and asked him if he might know anything about the fire next door.

"It's about damn time," Jones said and stepped outside with the help of a cane. "That wasn't no damn electrical fire."

It turned out Frank hadn't talked to Jones. The old man said his neighbors had been too busy spinning yarns and giving the deputy a hard time, and the deputy, for his part, wasn't interested in information that didn't make his job easier.

"Why not call the sheriff's department and make a report?" Harlan asked.

"Shit. I don't care *that* much. I just took care of the place so I wouldn't get no devil snakes in my yard. I can't stand no snakes."

Mattie pointed to a four-foot black racer draped over the bent fence that separated the two trailers. "That's the one I got today," she said.

Jones glanced at the snake and shivered. "If no one cleans this place up, it's gonna become a den for snakes and yellow jackets and all sorts of mean-ass shit." He shook his head.

"Why don't you think it was an electrical fire?"

"That's easy. I stripped the wires from the box. The last person who lived there—must've been two, three years now—he wasn't exactly a model citizen and I didn't like living next to a tinder box."

"So what caused the fire?"

"I have a theory but it's not of the practical sort your type would like."

"Try me."

"I think it was a haunt."

"A haunt?"

"A ghost. The night before the fire I had terrors and I couldn't sleep. There was some bad mojo in the air all the next day, so I stayed inside. Then around sunset I seen this shadowy figure glide out of the woods."

"It wasn't a person?"

"Didn't move like one. I tried to get a better look but lost him. And I got good sight. That's why I think it was a haunt."

"I have to ask again, why didn't you call the sheriff's department?"

"Is that your answer for everything?" Jones's voice went high-pitched with incredulity. "Hell, if I'd have called y'all, whatever deputy come out here would say I was a crank. You're probably thinking the same right now."

Mattie laughed but Harlan ignored her. "Maybe we would've looked in that trailer and found the culprit."

"We can speculate all we want but that don't change the reality."

"And you didn't see this . . . this figure leave?"

"Nope, but I heard a thunderous sort of growl come out those woods about ten minutes later. There's some bad shit in there, man. I've lived here twenty years. I know."

Mattie piped up again. "Maybe it was a car."

"I know what a car sounds like, girl."

"Maybe it was like a diesel truck or a muscle car or something. Hell, it could've been Henry. His engine sounds like thunder."

Harlan asked Jones if he could think of anything else, but the old man claimed that's all he knew. Harlan thanked him and promised to send out an arson investigator, though it was too late to do much good. At the very least they'd be able to confirm that the electrical box had been stripped.

"Does that mean you'll clean this mess up?" Jones asked.

"You've got to take that up with the property owner."

Jones snorted and ground his cane against the earth. "Then I don't give a shit what happens. The manager don't take my calls."

"Looks like you got to hire yourself a snake hunter," Mattie said.

"A dollar a snake," Jones said.

"Five."

"Two."

Mattie winked at Harlan and put out her hand for Jones to shake. "It's a deal," she said.

Mark forced himself back to sleep. He could hear Mary Jane watching television in the common room, but whenever she cracked the door, he closed his eyes. Around noon, she shook him awake and asked for cash to buy breakfast. Mark muttered to check his coat pocket and rolled deeper into the blankets, but as soon as the front door closed, he jumped out of bed. He needed to put what had happened at Chance's behind him and started by stuffing his soiled clothes in a garbage bag. Then he cleaned the apartment and took stock. He had the Oxy he'd been smart enough to hide from

Chance, though considering the way things had gone, the smartest play might be to flush the pills and be done with them. Not that that would work. Mary Jane would return and ask when they were leaving. At some point his father would call. None of Mark's problems would magically go away.

When he came clean to Mary Jane, she'd lose it. She might even leave for Canada alone. Mark couldn't blame her. He'd fucked up—plain and simple. Part of him actually hoped she'd leave. The apartment was becoming too small for the both of them. Mark wanted his privacy back. He didn't like hearing her flush the toilet or the way she chatted nonstop about nothing or how she left the television on even when she wasn't watching. He was no longer so confident in their plan. Canada was so far away and they'd be so dependent on each other.

He'd been stupid to drive out to Highsplint, but he'd be smarter now—no sob story, no drama—just business. He'd start by selling Oxy at the party Mary Jane mentioned. Even though dealing near campus was dangerous, it was good money—a couple of drinks and everyone wanted a pill. It would also keep Mary Jane off his back for at least one more day. Afterward he'd make a trip to Marathon and sell whatever Oxy he had left. After that they'd have a decent wad of cash and options.

Mary Jane returned with doughnuts and coffee and proclaimed that the sleepyhead had risen from the dead. She tried to hand Mark a long john but he waved her off. He hated doughnuts and was surprised she didn't know this about him. Mary Jane shrugged, but he could tell her feelings were hurt, which only annoyed him more.

She broke off a piece and chewed. "I tried to stay up, but you came home so late. How'd it go?"

"Fine."

"What do you mean 'fine'?"

Mark knew she wouldn't let the matter drop, so he sandwiched a lie within a truth. "He wasn't in a buying mood, so I'm going to sell tonight at that party."

"I thought you said it was dumb to sell to strangers."

"We need the cash, right?"

"Why don't we sell one of our cars?"

"Mine's leased in my dad's name, but if you have the title for yours, we can sell it."

"I guess technically it's my dad's."

Mark grabbed a coffee and took a sip. It was unsweetened and bitter. "Don't worry," he said. "We'll have a good time tonight. Celebrate. Like you said."

"We're supposed to be celebrating the cash you brought home."

"No. We were going to celebrate leaving Kentucky and we still are. Tomorrow we'll head north, stop by Marathon so I can unload the last of the Oxy, and then keep on driving until we reach the border."

"I don't want to go back there."

"You have to be flexible, MJ." Mark opened the top to his coffee and poured in three sugars.

"I have to be flexible because you can't do anything right."

Mark frowned. He opened a Ziploc of Oxy and held out a pill. "Here," he said. "It'll take off the edge."

"I don't want to take the edge off," she said. "And I don't want a fucking pill right now."

"Suit yourself." Mark dropped the Oxy in his coffee. "If you don't want to go to Marathon, I can go alone."

"That's not the point." Mary Jane finished her doughnut and rubbed her hands on her jeans.

Mark could make out a small oil stain from her fingers. He moved to rub her back and shoulders. "Let's not fight about it. Let's get stoned and watch a movie. Do something to take our minds off it."

Mary Jane shrugged out of his grasp and grabbed her coat. "I need to take a walk," she said. "Clear my head."

The door slammed and Mark said good riddance, but he found himself glancing at the clock on the microwave every few minutes, counting the time since she'd left. Suddenly, he was terrified of being left behind to fend for himself.

Lewis shifted on the couch to stave off the worst muscle strains. A couple of hours after their fight he'd heard Sophie come out of the girls' room and tiptoe to their bedroom. An hour later he tried the doorknob and it turned, the open lock Sophie's tacit invitation for him to apologize. Lewis watched her sleep, could just make out the mask over her eyes. Her lips were pursed and on her bedside table perched a bottle of sleeping pills. Lewis considered joining her but he doubted Sophie would just turn into him at night and reconcile. It wasn't that easy this time.

He started to feel like a Peeping Tom and shut the door, passed by the girls' room and thought better of checking on them. He made a sandwich in the kitchen and prepared for his hangover with Gatorade and aspirin, then returned to the couch where he belonged. He could've slept in the guest bedroom but this wasn't that sort of fight, the sort where you pretend it never happened. He wanted to be on the couch when Sophie woke up, wanted her to see that he'd suffered, too. It was all performance.

In the morning Sophie left with the girls. As she passed by with her rolling suitcase, she called him a bastard. Lewis figured they were headed to her father's house and that Trip would be around sooner or later to talk. It had happened like this once or twice before. The empty house made it clear how wrong he'd been. Ginny and Stella deserved better. Lewis should have confronted Trip, not Sophie. He'd taken the coward's way out.

His campaign for sheriff was over—that much was certain. A few phone calls from Trip and his support would vanish. He still had the name, but Trip had the influence. Lewis would find himself back at Riverside Security, his days spent talking trash with John Tyler, his nights spent longing for something more. He picked up the scattered pages of his father's will and threw them in the trash, then took a beer to the front steps and read the newspaper. There was something wonderful about a beer first thing in the morning. If it was going to shit, let it go to shit. Speed it up. He drained one and went back for another, started to feel more human as hangover faded to buzz. Around noon he drove to the gas station for another six-pack.

"Going fishing?" the attendant asked.

"Nope," Lewis responded. "Just getting drunk."

"Well, have a day of it, man," the attendant said and laughed.

When Lewis returned to the house, Trip's Mercedes was blocking the drive. Lewis gave his father-in-law's patented two-honk hello and stepped out holding a beer like a peace offering. Trip shook his head. He hadn't taken a sip in years. "It's a bit early for me," he said.

Lewis twisted the top off and turned the bottle up.

"Sophie came by."

Lewis nodded.

"I didn't think I'd find you here getting drunk. I hoped maybe you'd be trying to fix things."

"Like how you fixed things for my dad?"

Trip was standing in the dappled light of a maple tree, his face obscured by shadow. "If you mean the money I gave him to pay his debts, then yes, how I fixed things. Or if you mean the money I gave him to pay his electricity bill, then yes, I'm guilty there, too." Trip kicked at the fallen leaves of the maple. "But I'm not here to talk about your dad. I'm here to talk about you."

"I don't care what you have to say."

"You need to get your head out of your ass, son, and grow the fuck up. I'm not going to stand by and watch you mess up my daughter's life just because you found out your daddy wasn't father of the year. Besides, how much better could you have done?" Lewis wanted to answer the question but he couldn't. Trip seized his shoulders as if this were the moment their argument would turn into a heart-to-heart. Lewis barely recognized him. "I'm giving you the chance to be better," Trip said. "I'm giving you the chance to right your father's wrongs."

"You act like I should be grateful."

"I would be."

Lewis pushed Trip's hands away. "I'm not."

"The only thing keeping me from collecting what I'm owed is the fact we're family. For better or worse. So you're going to keep campaigning and win the election because it's good for the family. And you'll do as I say because that's good for the family, too."

"And what then? We pretend like none of this happened? We forget about how my father left my mother with nothing? How you helped him lose it all?"

"How do you want people in this town to remember your dad? Do you want your mother to pick up the paper and read every sordid detail? Because there's more." Trip ran a hand through his parted hair and it dropped right back into place. "And if that happens, you'll never become sheriff. And I can't have Sophie married to a loser."

"Sophie can make her own decisions."

"That's where you're wrong, Lewis. You've always been wrong about that." Trip knocked the beer from his hand and it clanged to the ground. "You're weak. That was your father's problem. When life got tough, he picked up a bottle. When things weren't good at home, he left. When he lost money gambling, he asked me to cover him." Trip scowled at the memory of it, picked up the beer and threw it against a tree, but the bottle bounced away harmlessly and came to rest under a bed of leaves. "Your father was weak but you don't have to follow in his footsteps."

"Fuck you," Lewis said and threw a haymaker that crashed against Trip's skull and sent him crumpling to the ground. Trip started spitting blood from his mouth, but as Lewis looked down, he felt nothing. He picked up the remains of his six-pack and drove away. The house no longer seemed his to call home.

Other than Holly, Harlan could trust two people to keep his investigation under wraps, which is why he found himself parked in front of Lyda and Jackson Finley's red brick Victorian once more. So long as he kept the affair quiet, he could ask them as many questions as he wanted. He'd learned this was how things worked in Marathon—no honest answers without a favor in return.

Lyda came to the door wearing cotton pajamas even though it was the middle of the day, her hair frizzy and undone. "Mr. Dupee, you've caught me unaware," she said, her voice brittle from sleep. "Are you returning the rifles?"

"I'm not," Harlan said. "But the crime lab has cleared them."

"That's good. I thought it was silly when you confiscated them in the first place."

"Do you mind if I come in?"

"Just forget how dreadful I look." She led him to the kitchen and sat at a table littered with old newspapers. "Jackson never throws anything away," she explained, stacking the papers to make room.

On an envelope beside the newspapers was the dashed-off note from her daughter. Harlan saw why its carelessness had irked Lyda in the first place. He tapped the envelope. "How's she doing, by the way?"

"Mary Jane? Haven't heard a word."

"Are you worried?"

"Worrying hasn't gotten me far with my daughter, so I've decided to let her be. Technically she's an adult, even if she doesn't act like one." Lyda balled the envelope in her fist as if it were trash and dropped it back on the table.

Harlan changed the subject. "I wanted to ask you about Wesley Craycraft and Trip Gaines."

"What about them?"

"Did Lew ever talk about them?"

"He was friendly with Wes, but it's like I said before, we didn't talk much about our lives."

"And Trip?"

"I don't think Trip was Lew's favorite, though to be fair, Lew didn't care for any of his family beyond his granddaughters. He said Mabel was a bore, Lewis was spineless, and Lewis's wife, Sophie, was a pain in the ass. That almost made me laugh, Lew talking as if he were parent of the year." Lyda looked down at the newspapers and sighed. On top she'd placed the edition from the day of Lew's funeral. A steely-eyed portrait of Lew as a young man stared back at them. Harlan couldn't help thinking she'd stacked them that way on purpose.

"Jackson told me you and Lew had a relationship in the past, maybe even before that photo of Lew looking thin was taken. How come you lied?"

"I don't recall the details of our conversation. I was still in shock from the funeral."

"Had the affair been going on all that time? Twenty years?"

Lyda flipped the paper over. "I really cared for him. That's what Jackson will never understand. I loved Lew. He was married with a kid when we met but I wasn't. Jackson and I were dating, the way kids do. I wanted Lew to leave Mabel but then I . . . well, it wasn't going to happen. Let's just say that. I married Jackson instead. I guess it would be accurate to say Lew and I have been on and off ever since. More off than on, though."

"Sounds complicated."

"Sad might be a better description."

"What made Lew stay with Mabel?"

"I think he loved her in his way. And there was Lewis, too."

"And what made you marry Jackson?"

She hesitated. "He asked."

Harlan figured Lyda had reaped what she'd sowed, but he couldn't help feeling a little sad watching her try and hold it together. "Back to Trip," he said. "He was paying off Lew's gambling debts. If they didn't get along, why would he do that?"

Lyda shrugged. "That's news to me but not exactly a surprise. I imagine a lot of people loaned Lew money. I can't tell you how much he 'borrowed' from me over the years. I once sold an antique lamp gathering dust in our basement to help him out."

"So you knew about his gambling?"

"What are you going to do? I tried to help." She rubbed her eyes, slipped an elastic band from her wrist, and tied her hair into a ponytail. "I guess I failed."

Harlan preferred the disheveled Lyda Finley sitting across from him to the actress he'd met the day of Lew's funeral. He believed her when she said she loved Lew but the rest was hazy at best. "Failure," he said and stood up. "At least we have that in common."

She tried on a smile. "So you talked to Jackson?"

"Did he mention it?"

"No. But he's been colder than usual."

"I had to," Harlan said. "You understand that, right? It's my job."

She nodded. "If you're interested in Trip, you should talk to

Jackson again. Trip was bothering him a while back. I don't know the details but Jackson complained about it once or twice."

"Point me in the right direction?"

"His office. Just climb the stairs to the top floor."

Harlan found Jackson listening to opera and staring out a small square window that looked onto the street when he walked in. "I thought I saw an official-looking car down there," Jackson said.

"Sorry to intrude. But I had a couple more questions."

"Do we really need to keep digging up these memories, Sheriff?"

"This isn't about that. Its about Trip Gaines."

Jackson laughed. "What do you want with that asshole?"

"I heard he'd been in contact with you. Why?"

"He wants me to sell him a piece of property." Jackson took a gold pen from his pocket and started clicking it with his thumb.

"What property?"

"I am the proud owner of a trailer park. The Spanish Manor."

"No shit," Harlan said. "I live next door."

"My father inherited that tract and all the acreage east to Mason County. After the mill burned down, he planned on building a house out there, but he never got around to it. Or he ran out of money. It was his idea to become a slumlord. I have a property manager who collects rents and handles the tenants."

"There was a fire out there the night Lew died."

"I know. If it's not one thing, it's another. I try not to get involved."

"It doesn't sound like you care for the place. Why not sell?"

"The land. It's the nicest track of riverfront property in northern Kentucky. You've been there."

"It's pretty, all right."

"The Spanish Manor is just the tip. All those woods that stretch east. They're pristine."

"What's Trip want with them?"

Jackson made his way to his desk and had a seat. "Says he wants to build a house. Retire and start farming."

"Become a gentleman rustic?"

"Something like that."

"Where would he get that kind of money?"

Jackson dropped the pen and let it make a mark on a pad of paper. "Exactly," he said. "No way he has that kind of cash without other investors, right? I don't trust it. Besides, the price of that land just went up."

"Why's that?"

"Mussels."

"I don't follow."

"You read the paper?"

"I do."

"Well, the docks for the paper mill are still in good shape. My father rebuilt them before the rest burned, so I figure that might be attractive to a certain gambling ship that needs a new home." Jackson put one finger in the air just as an Italian woman cried a mournful vowel over rising timpanis. "Beautiful," he said.

"Do you think Trip knew about the Silver Spoon's environmental troubles when he asked you to sell?"

"I don't know, but it doesn't matter, does it? The land is mine."

Mary Jane kept two steps ahead of Mark as they walked to the party. When he tried to catch up, she quickened the pace, and he played it off as if he didn't care. She couldn't believe he hadn't apologized, hadn't at least tried to make amends. As they got dressed for the party, he kept talking about how everything was going to work out but she was tired of false promises. The worst part was that Mark wanted to go back to Marathon and hadn't even considered how that might make her feel. When she tried to explain, he brushed off her concerns and said they needed the cash and it wasn't debatable. Mary Jane wished he'd take a leap of faith and leave that moment, but Mark wanted precise instructions, as if there were a set of prerequisites to running away. It was a difference between them that made her doubt whether life in Canada would be all she'd dreamt.

She followed the rumble of drum and bass to the front yard of a falling-apart triplex. The crowd was a mix of punk rockers, hippie girls in flowing skirts, and trust-fund kids sporting blazers. All held red plastic cups. A couple of jocks patrolled the grass, tossing a football in the scant streetlight. The revelry was welcome medicine for the numbed silence that had developed between her and Mark. She turned back to him and said, "I'm going to find Vince."

"Go ahead," he replied, fingering the bottle of pills he'd stashed in his pocket.

On the porch a pair of kegs floated in garbage pails of icy water and someone handed her a beer. Inside strobe lights flashed and shadows danced and pressed against one another. Hips clasped, legs wreathed. A dreadlocked boy walked in and Mary Jane thought maybe it was Vince, but this boy was shorter and wore khaki shorts and a collared shirt. A thin blonde hung on his arm, and as he walked by, he handed Mary Jane half a blunt and said, "Finish that for me, love." The girl laughed as they walked into an empty room and shut the door.

The pulse of a lazy drumbeat looped and Mary Jane leaned against the wall to feel it. Then a mousy girl with a long face and a crown of plastic flowers came out of the haze to share the spliff. She handed Mary Jane a pill that flashed butterfly in the strobe and popped one herself. "It's E," she whispered. Mary Jane swallowed the pill with the last of her beer and an airy sensation took over. When the blunt burned down to fingertip passes, the girl tossed it to the ground and stamped it with bare feet. Then she took Mary Jane's hands into her own and asked her to spin. And so they spun.

Lights pulsed and Mary Jane's body pulled back into nothingness, but the girl's hands kept her in the present, and through those hands Mary Jane felt the beat of her heart. Their spin slowed into an embrace and they fell cross-legged to the floor. Stars wandered the room, revealing flashes of the girl's face. There was laughter. The girl leaned forward, her bloodshot eyes briefly seen before she fell against Mary Jane's chest. "You're soft," she murmured. She seemed less girl than creature.

Above them, looming, crooked teeth glowed into a grin. Vince. "Join us." The girl's voice rose from Mary Jane's chest, its breathiness touching the soft skin of her throat. "Join." Vince's deep voice reverberated down as the drone of fuzzy guitars glided over a backbeat. His arms lifted them up. Two girls at once! The creature's crown fell and rolled like a coin, settling on a spot in the center of the floor where it was danced upon. Around them bodies lay prone on couches and slouched against walls. Mary Jane's feet followed Vince's to a bedroom decorated with lava lamps and posters of fleshy women and metal bands. Vince strummed an unplugged electric guitar and pulled a handle of vodka from the dark.

More faces appeared and the vodka circled. Mary Jane pulled out a bag of pills and handed it to Vince—the master of ceremonies. Madcap came into the room and checked her tattoo. "Remember to put lotion on it," he said.

The circle wanted to see and tendered their sincerest compliments. The room was aglow. Someone lit a pipe and the sweet smell of pot rose into the air as a glass tray with lines of Oxy passed clockwise. They broke bread. Everything was beautiful and rhythmic. Toke pass breathe smell smile snort pass breathe.

When the world fell into order, such wonderful things seemed possible.

Mary Jane felt herself float above the room, her eyes looking down like a traffic reporter in the sky. People laughed at a joke. Hers! And glancing backs of hands found thighs and laughter brought forth heaving bellies and chests and led to innocent kisses. Then someone broke the circle and others followed, but Mary Jane stayed—a blank look in her eyes.

Vince's touch brought her back. He traced the inside of her leg and Mary Jane held his hand there. The girl creature curled into them and her lips, disconnected things, found Vince and then Mary Jane. Lips upon arms and necks and lips upon lips. The lava lamp kicked onto its side—its dark glob suspended—and clothes separated from bodies and were tossed like bones to the fire. Offerings. Clunky, painful knockings. An elbow against the floor, the palm of a hand against her breast. All of it mixed with the ecstasy of skin touching skin, of not knowing where each body began or ended. Vince led them, guided Mary Jane down. She unbuttoned his pants, took him in her dry, sour mouth. Her swollen tongue throbbed a dull, comforting pain. The girl pulled off Mary Jane's jeans and underwear and reached under her own dress. There were too many sensations—the soft flesh of Vince, the tongue playing against her clit. Pleasure rising into one. Vince came in her mouth and Mary Jane leaned back, eyes lolling in her head like a blind man's while the girl brought her to climax. The door cracked open and Mary Jane turned to look. A familiar face in its sliver of light. "Mark," she whimpered as she came, her body shuddering as the door shut again.

"What's that?" Vince said, kissing her on the neck. The creature rose and took them in her arms. "Sshhh," she said. "Sshhh." The other two turned into sleeping lambs, but Mary Jane couldn't sleep. She didn't belong anymore. She fumbled in the scant light for her clothes. Her skin felt sticky. Vince mumbled, but the creature stroked his chest and soothed him to sleep. Mary Jane tottered away on shaky legs.

The partygoers in the living room danced a boozy ballet. She fell into a girl and laughed a sick laugh, fell into a boy whose push spurred her to another. A bumper-car room. She tumbled her way to the front door and steadied herself in its frame. Mark stood by himself in the yard, the street lamp revealing a bottle of booze in his hand. Mark in mourning. Over her! She staggered to him.

"I'm sorry," she said. The words came to her without thinking, not really her words. She wasn't sorry. She put a finger through his belt loop. "You know I love you."

"Fuck you," Mark snarled.

Mary Jane pushed herself into him. Mark's words couldn't hurt her. Words were meaningless. Fuck words. Fuck those. She risked a hand toward his crotch. You can have me too, it said. He pulled away, but she clutched him. He was such a flimsy boy.

"Don't," he said, but she didn't listen and his body responded.

"Do it!" someone shouted from behind them.

Mark's feet tripped backward as they moved around the side of the house and found space between two bare shrubs. Mary Jane pushed him to the ground and undid his belt. Her hands were dulled from the drugs and her body told her to stop, but she knew what needed to be done. Mark, spurred on by his erection, took over. Neither of them spoke. He pulled at her underwear with shaky hands, not wanting to continue, not wanting to stop. *How much can you hurt me?* they asked each other. *How much can I hurt myself?*

Mark pushed inside her and she closed her eyes. Her jeans hung useless from one leg as the trees hovered above. A rock burrowed into the small of her back but Mark didn't notice or care. With her head back, Mary Jane's tongue threatened to choke her, and the skin of her tattoo rubbed against the ground, a burning sensation each time Mark pressed down.

She opened her eyes as he worked, an amateur trying to make himself come hard and fast. His arms shook from the effort, but in his eyes there was nothing, a vacant stare, and he started to go limp.

"Quit looking," he said.

Mary Jane knew they couldn't recover from this. Mark softened but stubbornly continued to push, limp-dick fucking her, not willing to give in. Mary Jane started to laugh, not at him, but at the situation. She'd trusted a boy who didn't even know how to use his cock. She'd thought that he was the one to love her, the one to take her away and give her all the unnamed things she wanted, but he didn't even know his own body. At least she knew hers, had come to terms with it. It was imperfect, ugly even, but she could work it in ways Mark would never be able to work his.

His hand, open, slapped her and came back, knuckles across her cheek. Mary Jane laughed again as he buckled his pants. Mark strained for something to say, but she'd convinced him. Words didn't matter.

As he walked away, Mary Jane pulled her jeans up and let the cool air take the sting from her face. It was over. She'd leave Mark behind like she'd left her parents. She'd search for new places, new people. She'd haunt all their dreams.

She heard the sounds of the party being busted—loud voices, running feet, squealing tires—but she didn't move. The cops found her and two burly arms lifted. Mary Jane made a sound like vomiting, though nothing came out save a pearly white spit that stretched from her slack mouth. "Excuse me," she said. Her stomach reeled. They asked her what happened but she didn't want to remember. Sex? Sure. Rape? No. Drugs? Of course. Names? She didn't know. She was innocent. Innocent.

The cops sat her in the grass until the ambulance arrived, and

when the EMTs loaded her onto a gurney, she lisped, "Hi boys,"
but neither cracked a smile. She heard the word *intercourse,* which
made her smile. Such a silly word for fucking. The windows of
Vince's house were dark as they rolled her to the ambulance, and
she wondered if he'd looked for her. "Relax," one of the EMTs said as
he stuck her with a needle. Then the driver pressed the gas and the
liquid started to course through her veins—hot and sweet.

t e n

The doctor pumped Mary Jane's stomach and brought out the night's wreckage as a nurse injected her with knockout, and when she came to, she was greeted by her mother's creased face and thin lips. Mary Jane turned her head away and focused on the IV bag dripping clear liquid down a tube inserted into her forearm. On the other side of a pale-blue curtain the neighboring patient snored.

"You're okay, baby girl," Lyda said. "I'm here now." Mary Jane hoped she was dreaming, that she'd wake up in Mark's apartment and everything would be as it was before, but Lyda touched her hair and broke the illusion. "I'm here," she said again.

"Where's Dad?" Mary Jane muttered.

"He's at home."

"He wasn't worried?"

Lyda sighed. "That's not fair," she said. "He's worried but it's been a strange night. And you know your father. He's a little disappointed."

"That sounds about right."

"Shouldn't he be disappointed? The doctors said you could have died. And for what?" Her mother's words started to turn sour. "Do you know what it's like to be woken up in the middle of the night?

To be told your only child is in the hospital?" She shook her head. "What were you thinking? You weren't thinking, were you?"

Mary Jane yawned and closed her eyes, managed to ignore her mother's questions.

A nurse came by later and informed her that she'd been discharged but that a couple of police officers needed to talk with her first.

Lyda jumped up from her chair and said, "All she did was have too much to drink."

The nurse unfolded a wheelchair. "I have to usher you out when they're done. It's hospital policy."

Lyda intercepted the cops in the hallway. Mary Jane tried to listen but their voices were muted by the heavy door. On the other side of the curtain, her neighbor turned and moaned. Mary Jane didn't know what the police wanted but it didn't matter. There was nowhere left for her to run.

Lyda came back in the room. "They said you had sex last night. That you may have been raped?"

"I wasn't—"

"Why didn't you say something?"

"I don't have to tell you about my sex life."

"Mary Jane, this is serious. If anyone tried to force themselves on you—"

"They didn't."

Lyda placed a hand on her shoulder. "It's okay to talk about it. There's no reason to be ashamed."

"I wasn't raped!" Mary Jane screamed. "And I'm allowed to sleep with whoever I want. Just like you."

"What do you mean by that?"

One of the cops opened the door. "Ma'am," he said. "We need to talk with her alone. If you could step out into the hallway."

"But I'm her mother."

Mary Jane muttered the word "whore," though she couldn't be sure Lyda heard.

"I understand," the cop said. "But it's better if you wait in the hall."

Lyda patted Mary Jane's hand. "Just be honest with them," she said.

The cops wore cropped haircuts and crisp blue uniforms and strutted like boys she'd known in high school. Cocksure, the both of them, though the one who'd spoken to her mother had a paunch for a belly and puffy, tired eyes. "Mary Jane Finley?" he said, reading her name off a notepad. His partner rested one hand on his baton. He looked like he spent more time in the gym than fighting crime. Mary Jane tried not to shake beneath the covers. "Do you mind if I call you Mary Jane?" She shrugged. "We want to ask you a couple questions. I hope your mother explained that we're here to help."

Mary Jane didn't believe a word he said.

The second cop started in. "You had drugs in your system. You may not have known what you were taking, but it would help if you told us where you got them."

Mary Jane sat up, brought her knees close to her chest. "I don't really know."

The first cop checked his notepad. "It says here you were at a party. How'd you end up there?"

"I walked."

"Come on now."

"I mean it. I was walking and followed the noise."

"So you were alone?"

She nodded. Mark had been two steps behind but it was truer to say she was alone.

"Is that a yes?"

"Yes. I was alone."

"Had you taken any drugs before you went to the party?"

She shook her head. "No."

"So you got them there?"

"Yeah. It was really dark, though. Someone handed me a couple pills and I swallowed them. I guess that was a dumb thing to do."

The cop wrote in his notepad. "The person who handed you the pills. Do you remember them?"

"No."

"Male or female?"

Mary Jane remembered the mousy girl with the crown of flowers, her soft lips and downy skin. "A girl," she said.

The cops shared a look. "Did you know her?"

"I don't even live here. I don't know anyone."

"So you just walked into the party uninvited?"

"Sure. Why not?"

The meathead cop jumped back in. "This girl. Did you get a look at her?"

"Like I said, it was pretty dark."

"Anything you can tell us would help."

"I think she had long hair. And a soft voice. I remember that."

"What was she wearing?"

"I don't know. A dress?"

"You don't remember anything else."

"We only met for a moment."

"Strange."

"Yeah," Mary Jane said. "Strange."

Mary Jane's confidence grew with each lie she fed them. They weren't here about Lew. They didn't know her. To them she was just another dumb girl who'd OD'd. She caught sight of her mother's face in the door's sliver of glass and threw her a smile.

"Just a couple more questions," the pudgy cop said.

She nodded.

"Do you want a glass of water?"

"No thanks."

"Okay then." He smiled at her. He was trying his best. "You told the officers last night that you had sex. Is that true?"

"Yes."

"This is tough to ask, Mary Jane, but was the sex consensual?"

She hesitated.

"What I mean is, did someone force you—"

"No."

"There's no reason to be afraid."

"I'm not."

"A lot of times victims—"

"I'm not a victim."

"Okay."

"I wanted to have sex with him."

"With who?"

"The boy."

"What's his name?"

"I don't remember."

The cop sighed. "What did he look like?"

"He was cute."

"Mary Jane."

"It was consensual."

The first cop nodded. "Why don't you go wait in the hall," he said to his partner. "Mary Jane, we have a kit that lets us test for DNA in case you decide you were taken advantage of. It would help us find that person. It would be a nurse who collected the sample, not me or my partner."

"I wasn't raped."

"Your mother thinks we should get the sample."

"I don't care what she thinks."

"If we don't do it now, we won't be able to later."

"I wasn't raped. And if that disappoints you, I'm sorry."

"Okay." The cop put up his hands. "Thank you for your time." He pocketed his notebook and paused at the door. "You know you're lucky we found you. You understand that, right?"

Mary Jane nodded. "I feel very fortunate," she said. Anything to get him out the door.

Holly had her feet propped up on a box of case files and was playing solitaire. "Quiet morning?" Harlan asked.

"We could use more like this."

"You *have* looked pretty worn down recently," he said before suggesting she take the day off.

Holly replied that Harlan didn't look so hot himself and maybe he should keep his opinions to himself. He responded by pulling out a pack of Bugler and said, "I'm going to set in my office and ruminate. Chances are I might roll one of these and I'd appreciate it if you don't harp on me, okay?"

"It's your funeral," Holly replied.

On the top of Harlan's desk was a folder with a Post-it that said, "Thought this might be of interest." Inside he found a report on Trip Gaines. Except for a couple of speeding tickets, the doctor's arrest record was clean, but there were loads of documents from the state medical board. Harlan had heard rumors the doctor ran into trouble before moving to Marathon but he'd never paid them much mind. He avoided doctors or anyone else who might tell him to change his ways. Apparently, the board had been split over whether or not to let Gaines practice because of two malpractice suits brought against him in Ohio. There was testimony from Gaines about his troubles with alcohol, and his ultimate recovery through the twelve steps. He talked about raising his son and daughter as a single parent, talked about how his trials and tribulations reminded him why he loved medicine in the first place. He wanted to help people. His father had been a doctor in rural Ohio, the kind who doled out care in exchange for fresh vegetables and baked goods. It sounded like a story out of a movie. Harlan wondered where the Mercedes, designer sunglasses, and holier-than-thou attitude fit in to Gaines's portrait of a selfless medicine man.

He closed the folder and smoked one cigarette after another in silence. He couldn't fit the information on Trip Gaines back into Lew's murder. There was money and shady business dealings but no endgame. The tobacco dried his mouth and the stale smell of tar stained his fingers. The dispatch stayed quiet and the streets outside stilled. Even the fall breeze buffeted down to a whimper. Ash fell onto Harlan's lap, fell to his feet, but he didn't care enough to dig up an ashtray. Time passed. At some point, his phone rang—a shape on the desk screaming out like some wretched child.

"Sheriff here," he said, his voice creaking like a brittle door.

"Sheriff, this is Sam Boggs over in Deerhorn. I got a couple boys pulled a bag off the creek bank. It's got a .308 in it. Fits the Teletype you sent out."

Harlan wondered what his murder weapon would be doing in Deerhorn, but without any better leads, it didn't matter. He told Boggs he'd be there as soon as he could.

Deerhorn was a sleepy one-street town a little over an hour from Marathon. The only buildings were a couple of wood-paneled municipals, a Gulf station, and a Rax that served up dry roast beef sandwiches and whipped-cream desserts. Harlan got the sense that the town would never grow again, that, in fact, it would shrink until one day it vanished completely—its last resident dead or moving on like the lone survivor at the end of days.

At the sheriff's department, he found Sam Boggs listening to Dwight Yoakam and sweeping dust bunnies into neat piles. "I must look like the goddamn maid," Boggs said as a means of introduction.

"I'd trade places," Harlan replied.

"No deal. I'm too old to go solving murders." Boggs was silver-haired but fit. He kept his hair cut close and his grip strong. Harlan pegged him for a soldier. Vietnam? Korea? "Thanks for taking this off my hands," Boggs said as he handed Harlan the transfer document and a box with contents marked in plastic bags.

Harlan noted the rifle. The barreled action had been unscrewed from the stock. It was a common Winchester, could have been bought at any gun show, store, or pawnshop. Beneath it was a tripod and a single bullet casing, a bag with white residue, and some soggy trash.

"I don't know how much any of that means to you," Boggs said. "I figure it's a hunting trip gone bad, but that powder's either pill dust or cocaine. Pills, most likely."

"Why do you think that?"

"We've been fighting that shit for a year or two now. Seems like every other person I arrest is hopped up on pills. I asked my brother who's a cop out in Tucson if they have the same problem but he told me they have the cartels and we have Purdue and Pfizer."

"I just started hearing about it in Finley."

"Watch out," Boggs said. "It only gets worse."

Harlan borrowed a vinyl glove and examined the evidence. The empty cartridge was promising. He hadn't found one along the ridge in Marathon and it wasn't like a hunter to clean up after himself. Boggs had done a good job preserving the lot, even managed to dry out the water-sodden food containers and a receipt.

Harlan returned the bags to the box and hefted it up. "I appreciate this," he said.

Boggs picked up his broom and returned to sweeping. "Glad to get it out of my hands." As Harlan walked outside, Boggs called out, "Safe home" while Dwight continued to croon about being a thousand miles from nowhere.

———

Lewis woke to the tap-tap of his mother's bony fingers. "Get up, get up, you sleepyhead," she sang. "Get up, get up, get out of bed." Lewis groaned and burrowed deeper into the sheets, but Mabel continued to tap-tap away. "You're not sleeping off a hangover in my house," she said. "I laid out clean clothes and a towel in the bathroom. Shower and then come eat."

Lewis opened his eyes and tried to piece together how he'd ended up in his childhood bed. After punching Trip, he'd driven to the river to drink in solitude, and when all he had were empties, he'd driven to the gas station for more. He remembered calling Sophie from a pay phone. Ended up leaving a drunken message on her father's answering machine—apologized, defended himself, apologized again, said he loved the girls. Then he called their house and did it again. It was all so dramatic. A marriage, not some high school romance, and yet he acted like they were one and the same. He had a vague recollection of having driven to his mother's house, though he couldn't remember if she'd come to get him or if he'd knocked and asked to be let in.

His bedroom was unchanged from when he was a kid, had the same pennants and posters thumbtacked into the wall, the same trophies atop the dresser, the same linens on the bed. It felt like the room of a boy who'd died young.

A new toothbrush sat on the bathroom sink along with a set of hotel soaps and shampoos. It was as if his mother had been preparing for this day. The clothes she'd left out were leftovers from high school—snug—though aside from a few extra pounds, Lewis cleaned up well. He almost looked like he did before his marriage, when the world was still his oyster and he held the knife, but Lewis knew better than to think time could go backward.

He wandered to the kitchen, found eggs, bacon, and strong

coffee on the table. His mother sat reading the newspaper and began chatting about insignificant things. "The weatherman says it's going to storm again," she said. "I hope he's right because my new garden could use a drink."

Her small talk pained him. Lewis couldn't pretend like this was just another day. "I punched Trip," he said.

"I know. You went on about it quite a bit last night." Mabel sipped her coffee. "I think today is a better one for amends, so you and I have an errand to run."

"What's that?"

"We're visiting your father."

Lewis couldn't imagine why, but he didn't argue. It didn't seem his place, considering. He chewed his breakfast slowly, his stomach gurgling as each bite settled. When he finished, his mother took his plate and said, "It's nice to have someone to cook for, and since the house is all we have left, I'm glad you're putting it to use." He couldn't tell if she was being sarcastic or sincere.

As they left, Mabel picked the lone rose from her new garden, stepped over a beer bottle on the lawn, and made her way to the Explorer, which was parked crooked in the street. If she had a lecture about driving drunk, she kept it to herself. "The Plymouth won't start," she explained, and though Lewis could have said, "I told you so," he didn't.

There were only two other cars at the cemetery, both of them in spots reserved for employees. As Lewis and Mabel walked toward his father's grave, a heavyset groundskeeper sped by on a riding mower. He took breakneck turns around the shrubs and scraped against one of the vaults that lined the water like ancient fishing shacks. A second groundskeeper, a Hispanic kid with a pockmarked face, pushed a beat-down Briggs & Stratton wherever the riding mower didn't fit.

"Not very restful, is it?" Lewis said.

"You take everything personally," his mother replied.

It was a large cemetery for a small town, as though what Marathoners excelled at best was death. His mother kept stopping to read names and dates. "You knew the McGreevys, right? Went to school with a McGreevy?" Lewis nodded. She placed her hand on the cool stone of a mausoleum decorated with a lion's head. "Your father wanted one of these," she said. "And he wanted all his sons and daughters and their sons and daughters buried in there with him, like some king of kings."

"What happened?"

"I had my tubes tied after you."

Lewis hadn't known this but he couldn't bring himself to ask her why.

The grave sat on a grassy knoll overlooking the pond. "I bought the plot next to him," he said. "For when the time comes."

"How thoughtful."

"I figured—"

"When I die, you can scatter my ashes where I grew up," she said. "Your father won't miss me."

"But you haven't been back there in ages."

"It'll be about time for a visit then." His mother bent at the knees and laid the rose in front of the headstone: LEW MATTOCK 1946–1998. SHERIFF 1986–1998. The hem of her long skirt gathered moisture from the grass.

"Maybe we should give each other time alone," Lewis said.

"No," Mabel replied. "We do this together."

Lewis felt stranded as she began to speak. "I thought you were too tough to die," she said. "Too stubborn, really. You should have warned me this might happen." Lewis looked across the pond, watched a heron settle on a water lily. "We could have done things differently." The heron dipped its beak at something in the water— an insect, a piece of algae. "I'm sorry we didn't get that chance."

His mother's voice started to tremble. Lewis felt like a trespasser to sadness. "I brought a flower from my new garden. I know it's silly. You couldn't care less about flowers. Maybe next time I'll bring a steak." She reached back for Lewis's hand. "Your son plans to run for sheriff." She wiped her eyes. Lewis looked for the heron but it had flown away. "You'd be proud of him."

She stood and waited for Lewis to speak. He felt like an actor on a stage. He leaned close and whispered, "Take care, Dad. Be good." He wanted to say more, wanted to tell him he loved him, but when the time came, it seemed like too great a lie. He'd run out of words. He turned to look at his mother and she nodded and wiped a single tear from her eye. Then he put his arm around her and shepherded her back toward the noise of the mowers, back toward their new lives.

Mary Jane balled a sweater against the passenger-side window and counted mile markers. The leaves on the trees, the same trees she'd passed a week before, were still painted in hues of red and orange, but on the ground beneath them brownish piles of dead had formed. Horses huddled in packs to protect themselves from the cold and a heavy gray sky swallowed the horizon. As they passed the sign marking twenty-six miles to Marathon, an announcement by Miss Kentucky came on the stereo reminding people to buckle their safety belts. It was followed by a campaign ad for Lewis Mattock that Mary Jane's mother turned off. Neither of them said a word.

At the house, the first order of business was a search of Mary Jane's room, which turned up a stale dime bag and a couple pills that Lyda flushed down the toilet. She made Jackson bear witness like it was a holy affair. Mary Jane didn't care for the show and she didn't think her father did either. Jackson perched awkwardly on the ledge of the tub and wrung his hands the entire time. He glanced at Mary Jane, managed to ask if she was okay, and then excused himself—more distant than ever. Even her mother's heart wasn't in it. Lyda looked ghostly. She kept asking Mary Jane why. Why had she acted so recklessly? Why was she sleeping with strangers? Why was she doing drugs? But Mary Jane couldn't explain why. Her parents had spent years looking past her stumble-home arrivals, her deep-seated sadness. How could she explain that none of this was surprising? And they didn't even know the worst of it. Mary Jane carried secrets that would break them.

Lyda started in on another question, and Mary Jane's stomach churned and she managed to reach the toilet just in time to vomit. The fluids from the hospital had kept her from crashing but now she felt ragged. Her mother had cruelly emptied the medicine cabinet, hiding the aspirin and sleeping pills. There was no relief but at least the vomiting quelled her mother's need to ask why. After handing her mouthwash, Lyda helped Mary Jane crawl beneath the covers of her bed. "This too shall pass," she said.

It was still the middle of the day and no matter how hard she tried, Mary Jane couldn't manage sleep. Her mind raced. Her skin ached. Her breath quivered. Images of Mark flashed into her head. And Vince. And Lew. Images of her mom. Her dad. All of them coming to pay their regards.

Her bedroom was a prison. It gave the illusion of freedom—no bars on the windows, no chains on the door—but there was no place to go. Lyda checked in every hour or so and asked if she needed anything, though this was just a pretense to spy. Her father didn't make any similar attempt. At some point a black bird flew into her window and fell to the sill. Mary Jane sat up and watched the bird flap back to the power line, where it perched as if nothing had gone wrong. She looked at the hole she'd cut in her window screen and made up a new lie. A bird flew into it. It didn't sound believable, but the truth rarely sounded as good as the lie.

Lyda talked about recovery programs and counselors, even brought out a couple of brochures from the hospital. Mary Jane clutched her teddy bear, his battery bay free of both drugs and batteries. She half-hoped that he'd speak up in her defense, but he didn't speak. Mary Jane wanted to tell her mother that drugs weren't the problem—they'd only been the solution—but her parents would do what they wanted with her now. And she'd let them. She'd failed. She was a girl who couldn't even manage to run away, who'd committed unforgivable sins, a girl who deserved whatever tragedy came her way.

She left the bedroom to use the restroom and release more terrible into the toilet, and only after she felt empty did she manage to shower. Back in her room, she let the towel fall away and stood in front of the mirror. She still wasn't clean. She could smell the sweat and sick and sex on her skin as she examined the bruises from the IV, the splotches on her backside where Mark had ground her into the earth, the puffy spot where his knuckles met her cheek. Then she scratched behind her left knee with her right foot and did a pirouette. Hers was a strange body—thick legs and swollen boobs beneath rounded shoulders. Parts of it she'd mastered while other parts felt like they belonged to another person entire.

In her desk she found a pair of safety scissors, things made for grade-schoolers, and started cutting. She planned to chop her hair off but stopped just below the ears because she liked the way it looked. It was a style from the past, given to girls who wore letter jackets and had doors opened for them. Then she put on a skirt and blouse that matched the hairstyle and imagined herself on black-and-white film—the very picture of innocence.

Mary Jane was no one and therefore she could be anyone, but it was exhausting, living with such uncertainty. She didn't recognize the girl in the mirror but neither did she recognize the one in the photos taped to that mirror—the mother's daughter wearing a

robin-blue dress and glittering tiara. Her hair had darkened since
then, her face broadened, her body grown. She'd failed at becoming
the woman the photos promised. She no more recognized herself
now than she had the day she shot Lew or anytime before that. So
much had happened and yet nothing had changed. How could she
be guilty when she didn't even know who she was?

Harlan drove straight from Deerhorn to the crime lab in Frankfort. The tech, a thin-nosed woman dressed like a scientist, said
they'd analyze the evidence and search for prints before seeing if
the gun fired. "It will be a couple days," she said.

"Can't you fast-track it?" Harlan asked.

"There are protocols," she replied. "And while it's not rocket science, it's not far from." Harlan shook his head. Protocols. He cringed
at the word. They seemed to get in the way of people doing their jobs
more than they ever helped. Harlan watched as the lab tech started to
catalogue the evidence. "Someone liked Big Macs," she said. Harlan
asked what she meant and she showed him the fast-food receipt.
"Big Mac, fries, and a Coke." At the top was a phone number with
a northern Kentucky area code. He asked for the telephone.

A girl answered and said, "McDonald's, Highway 68. How
can I help you?" Harlan asked where exactly they were located
and she said just down from the Walmart and that they'd be open
until ten.

"In Marathon?" he asked.

She seemed surprised by the question. "Yeah," she said. "In
Marathon." Harlan hung up and asked the tech to examine the receipt and copy down as much information as possible. After a little
work, he knew the store number, the server's name, and the total.

"I bet the person knew the server," the tech said.

"Why's that?"

"There's an apple pie wrapper among the evidence but it wasn't on the bill."

"Good find," he said.

"Rocket science," she replied.

Harlan stepped back in his cruiser and drove past the capitol building on his way out of Frankfort, chain-smoked until he had to pull off near the outskirts of Lexington for gas. He was greeted by an intersection of fluorescent flash and arrow and pulled into a crowded Shell station. It had once been farmland. It had all been farmland. Now it was gas stations and fast-food joints and hotel chains. Now it was boxy houses built over fields that had been plowed for centuries. The city seemed to attack the land like a virus, spreading a little more each year. Harlan wondered how God could look down and not cringe. Rivers polluted. Mountains leveled. People fenced in by the ring roads they'd built. Kids smoking, huffing, shooting up. And Harlan was no better. He hid in his hovel and smoked pot to forget the past. Less than half his life over and in so many ways he'd given up.

The lit parking lot of Walmart shimmered as he came into town—Marathon's sad way of announcing itself. The inhabitants of an RV had set up chairs in a circle as if camping in some pristine wilderness. Shopping carts were scattered about, one rolling down an empty row pushed by unseen hands. Harlan pulled into the McDonald's next door and eased around the line at the drive-thru.

He couldn't remember the last time he'd eaten. His gut was twisted with hunger, but even as a kid, the rare trip for a burger and fries ended with him vomiting and his father belting him for not appreciating the Happy Meal like a normal child. He headed inside and pretended to study the menu. He planned to ask the manager for security tapes from the day of Lew's murder, but as he approached the counter, he noticed a familiar face working the drive-thru. He checked his notes for the name of the server. Tara. The girl he and Paige had seen leaving the dirt track.

"That girl at the drive-thru," he said to the cashier.

"Tara?"

"Yeah, that's it. Tara. I'd like to chat with her."

"You gotta talk with the manager about that."

"Okay."

The cashier stood like a stump, hands perched above the till.

"So, I want to talk with the manager," Harlan said.

"Oh. Sure." Harlan shook his head as the kid lumbered toward the break room.

A dyed redhead with her pants hiked up like an old man came out a minute later and asked how she could help. Harlan mentioned Tara and followed the manager's eyes to the girl, who was deep in the trance of her work. "She's not in any trouble," Harlan said, anticipating the next question.

The woman looked unconvinced. "I'll send her on her fifteen," she said before asking if he wanted something to eat.

Harlan felt his stomach grumble again. "How about a cheeseburger and a soda."

"Like a number two?"

"Just one cheeseburger and a Coke would be great."

A couple minutes later, Tara carried a tray over and took the seat opposite Harlan in a red vinyl booth. He thanked her and opened the wrapper. He examined the piddly burger skeptically before taking a bite, but God, he'd been hungry. He took another bite and the burger was half-gone. "We met the other day," he said. "You were leaving the dirt track."

Tara nodded.

"This isn't about that, though."

She nodded again.

"You've been giving away free food."

The girl shook her head. "I haven't—"

"Tell the truth now."

Tara looked away, fidgeted with the hat atop her head. She'd tried to cover the grease stains with pins. The Golden Arches. The Hamburgler.

"I'm not here to cause you trouble," Harlan said. "I just want to chat."

"Every now and then," she whispered, her eyes darting toward the manager, who tried to look busy but was watching them intently. "Everybody does it."

"It's okay," Harlan said. "I'm just gonna ask a couple questions. I know the other employees do it, too." He fiddled with the salt and pepper shakers. "So do you only give freebies to people you know or is it anyone who comes in?"

She stared at her fingernails as though there was something interesting there. "It's not anyone."

"Tara," he said. "Look at me."

"Just friends," she said. "I'm not like a criminal. I'm just a good friend."

"And you have a lot of friends?"

Her eyes returned to her nails. "Not too many."

"Don't worry," Harlan said. "Your manager over there, she doesn't know what we're talking about. This information came from someplace else. And I want you to keep this job, but I need you to be honest with me."

Tears started to well up in the girl's eyes. "I need this job," she said.

"Now, come on. Don't do that. Don't cry. This can be between us. I just need you to tell me who you've given free food to in the last couple weeks. Can you do that?"

Tara sniffled, composed herself. "Sure. There's this boy I used to date, Tyler Darnell. He keeps coming by and I give him free stuff to get him out of my hair. And my best friend, Jana Jarboe. And I guess Mary Jane came by, too. That girl you saw me with at the dirt track."

"Mary Jane Finley?"

"Yeah. We aren't close, but she came through a couple days before I saw you and that woman deputy. I gave her a dessert we were going to time out. It was actually a joke. I mean Mary Jane's kind of piggy." She hesitated. "Maybe that's why she called me the next day to hang out."

"Is that everyone?"

"My mom. She's the biggest mooch of all. Tonight she asked me to get her a fish sandwich and fries. Extra tartar sauce."

Harlan wrote the names in his notebook. "Why don't you like Mary Jane?"

"I don't know. She's a rich girl who's always trying to act normal. And everyone in her year graduated and she's still hanging around. It's weird. And when she gets all fucked up, she lies. Like the other night at the dirt track she was drunk and told me she had a boyfriend and they loved each other and were going to get married and have babies."

"A boyfriend?"

"Yeah. Mark Gaines."

"The doctor's son?"

"Yeah. But he's down at UK, so I know Mary Jane's lying. Like I said, she's a weirdo."

"What do you know about Mark?"

"Not much. He drives a fancy yellow car."

"But he's not close with Mary Jane?"

"They dated way back when she was a freshman or something. It's pathetic, really, the way she lies like that."

Harlan nodded. "Do me a favor. Have your manager come over here. I'm going to tell her a little white lie about our chat. But don't make me come back, Tara. Stop giving away food."

The girl sniffled and wiped her eyes clear of the tears that had never come. "Okay."

The manager shared a couple of words with Tara before coming over. Harlan thanked her for the meal and asked if they kept security tapes; she claimed not to have access and gave him the name and number of the proprietor.

After he left the McDonald's, Harlan headed east and roamed the county roads. He didn't want to go home and fall asleep on the same unwashed sheets in the same shabby house, so he drove. And drove. A soft rain fell and slicked the blacktop, and as his windshield wipers whipped back and forth, the mile markers and trees flashed in his headlights before they turned into nothings and disappeared like the earth was being swallowed by the coming dark.

eleven

Lewis opened the front door and allowed himself the fleeting fantasy he'd find Sophie and the girls inside and life would return to normal. Instead he found an empty house—dark even though it was the middle of the afternoon. The evergreens left by the developer blocked the sun and the windows were too small to brighten the rooms. The builder had meant for the place to feel like an upmarket cabin—wide cedar floorboards and high ceilings—but standing inside the living room simply made a man feel small.

The girls' favorite stuffed animals were missing and Sophie and Lewis's bed was unslept in. Lewis played the answering machine, and as soon as he heard his voice slurring an apology, hit Delete. In the kitchen he made a pimento cheese sandwich and drank the last of the milk. His stomach was wrecked but recovering. It was time to stop drinking and get his health in order. The rest would follow. He packed a bag of toiletries and a couple of changes of clothes. Anything more would be admitting something he didn't want to admit. Then he checked that the windows and doors were locked and turned down the thermostat. It reminded him of leaving for a family vacation, only there was no family.

He drove to Trip's house and parked behind Sophie's Volvo. The girls were playing in the yard and Ginny came up to him while Stella ran inside.

"Hey, Pumpkin," he said.

"Hi, Daddy."

"What were you and Stella doing?"

Ginny twisted her leg like she had to pee. "Why'd you hit Grandpa?"

Lewis appreciated that she hadn't yet learned to speak in slanted adult ways. "It was a misunderstanding."

"Mom's *real* mad."

"I know."

"It's okay." There was a film of wet over her eyes. "You just need to say you're sorry."

He bent down and gave her a hug. "I know. I will, honey."

Sophie came out of the house in a new dress and leather jacket. She always went shopping when things got rough. Ginny led him to the front steps but he waited to be invited up. Sophie looked down. "Go on inside, Ginny," she said. Lewis caught Stella craning her neck around the open doorframe. He smiled but she didn't react. Sophie closed the door. "You did this to yourself," she said.

Lewis didn't deny it. "Can I come in?" he asked.

"Daddy doesn't want to see you."

"And you?"

"I'm talking to you, aren't I?"

"How about we talk on the steps then?"

Sophie folded her hands behind her legs to keep her dress in place and sat. A lady through and through. She was too conscious of her every move to ever embarrass herself, a habit that had the effect of putting Lewis on edge. He sat beside her but not too close, and they allowed themselves one of those silences that people take before important conversations. They looked into the distance as if to make sense of the world. Lewis let the moment play out, but it all looked the same to him. Grass, trees, house. Hills, house, trees. "I'm sorry for the other night," he said after a while.

"I don't know what you expect from me. Your father died and you're upset, but you shouldn't take that out on me. Or my dad."

"My father lied to me, Sophie. To everyone. And your dad, he knew the truth but he never said a word. Don't I have a right to be angry?"

"Daddy tried to protect you. Protect us. Deep down you wanted to be just like your father. What would telling you or me or anyone about his gambling have accomplished? It would've broken your heart."

Lewis started to argue against this but stopped. He didn't particularly feel like being analyzed as if he were on one of Sophie's talk shows. He could get over his father's failings—most sons do—but he couldn't get over the lies. He tried to change the subject, searched for common ground. "How are the girls?" he asked.

"They like it here."

"And you? How are you?"

She let out a deep breath, brushed back her hair, and set her mouth. She could turn from vibrant to lifeless in an instant. "Don't be so dramatic," she said. "It's been a couple days. I'm fine. And no matter what, I'll be fine. Just apologize and start campaigning again. We'll figure out the rest."

"So that's the main thing, the election?"

"For the moment."

"And the girls? Aren't they more important?"

Lewis hoped Sophie would realize how callous she sounded, but she stared right through him and said, "They're just kids, Lewis. Feed them, bathe them, put them in front of a movie."

"It's that simple?"

"It's simpler than you make it out to be."

"I guess you have all the answers."

She stood and swiped the back of her skirt for any stray bits of dirt. "If you're ready to apologize, come inside. I can talk to Daddy with you. That way we can skip the melodrama."

"Are you coming home?"

"Not yet. I have things to work out here."

Lewis looked up to Trip's second-floor bedroom, imagined him looking down like some lord. He was tired of playing second fiddle in Sophie's life; it would always keep them a little ways apart. "I'm not ready to apologize," he said. "And I'd like it if you and the girls stayed at our house, but I suspect you'll do what your father says."

"This is how you want it?" she asked. There was no feeling in her voice. No love. She'd loved him once. He knew that. He knew because he'd loved her, too. Real love. Full of passion and promise. He wondered when they'd become so static. He could have hugged her, could have let her know he remembered the nights they'd danced without music, the mornings they'd stayed in bed just to hold each other, but instead he sat there like a tree. "All you have to do is apologize," she said.

"No," he replied, "I'd apologize, and then I'd have to lead my life how your father says, and I suppose the girls would have to do the same, and that's not what I signed up for. I didn't marry your father. I married you."

"Well, I didn't sign up for a husband who gets drunk and falls apart the moment something goes wrong. I guess we don't always get what we want."

Lewis smiled despite himself. The words coming out of her mouth—Mick Jagger's words—tickled him.

"What's funny about this, Lewis?"

"Nothing. It's just . . . that's a Stones song." He half-sung it for her. "'You can't always get what you want. But if you try sometimes . . . you get what you need.'"

Sophie looked at him as though he were speaking another language.

"Sorry," he said. "It was just a—"

"Grow up, Lewis," she said and turned away.

"Sophie, hold on—"

He reached out, but she didn't hesitate, and the door slammed. It felt like the end to a fight over some minor misunderstanding, not the life they'd built together.

Lyda Finley marched out of the house and up to Harlan's cruiser before he had a chance to step out. "What do you want now?" she asked, unable to hide her annoyance. Harlan couldn't blame her. Even he was starting to feel like a nuisance.

"I came by to see if Mary Jane has been in touch."

"She's upstairs in her room."

"I'd like to ask her about a friend of hers."

"Is this about what happened in Lexington?"

"I'm sorry?"

"The police in Lexington talked to her after she had her stomach pumped. I didn't know they'd contact you."

Harlan feigned awareness. "It's just a formality," he said. "What did they find in her system again?"

"What didn't they find? Booze. Something called Ecstasy. A prescription drug. She's lucky to be alive. Oh, and she got a tattoo."

Harlan smiled at this last detail. "A lot of kids overdo it once and learn their lesson."

Lyda glanced up to the top floor. "Jackson won't be happy you're here."

"I'll be quick."

"Give me a minute to check on Mary Jane. She's still not feeling well."

Harlan watched Lyda steal back to the house, the pep gone from her step. He turned the rearview mirror on himself and rubbed the exhaustion from his face. His eyes were sunken and his skin

brackish. He'd ditched his crumpled uniform in favor of a simple
T-shirt that made him look less official, less scary.

He didn't know how to best approach the girl or where to begin. He wasn't even certain the gun from Deerhorn was the murder weapon or that Mary Jane had been the one to toss it in the
creek, but she was his best lead. The fact Tara had mentioned Mark
Gaines piqued his interest even more. The investigation kept circling back to the Gaines family but he didn't know why. It was a
tangled web and the tangles had to mean something.

Lyda led him up the wide staircase with its beautiful oak banister and pointed him down the hall. He knocked softly on the door
and it inched open. "Mary Jane," he said, poking his head in. She
looked sick—her skin melted like a wax doll's, with a bruise along
the cheek. Under different circumstances, Harlan could see that
she'd be pretty. Hers wasn't the sharp beauty of her mother but
something more natural. He said her name again and she looked up.
She seemed fragile, soon-to-break, and he felt cruel before he even
asked a question. "I was told to check in on you," he said.

Mary Jane didn't respond.

"I heard you had a pretty wild night."

"Not that wild."

Harlan nodded. "And you're doing better now?"

She tilted her head to take in the room. "Yeah. I'm great."

Harlan sat along the bottom of her bed.

"What were you doing in Lexington?"

"Visiting friends."

"Friends who got you pretty messed up."

"I went to the party alone."

"Oh. Where were your friends?"

"I don't know."

"You sound a little confused."

"I'm not confused." A touch of anger crept into her voice.

Harlan needed her to relax. "You mind if I set here a spell?" he asked. Mary Jane shrugged and he prattled on about whatever came into his head—the weather, his neglected house, growing up in Marathon, his lackluster parents, anything to keep the conversation from stalling out. "I guess I'm the one who's confused. And I'm a lot older than you, so I should have my shit together." His hands fidgeted. "Hell, I'm wanting a cigarette right now even though I know they'll kill me."

"You wouldn't want to smoke if you'd had your stomach pumped."

"Probably not. But I'm fairly addicted, so you never know." He stood up from the bed and walked to the window, looked outside to where a neighbor was putting up Halloween decorations—plastic pumpkins, a store-bought scarecrow. "So I heard you got a tattoo."

Mary Jane muttered something he couldn't make out as he rolled up his sleeve and showed her the mess of ink he'd gotten from a cousin with a guitar-string gun.

"What is *that*?" she said.

"It was supposed to be the logo of this band I loved. Led Zeppelin. For a while it might have looked that way but not anymore. I'm sure yours is better."

"It's a woman hiking in the woods."

"That's cool. So no regrets?"

She hesitated. "No regrets."

Harlan rolled his sleeve back down. "Do you mind if I level with you, Mary Jane?"

She shrugged.

He hoped that if he danced around the subject of Lew, she might fill in the gaps, give him something to work with. "I've had a tough couple weeks. The previous sheriff got shot, which I'm sure you heard about, and I keep hitting dead ends. See, there were a lot of people mad at Lew when he died. And they all had their reasons, but no one wants to talk about it. And I just want to know *why* he died. I don't even care who did it." Mary Jane faked disinterest but her pupils tightened. "Do you know what I'm talking about? Did you know Lew?"

"No. I mean I heard he was . . . you know."

"Yeah, well, I figure maybe if I can't solve this Lew thing, I can help you. 'Cause I'm worried about you. I see you leaving the dirt track, where I know bad things happen to good people. Then your mother tells me you've run off. And now you've gotten your stomach pumped. Tell me how I can help."

"I don't need help," she said, but her heart wasn't in the lie.

Harlan stifled the impulse to reach out and stroke the stray hairs from her sweaty face. She wasn't much older than Angeline had been when they'd met—just a girl doing her best impression of a woman. Angeline. If she'd lived, she'd be twenty-six and maybe she and Harlan would have made a life together. Pets. Children. Dinner parties. The whole ever-loving bit. And she would have done it all with grace. She did everything with grace. He'd loved watching her navigate the world.

Harlan closed his eyes and pressed his palms against his eyelids. "I'm so tired," he said. "When you sign up to enforce the law, you're supposed to do what the books say. When a law is broken, you arrest the person who broke it. But it's more complicated than that." He paused, backed into the question he'd wanted to ask all along. "I was at that barbeque when Lew was shot. Do you remember where you were?"

She answered without hesitation. "A movie." It was a practiced response but she'd been too nervous to play it cool. Her eyes darted around the room, settled on anything but him.

"What movie?"

"That Will Smith one. With the aliens."

"You like it?"

"It was okay."

"Was anyone else with you?"

"I went alone."

"Really?" Harlan said. "Me, I like going to the movies alone. But I'm a loner. That's a rare quality in someone your age."

"I guess."

"Did you do anything else? See any friends?"

"I saw my friend Tara."

Harlan nodded. "Was this at her house or at work or—?"

"I'm really tired."

"I know," Harlan said. "Just humor me a bit longer."

"At work."

He nodded. "And no one else was with you? A boyfriend, maybe?"

"I don't have a boyfriend."

"What about Mark?"

Mary Jane lost a beat, tried to recover. "Mark?"

"Gaines," Harlan said. She froze, blinked at him, said nothing. He'd hit the magic words. "What did Mark do to you in Lexington?"

"Nothing. We had a fight."

"Did he hurt you?"

She hesitated. "No."

"Tell me about him."

"What do you want to know? He's a jerk."

"Why?"

"He just is."

"Was Mark the one who gave you the drugs? Is he the reason they pumped your stomach?"

Mary Jane looked away.

"You don't want to tell me?"

"No."

"Why not?"

"Because there's nothing to tell."

"You can talk to me, Mary Jane. I won't let Mark or your parents or anyone else hurt you."

She shook her head. "I don't know what you're talking about." Then she said it again, softer. "I don't know." She pulled the covers up over her head. "Please, just leave me alone."

He'd lost her.

Harlan touched her shoulder beneath the sheets, pulled them down slightly, and made her look at him. "I'm gonna leave, Mary Jane, just like you asked, but promise me you'll call if you need anything." He placed a card on the bedside table, wrote his home number on the back. "I don't care what you want to talk about. Could be Mark, could be your parents, could be the weather. It doesn't matter. I'll listen."

She lay there, still as a corpse, so Harlan shut the lights on the way out and let her rest. Then he left the house without a word to Jackson or Lyda.

He felt himself getting closer to solving the case, but he couldn't quite make himself believe that Mary Jane pulled the trigger. And he didn't want to trade her life for Lew's. Lew had been corrupt. A cheat. Mary Jane was confused. Young. Maybe Holly was right and it had become personal for him, maybe he wanted revenge for what Lew had done to Angeline, but it wasn't that exactly. It was about right and wrong and Harlan's mistake had been believing the law had something to say about that.

Even if he brought Mary Jane in on suspicion, without stronger evidence, he wouldn't be able to charge her. And if the gun wasn't a match, if he was wrong, all hell would break loose. In the end, all he really had was a bag of McDonald's trash, a Winchester, and a hunch. It wasn't enough. Not yet.

After the sheriff left, Mary Jane heard her mother climbing the stairs to her room. Her hands clenched into fists. She'd tricked the cops in Lexington but this one knew something, and he wasn't visiting because she'd gotten her stomach pumped. He'd known about Mark. But how? And he talked about Lew, but what was he hinting? If he knew something, why didn't he just arrest her? Lyda looked in and said her name softly, but Mary Jane played dead. When the door closed, her fingers relaxed. There were four pink grooves on each palm where her nails had burrowed into the skin.

Lyda continued up the stairs to the third floor office. If ever there was a time to run, it had come, but as she rolled out of bed, the world around Mary Jane swirled and in the hallway she had to drop to her knees. She heard voices and thought she was hallucinating, but they kept on—became familiar—until gradually she made sense of them. Her parents. Arguing. She crawled to a vent along the floor and a memory clicked. As a child, she'd listened to her parents argue through the same heating vent.

Jackson was complaining about the sheriff. He said that it was all Lyda's fault, which didn't make sense to Mary Jane. The sheriff had been there to see *her*. But her mother kept apologizing, as if it were true. "For twenty years you've made me look like a fool," Jackson said. "And now he knows. And who knows how many other people will find out." Something slammed and her father's voice started to rasp as it rose. "And for what? For fat Lew Mattock?"

Mary Jane craned closer, unsure of whether or not to believe what she'd heard. Her father knew about the affair, and her mother kept apologizing in starts and stops as she sobbed, a language more utterance than word.

"It's my fault for marrying you," Jackson said. "I knew better. But Dad wouldn't allow it. What would people say if I left my pregnant girlfriend to fend for herself?" His voice weakened. He was trying not to cry himself. "And I wanted to believe, Lyda. Really, I wanted to believe that it was over with him. That you loved me. That she was mine. But she isn't. She isn't mine."

"You don't know that."

"I do. It's written on her face. Every time I look at her, I see him looking back at me. It's easy to delude yourself when they're young. Babies look like babies. Little girls aren't much different. But she's older now. And I see it."

It took a moment for Mary Jane to realize they were talking about her. She was the reason her father had proposed to her mother. She caused their terrible sham of a marriage. Her heart dropped into her stomach and she opened her mouth to vomit but all that came out was a dying noise. She curled into a ball and plugged her ears because she couldn't bear another word, rocked back and forth and choked on her tears. Suddenly, the great sadness of her life seemed to have reason. She'd never been wanted.

Her father—no, Jackson Finley—was telling the truth. It was written on the wall in his office. Generations of Finleys. None of them like her. All her failures, her blemishes, her heavy skin, her inability to fit in, all of it had been there from the moment she was born. All of it had been fated. She was the daughter of a bastard, a man she'd hated so much that she'd . . . Mary Jane tried to shut the memory out—the trigger, her breath, him standing in the crosshairs—all the images running together to make a muddy world.

She stood on shaky legs and banged against the wall, reached the stairs and clutched onto the banister for support. She scrambled down but her legs couldn't carry her, not all the way, and the base of the stairs came careening toward her before it all went black.

Harlan got word from the proprietor of the McDonald's on Highway 68 that the security tape he needed had been recorded over. The guy, who lived an hour away in Covington, blamed the manager and said it was his policy to keep the tapes for a month before reusing them, but he had a hard time making employees follow rules, and if there was anything else he could do to help, just let him know. Harlan slammed the phone back on its cradle and asked Holly to bug the crime lab to hurry the fuck up.

Then he drove out to Leland Abbot's to see what he could dig up on Mark Gaines. Leland denied drugs were sold at the track, but that was an act performed for the benefit of the authorities. He just needed motivation to talk, a carrot or stick.

Something bad had happened between Mary Jane and Mark, that much was certain. There was the bruise along her cheek, the panic in her eyes when Harlan said his name. There were the drugs pumped from her stomach and the pill dust from Deerhorn. And then there was Trip Gaines, looming above it all. The doctor.

Harlan found Leland outside his trailer holding a drill and building a mess of a deck with untreated two-by-fours. "That looks like shit," Harlan said, crouching to examine the shoddy craftsmanship. "Bob Vila you're not."

"Fuck that guy. He's a know-it-all."

Harlan jostled a loose board. "You think about our chat the other day?"

"Not particularly."

"Why not?"

"I don't remember you giving me much to think on. The way I remember it you made some threats and then took off."

"After you tried to bribe me."

"That was a misunderstanding."

Harlan put out his hand for the drill and secured a loose board. "I've reconsidered," he said. "You can buy me off. But not with cash."

"What do you want? Stock options?"

"Information on drug dealers."

"I don't know any."

Harlan drove another screw home and put the drill down. "Then expect to see a deputy camped outside your place tonight."

"How long can you keep that up?"

"I'll do it myself if I have to. I love getting overtime."

Leland scratched at the back of his neck. "Why do you have a hard-on for me?"

"Why don't you listen to me the same way you listened to Lew?"

"Lew's price was cheaper." Harlan shrugged and Leland cursed under his breath as he took a seat atop the toolbox. "Okay," he said. "I'll hear you out, but be quick."

Harlan rolled a cigarette and handed it over to Leland, took his time and rolled one for himself as well. "Some of what you said the other day is true. It's not necessarily in my best interest to break up your pleasure park. It keeps the riffraff localized and all, but I need to do some police work out here every now and again—bust drunk drivers, pocket some drugs. Just enough to keep people honest. That's in your long-term interest, too. You're one fuckup away from another jail stint."

"What other people do isn't my business."

"They do it on your property, it becomes your business. Now, I don't care to get you in trouble, Leland. I figure we can work together. I give you a heads-up before I do any policing out here and you make yourself scarce."

"And what do you get in return?"

"Information about a kid up to no good."

"Who's that?"

"You ever hear of Mark Gaines?"

Leland laughed. "The doctor's boy."

"I know it seems far-fetched—"

"It's not."

"What do you mean?"

"You're asking a lot, Harlan."

"I'm offering a get-out-of-jail-free card."

Leland stood up and paced a circle, stretched his limbs. "That little motherfucker deals out here from time to time. He and the other druggies hide out in my woods—they call it the enchanted forest or some shit. My pops called it tick heaven. I'm not saying I have a part in this. It's just that running them off my land is more hassle than turning a blind eye."

Harlan nodded but he didn't buy the bullshit. If there were drugs being sold, Leland would make sure he got a piece. "How often does Mark deal?"

"Shit, I don't know. There's not a schedule. But Halloween's coming up. You don't need me to tell you that's a big-time holiday for druggies."

"So he might be out here soon?"

"Might be."

"Quit playing coy, Leland. Help me catch this kid and you and I can live in relative peace."

Leland threw his smoke to the ground and picked up the drill. "I'll see what I can do, but I need a favor first."

"What's that?"

"That ratty girl who claims to be your friend got all fucked up last night and damned if she isn't sleeping it off in my place as we speak."

"Mattie?"

"Is that her name?" Leland grinned. "All I know is she puked in my bathroom."

"You didn't?"

Leland drilled another screw. "Didn't what?"

"Take advantage?"

"Jesus, Harlan. She's just a kid. What kind of guy do you take me for?" Leland spat on the ground. "Kids come out here uninvited and when they get messed up, I end up taking care of them like some goddamn babysitter, so you finish the nanny job and take her the fuck home."

Harlan stepped past Leland into the trailer. Mattie was curled up beneath a blanket on the couch. He shook her awake. "Let's go," he said. She didn't make a fuss or seem surprised to see him, and when she pushed back the blanket, he was glad to see that her clothes—even her shoes—were on. She folded the blanket and put it back on the couch before following him outside.

"Goodbye, sweetheart," Leland said as she passed by. "Next time try not to vomit in my house."

Mattie mumbled an apology.

Harlan opened the door for her and looked to Leland. "I'll hold you to your end of the deal."

"Expect a call, Sheriff."

The silence inside the cruiser turned awkward as they drove away. "He didn't touch you, did he?" Harlan finally asked.

"Who?"

"Don't play dumb, Mattie. Leland."

"I'm not playing dumb, Harlan. Leland isn't like that."

"You know him well then?"

She picked at a fraying spot on her jeans. "Well enough."

"I don't like the life you lead," Harlan said.

Mattie ignored the insult and asked him to take her to his place, but he refused, and when he pulled into the Spanish Manor, she jumped out while the car was still moving. Harlan hit the gas, caught up, and told her to stop. He had to end whatever kinship was growing between him and the girl. It could only bring trouble, and he couldn't go saving every hopped-up kid with an ounce of potential.

"You're sixteen years old," he said. Mattie nodded, her bone-white skin translucent and fragile. "Whatever you feel for me has to stop."

She lowered her eyes.

"It's not right."

"You think too much about right and wrong," she said.

"We're not friends, Matilda." There was a sting to the words because they weren't true. In some strange way, Harlan felt he and this girl needed each other, but he couldn't admit that to Mattie and least of all to himself. "Clean yourself up and leave me alone."

She pawed the ground with one foot as if she'd dropped something and was hoping to catch glint of it. "I knew we wasn't ever gonna fall in love, Harlan," she said, her voice trembling. "I just liked imagining that if things were different . . . if I were older and not such a fuckup or you weren't the law, we might be friends. You could have let me hold on to that. You don't know how hard it is to find a friend." She peered down the gravel road that led her home. "I gotta go," she said.

Mark turned on the television and ate pizza cross-legged atop the scratchy comforter of his Day's Inn bed. In the parking lot the neighbors, a couple of guys who were in town on a construction job, sat on the tailgate of their truck and drank. They were getting rowdy on malt liquor and cheap cigars, and at some point, they turned on the truck's stereo. Mark considered telling them to knock it off, but he knew that no matter what he said, they wouldn't stop. He called the front desk but no one answered.

The motel was on the outskirts of Lexington, the sort of place you pulled off the interstate to find, but the parking lot was full. Mark wondered what had brought so many people there, wondered where they were headed. He didn't even know where he was headed. He'd run from the party and escaped but something in his gut told him to circle back. That's when he saw Mary Jane being loaded into an ambulance with two cops nearby. He'd gone straight to the apartment, packed a bag, and left. Now, he kept watching the local news, as if something would show up and tell him whether or not the coast was clear, but nothing ever did.

If he were a betting man, Mark would double-down on Mary Jane's ability to keep a secret, but he couldn't gamble his life on it. He didn't know where she was or who she was with or what questions they were asking. Besides, if Mark were a betting man, he never would have guessed Mary Jane would cheat on him. After he'd caught her, something changed in him. He'd wanted to hurt her. And when he couldn't find any other way, he'd hit her. The violence surprised him—probably him more than her. It seemed ridiculous that the day before he'd felt beholden to Mary Jane, that he'd planned on running away with her to Montreal. At least now he was on his own. Free.

Ever since Lew died, he'd been making mistakes. He hadn't handled the situation with Mary Jane. Or with his father. Or Chance. He thought about going back to his dad and asking for help, but he couldn't trust him, and he couldn't exactly come clean about Mary Jane. His dad was a powder keg ready to blow.

The drunken assholes outside his motel room decided they liked a particular song and cranked it up. The gravelly warble of a country singer filled the air. "Shut the fuck up," Mark muttered before trying to drown their noise with the volume of his television.

He counted the money he had left. He couldn't afford to keep staying at the Day's Inn, couldn't afford to stall out. It was always the same problem—not enough foresight, not enough means. He needed to make a run for it without Mary Jane. Maybe he would head south instead of north. Mexico was a place to start over. Or maybe he'd head west and change his name. In his Intro to American History class, he'd learned that the pioneers were men with checkered pasts, men who'd sought new beginnings.

A beer bottle broke in the parking lot and Mark stood up from the bed. He turned the doorknob and almost stepped out but reconsidered, pulled back the curtain to sneak a look. The men were tossing their empties toward an open Dumpster, arcing the bottles over his Mustang. He wanted so badly to confront them but he returned to the bed and picked up his planner instead. It was a small token of the life he'd left behind. The planner made his life seem so innocent—class, homework, a note to go to French club. He tried to pretend that he'd been the person depicted in those pages, but the beeping of his pager interrupted his reverie. It came from a number he recognized and he called back. Leland Abbot needed pills for Halloween. And Mark Gaines needed gas money.

twelve

As soon as she walked in, Harlan called Holly into his office. He'd been up all night organizing the case, had compiled a folder with the autopsy report, Pedersen's bounced check, the Deerhorn evidence, and notes from his conversations with Little Joe, the Finleys, and Tara Koehler. "I want everyone on duty tonight," he said. "I'm going to arrest Mark Gaines and it's all hands on deck."

"What's Mark Gaines have to do with anything?" Holly asked.

Harlan explained how the evidence pointed back to Mary Jane and Mark. He couldn't arrest the girl without the crime lab's confirmation, but he'd worked out a deal with Leland to set up Mark.

"And you think this links back to Lew's murder?"

"I do. Trip was paying Lew's debts for a reason. And then I find out Mark is dealing drugs."

"But where's Lew fit into it?"

"Maybe Trip paid him to turn a blind eye to Mark's drug dealing. Lord knows Lew needed the money. Or maybe all three of them got caught up in something that spun out of control. If I bring Mark in on a drug charge, he might just fill in the gaps."

"What about bringing in the girl, too? Don't forget about her mom's affair. That's a strong motive."

"Once the crime lab confirms we have the murder weapon, I'll bring in Mary Jane. In the meantime, I don't want to tip everyone off." Harlan handed over the folder of evidence. "I don't know who pulled the trigger, Holly, but I'm pretty damn sure both those kids know something."

Holly spun the gold band on her ring finger. "It sounds far-fetched."

"Don't I know it."

"And you trust Leland?"

Harlan sighed. Ever since Lew died, he'd been looking for some-one he could trust, and what he ended up with was Leland Abbot. Somehow it made sense. "I guess I have to."

Holly held the folder as if it were live-wired. "If this falls apart, you're gonna be wading in deep shit."

Looking at the battered case file, Harlan couldn't help feel-ing proud. "And if it solves this murder, I just might win an election."

"What else do you need from me?" Holly asked.

"Run the dispatch tonight. I'll take Paige with me to the dirt track, but I don't want the other deputies to know what's going on until I have Mark in custody. After that the dominoes will fall and we'll need help."

Holly paused at the door on her way out. "Sometimes this job," she said. "It makes me think the worst about people."

Harlan didn't disagree.

Mary Jane woke up next to her mother, who was fast asleep and snoring. She didn't remember how she'd ended up back in her room but one touch to her forehead confirmed that she hadn't dreamt the events leading up to it. There was a knot where she parted her hair.

The window was open and a damp blanket of air settled, and

her breath felt shallow as a ghost's. She slipped out of bed, careful not to wake Lyda, and nudged open the closet, counted the many Mary Janes that dangled there. Belle of the Ball Mary Jane dancing the night away in a champagne gown. Beachcomber Mary Jane lounging by the sea in a swimsuit. Rocker MJ in a ripped T-shirt and jeans. Today, it seemed important to find the right Mary Jane. She started with jeans and a gray V-neck stretched thin from wear. Over that she added a flannel shirt that had been Pappy's. She'd worn the flannel every day for a month after he died. Even now she touched the fabric and whispered hello. Then she ran a brush through her hair, pulled it behind her ears, spread cover-up over her bruises, and added lip gloss. When she looked in the mirror, the girl that looked back was the truest Mary Jane she knew.

She had a headache, a stomachache, jitters from withdrawal, but she wouldn't let the pain overcome her. She opened the jewelry box on her desk and pocketed her last hidden Oxy, glanced back to make sure Lyda was still sleeping. She decided to write a note—an explanation. She held a pencil over a piece of paper but struggled to find the right words. The thought that came to her was one countless teachers had written on her report cards. It didn't matter whether Mary Jane was a grade school chatterbox, a middle school prima donna, or a high-school outcast, her teachers wrote the same seven words over and over. *Fails to live up to her potential.*

When she finished the note, she placed it somewhere hard to find, and crept down the stairs, gripping the banister with both hands, careful not to make noise, careful not to stumble. On the porch, she took out the Oxy and held it like a gemstone. She wanted to be better than this. She wanted to be stronger, strong enough to flush this pill down with the rest, but she wasn't that strong. No point in pretending. She crushed it with the base of her mother's lighter and snorted the dust. It felt right.

She could have turned back, could have walked into the house and slipped beneath the sheets and slept until the sheriff came to get her or her parents sent her away to rehab, but she wanted control over her own destiny. Downtown lay ahead like an apparition, and she followed streets that sloped toward the river. The diner's fluorescent Mountain Dew sign flickered, and through a layer of dust on the window, she watched two men sip coffee. The cook stepped out for a cigarette. Her jet-black hair was tied in a bun and she wore an apron that said, SCREW HOME COOKIN'. Mary Jane nodded hello. A newspaper trapped against a nearby bench flapped in the breeze.

The pavement turned to rubble as she reached the edge of town. In lots where brick row houses had been razed, vacant trailers perched above weedy, rock-strewn ground. When she reached the river's edge, Mary Jane traced her fingers over the graffiti of the town's half-built floodwall. She thought about how if you build a wall to protect yourself, you just make it worse for someone downriver, someone without a wall of their own.

She scrambled along the banks of the Ohio. It had rained overnight and debris dredged up by the floods floated by. Tree branches crested like snakes and runs of yellow mud from the bottoms surfaced as foamy crests of smogwater circled in the swells. Mary Jane tossed a stone into the riffling current and made her way along a sand shoal to the base of the bridge that crossed into Ohio. A dead bluegill—a tiny, ugly thing—had washed up along shore and been gnawed at by turtles. She grabbed the rusted iron rungs bolted into the bridge support and climbed. It was a game they'd played as kids: Who could climb the highest? And when heights no longer frightened them, they'd tossed rocks at the climber. And when those rocks became too small, they'd found larger ones.

Ochre flakes broke off the rungs and fluttered to the ground like dying moths. Mary Jane's feet slipped along the wet and gusts of wind broke across her face and whipped her hair. She paused to rest, put the flat of her hand against the cool concrete. When she looked down, she was not afraid.

When she reached the top, she grabbed the cool wet metal of the bridge's railing and pulled herself onto the asphalt. She was surrounded by the sounds of a world without people. The wind moved in circles and she put her arms out as if they were wings. The river rushed and a pair of waterbirds called out to each other. Mary Jane watched them wheel in the swirling winds, their bodies going whichever way the breeze took them, their necks craning down in search of fish.

She sat atop the railing as the fog lifted. The sun played hide-and-seek with heavy gray clouds and a soft rain started to fall. She licked her lips and tasted the wet. Before her was the river, cutting farther west than she'd ever make it. They'd misunderstand her no matter what she did, but she hoped this might save them from the truth; she hoped that once she was gone, the story of what she'd done would disappear with her. She'd been so wrong. She'd done terrible things and pretended there weren't consequences. She'd done terrible things because she was afraid of being alone.

A waterbird came up from the river with a fish in its beak, and Mary Jane imagined a world of every action's opposite. In that world, the bird would miss the fish, or perhaps the fish would get the bird. In that world, she never would have run to Mark in Lexington. She never would have run because the bullet that killed Lew would get swallowed back in its chamber. The gun would be in someone else's hands, some hunter who missed his shot, and the bullet would lodge into an ancient tree, which would scar over and bury the guilt inside. Mary Jane pictured that tree, deep in some woods she didn't know and had never seen. She went on like this, into a world where she hadn't become just another face in the crowd, a world where the best hadn't been first and the worst hadn't been last. There were better worlds out there. She just didn't know how to reach them.

She didn't say goodbye, didn't offer a prayer, but she kept her eyes open and paid witness. She tilted forward and let go. The sky became a blur until the snap of hard water ripped through her and she gasped and choked as the cold worked back from her fingers. Then her arms went weightless and her heartbeat slowed. And slowed. The current took her.

Every landmark Mark passed, every mile that brought him closer to Marathon, made him sicker. When he reached the county line, he looked away from the sign that spelled out Mary Jane's last name in all caps. He'd been forced to check out of the Day's Inn by three and reached Leland's early. It was eerily quiet as he parked, so he hiked into the woods to collect his thoughts and waited for the sun to set. In the branches of a nearby shrub a spider spun its web. He watched it climb up and down a seemingly invisible thread of silk, watched it pivot and turn as if in thin air. He counted the pill bottles in his bag and squeezed them in his hand. He didn't want to keep dealing drugs but he had no choice. Leland offered him a lifeline, and after he sold his stash, Mark would become like that spider. He would travel invisible roads. He would look out for himself and no one else. And for that reason he'd survive.

Where he'd go, he didn't know. What he'd do, the same. He'd repent. Or try. It wouldn't do much good. It took a lot for a person to realize the evils they were capable of, but Mark knew. If his father had sought to create a monster, he'd succeeded. Monster born of monster. Mark would never not feel shame. Maybe after he settled someplace no one had ever heard of, he'd call the newspaper and rat his dad out, write a note to Mary Jane and apologize for letting things get so broken, do his best to make amends. But none of it would wash the blood from his hands.

He thought of Chance's last words: *I do nothing upon myself and yet I am my own executioner.* They seemed to suggest a world full of innocents. And perhaps they were all innocent—himself, Mary Jane, Lew, the elderly people selling their prescriptions to keep the heat on, the kids popping pills to get high, even his father—but it seemed more true to say the opposite, to say, *Because of what I do upon myself, I am my own executioner.*

Harlan and Paige drove her rusty Datsun up the switchback into Leland's property. He was wearing a flannel and jeans and Paige had on a short skirt over black tights and a suggestive top, but still Harlan worried they'd be pegged for cops. The idea of going undercover in a town as small as Marathon was ridiculous.

"Remember this place?" he asked.

"Looks better during the day," Paige replied.

The parking lot's ruts had muddied from rain and the Datsun's wheels spun and the steering wheel jangled. "This thing's almost as bad as my truck," Harlan said.

"Almost."

A steady stream of cars followed them in. The racetrack had turned into a soupy mess lit up by floodlamps like the ones rich boys put atop their jeeps. A couple of ATVs cruised at low speeds, and spectators tossed their empties onto the track, which the drivers took aim for and crunched into flat pieces of aluminum that refracted the light. An attempt at a PA strung along slanted poles crackled out a country song.

Girls in midriff shirts stalked the grounds, their heavy makeup turning them into little Lolitas. The older women dressed the same but their bodies had become skeletal from hard living, their faces carved with deep tracks and sunken cheeks. The worst had thin, tattered hair that had been dyed so often it looked burnt. Half the men looked like farm boys while the other half wore jerseys and fake diamond jewelry, the latter's high-pitched voices spouting a language foreign to Finley County, a language learned from television and rap videos. Harlan looked at Paige and felt a pang of guilt. He hadn't told her the real reason for their visit, had lied and said they were just out there to get a feel of the place. Eventually, Paige might come to understand why he'd cut a deal with Leland, but she'd never fully agree with the decision.

A group of kids caked in white makeup and boasting safety pin piercings pushed through the crowd and congregated on the gate of a pickup beside the Datsun. People heckled them and the kids seemed to feed off the anger, but when they spoke to one another "Oh my Gods" and "likes" peppered their speech—just like any other group of teens. Three country toughs in ripped shirts, one sporting a Confederate flag on his cap, walked by and gawked at them. One of the ghosts—a girl with straight black hair—screamed, "What the fuck are you looking at, hillbilly?" The redneck didn't take the bait, so she turned her gaze to Harlan, and said, "You too, asshole."

"Come on," Harlan said to Paige. "Let's go."

Paige hesitated, so Harlan pulled her toward the dirt track. "I don't like those vampire freaks," she said.

"They're just kids. Doesn't matter if they whistle Dixie or paint their face. They're just trying to fit in."

He bummed a couple of beers from a guy with a cooler full of them and handed one to Paige.

The smell of dope drifted toward them, and he followed it to a group of women passing a joint. One of them made eye contact and beckoned him with her slouch. He drained his beer and stomped it into the ground as she came over. From afar she'd had the outline of a beauty but up close it disappeared. Spray-on tan, blue-veined arms, loose skin on a skinny frame. She offered him the last of a blunt. "Toke?"

Harlan shook his head.

"Boring," the woman said and walked away.

"You gonna let people smoke dope night in front of you?" Paige asked.

Harlan realized he needed to come clean or else Paige would blow their cover. "Our goal," he said, "is to not draw attention. In a minute we'll make our way up to Leland's trailer, and a little after seven, I'm going to bust a kid that's dealing drugs. You're going to stay outside unless something goes wrong."

"How do you know the guy you're looking for will be there?"

"A little birdie told me."

"And what about Leland?"

"Who do you think the birdie was?"

Faces floated by, all with a hint of familiarity but none with names Harlan could have called out. "If people recognize you, say you're off duty," Harlan said. "And keep a beer in your hand. It'll help you fit in."

"At least I look the part," Paige said and pulled down on her skirt. They headed up the hill past the old Abbot place. Next door the shades of Leland's trailer were drawn. The farmhouse's garden had reverted back to wild and become a den for rodents and chirping insects. They passed rotted trellises snared by roses whose canes ran across the ground like rows of shark's teeth. "What a shithole," Paige said. Harlan tried to remember the house as it had been when he was a boy, told her it hadn't always been so run-down. They passed through tall, gone-to-seed grass and came upon a notch they could use as a lookout. Deep in the woods there was light from a bonfire that reflected off mirrors strung in the trees. The ether of voices and scurrying sounds of night slipped to them. "They call that the enchanted forest," Harlan said.

A little before seven, a shadow stepped out of the woods, made straight for Leland's trailer, and knocked on the door. Leland flipped on the outside light. "Is it him?" Paige asked.

Harlan grabbed her arm and squeezed. "Shh," he said. And then, "Yeah. It's him."

Harlan crept up to the trailer after Mark went inside. He thought about pulling his gun, thought about kicking the door in, but realized there was no need. Instead, he took a deep breath and turned the knob.

He saw Leland first and then Mark, who stood up from the couch as if to run, though there was nowhere to go. Harlan rushed at him and yelled "freeze" and "police" and all those things movie cops yell before tackling Mark to the ground.

"Damn," Leland screamed. "Take it easy."

Harlan slapped handcuffs on the kid and rolled off. He was breathing heavy as he brought Mark to his feet, all the adrenaline draining out of him, the soreness setting in. Paige sauntered in a minute later, collected the drugs, and read Mark a monotone Miranda rights. The kid nodded his head ever so slightly when she asked if he understood.

They marched him to Paige's car, hoping not to draw attention. Mark didn't fight or make a scene, though. He watched his shuffling feet as if he were going to the gallows. In the parking lot, Harlan noticed a yellow Mustang. "That your car?" he asked. Mark didn't respond, so Harlan told Paige to search it and wait for a tow. He could take Mark in alone.

The kid bent willingly into the Datsun, so Harlan let him ride in the front. As they drove into town, Harlan looked out at the black river. He imagined the look on Trip Gaines's face when he found his son in custody, but it didn't bring him the pleasure he thought it might. The boy next to him was scared shitless, fragile as a misplaced vase. Harlan had a million questions he wanted to ask but they all had to wait.

He led Mark to a holding cell until formal charges could be filed, called over to the diner and ordered a burger and fries to help put the kid at ease. Frank, who was sitting on the couch with a bemused look on his face, asked what the hell was going on. Harlan said he'd explain later.

Mark's dinner arrived around the same time Paige came back with evidence from his Mustang, including a prescription pad of his father's that she found in the glove box. Harlan stepped into Mark's cell with food in one hand and the prescription pad in the other. "What are you doing with this?"

"I don't know anything about that."

"This isn't just about a drug charge," Harlan said. He risked a little white lie. "I have the gun that shot Lew Mattock. You're gonna be charged with murder."

"I didn't do it," Mark whined.

"Who did?"

Mark looked down at his feet. Harlan slid the Styrofoam container of food across the floor to him. "Come on, Mark. Do the right thing."

Mark opened the container and chanced a fry. "Just let me eat."

Harlan relocked the cell. The kid hadn't asked for a lawyer, but Harlan needed to be careful and wait until he was formally charged before pressing him too hard.

Paige stepped out of the bathroom wearing her uniform and holding the skirt and halter-top as if they were covered in grime. "Wild night," she said.

"It's about to get wilder," Harlan replied. "I want you to go arrest Trip Gaines." With the prescription pad as evidence, they'd be able to charge Trip and hold him until he posted bail, which would give Harlan more time with Mark, who seemed primed to break at any moment.

"Are you serious?" Paige asked.

"Tell him he's suspected of drug trafficking and take him to Mason County. I'll call Sheriff Hart and secure you an empty cell. And take Frank with you. He's bored."

"You sure you don't want to do it, Harlan? I mean, this isn't something I've done before."

"If I go out there, I might belt the motherfucker, and I don't want to mess up our chance at a conviction. Besides, it'll give you both a good story to tell."

After they left, Harlan took in the momentary peace and quiet with Holly. "Is Del out on patrol?" he asked.

"Yep."

"You mind staying here with the kid? I have one last person I need to see."

Holly nodded. "Of course. I couldn't fall asleep tonight no matter how hard I tried."

Lewis headed for the Fifth Amendment, a mobile-home-cum-bar with a rough reputation and views of the river. He'd been at home watching television when Harlan called. He figured if Sophie wasn't going to stay there with the girls, there was no reason to keep the house shuttered. Lewis explained to Harlan he wasn't drinking and didn't particularly feel like socializing, but Harlan said it was important and that while Lewis might be on the wagon, he himself was in need of a beer. When Lewis tried to find out what he wanted, Harlan was vague and shifty, and ended the conversation by saying, "See you in about twenty," as if Lewis had never expressed hesitation.

By the time Lewis arrived, Harlan had taken up residence in front of the taps. The place was otherwise empty save a couple of disability-check drunks. Lewis took the stool next to Harlan and ordered a Coke. The bartender, an old-timer who Harlan claimed kept a shotgun behind the bar and shells in his pocket, fizzed the drink out in a plastic cup and added a straw and a cherry. Lewis picked up on the sarcasm and said, "Fuck it. Give me a Budweiser." The bartender nodded and poured the Coke down the drain.

Photos of the UK basketball teams going back to the '50s lined the walls, the white faces of the past giving way to the black faces of the present. A couple sepia-toned photos of family hung behind the taps. Harlan asked about them, and the bartender said he'd bought the photos at a junk sale, claimed he didn't even know the people. "You believe him?" Harlan asked Lewis.

Lewis studied the photos. "Not really. If they were junk, why hang them where you see them all the time?"

"I suspect you're right." Harlan raised his glass. "To having a good eye."

Maybe it was because his home life was unraveling and he welcomed the distraction or maybe it was the setting or something in the way Harlan carried himself off duty; whatever the reason, Lewis felt at ease. It was almost as if he were catching up with an old friend. "You think they know we're candidates for office?" he asked, nodding his head toward the drunks.

Harlan put his palms on the bar and stretched his back straight. He sure was a tall son-of-a-bitch. "You drumming up votes?" he asked.

"Nope," Lewis said. "To be honest, my campaign is in shambles. I've been drunk every day since my dad died. I got into a fight with my campaign manager, who happens to be my wife. And I punched my biggest backer, who happens to be her father." He laughed at the ridiculousness of it. "Apparently, I'm not the best at running for office."

"Hell, Lewis. I had no idea. You sound right nice in those radio ads."

"Trip's handiwork."

"And you hit him?"

"Knocked him down with one punch."

"What for?"

Lewis shrugged. "It's hard to explain."

"That asshole probably deserved it."

Lewis watched Harlan's slender fingers work a rolling paper around a mound of tobacco. "So why'd you call me out here?"

Harlan licked the paper and picked stray threads of tobacco from the end. "I guess Trip's part of the reason," he said and lit the cigarette.

Lewis tensed up. "So this is about the election?"

"Not really. The reason I called you is to let you know I arrested Trip's son tonight." Harlan blew smoke toward the ceiling, which had blackened from years of other people doing the same.

"Mark? What for?"

"Dealing drugs."

"No way."

"He's in some deep shit, Lewis."

"But Mark's a good kid. . . . I mean why would he—"

Harlan frowned. "I'm not sure he came up with the idea. We found one of Trip's prescription pads in Mark's car."

Lewis shook his head. "Why are you telling me this? I mean, what's your angle?"

"I don't have a fucking angle," Harlan said. "I just thought you should know." He drained his beer and banged the empty glass on the bar. "I'm not messing with you, Lewis. A deputy is bringing Trip in as we speak. Mark's already in jail. I'm giving you a heads-up because this shit is going to turn your life inside out."

Harlan motioned to the bartender for another round. The glass in Lewis's hand was half-full but he followed Harlan's lead and drained it in one go. He couldn't wrap his head around what Harlan was saying, but he also couldn't convince himself it wasn't true. He'd never trusted Trip. And there was the Mercedes and the new-found wealth—the loan he'd given Lewis, the down payment on his and Sophie's house, the money to pay his father's debts. If what Harlan said was true, much of Lewis's life had been built on the back of Trip Gaines's wrongs. When he finally replied, he said, "My daughters are at Trip's with their mother."

"I wouldn't worry about that," Harlan said. "Trip's smart enough to keep quiet and let his lawyer deal with the charges."

Lewis pointed to Harlan's pack of Bugler. "Roll me one of those?" Harlan set to work and Lewis asked the question he'd been avoiding. "Do you think this has anything to do with my dad's murder?"

Harlan took his time with the cigarette. "I think your dad knew Mark and Trip were dealing drugs, but as far as his death is concerned, I'm looking for a different suspect." He handed over the cigarette and lit a match.

Lewis leaned forward. "Who?"

"I can't tell you that, but it's not going to be some feel-good story when it comes out."

Lewis inhaled, leaned back, and coughed. "So my father was crooked?"

"Truth told, I thought that's why you were running for sheriff. Keep it in the family and all. But I don't believe that anymore."

"Why not?"

"You'd have to be the best damn actor I ever met, Lewis. And that's just not the case."

Lewis stabbed his barely burned cigarette in the ashtray and excused himself. He needed a moment alone.

The bar's bathroom smelled like stale piss and shit. Phone numbers and juvenile drawings of big tits and big dicks covered the wall. A mound of cigarette butts sat in a plastic tray atop the urinal. Lewis closed his eyes and tried to let his mind go blank, focused on the sound of his stream hitting the urinal cake. One of the bleary-eyed drunks stumbled in and wheezed, "Don't shake her too much, Youngblood."

"Just once," Lewis replied.

"Once ain't enough."

When Lewis opened his eyes, the world careened toward him. He glanced over at the drunkard as he removed his gray member. The man put the palm of one hand on the wall for support and swayed. Piss splattered and kicked down to his feet. Lewis finished up and returned to the bar, where Harlan had another round waiting.

As Lewis stepped out of bathroom, Harlan noticed that his face had gone pale and that his bulky body listed more than it moved with any sense of direction. Harlan could tell a dam was about to break inside the poor man. When Lewis had asked if Trip was involved in Lew's murder, he'd tried to plug the hole. Lewis was in no position to think rationally about his father or Trip Gaines, and while Harlan had his suspicions, they'd remain that until he got Mark talking. He hoped Lewis would be able to recover. He knew about the sorts of disappointments fathers leave sons.

"I'm going to drop out of the election," Lewis said as he sat back down. "I don't deserve it. My father. My father-in-law. You deserve it."

Harlan shook his head. "Nobody *deserves* it, Lewis. You just get the job and do it."

He watched as Lewis ran a finger through the condensation on his beer. "If you knew he was corrupt, why didn't you confront him?"

"Your dad?"

"Yeah."

"I didn't know back then. Part of me wishes I still didn't. It wears you down, learning the things people do."

"So what now?"

"Life goes on. A little messier for a while. Maybe you drop out of the election, maybe you don't. I don't care. Maybe I hire you on as a deputy 'cause we're one short and I teach you how to do the job." Harlan laid a twenty on the bar, tapped it. "I've never told anyone this but a woman I loved, the only one I ever loved and probably ever will, your dad wrote a note asking for her killer to be let out of jail. Just a couple years and he was free. Maybe that's why I'm telling you all this. 'Cause at some point it's got to stop being about winning elections and start being about doing what's right. And trust me, that's a gray area." Lewis didn't say a word, so Harlan picked his hat off the bar and finished his beer. "Take all that bad shit I told you and let it go. Don't let it sink you. And when you're not buying up newspaper ads or radio ads or punching your father-in-law or whatever the hell it is you do in your free time, drive around this county with me and see it through my eyes." Harlan put a hand to Lewis's shoulder. "Buck up, Lewis," he said. "You're not him. You never were."

Harlan ordered a six-pack to go and popped a beer as he drove home. The maples and oaks still clung to a smattering of leaves, but the height of fall had passed and swirling winds blew debris across the road. It was almost November and the ash were bare. Sickly. There'd been years when fall had passed him by, when he hadn't taken notice until it was too late, but he'd learned there are things worth appreciating in this world and autumn in Kentucky is one of them.

It was near midnight by the time he pulled into his driveway. The houselights were on and the hood of his truck was open with a lamp clipped to it. Harlan grabbed the remains of his six-pack and followed the sound of a dog barking to the porch, where he found Mattie's brindled mutt chained to the door. The dog was a big-headed, small-bodied mongrel with a raspy bark and overgrown paws. He sat and stared at Harlan with a slight underbite and goopy brown eyes, his tail curled up behind him like he had something to show off.

Mattie came out of the house, spatula in hand, and pretended like she was surprised to see him.

"So now you broke into my house?" he said.

"It was open," she replied.

Harlan leaned down to scratch the mutt behind his flea-ridden ears. The dog was a sucker for attention. "Who's this?"

"That's Floyd."

"Hello, Floyd," Harlan said. "What are you and Mattie doing here?"

"Well, Harlan," Mattie said in what he supposed was her approximation of the dog's voice. "Mattie was fixin' your truck but she hasn't finished. And she's been waiting for you to get home so she can cook dinner."

Harlan straightened back up. "Mattie, you don't have to—"

"No," she said, stopping him. "I'm sorry about the other day at Leland's and the way Henry treated you and . . ." In the moonlight, he could see the wet forming in her eyes. "And I don't really want to talk about it except to say you've been a good friend to me and I don't have too many friends, so I'd like to keep counting you as one. And I think you need a friend every once in a while, too, so I thought maybe I'd fix your truck and cook you dinner, and then if it's all right, we can put the past behind us." She wiped her sleeve across her face and sniffled once.

Harlan should have told her to go on home but he didn't. He'd befriended the girl and he had to accept that for what it was. Maybe her apology was meaningless but he believed her. Or he believed in her. She reminded him of Angeline. It wasn't physical. Mattie was just a girl, a rail. Angeline had been a woman, generous and full. It was something in the way Mattie approached the world, the way she pivoted when things didn't go her way, the way she put Harlan at ease. There was something of Angeline in Mattie because she trusted Harlan and thought maybe he could help her through this hard life, and there was something in Harlan that thought that might be true and so he did as she asked and let the past go. "Where'd you get this mutt?" he said.

"I found him near the river looking half-starved and mangy as hell."

"He's still that."

Mattie ignored the insult and bent to scratch the dog. "Don't listen to him, Floyd." The mutt rolled over and she rubbed his raggedy stomach.

"What kind is he?"

"What kind ain't he?"

"Why Floyd?"

"I don't know. When he looks at me, he kinda seems human and a little bit sad. Like a Floyd."

Harlan unhitched the dog from the door and walked him around the yard. The mutt bounced ahead of him like some danged rabbit and stopped at every stray pile of leaves and patch of tall sedge to pee until long after he ran out of piss. Then he crapped in the grass. "Good boy," Harlan said.

Back inside, he found Mattie cooking with his lone skillet. She flipped a pair of catfish filets and the raw sides touched down. "I'm guessing you don't cook much," she said.

"Why's that?"

"There ain't nothing in your fridge."

"I'm due for a trip to the store."

He carried his beer to the porch, put a warped tape in the cassette player, and listened as the Boss's voice cried out into the night, yelling over and over: *Adam raised a Cain. Adam raised a Cain.* Inside, the filets sizzled and the pan spit oil. There was a haze around the moon—icy skies that promised storms come morning.

Mattie came out after a couple minutes with two plates of blackened fish. Harlan wolfed down his plate and complimented the
chef. Mattie gave more of her fish to the mutt than she put in her
mouth, and when the dog came begging his scraps, Harlan held
them in his fingers and let the beast lick them clean.

thirteen

The gray-haired woman who ran the sheriff's department came into Mark's cell with a bedroll and a blanket. Mark was curled on the ground, his arm pinned beneath his head to keep it from pressing against the concrete. He opened his eyes as she set the bedding down. This was his best chance to make a run for it. He could get past the woman. After that it was a short run down the hall and out the front door. It wasn't exactly Alcatraz, though Mark couldn't be certain there wasn't someone else in the office, and by the time he was done debating whether or not he could make it, the woman was crouched beside him and running her fingers through the hair above his temple. "Honey, you should sleep on this mattress," she said. "It isn't much but it's better than the floor." She had an airy touch that put Mark at ease and his dreams of escape vanished. He just wanted her to stay with him. "Come on," she said. Mark sat up and scooted onto the bedroll. "Isn't that better?" He nodded. "Do you need anything else?" He shook his head. "Don't hesitate to ask. I'm just down that hall. You call out if you need anything." Mark managed to say thank you softly. The woman frowned as if she were sad. "I can't turn off all the lights but I'll make it less bright in here." She stepped out and locked the cell door again. A minute later every harsh fluorescent save one flickered and went dark. Mark closed his eyes.

He wished he could sleep but his mind raced with thoughts too frantic to capture. Every time he shifted, part of him came off the bedroll, and in the middle of the night just as he started to nod off, the female deputy came back full of energy, talking about how shocked Trip Gaines was when she arrested him and how he started demanding a phone call like it was a movie. Mark wondered if he should have asked for a phone call, too.

His entire life Mark had been a follower. He did what his father asked, believed his sister when she told him he was worthless, tried to make Mary Jane's pipe dreams reality. And all because he didn't have an opinion of his own. That need to please, more than any-thing, was why he found himself in a box that echoed when he rustled the blanket or coughed or started to cry. It wasn't dealing drugs that had doomed Mark; his lot was cast by the boy who too often said, *Hey, Dad, watch this.* Who pleaded, *Hey, Dad, look at me.* Who whispered, *Look* . . . If he could go back in time to change things, he would . . . but how far back would he need to go?

Mark's stomach thundered and the stench inside him roiled as he clambered across the floor to sit on the aluminum toilet. He sti-fled his sobs with the blanket as his guts clenched and unclenched again and again. He heard the steps of the gray-haired woman come down the hall. She called out, "Are you okay?" And then, "Can I get you anything?"

Mark cried out, "Just leave me alone," as the toilet filled with the muck inside him. And when he didn't hear her walk away, he yelled, "Leave me the fuck alone," which did the trick. About ten minutes later, after he'd emptied his stomach and flushed, she returned without a word and slipped a plastic cup of ginger ale and another blanket into the cell. And even though Mark wanted to tell her he didn't need her pity, he was overcome by her kindness, and thank-ful that anyone might think he was still worth helping.

He sipped the soda and chewed on the ice, started to feel human again. He decided that when his father came marching in with bail money and a lawyer, he would turn them away. He had nothing to offer now but the truth. He was guilty. His father was guilty. The truth might not fix the situation but it was as close to redemption as he'd ever come.

Harlan wanted to check on Mark but Holly, who was on the phone, pointed him to his office instead. She cupped the mouthpiece and said, "It's Tom Gabel. He needs to talk with you." Gabel was the two-term sheriff of Brown County across the river in Ohio. As she removed her hand, Holly said, "I know, Tom. Anything in the river is our responsibility. We've done this before. Harlan just walked in. You can talk him through it." Holly shook her head. "Good luck," she said.

As soon as Harlan picked up, Gabel said, "I think we have a body in the river."

"Why do you think that?" Harlan asked.

Gabel launched into a story about a couple of teenage lovebirds who'd seen a person jump from the bridge the day before. Apparently, the kids hadn't planned on telling the authorities—because they were scared or they didn't want their parents to know they'd snuck out—but they told some friends and those friends told other friends and eventually a concerned parent caught wind and called him.

"So it's been what," Harlan said, "twenty-four hours?"

"Sounds about right."

"Have you talked with the witnesses?"

"They say the person was alone, couldn't tell male or female, and they didn't see the body surface." Gabel explained that he didn't want to add to Harlan's troubles, but technically the river was Kentucky's jurisdiction as determined by the Supreme Court in 1793 and upheld in 1966—the gist being the body was Harlan's responsibility and not his.

Holly appeared in the doorway and said, "I've got the crime lab on line two."

Harlan cut Gabel off. "I'm aware of the legal precedent, Tom. I'll get our Staties to search the riverbank. And I'll want to talk with the witnesses myself. I'm sorry to cut this short, but I've got to take another call. Let me know if you get a notion of who I might find in the river."

Harlan switched lines to the crime lab and asked for news.

"Sheriff, you've got a match," the tech said.

"You're sure?"

"Yep. We couldn't pull any prints but after a little TLC, we were able to fire the gun. We matched test bullets to the one you pulled. I'll be faxing the report over in a minute."

Harlan thanked the woman and grabbed the keys to his cruiser. "We found the murder weapon," he told Holly on his way out the door. "I'm heading to the Finleys. Get me a warrant as soon as the fax comes through. Oh, and a state police boat to search the river."

"Are you bringing the girl back here?"

"Yeah. We can put her in the box. That'll let Mark get a good glimpse of her."

Jackson Finley answered the door and asked Harlan what he wanted. There were deep bags under Jackson's eyes that matched his jowls.

"I'd like to talk with Mary Jane."

"Wouldn't we all."

"What's that mean?"

"She's gone. Again."

"Where?"

"I don't know. Mary Jane likes to make us worry. It's her preferred form of rebellion. I'd wager she's out blowing off steam."

"Last time she did that she ended up in a hospital."

Jackson shrugged.

"I think we should talk," Harlan said. "You, me, and Lyda. See if we can figure out where she might have gone."

Jackson pointed him up the stairs. "My wife's asleep in Mary Jane's room. I think she stayed up all night worrying."

Harlan took the stairs in pairs as Jackson trundled up behind him. Lyda was curled on top of her daughter's bed, clutching a pillow. Harlan waited for Jackson to wake her, which he did by rubbing her arm softly. She muttered nonsense and Jackson took a moment to explain the sheriff was looking for Mary Jane. Lyda sat up and yawned. "Wait, what? Did you call him?"

"No. He just showed up."

Lyda turned to Harlan, rubbed the sleep from her eyes. "How did you know she was missing?"

"I didn't. I just found out." Harlan wondered how much of the truth he should tell. He didn't want Jackson or Lyda getting defensive. He thought about Mark curled up in the drunk tank and said, "Mary Jane is friends with someone who's in trouble. I came to see if she could help me help them."

"Do you think this friend has something to do with why she ran off?"

"Could be."

"Who is it?"

"That I can't tell you, Mrs. Finley." He hadn't consciously reverted back to using her formal name, but he was aware of the change in his behavior. Call it professional distance. "We all have the same goal," he said. "And that's to find Mary Jane."

Lyda nodded and Jackson did the same.

"So how long has she been gone?"

"Since yesterday morning."

"It's like I told you," Jackson said. "Mary Jane taking off isn't a surprise."

"Did you look for her?"

"I called everyone I could think of. I even drove to Lexington to see if I could find her car."

"And no luck?"

She shook her head.

"Can you get me the information on the car? Make, model, plates? VIN if you have it?"

"Sure," Jackson said. "I have the title in my office. But honestly, Sheriff, I think we're overreacting."

"Better safe than sorry, right?"

"She didn't leave a note," Lyda mumbled.

"What's that, Mrs. Finley?"

"A note. Mary Jane usually leaves a note on the kitchen table. This time there wasn't a note."

"That doesn't mean anything," Jackson said. "It's not like she's otherwise dependable."

"I know my daughter," Lyda said. "Something's wrong."

"We'll need you to get us in contact with friends and acquaintances, give us as much information as possible." He scanned the bedroom. "And I'd like to examine Mary Jane's room, see if I can find anything to help us track her down. Is that okay?"

"Whatever you need," Lyda said.

Jackson shrugged. "Sure." He stood up from the bed, anxious to leave. Harlan shook his hand, went to do the same with Lyda, but as she stood, she fell forward and started to cry into his chest. Harlan draped an arm around her and they stayed that way until Jackson took her by the shoulders. "It's your fault," she said as Jackson led her away.

As he searched the room, Harlan tried to divorce himself from the proceedings, tried to pretend this was just a missing persons, tried to forget that he'd been here days before, tried to forget about the body in the river and whether it might be Mary Jane. For now the two were separate. There was a girl, wanted by the law, on the run. There was a body in the river.

The room's décor was a contradictory mix of girlish sentiment and punk rock, the Disney of yesteryear giving way to the grunge girl of today, though neither dominated the other. It was as if Mary Jane was caught between two versions of herself—the dutiful daughter and the rebellious woman. Along the doorframe of her closet there were hash marks to track how tall she'd grown and when. Harlan followed her rise from toddler to adult, from just over three feet to her full five seven. Then he examined the picture frames atop the desk. Every single photo was from when Mary Jane was a child, smiling wide despite a slight gap in her front teeth.

On top of her nightstand, Harlan found his card in the exact spot he'd left it. Mary Jane hadn't even picked it up out of curiosity. In the drawer of the nightstand he found a road atlas of the fifty states and opened it to Kentucky. A blunt pencil had traced a line over the bridge into Ohio, so he flipped to Ohio and found the path again, followed it north into Pennsylvania, New York, and finally Ontario, which he found in an addendum. As he flipped to Ontario, an unsealed envelope with the words *to whom it may concern* fell to the ground.

Harlan pulled the paper from the envelope, a piece of pink-bordered stationery of the sort used to write thank-yous. There were only five words, a single line written just above the center of the stationery. "Never lived up to potential."

He read it once to himself, then out loud, tasted the words on his tongue. There was something ominous about the past tense, the terseness. She'd signed her full name in cursive below the line and the year, a final flourish. Harlan turned the paper over in his hands, looked for more. If it was a suicide note, it wasn't exactly straightforward. It could just be a goodbye, an explanation for why she left. The atlas itself gave Harlan hope that Mary Jane was still out there—running.

He went to the window as if by some magic he'd see her on the horizon. It was open and he examined a hole cut in the screen. He wondered where she hid the pipe and searched the room some more, rummaged through piles of dirty clothes, looked behind books on the shelves. In the closet he found a stack of shoeboxes, each one with the word *memories* written in permanent marker on top. The boxes were filled with keepsakes from Mary Jane's youth—Valentine's cards from every kid in class, drawings she'd pulled from school notebooks, seashells and arrowheads. He hoped for a diary or some other tangible evidence, but it wasn't until he reached the last box that he found anything recent. Inside were doodles making fun of teachers, pages of Mary Jane trying different signatures, an attempt to write Mark to tell him she loved him.

He tucked the unsent love letter and five-word note into the atlas. It was hard for Harlan to look around the room and think of Mary Jane as anything more than a lost girl, easy to forget she was a murder suspect. He'd need to put out an APB and alert the authorities along her route north, get in touch with border control. And if she didn't turn up, well then he'd need to search the river.

He walked down the stairs and found the front door open. Lyda was waiting for him on the porch, smoking a cigarette. Harlan held up the atlas. "I found this in her drawer. It's probably nothing but I'd like to study it some more."

"Of course," Lyda said. "Anything that helps."

"A recent photo would be good. For the missing persons."

"Give me a minute." She stabbed out her cigarette and disappeared inside, came back with her pocketbook and pulled a small photo from a plastic shield.

"What's this?" Harlan asked, pointing to a number along the photo's bottom.

"It's a school photo. That's so you can place an order, which I would have done had Mary Jane shown me it. I found the picture in a pile of her things months after it was taken." Lyda took the photo back and studied it. "I can't believe the photographer got her to smile."

Sophie called Lewis and asked if he could look after the girls. At first she lied and said she needed to run errands, but then, without him prodding, she came clean and told the story of her father being led away in a squad car. "Arthur Blakeslee is driving in from Cincinnati and I need to go with him to bail Dad out."

"That's crazy," Lewis said, trying his best to sound surprised. "What's going on?"

"I don't know."

Sophie sounded lost and Lewis felt a pang of guilt for not warning her, for not reaching out.

"I'm sorry, Sophe," he said. "Bring the girls. I'll watch them for as long as you need."

She pulled into the driveway twenty minutes later. Ginny and Stella jumped out and started playing tag in the yard. Lewis risked a kiss on Sophie's cheek. "Thanks for taking the girls," she said.

"I'm happy to."

"I won't be long."

Ginny and Stella were circling a tree. He couldn't tell who was chasing whom.

"Are you okay?" he asked.

"No. Not really. Everything is falling apart."

Lewis nodded. "I know."

"First your dad and then us fighting. And now whatever's going on with my dad. And my brother. I didn't mention that. Arthur called me on the phone right after I hung up to tell me Mark was arrested, too."

"Is it related?"

"I don't know. I don't know anything. I just want life to go back to normal."

There were tears in Sophie's eyes, and Lewis wrapped his arms around her. She shook against him like water lapping to shore. "It'll be okay," he said. "We'll get back to normal. Whatever that is."

The girls stopped playing tag and watched them. Lewis wondered what was going on in their minds, wondered how much they understood. Sophie stilled and he dropped his arms to his sides. "Thank you," she said under her breath.

Lewis crouched down like a catcher and called to Ginny and Stella, but each girl hesitated. "Did they see what happened with your father?"

Sophie shook her head. "They were asleep."

Lewis stayed in his crouch, kept looking up at Sophie. The gray sky loomed stark and close behind her. "And you still think they're fine?"

"Fine, yes. But not good. You were right about that."

Lewis shrugged. "Maybe having to be right or wrong is what caused our problems in the first place." He shredded a rust-colored maple leaf in his hands, twirled its veiny remains. "Right now, I'd settle for fine." He called the girls again, clapped his hands together. Ginny came first and Stella followed. It was always Ginny first. Lewis needed to work on that; he needed to earn Stella's trust as well.

"Do you girls want to see Grandma's new garden?" he asked as he hugged them. They each nodded. Sophie helped him settle the girls in the Explorer, and after she closed the back door, he wished her luck and asked her to call him with news. She waved at them as he backed away, and Lewis watched her and wondered what his life would be like if he hadn't married Sophie, if he'd be happier or sadder, if she was someone he'd remember fondly. The high school girlfriend. The first girl he'd ever loved. Maybe he'd have led the same life but with a different person. Or maybe he'd be lonely. And what about Sophie? Would she have been better off without him?

"What are you doing, Daddy?" Ginny asked.

Lewis looked in the rearview mirror. Both girls sat shock still. He'd almost forgotten they were there. "Oh, nothing much." He'd only spent a couple of days apart from his daughters, but it wasn't until that moment, that glance in the mirror, that he realized how much he'd missed them. Maybe a better father wouldn't have needed the time apart. He wasn't sure. All he knew was that he wanted to be with them now.

He guided the Explorer onto a highway pull-off next to a plaque.

"Why are we stopping?" Ginny asked.

"A little fresh air."

He helped the girls out and they looked at the creek below. Mounds of leaves had piled beneath the trees, and in the distance a log cabin lay in open view. The girls peppered him with questions.

"What's that?"

"A cabin."

"Whose?"

He read the plaque. "A family. The McGoverns."

"Do you know them?"

"No, sweetie. This was in pioneer times. Way back before cars or television."

"Before TV?"

"Yep."

"What did they do?"

Lewis made up a story. "They worked. They hunted and gathered, mended clothes. They played games and took long walks."

"Why'd they leave?"

"It says here they didn't want to be near other people."

"Why not?"

"I guess they were happy by themselves."

The girls stopped talking and tried to mimic how Lewis looked deeply into the valley. He imagined how their lives would have been different in earlier times. Maybe things were better then.

"Are you and Mommy getting a divorce?" Ginny asked.

"Where'd you hear that?"

Ginny didn't answer.

"I don't know anything about that," Lewis said.

"Do you love Mommy?"

"Yes. Yes, I do."

"What's divorce?"

"It's when two people who live together decide not to anymore."

"What happens to their kids?"

Lewis thought before answering. He wasn't saddened by the question so much as unsure how to respond. The girls weren't distraught or suffering; they were trying to understand. He tried his best not to lie. "They grow up," he said. Each girl nodded like she understood.

When he settled them back in the Explorer, Lewis let the girls sit in the front. A soft rain broke down from the clouds, and he showed them where the windshield wipers were and how they worked, and as he drove, he draped his arm over the seat so that he could hold them all together as the world raced by.

Harlan parked next to the same unfinished A-frame he had the day after Lew died. No more work had been done. The house would stand exposed all winter long. Bored kids would congregate there, tag the beams, leave empty bottles and the remnants of fires. Nobody would complain or care.

He hiked the worn path back to the spot where Mary Jane shot Lew. It was wishful thinking, but he hoped he might find the girl there. It made sense to him, returning to that moment when a life went off the rails. And if she was out there, sitting on the bald rock and staring out over the river, he would let her have her moment's peace. Hell, he might even join her.

The ground was soft and forgiving underfoot and Harlan barely made a sound as he walked, but when he came out of the woods, the clearing was empty. He sat down on the rock and started to roll a cigarette, then decided against it and let the tobacco scatter in the breeze. He picked up a few small stones and pitched them over the edge.

They hadn't yet found a body in the river but each passing hour made Harlan more and more certain it was Mary Jane. He tried to convince himself he'd done right, handled the case right. Mark Gaines and his father were in custody. He knew who pulled the trigger and had an APB out to arrest her. He'd uncovered the truth, or most of it, anyway. He'd done his job. By all accounts, he should have been proud—it was good police work—but he didn't feel proud. The girl, if she was dead, that was on him.

All his life, Harlan had searched for a code worth living by, a guiding star, but he was a man who hedged bets, who believed a little in everything and therefore stood for nothing. He'd wanted to place his faith in the law, to place it in God, place it in himself, but he wasn't a true believer. Other people found mentors or gave themselves fully to a cause or a person or the bottle, but Harlan had always kept a part of himself back. Out of fear. Out of doubt. It was the reason he'd failed Mary Jane. He'd allowed himself an ounce of doubt and it had drowned her.

When the dust settled, he would be able to stand before a crowd of voters and claim he'd delivered justice, but that would be a lie. There was nothing just about what he'd done. What was the point of reckoning? Harlan had never wanted to punish people. He wanted to save them. He wanted to be there the moment before Mary Jane pulled the trigger, wanted to let her know that if she put the gun down, he'd let her go. Mary Jane was somewhere out there—on the road? in the river?—and what had he done to help her? What had he done?

If the good book was right, maybe there was some St. Peter at the gate separating the righteous from the wicked and if only Harlan could believe that, or believe that there was a man whose judgment was honest and absolute, then maybe the wet world before him wouldn't seem such a terrible place. But he couldn't imagine there was much reward for stumbling through this life, and he wasn't sure he wanted the reward anyway.

epilogue

Harlan managed to have Mark Gaines transferred to a juvenile facility in the southern part of the county even though he was nineteen, a carrot that he hoped would maintain the kid's cooperation. Mark kept refusing visits from his father, who was out on bail, and told Arthur Blakeslee, his father's lawyer, that he'd be using a public defender. He agreed to tell the whole story in court and a plea deal was drawn up. Harlan was there with the lawyers for Mark's first deposition. The story Mark told was long and wieldy—it started with his dad's medical practice and Mark's ability to get pills, moved on to Lew and his father's partnership, Mark's scheme in Lexington, and the startling wealth that came from dealing pills, all of which sowed the seeds of distrust that ended in murder. He even copped to setting the fire at the Spanish Manor to help Mary Jane escape. When the kid finished talking, Harlan could see that he expected swift punishment, but this was just the beginning and Harlan didn't know how to tell him the guilt wouldn't go away. "I'm so sorry you and Mary Jane went through this," he said, patting Mark on the shoulder. "But you should have fought back."

Each day Harlan sent one of the deputies to search the banks of the river for a body. He hoped they found it before the vultures or snapping turtles did their damage. Eventually, word got out that it was Mary Jane Finley in the water, and it seemed like the entire town joined the search, but they all came up empty. The only things anyone in Marathon could talk about were the case against Mark Gaines and his dad or the Finley girl's suicide. The details were meant to stay sealed but rumors spread.

Right after Trip posted bail, he started bad-mouthing Harlan to the *Marathon Registrar*. Each issue included an editorial by Stuart Simon about the various ways in which Harlan was tarnishing Lew's legacy. Harlan tried to shrug off the criticism. The case against Trip seemed primed to go federal—there were even charges of fraud concerning the Silver Spoon and Trip's attempted land grab. Harlan had done the job he was supposed to, but no one thanked him for it. He wanted to believe that when Mary Jane turned up, life would go back to normal, but it wouldn't.

The authorities in Lexington found her car and thanks to a bevy of parking tickets from a diligent meter maid, they confirmed it had been parked since before her disappearance. Holly didn't like to talk about Mary Jane, but sometimes when she looked at him, there was a sadness in her eyes that made Harlan shudder with guilt. He drove by the Finley home at the end of each night, hoping for some glimpse of Lyda, but the blinds were always drawn and the only light came from two small windows near the roof.

During his rare hours off, Harlan would walk the riverbank with Mattie and her mutt, pretending to search for the body. In truth, it was just an excuse to be away from other people. He'd done all this before. He'd been about Mattie's age when his daddy fell in the river, had searched the riverbank without end until one day the sheriff came by asking for someone to identify the body. His mother refused, saying she wanted nothing more to do with the man, so Harlan had gone. He could still see the red splotches where fish had nibbled his father's flesh, the cuts from branches and rocks, his father's dead, yellow eyes and bloated neck. He remembered wondering why he needed to be there at all. The sheriff had arrested his daddy enough to recognize him. All Harlan said was, "That's him." The sheriff said, "I know, son."

As the days passed, Harlan and Mattie's search for the body moved farther and farther into the woods. Mattie liked to point out birds and woodland creatures. They rested for long stretches, and Harlan let Mattie use his knife to whittle sticks into nothing. She rolled him loose cigarettes that burned too fast, and he built small campfires that she tossed twigs into just to watch them burn. Sometimes he left her and hiked down to the river to swim in the stills. The cold water seemed to remind him he was alive.

The election came and went. There was record low turnout but Harlan managed to eke himself a win. Almost immediately he named Paige his second-in-command and deputized Lewis after he promised not to get involved with his father-in-law's case. Lewis seemed perfectly content writing speeding tickets and patrolling county roads before the roosters cried at dawn. He was actually good company around the office, a bridge between Harlan and the other deputies. He liked bantering with Frank and Del, treated Paige with deference, picked Holly's brain about what makes a good deputy. It had to have been a strange time for him. Lewis's wife had moved back into their house to get away from her father, but Lewis and the girls were living with his mom. Lewis and Harlan met every couple of days to chat about how he liked the job but it always turned to more personal matters. Lewis explained that his marriage was on hiatus, but whenever he dropped Ginny and Stella off to visit their mom, Sophie would invite him in for coffee. Her life was in shambles—her brother in jail, her father out on bail. She didn't know what was happening or why. Apparently his daughters liked to ask when they were moving back home with Mommy, and every time they did it threatened to break Lewis's heart, but he claimed that Sophie was becoming a better woman and that maybe he was becoming a better man, and in time maybe they could be better to each other.

Harlan talked about retiring even though he'd won the election, thought about handing the reins over to Paige. He'd lost his faith in the law. The law hadn't been able to save Angeline from her father or save Lew from himself or save Mark and Mary Jane from whatever darkness haunted them. All the law could do was punish after the fact. At best it could keep the town from destroying itself, and it could barely manage that. Harlan thought maybe he'd go back to school, get a social work degree, start trying to save people before they did wrong. At least it would give him something new to believe in.

Eventually, he called in a diver to search the river for Mary Jane. He thought that, at least, might give the town some closure. The search turned into a long day of setting the trawler, releasing the diver, and watching him come up empty-handed. A bunch of Staties sat around the boat trading dirty jokes and dropping nips of whiskey in their coffee. No one spoke to Harlan. Despite a cold misting rain, a pack of locals watched from the bridge—lined up like birds on a wire. At some point Harlan began to wonder if Mary Jane's body was in the river after all, if it wasn't just another trick. He wanted to believe that she was out there somewhere—alive— but late in the afternoon, the diver surfaced and gave a thumbs-up. Harlan stood among the Staties and listened to his report. "She's caught on a rock with all these initials carved into it," he said. "Damnedest thing I ever saw." The Staties threw out a wide net and the diver went down once more. People on the bridge cheered.

Harlan knew the rock. When he was a kid and the river was low, it rose like an island above the surface. People boated out and carved their names and the names of their loved ones into it. And then when the water rose again, the rock vanished. It had come loose years before and sunk to the bottom. Harlan's own initials were on the rock. And who knew how many others? And who knew how long it would be before all their symbols were worn away?

Harlan looked up at the bridge and saw Henry Dawson standing among the birds. Mattie was nowhere to be seen, and he had a sudden urge to find her, to jump from the boat and swim to shore and search her haunts to make sure she was okay. The anxiety crippled him and he took a seat just as the sun peeked out from behind the clouds. The mist from the boat's spray danced before him like a million atoms of space and time, like all the world's chaos and possibility. One of the Staties put a hand to his shoulder and said, "It's okay, Sheriff. It's over now."

Dredge the bottom of any river and you'll find things forgotten, things left behind, things pitched over the rail or fallen from the sky, things carried by the wind and worn down by time. Dredge these things up and you'll have more questions than answers, but the river will keep moving, keep changing, keep pushing so that nothing has its final resting place, so that nothing is ever finished or complete but just sitting there, trapped in the mud, waiting for some swell to lift it, to carry it along some new current, waiting for some hand to loose it from its snag, so it can float weightless to the top, new and pale and clean again.

acknowledgments

This book has brought me into contact with many amazing people, and whatever this novel's charms, they are indebted to that community.

Thank you to David Hale Smith for boarding the ship and Will Anderson for bringing it into port.

Thank you to Liz Parker, Katie Gilligan, and Jamie Levine for guidance along the way. And to the team at Thomas Dunne, including Justin Velella, Paul Hochman, Emily Walters, and Susannah Noel.

Thank you to the Michener Center and all the writers I met there. To Artcroft and the VCAA, which gave me time and space to work.

To my friends and confidants: Gregory, Smith, and the Billy Goat; Kevin and Jessica; Mac and Tate; Adam, Aja, and James; P.F. and Peter; Dan and Ronnie; Yaakov, Scott, and Nick.

To kind strangers like Sheriff Patrick Boggs and his father, Bill, who taught me so much about the place that was once called Limestone.

Thank you to my family: John, Marty, Emily, and Sarah. I'm a fortunate son.

To my spiritual adviser, the Right Reverend Parker.

And finally, to Becca and Poe. Love. Always.